Rome

BY JAY CROWNOVER

Rome

Jet

Rule

Rome

A Marked Men Novel

JAY CROWNOVER

wm

WILLIAM MORROW

An Imprint of HarperCollinsPublishers

HarperCollins books may be purchased for educational, business, or sales promotional use. For information please e-mail the Special Markets Department at SPsales@harpercollins.com.

FIRST EDITION

Library of Congress Cataloging-in-Publication Data

Crownover, Jay.
  Rome : a marked men novel / Jay Crownover. — First edition.
    p. cm
  ISBN 978-0-06-230242-7
  1. Man-woman relationships—Fiction. I. Title.
PS3603.R766R66   2014
813'.6—dc23
                                                    2013035986

14 15 16 17 18   OV/RRD   10 9 8 7 6 5 4 3 2 1

Dedicated to all the men and women who are serving or have served our country in any branch of the armed forces. Thank you for your service.

Also to the families, friends, and loved ones who love and support their service members while they are near, far, and everywhere in between.

FIRST OF ALL, I want to say that I have nothing but respect and admiration for the men and women of our armed forces. I think it is admirable to choose to serve for the good of others. It's selfless, heroic, and all-around commendable.

I live near Fort Carson, in a town that is full of men and women on active duty. My grandfather was in the army, which led to my mom being taken all over the world when she was young. My cousin served overseas in the army and he is a delightful, truly wonderful young man who did not come back entirely unaffected by his experience. My most recent job was at a bar located near a university here in town that served as the unofficial hangout of a group of ex-soldiers who were all back in school on the GI Bill, building their postservice life. I've heard the stories, good and bad. Seen the highs and lows that getting out of the service can bring. That being said, *Rome* is in no way meant to be a portrait, in a generalized or documentary way, of the kinds of lives these military people lead.

Rome is a man on a journey, just like we all are, and he's only trying to do the best he can. Any liberties I have taken with the truth are my own doing and only designed to develop his character and tell his tale.

Thank you all and happy reading!!!

Jay

Rome

CHAPTER 1

Cora, The Fourth of July

I T'S MY FAVORITE THING ever to have all the people I love in one place at the same time. Pair that with a day off from work, cold beer, barbecue, and fireworks, and I couldn't be a happier camper.

And I would have been ecstatic, if only a dark, looming, man-shaped cloud wasn't bound and determined to rain all over my parade.

It was a long holiday weekend and everyone from the tattoo shop I worked at, plus the other boys, Jet and Asa, as well as the girls, was gathered in the backyard of Rule and Shaw's brand-new house for a barbecue and a house-warming. Everyone had a beer in hand; Rule and Jet were manning the grill, looking slightly ridiculous while doing it. It was supposed to be fun and relaxing, only someone had missed the memo.

I was rolling my sweating beer can between my hands and trying really hard to keep my mouth shut because in a few short minutes I'd determined that Rome Archer had to be the least fun person I'd ever met. Sure, the guy had just gotten home from a war zone and was dealing with some pretty serious family drama, but that didn't excuse the fact that he seemed bound and determined to infect the rest of the festivities with his vile mood.

Ever since he had walked in the back gate, he had been alternately scowling and sniping at anyone who got within spewing distance of that unchecked fury. He had on mirrored aviators, so I couldn't see his eyes, but I could practically feel the disdain and dissatisfaction pouring off of his massive body. I had never met anyone who I could actually describe as "hulking" before Rome started hanging around, and like the green monster, his temper seemed to be something everyone else feared. I was getting sick and tired of watching my friends tiptoe around him and try to placate him.

Hell, he should be jumping for joy that his horn dog of a sibling had settled down and was making a real commitment to someone, that Rule had found his perfect match and was a better man for it. But no, all Captain No-Fun could do was sneer and grunt at anyone trying to make conversation.

No, I was pretty sure I was not a particular fan of Rome Archer in any way, shape, or form, be he a war hero and beloved older sibling, supposed nice guy, or not. I personally thought the man was going out of his way to be an ass hat and make everyone else as miserable as he seemed to be.

The boys who grew up with him and even my girlfriend Shaw kept repeating the litany that the ex-soldier really was a great guy and that he was just struggling since coming home. I wasn't sure I believed it because nothing I had seen thus far indicated he was anything but a grumpy, slightly unhinged bully. Which was a shame because the guy was gorgeous, like it-hurt-to-look-at-him gorgeous. All the Archers had some kick-ass genetics, but where Rule, my coworker and best friend, was gifted with all kinds of troubled, bad-boy swagger, Rome was straight-up masculine perfection.

He was tall, way taller than the other guys, which was saying something since none of the crew was exactly petite, and he was big. He was broad and strong and strapped with muscles that looked like they had been used for survival not just show. He had short, dark hair cropped close to his head, and over the reflective lenses of the sunglasses there was no missing a jagged white scar that hooked through his eyebrow and down next to his eye. His face had a vivid intensity about it that just made him stupidly hot, even without the body that was bound to make the opposite sex dumb. I bet if he ever bothered to smile, panties across the nation would melt.

I looked up as one of my other coworkers, Nash Donovan, popped up behind me and rested his hands on my shoulders. Nash was Rule's best friend and currently living with the mountain of doom and gloom I was sitting next to on the lawn. The camp chair he was sprawled in looked like it was going to snap under his considerable bulk at any minute. I couldn't imagine a guy as mellow and laid-back as Nash living with someone so dour and grumpy, but considering he and Rule pretty much hero-worshipped the guy, I figured it would behoove me to just stay out of it for as long as I could.

"How goes it, Tink?"

It was a simple question, but there was a lot behind it. I recently found out my first love, the guy who was responsible for shattering my young heart into a million irreparable pieces, was getting married at the end of the summer. I was having a hard time with it and all the guys from the shop were worried about me, because I was typically unflappable.

"Oh, you know, still looking for Mr. Perfect."

That was my default answer. In order to prevent the same mistake, to prevent myself from giving my heart away so carelessly, I was bound and determined to wait for a guy who was all in with me. I wasn't settling for anything less than perfection, even if I had to wait forever to find it. The idea of compromising and ending up as lost and broken as I was when things with Jimmy didn't work out was too terrifying to consider.

"Tink?" Rome's voice was gruff and as rough as the look on his handsome face.

Nash snickered and moved to take a seat on the other side of the older Archer.

"Tinker Bell. She looks like a punk-rock version of Tinker Bell."

A dark eyebrow lifted behind the sunglasses, and I smiled sweetly at him. I do look kind of like a cartoon fairy. I'm short, have spiky blond hair that kind of ends up all over the place, and my eyes are two different colors. I also have a riotous sleeve of flowers and filigree tattooed from the top of my shoulder to my wrist on my left arm. It's brilliant and bright. I love the vibrant ink and often changed the stud in my eyebrow ring to match the different colors. The nickname suited me, and I didn't hate it when the boys used it because it showed me they loved me as much as I loved them.

Rome whipped his sunglasses off and rubbed his hands over his eyes. When he was done I could see that not only were his eyes the most beautiful, clear blue that I had ever seen, but they were also rimmed in dark circles and bloodshot with lightning bolts of red. He was most definitely a babe, but he looked like shit.

"I shouldn't have come. This is all so wrong. Everyone pretending like Rule and Shaw playing house is something to be excited about. It's all just going to blow up, they are going to end up destroying each other, and I'm going to have to be the one to clean up the mess."

At first I thought I heard him wrong, but I saw Nash wince and Rowdy, one of my other boys from the shop, tense up. So far he seemed to be the only other person at this ramshackle gathering who hadn't been initiated into the Rome Archer fan club. That was a good thing because Rowdy was probably the only guy in the group who could give the soldier a run for his money physically, should he decide to be a handful.

"Dude, chill out. Be happy for Rule and Shaw. That's your family." Nash was always the most practical of the bunch, but I could hear the underlying tension in his voice.

I flicked the tab on the top of my beer and narrowed my eyes. I wasn't about to let this guy rain on my friend's day, even if he seemed determined to. Those eyes that really were too pretty to be in such a sour-looking face narrowed at Nash, and I could literally feel the heat of uncoiling anger rolling off those wide shoulders. So far I had been quiet, I had watched and judged. I had sipped my beer quietly and let everyone else try and get this guy to loosen up. I was here for fun, to enjoy having all my friends in one place, to celebrate the cohabitation of two people I adored and the recent wedded bliss of two more people I loved and considered my own. My group of friends was quickly pairing off and to me that was worth throwing a party for. I knew how hard it was to find a perfect match, and I loved that people I cared so much about were doing exactly that. Captain No-Fun better get with the program real fast or it was going to get ugly.

"None of this is good for anybody. I don't know what I'm doing here. This is all such a joke. None of you know what you're doing or what the real world is like."

I saw Nash blink in surprise. I saw Rowdy climb to his feet and I knew instinctively it wasn't Rome he was going to go after.

I narrowed my eyes just as those baby blues swung my way. Maybe he thought I was safe because I probably only came up to his breastbone. Maybe he thought I was sweet because I had on a bright pink halter top and short, white shorts and looked like I was unassuming and nonthreatening. Maybe he thought I was meek because I hadn't bothered to say anything to him since he'd thundered in and proceeded to ruin my lovely holiday. I lifted the eyebrow that had the pink crystal in it and met him glare for glare.

Whatever he thought or was thinking, I'm sure I proved

him wrong as I calmly got to my feet, leaned over in his direction, and upended the last of the beer that was in the can I had practically crushed in my fist over his head. The beer slid down his shocked face in slow motion as I got so close our noses were practically touching.

"You are such an asshole!" I knew the volume of my voice carried all the way across the yard, and I could hear feet running in our direction. Those electric eyes blinked at me and I could have sworn I saw something break through the thundercloud lurking in there. I was about to launch into a lecture on manners and respect and being a jerk for no apparent reason, but a heavy arm locked around my waist and hauled me back against a hard chest.

The big guy climbed to his feet, but before he could make any move in my direction, Rowdy stepped between him and where Nash was hauling me bodily toward the deck and away from the soggy, frowning giant.

I pointed a finger in his direction and watched as he flicked boozy moisture out of his eyes. "We don't need all that negative, Captain No-Fun. Why don't you go spread your gloom and doom somewhere else? Hell, you can take that crap back to the desert, for all I care; we were all getting along just fine without you. Just because you can't find anything to be happy about doesn't mean you need to crap all over what everyone else is trying to do here today."

I let out a huff when Nash gave me a none too gentle squeeze that was a warning to pipe down, so I returned the favor by jabbing an elbow into his ribs. He grunted and deposited me on the deck in the spot Shaw had just vacated.

We all watched silently as Rule got up in his brother's face. I wanted to holler at Shaw to stay out of it, but if Rule went loco, she was the only one who was going to be able to put that fire out. I felt kind of bad for stirring the pot when I didn't even really know the guy that well.

Loud male voices exchanged ugly words, and we all held a collective breath when Rule reached up and shoved Rome back a step, knocking over the lawn chair. Rowdy scooped up Shaw and moved her out of the way and I felt a twinge of guilt for starting such a scene when we were supposed to be at a celebration.

The brothers were fairly evenly matched in height, even if I knew Rule had his older brother dead to rights in the bad attitude department, but Rome was undeniably taller and built like a beast. If he really wanted to put a hurting on Rule, it was going to get unpleasant and the other guys were going to have to get involved. I bit my lip and tried to wiggle free from Nash's iron grip but he just squeezed me tighter.

"You poked the bear, Tink, so you better hope someone can put him in a cage."

I gasped and fought the urge to cover my eyes when Rome simply reached out and shoved Rule to the ground with a palm on the center of his chest. He lowered his voice and said something that none of us on the deck could hear, but I saw Shaw burst into tears and turn into Rowdy's chest. I could have sworn those blue eyes sought out mine before he turned on the heel of his heavy black boot and stormed out of the backyard. The gate he exited through rattled on its hinges, and the roar of the motorcycle engine drowned out any other noise as Rule got to his feet and collected his crying girlfriend.

Nash gave me one last squeeze and finally let me go.

"You just can't help yourself, can you, Cora?"

I crossed my arms defiantly over my chest and took a seat next to the only member of our little group who seemed unfazed by the drama. It probably didn't hurt matters that he was in a full walking cast and still had a whole slew of broken ribs and bumps and bruises from his epic beat-down. Asa Cross was an enigma and had enough of his own drama that ours probably seemed silly and uninteresting to him.

"He's an ass."

Nash shook his head at me and his periwinkle eyes looked reproachful.

"No, he's not. I don't know what's going on with him, but ever since he got back and got out of the army, he's been acting weird. He's a good guy. You know I wouldn't defend someone that I didn't truly believe that about."

I rolled my eyes.

"He's being terrible to Rule and Shaw, and I'm not going to just watch."

"That's a family matter. Rule can fight his own battles, and he isn't going to let anything happen to Shaw. Just calm down, okay. We got this. Rome isn't . . . whatever this is, all right?"

I sighed and took the slice of watermelon the golden-eyed heartthrob that I had inherited as a roommate within the last month handed me. I winked at Asa and waved Nash off.

"I love you guys. He needs to pick on someone his own size."

My hair got ruffled as Nash made his way off of the deck to go check on his friend.

"Like you?"

"Is that a short joke?" I didn't get an answer as he disappeared down the deck steps, but his deep laughter followed him. I made a face as Jet and Ayden, the two newlyweds I shared a house with along with Ayden's wayward brother, caught my eye. They were snuggling and too cute to ignore.

"See . . . like I always said, you two are just perfect. That's what I want."

I knew I sounded wistful, but I couldn't keep the longing for that kind of love, that type of connection, out of my voice. I thought I had had it once, and when I realized I didn't, it nearly broke me.

"I keep telling you that your expectations are too high." Jet tried to sound lighthearted about it, but he didn't know about my broken engagement or the fact that my ex-fiancé was planning on getting married at the end of the summer.

"Love isn't perfect. It's hard work and sometimes it's more effort to be in love than it is to just run away. If you keep looking for perfect, the real thing is going to pass right by you."

I waved a hand at him because I knew he was speaking from a place of experience. His road to Ayden hadn't been without a pit stop or two in Stupidville, but they made it and I could only hope for such a beautiful outcome. I took my seat back by Asa and I could swear he was mentally taking notes on all of us. Those gears behind his gold eyes always seemed to be turning.

"I'll know it when I see it."

I said it to Jet, but really I was reaffirming to myself that I would know it this time when it came along. I wouldn't be fooled by a pretty face and promises of devotion. I wouldn't end up anyone's joke or castoff ever again. The fact that so many of my friends were stumbling headfirst into their happily-ever-after gave my tired heart hope that I couldn't be far behind.

When the wedding invitation Jimmy had cruelly sent in the mail landed in my hands, it was a wake-up call. I had loved a guy who had cheated on me, lied to me, made me a laughingstock, with everything that I was. I wanted to spend my life with him, build a business with him, and have children with him. All of it. He, on the other hand, had wanted to have sex with his tattoo clients and lead me on for as long as possible. If I hadn't had to go back to the shop one night because I forgot something and walked in on him with a girl who was barely out of her teens, there was a good chance I would be married to the rat bastard right now.

Still, to this day what hurt the most was that everyone knew. The people I thought were my friends, the coworkers I thought of as my family, they all knew and no one had said a word. They let me play the fool, let Jimmy put me at risk, use me and humiliate me without as so much as a peep. It was awful. If my dad's old buddy Phil hadn't come to town to visit him when all of it was falling to pieces, I don't know where I would be now. The guys at the shop had saved me.

"Ayd and Jet just snuck out through the side gate. Looks like you're gonna have to get the gimp home."

I looked at Asa and then at the gate, which was indeed swinging shut. I made an offhand comment about being newlyweds but didn't get much further because Shaw plopped down next to me on the patio furniture and wiped at her wet cheeks with the back of her hand. The rest of the guys followed, carrying the now-burned remains of the barbecue Rule had been working on.

I reached out to pat my friend on the leg. Shaw was a beautiful girl. She had this ethereal, otherworldly beauty that took a minute to get used to. It made my heart twinge in sympathy to see her big green eyes look so sad. No one wanted to make Shaw cry, it was like kicking a fairy-tale princess when she was down.

The guys all gathered around the food and popped the tops for another round of beers. It looked like they were going with the time-honored, male way of dealing with things by ignoring the entire thing. Not that I could blame them. None of them seemed to want to call Rome out on his ridiculous behavior and I knew all of them well enough to know that stubborn didn't even begin to cover how they acted when they made up their minds about something.

"You okay?"

Shaw blinked at me and gave me a lopsided grin. It was just her way to always want things to be okay for everyone.

"I'll live. Part of me thinks they should just beat the crap out of each other to get whatever is going on between them out in the open. But I don't think Rule would know when to back down and I think Rome could kill him if he lost control.

I don't know what happened to him this last tour, but that guy is not the guy I grew up with."

I lifted my eyebrow and took the plate Rowdy handed me as he sat down across from me and put his feet up on the arm of my chair. I made a face at him, but he was forgiven when he tossed me a beer.

"You know, everyone keeps saying that, but I met big brother a few times before and he never struck me as a barrel of laughs. The guy has always been wound up pretty tight."

Shaw took the plate Rule handed her and scooted over on the bench seat to make room for him next to her. They were an odd pair at first glance but the love they shared was a tangible thing and I tried really hard not to be jealous about it.

"It has to do with more than Remy." Rule's deep voice was gruff and I could tell he was stewing over the latest run-in with his brother.

I cracked open the beer and offered my own two cents. "Who cares what it has to do with? He's a jerk face for no reason. Screw him."

Rowdy shook his head at me and Shaw and Rule both rolled their eyes. As usual, it was up to Nash to be the voice of reason.

"We don't just write off people that we care about, Cora. You know this."

I did. This group was fiercely loyal and honest to a fault, which is why I loved them like I did. I just hated to see one person causing so much strife with so many different, wonderful people.

"I gotta say I'm glad he doesn't have your temper, Rule.

I think one solid hit with those mitts of his and I would've ended up like Asa over there." Rowdy indicated the southern playboy with a tilt of his beer.

Asa had taken a beating so bad that he had been in a coma for several weeks. It was a miracle he had come out of it as unscathed as he had.

Rule grunted and put his free arm around Shaw as she leaned into his side. They really were too cute for words. I had to bite back an envious sigh. Rule glanced at the gate Rome had just stormed out of and stated, "He's never been much of a brawler. I mean, when we were younger he would wade in when Nash and I started shit, but he was never the type to start anything himself. That's why I don't get what is going on with him lately. I'm about sick of it, though."

Nash snorted a laugh and pointed at me with the end of his fork. "To be fair, Tink kind of started it today. Was dousing him in beer really necessary?"

I tried to look innocent. It wasn't really a look I could pull off very well, so I gave a helpless grin.

"I could've punched him in the nose, but there wasn't a stepladder anywhere handy."

That got a round of laughs from everyone, because I really was tiny compared to the older Archer and laughter worked wonders at lifting the black mood he had brought. We finished eating and had a few more drinks; at least they did. I had to drive Asa back to the house and there was no way I was going to risk a DUI on such a checkpoint-happy holiday. The guys waited until it was dark and wandered off into the yard to light fireworks, because really they were all just big kids covered in ink.

I found myself alone with Shaw on the deck once again and noticed that despite the lingering sadness on her pretty face, her happiness practically emanated from her. I put an arm around her shoulders and rested my head against hers. I was older than Shaw. The poor girl had been through the ringer in the last few years, so I knew she deserved every single bit of happiness she was feeling at this moment.

"You did good, kiddo. You got the guy, the house is amazing, and all of this is good stuff. Don't worry about anything else. You and Rule live in this moment and forget about the rest."

I felt her laugh and she reached up to squeeze the hand I had thrown over her shoulder. The sky lit up with a bunch of different colors and male laughter floated up from the yard.

"Sometimes I feel selfish. I got everything I ever wanted and it isn't always perfect but the good days always outnumber the bad. I feel like I'm not allowed to ask for more." She sighed so heavy I could feel it. "Now Rome thinks it's all a joke and that hurts, I don't know why he's so mad. I've loved Rome like a brother as long as I can remember, so it hurts in more ways than one."

"It'll work itself out, you'll see." And I would be happy to help it along if I had to.

She was quiet for a really long time and we just watched the mini-explosions and smiled at the boys, who were clearly having a blast. Maybe one of us should have mentioned that drinking and fireworks weren't a great idea, but Captain No-Fun was gone and I wasn't going to be the good-time police.

"Did I ever tell you that you're the smartest person I know, Cora?" Shaw's voice was quiet but I took it as a compliment considering the girl was well on her way to becoming a doctor.

"I just call it like I see it."

I did. I was from the East Coast, downtown Brooklyn to be exact, and I was the only child of a career sailor who had no clue what to do with his rebellious daughter. I loved my dad, he was my only blood relative, and I knew that he loved me in return. But we didn't connect, and as a result, I learned from a young age to speak plainly and not pull any punches. It was the only way the two of us could communicate. So if someone needed to get to Rome Archer and tell him to get his fool head out of his ass, I was more than willing to be the person to do it. I didn't idolize him, I wasn't scared of him, and whether he was a giant or not, I wasn't going to stand by and let him continue to cause so much grief for the people I cared so much about.

CHAPTER 2

Rome

I COULDN'T BELIEVE THAT crazy little sprite had the nerve to dump beer on my head. First of all, she barely came up to my shoulder, and second of all, she looked like a walking, talking piece of candy. Everything about her was so colorful it almost hurt to look at her.

I should be furious at her, but she was right, I was an asshole. There was no reason to talk shit to Nash, no reason to get into it with Rule. I was just looking for a target to vent my frustrations at and those were the people closest to me. Maybe it was easier to unleash my aggravation at them, because I knew instinctively they would forgive me. I needed to find a place to have a drink and try and get my head together. A place that was dark and quiet and where no one expected me to be anything, or act a certain way. I was tired of not meeting expectations. I was not an idle man by nature. I was used to action, used to being in charge and taking the lead, and the only things I had managed to be on top of since coming back to Denver was pissing off everyone I encountered and drinking my considerable body weight in vodka. I was on a downhill slide that was bound to have an ugly-as-hell impact at the bottom and I knew it, but I felt powerless to stop it. Today was the proof of that.

I pulled into the first bar that looked like it could handle the mood I was in. Independence Day, my left nut. I had had about enough of the revelry and good cheer to last me a lifetime. I just wanted to bury my head in the sand and go back to a point in time that felt comfortable and familiar. I hated feeling like a visitor in my own life, and no matter what I told myself when I woke up in the morning each day, I couldn't shake feeling like everything I had come back to after my contract with the army was up was a life that belonged to someone else. My family didn't feel right. The new dynamic in my relationship with Rule didn't feel right. Trying to get used to Shaw being taken care of by my wayward and reckless little brother didn't feel right. Crashing with Nash while I tried to get my shit straight didn't feel right. Not having a job lined up or any clear direction of how to support myself doing something other than fighting a war quite possibly felt the most wrong out of it all.

The bar was dark and not a place for those out for a fun Fourth-of-July cocktail. In the back, around several well-used pool tables, was a bunch of guys in biker gear sporting colors and looking like they meant business. Toward the front were several older men who looked like they never even got off the bar stool to go home and shower. Neil Young was blasting on the house speakers even though no one seemed like the type to sing along. This was not a place for the hip and trendy urbanites that flocked to Capitol Hill when the weather finally warmed up. I took a spot on an empty seat at the bar top and waited for the guy manning the bar to wander down to me.

He was almost my size, which was rare, only he had a solid thirty years on me. He had a beard that looked like it could be the home to a whole family of squirrels, eyes the color of charcoal, and the grim countenance that could only be found in men who had seen the worst the world had to offer and came out the other side. I wasn't surprised at all to see a marine tattoo inked on his bulky forearm when he propped himself up across from me and put down a battered coaster in front of me. I saw him size me up, but I was used to it. I was a big guy and other big guys liked to figure out if I was going to be the kind of trouble they could handle or not.

"Boy, you already smell like a brewery. You sure you need to have another one?"

I frowned until I remembered the little blonde pouring her beer over my head. She could have found a better way to make her point. I thought as I remembered the soggy state of my T-shirt. I didn't know what to make of Cora Lewis. She was around a lot. We never really talked much. She was too loud and tended toward the dramatic, hence the Coors Light shower I had just received. Being around her made my head hurt and I didn't like the way her mismatched eyes seemed to try and pick me apart.

I took my sunglasses off the top of my head and hooked them in the collar of my T-shirt.

"I picked a fight with the wrong pixie and she poured her drink on my head. I'm straight."

The guy gave me a once-over and must have deemed

me okay because without my asking a tankard of beer was set in front of me along with a shot of something amber and strong. Typically I was a vodka drinker, but when the burly brute poured himself one and wandered back over to where I was seated, I didn't dare complain.

He lifted a bushy eyebrow at me and touched the rim of his shot glass to my own.

"You army?"

I nodded and shot back the liquor. It burned hot all the way down. If I wasn't mistaken it was Wild Turkey.

"I was. Just got out."

"How long did you serve for?"

I rubbed a hand over my still-short hair. After wearing it cropped close to my head for so long, I really didn't know what else to do with it.

"Went in at eighteen and I turn twenty-eight at the end of this year. I was in for almost a decade."

"What did you do?"

It wasn't a question I normally answered because frankly the answer was long and anyone that hadn't served just wouldn't get it.

"I was a field operations leader."

The bear of a man across from me let out a low whistle. "Spec ops?"

I grunted a response and picked up the beer.

"I bet they were sad to see you go."

The thing was, I think I was sadder to see *them* go. I wasn't cleared for active duty anymore. My shoulder had taken a beating when we rolled over an IED on my last deployment and there were all kinds of shit rattling around in my head, constantly taking me out of the game. Sure, I could have taken a desk job, stepped down, and trained the generation coming up after me. But I wasn't the best teacher and being tied to a desk was the same thing as retirement to me anyway. So I got out and now I had no fucking clue what I was going to do with the rest of my life.

"What about you?" I motioned to the tattoo on his arm. "How long did you put in?"

"Too long, son. Way too long. What brings you in here today? You aren't one of my regulars."

I cast a look around the bar and shrugged. For now this place was a perfect fit for my mood.

"Just out having a drink to celebrate America like a good patriot."

"Just like the rest of us."

"Yep." I had to fight the urge to chug the beer down and order him to keep them coming.

"I'm Brite and this is my bar. I ended up with it when I got out and started spending more time in the bar than I did at home. I've been through three wives and one triple bypass, but the bar stays true."

I lifted the eyebrow that had the scar above it and felt the corner of my mouth kick up in a grin.

"Brite?" The guy looked like Paul Bunyan or a Hells Angel; the name didn't really fit.

A smile found its way through that massive beard and pearly-white teeth that were the only bright spot in the dim bar.

"Brighton Walker, Brite for short." He extended a hand that I shook on reflex.

"Rome Archer."

He dropped his head in a little nod and moved down the bar to help another customer.

"That's a good name for a warrior."

I closed my eyes briefly and tried to remember what it was like to feel like a warrior. It seemed like it was a million miles away from this bar stool. The music switched to AC/DC and I decided this was my new favorite place to hang out.

I was on my Harley, so I should probably cool it with the booze. A DUI would just be the icing on the crap cake I was currently being served on a daily basis, but as the beer mixed with the potent bourbon from earlier, none of that seemed to really matter anymore.

At some point I did another shot with Brite and the bar stool next to me was abandoned by the grizzled old man that had been complaining about his wife and his girlfriend for the last hour and quickly occupied by a redhead with too much makeup on and too little clothes. Had I been three less beers in, I would've seen her for the trouble she was. As it was, Brite told her to scram, advice she promptly ignored. She was cute, in that *I'm a good time take me home* kind of way, and I couldn't remember the last time I had randomly picked anyone up from a bar. When I was overseas there had been a female intelligence officer who'd been down to be friends with benefits whenever we were in the same place at the same time, but it had been months since I had seen her. Maybe a quick, sleazy hookup was just what I needed to break through the black cloud that had been hovering over me since my return.

"What's your name, sugar?"

Her voice was squeaky and hurt my head but I was loaded enough to ignore it.

"Rome."

I saw her heavily made-up eyes dart back to someplace over my shoulder and that should have been my first clue that this wasn't going to end up all fun and games.

"That's a different name. I'm Abbie. Now that we're friends, why don't we get out of here and get better ac-quainted?" She ran a painted fingernail over the curve of my bicep and for some reason the bloodred color of it made other images of things that same color start to flash behind my already hazy vision.

I started to pull away, to get those hands that were making bad things happen in my foggy brain to let me go, when a heavy hand fell on my shoulder from behind. I was a trained soldier, but more than that, I was a man who had a brother born and bred into trouble. I knew what trouble looked like from a million miles away. I knew what trouble felt like, what it moved like, how it sounded, and yet I had kept right on drinking and ignored all the signs as it built up around me. Out of the corner of my eye I saw Brite frown at whoever was standing behind me, and even in my stupor of bourbon and beer I knew this wasn't going to be good.

Sighing under my breath, I shook off the talons that had me seeing blood spilling out of a young soldier's throat onto the desert sand and turned around so that I was leaning back on the bar with my elbows. It shouldn't have surprised me to see that almost the entire back poolroom of bikers was now gathered around me and the bar area. The guy with his paw on my shoulder was a scrawny little fella and I felt my boozy brain register that he wasn't wearing the club's colors, which meant he was either a hang-around or a prospect, and I was the lucky bastard he had picked to try and prove his worth with. Sometimes it sucked being a big-ass dude.

"Can I help you?"

The redhead was long gone and Brite was making his way around the end of the long bar. The old guys stayed posted up and ignored the brewing hurricane like only life-long drunks were capable of doing.

"You trying to start something with my girl, GI Joe?"

It was boring and so predictable that I had to roll my eyes. I had been in enough shithole places in the world to know that a bar brawl was a bar brawl, but throw in a wanna-be biker and it could get really foul.

"No. I was trying to get drunk, and she interrupted me."

I don't think they were expecting that because a couple of titters ran through the group. Scrawny puffed up his chest and reached out a finger to poke me in mine. Normally I could just walk away from this kind of thing. I was typically a levelheaded kind of guy. I didn't fight unless it was in defense of something I really and truly believed in, or in defense of someone I loved, but today was the wrong day to goad a reaction out of me.

I swatted the guy's hand away and did a quick survey of the room. I didn't see any visible hardware, but bikers were known for stashing knifes in hard-to-see places, and Brite seemed like a cool enough guy. I didn't want to trash his place if I could help it.

"Look, dude, you don't want to do this, and I really don't want to do this. We both know you sent the chick over here to try and start shit, so just leave it at that. I'll bounce, and you and your buddies can go back to smoking up and shooting pool. Nobody has to bleed or look stupid. Okay?"

In hindsight, trying to drunkenly reason with a bunch of bikers probably was bound to have a low success rate. Between one blink and the next I had a bottle broken over my head and found myself in a serious choke hold. Scrawny Guy looked like he wanted to kill me and the rest of his crew was just hanging back waiting to see what he could do. I didn't really want to hurt the guy, but the bottle over the head had taken a nice chunk of skin off with it and a river of red was steadily flowing into my eyes. Just like with the red nail polish on the tramp's fingers, the sight of my own blood took me to another place and time, and it wasn't me struggling with a stupid, show-off biker, it was me battling for life, for freedom, for the security of my family and friends at home. Just like that, the poor kid had no idea what hit him.

I already had a distinct size advantage on the guy; throw in the fact that I was a soldier who'd been battle-hardened and trained by the country's best, and it got nasty and bloody fast. It didn't matter that the numbers were so obviously skewed in the biker's favor, I was getting out of the bar in one piece no matter what I had to do to make that happen.

Bar stools were broken. Glasses went flying. Heads

banged against the floor. I think at one point I heard someone crying, and somehow when it was all over I was hunched
over with my hands on my knees, blood now dripping not
only from my lacerated head but also my hands, and a nasty
knife slice across my ribs. The bikers had scattered, for the
most part, and I wasn't surprised to see Brite holding a baseball bat and glaring at me.

"What the hell was that?"

I would have laughed, but I think the knife cut in my
side was worse than I'd originally thought.

"A really shitty 'thanks for your service'?" My humor was
not appreciated, as the older man swore at me and pulled me
painfully into a standing position.

"Doesn't look like that little punk is gonna get patched
in anytime soon."

I got a critical once-over and was met with a sigh.

"You need a doctor."

It wasn't a question.

I tried to wipe the blood off my face with the back of my
hand but just ended up smearing it all across my face while
my side steadily leaked onto the floor.

"I rode in. Don't think I can handle the bike right now."

He shook his head at me and put two fingers in his
mouth and let out an earsplitting whistle.

"Everybody drink up and get out. Consider this last call."

A few diehards grumbled, but it only took five minutes
before Brite was locking the front door, hauling me out the
back door, and shoving me into the battered cab of an old
Chevy pickup truck.

I rested my head back against the seat and gave the older man a rueful grin.

"I'll pay for any damage to the bar. I'm sorry about that."

He snorted in response and gave me a narrow-eyed look. "Try not to bleed out before we get to the emergency room, son."

Like I had a choice.

"The Sons of Sorrow hang out in the bar all the time. The old-timers are a good group of guys. A bunch of them are ex-military and get what my bar is all about, so I don't usually gripe about them coming in. It's all the younger kids trying to make a name who stir shit up. It wasn't the first time blood has been spilled on that floor and I doubt it'll be the last. You come see me when you sober up and get all sewed back together and we'll talk about what you can do to repay me for the damages. Gotta tell you, you're one hell of a fighter, son."

I would have shrugged but the slice on my ribs was starting to burn and I was having a hard time ignoring the sticky, warm blood oozing between my fingers, so I just grunted in acknowledgment.

"I'm really not. I hate fighting, I did it for a living for too many years, but the only way to come out alive is to be better at it than the other guy."

I closed my eyes and silently prayed we didn't hit any more red lights. My vision was starting to blur around the edges.

Brite's voice was gruff as we pulled into the parking lot of the emergency room. "That's a damn shame, son."

I didn't have a response because he was right. It was a shame.

I didn't get admitted right away. I guess a knife wound and a split-open scalp took a backseat to fingers blown off by fireworks on the Fourth. I didn't want to keep Brite waiting, so I called Nash and left a garbled message that I was going to need a ride at some point in the night. I knew I should have called Rule or Shaw, but I just wasn't up to dealing with that headache right now. And I knew Nash would come with no questions asked even if I had been a royal ass earlier in the day.

"I gotta leave my bike at your bar tonight. I would appreciate it if you kept an eye on it for me in case Scrawny is a sore loser."

Brite nodded and again I saw that flash of white buried in that massive beard. "Well, I would say it was nice to meet you, Rome Archer, but of all the things I've been in this life, a liar has never been one of them."

We shook hands and I promised that I would touch base with him when I was in more functioning order.

I had to wait longer than I was comfortable with to see someone, and by the time they took me to the sterile little room and pulled the curtain around the bed, I was pretty sure I was staying conscious by the sheer force of my will alone. I was peeling my ruined T-shirt off over my head when the curtain moved back and a really pretty nurse holding a chart came in. She had her head bent over whatever she was reading and it gave me to opportunity to check her out. She had long copper hair twisted in a braid away from a truly lovely face. She looked a couple of years younger than me, and I couldn't help but appreciate that she was rocking some kick-ass curves under those boring scrubs all medical professionals seemed to wear.

"Hey."

She looked up at the sound of my voice and blinked wide, dove-gray eyes at me. I don't know if it was the sight of my naked chest or the fact that I was now covered head to waist in blood that had her looking apprehensive.

"Hello, Mr. Archer. It looks like you had a rough night."

"I've had better, that's for sure."

She snapped on some latex gloves and came over to stand beside me.

"Let's have a look at what kind of trouble you got your-self into, shall we?"

She poked and prodded at my head and I tried not to stare at her boobs. She really was a pretty girl and it made the sting of her jabbing at my newest battle wounds hurt just a little less.

"What's your name?" I didn't really need to know it, I probably would never see her again after I got stitched up, but her eyes were just so soft and pretty I couldn't help but ask.

She gave me a friendly smile and looked like she was about to oblige me when the flimsy curtain was yanked back and Nash came barreling through. His cornflower-blue eyes were on fire with a mixture of anger and concern. The flames tattooed on the side of his head were standing out as the vein under them throbbed in irritation.

"Do you have any idea the kind of hell I'm going to get from Rule when he finds out about this? Goddamn it, Rome, what the fuck is wrong with you lately?"

I was going to respond when his attention switched from me to the lovely nurse who was staring at him with her mouth hanging slightly open. I was used to Nash's dramatic look and larger-than-life presence. He and Rule had always drawn a lot of attention, so it never fazed me, but the pretty little nurse suddenly looked like she was seeing a ghost and it looked like Nash was trying to place where he might have seen her before as well.

"I just need to get stitched up and then you can yell at me on the way home."

The nurse cleared her throat and tossed her now-bloodstained gloves in the trash. "You're probably looking at staples for the laceration in your head. It's pretty nasty and deeper than it looks. The slice on the side is pretty clean, so you might get away with just a topical, liquid suture on it. The doc will be in shortly."

Her entire demeanor changed with Nash in the room. I could tell he noticed something was off with her as well. He scrunched up his nose and stared at her until she was uncomfortable enough to look up at him.

"Do we know each other?"

She shook her head so hard that she dislodged the pen she had tucked behind her ear.

"No. No I don't think we do."

He scratched his chin and narrowed his eyes at her. "Are you sure? You look really familiar to me."

She shrugged and fiddled with the stethoscope that dangled around her neck. She was hot, and if I was so inclined, I could see working up some really nice nurse fantasies where she was the main attraction.

"I get that a lot. I must just have one of those faces. I have to run. No rest for the wicked." She gave me a little grin and disappeared around the corner, leaving both of us staring after her, me in pure male appreciation, Nash in puzzlement.

"I swear I know that chick from somewhere."

"She one of your one-hit wonders?"

"No. Maybe Rule's pre-Shaw?"

I snorted and contemplated the ceiling while my head and side continued to burn. "She seems too smart to fall into that category."

"Maybe. It's going to drive me nuts until I figure it out. What the hell happened to you tonight? Picking a fight with Rule wasn't enough, you had to take on a whole biker bar?"

"'Merica!" I gave a bitter laugh at my lame joke.

He scowled at me and took a seat on the doctor's wheelie chair, dwarfing the thing.

"Seriously, Rome. You need to knock this shit off."

I didn't have to answer because the doctor chose that moment to come in. He was a guy in his fifties who clearly was at the end of a long shift because he was no-nonsense as all get-out and wasted no time it fixing me right up. When he was done he gave me a serious look and told me I might want to lay off the booze considering my blood test came back potent enough to start fires, and all I could do was silently agree.

He scribbled a prescription for painkillers that I hoped I wouldn't need to fill since I was already struggling with my reliance on another dangerous substance, and told me the nurse would be back in a few minutes to discharge me. I was stoked about having one more chance to get my flirt going, but as soon as she stuck her head back in, it was clear she was all business and wanted nothing more than to see us go.

"Take care of yourself, Mr. Archer, and thank you for your service to our country."

She spun around to leave when Nash suddenly hopped to his feet and snapped his fingers. It made the nurse wince and made me frown.

"I knew I knew you! We went to high school together, didn't we? Aren't you Saint Ford?"

We could have heard a pin drop she went so still and got so quiet. She stared at him like he had just crawled out of the sewer.

"I am. I'm surprised you recognized me, most people don't."

He tilted his head to the side and gave her a considering look. "Why did you say we didn't know each other, then?"

She cleared her throat and fiddled with the end of her braid. She was clearly very uncomfortable with the conversation.

"Because high school was a million years ago and I was a very different person then. It's not a time that comes with the fondest memories; in fact I prefer to pretend it never even happened. I'm sure that's not something a guy like you can understand. Have a nice night; try to avoid any more knife-wielding bikers if you can, Mr. Archer."

She swept out in a haughty cloud, leaving both of us dumbfounded and gaping at each other.

"Whoa. Were you a dick to her in school or something? That was a whole lot of hostility for something that happened so long ago."

He shrugged and helped me get up onto my feet. I wobbled a bit from the mixture of alcohol and blood loss, so he didn't let go until I was steady.

"Probably. Rule, Jet, and I were a bunch of punks. Remy was the nice one."

"What do you mean, "were"? You probably teased her for being fat or something."

He had the good grace to look ashamed. "That is entirely possible. I wasn't exactly in a great place when I was in high school either. There was too much stuff going on with my mom and that idiot she married for me to really give a crap about anything or anyone else. Man, that blows. She's a total babe now."

I didn't even consider putting my blood-soaked shirt back on as I hobbled out of the emergency room.

"She sure is."

We got to Nash's fully restored '73 Dodge Charger and I slumped down in the seat. It wasn't the worst Independence Day I could remember having, but it sure wasn't one of the best either. All I wanted to do was crawl into bed and forget about everything, not that that seemed to be working out for me so great as of late.

"Listen, dude, I'm sorry about today. I'll touch base with Rule and make things right. I'm just a little off balance right now."

The massive motor rattled so loud it made my teeth hurt.

"We all get that. You just aren't giving anyone a chance to try and help set you straight."

"I'll chill out." I wasn't sure how I was going to go about that exactly but I knew I needed to get on it. "You can tell the rabid pixie to back off."

He laughed. "No can do, my friend. Cora is like a pit bull; when she sinks her teeth into something or someone she doesn't let go. You might want to try and apologize. She just wants to look out for all of us and she does a good job of it."

I closed my eyes and let my head drop back on the seat.

"I remember when that was my job."

Heavy silence filled the car and I didn't think he was going to say anything else about it, but after a minute he muttered, "You went off to save the entire world, Rome, we just did the best we could while you were gone."

Just like being a big guy often had its disadvantages, wanting to be a hero to everyone and anyone often had the same dangerous pitfalls. I got used to everyone needing me, to them relying on me, and now that I wasn't needed anymore I simply just didn't know what to do with myself. That honestly terrified me more than any war zone or bar brawl with armed bikers ever could.

CHAPTER 3

Cora

SUMMERTIME WAS ALWAYS BUSIER at the shop. It was the Tuesday after the ill-fated barbecue, and the ink bunnies were out in full force. The warm weather and lack of clothes led to people wanting to get all kinds of adornment in all kinds of interesting and visible places, and I swore to God that ever since Rule had officially gone off the market, the girls who came in to get work done specifically by him had doubled in number. I would never understand the allure of wanting something you clearly couldn't have, but I had to admit it was a riot to watch them try to get it.

The Terrible Trio were booked solid for the next six weeks, as were the other three artists who rounded out the crew at the Marked. I wasn't as busy since I had to schedule appointments around my other obligations at the shop. Today a young guy had wandered in talking a big game about getting a full Jacob's ladder, but hadn't even made it past the point where he actually had to take his pants and underwear off to let me get at the goods. That happened a lot, so I found myself with an hour of downtime that I was using to stalk Jimmy on Facebook.

For the last five years Jimmy only popped up in my mind when something or someone reminded me of him, but ever since that wedding invitation showed up in the mail, I was obsessed. It was like all the old hurt, the old embarrassment, was fresh in my mind and all the wounds he had left me with were opened back up and bleeding. I really owed that jackass a punch in the nuts if I ever saw him again. I hated to admit that the girl my ex was going to marry really was lovely and that they looked happy together, but then I remembered that he and I had looked that way as well at one point in time and it hadn't kept him faithful to me.

The guys were listening to some really loud punk rock and I wasn't really paying attention because I was lost in my own memories when I realized someone was leaning on the counter across from me. The waiting area had people milling around waiting for their friends or family members to finish up with their appointments, but I hadn't heard the chime of the bell over the door ring to indicate a new arrival. At first I thought it was a walk-in wanting to set up a consult, but it was only when I had to lift my gaze up, and then even farther up, that I realized it was not someone I was particularly happy to see. My feelings must have been reflected on my face because the hard mouth I was used to seeing in a harsh downturn actually kicked up on one side in a grin that transformed Rome's entire face.

There was no denying the Archer brothers had won the genetic lottery. Whereas Rule's good looks were camouflaged under self-adorned artwork and flare, Rome's were totally in your face and impossible for all the girly parts of me not to notice. If the army wanted to guarantee the recruitment of every ninety-pound weakling from here to Brooklyn, all they needed to do was slap Rome Archer on their recruitment posters. He just emanated a sense of "take care of business" that was heady, and I shouldn't have found it attractive, but I totally did. He was as gorgeous as he was annoying.

I cleared my throat and clicked off the browser.

"You look terrible." And he did. He had a black ball cap on with a white Broncos logo on the front, but even under the shadow of the brim I could see that he had the shadow of a bruise under one eye and that the knuckles of the hands he hand placed on the counter where he was leaning were torn up and covered in scabs. All that aside, his eyes were still the bluest blue I had ever seen and that tiny little grin did more to make him look like an actual, breathing human than I think a full-on smile ever could.

The eyebrow under the scar twitched a little and he rapped his fingers on the marble that separated us.

"You have really pretty eyes."

I blinked those eyes in surprise because I wasn't expecting that. So far all this guy had shown he was capable of emoting was vitriol and angst. The compliment seemed out of left field.

"Ahh . . . thanks?" My eyes were two different colors. The left was a bright, iridescent turquoise that was indeed really pretty, the right was a hazel brown that fluctuated between hot-cocoa brown to the color of espresso at any given moment. People commented on them a lot, but I never would have figured Rome to be one of them. In fact I think it was the first thing he had every spoken directly to me. I was good with words, so I didn't love that him being nice made me tongue-tied.

"Do you think you can grab my brother for me? I need to talk to him really quick. I have an entire post–Independence Day parade of repentance I need to get through today."

I stared up at him in surprise. In my experience big, gruff ex-soldiers weren't the type of guys who readily admitted accountability when they messed up. I wasn't sure what to make of that, or really of him. I did know his looming presence and those too-blue eyes were making me kind of uncomfortable, but not in the *he's a big jerk* kind of way, more in the *I really want to see him without a shirt on* kind of way.

I cleared my throat again and looked back into the shop. Rule was wiping the clear goo on the fresh ink he used to protect the tattoo for the client until they got home. He was watching Rome and me interact with a frown on his face and I noticed that Nash and Rowdy all wore similar expressions. I didn't know if the sour looks were directed at me or at Rome, but I didn't like it either way and gave them all a glare back. I swiveled around in my chair and looked back up at Rome. He was watching me with a look of curiosity on his face and I almost wished I knew him better so I knew what it meant.

"He'll be done in like fifteen minutes if you want to hang out. He has another appointment right behind it, though, so try and keep the murder and mayhem to a minimum."

He snorted and pushed off the counter. I hated to admit

it, but I couldn't pull my gaze away from the muscles that
were rippling along his huge biceps, visible under the sleeves
of his black T-shirt. I wasn't the kind of girl who was attracted to bulging muscles and a rock-hard physique, at least
I never thought I was until I couldn't pull my eyes off of all
the sinew and flex that was Rome Archer. He was just too
big, too much, and way too all-American to be sending all
those kinds of tingly things running under my skin.

"I'm not exactly sure why, but I feel like I should apologize to you as well. Even though I'm the one that ended up
covered head to toe in beer."

I winced a little and tried not to squirm under the scrutiny of those piercing eyes. I tugged on my ear and looked
away. The smooth surface of the plug in the lobe rubbed
back and forth between my fingers.

"I have a tendency to overreact at times, and you were
being unbearable. Every one of those people loves you and
has worried about you for years and years while you were
gone. The least you can do is return that affection."

He had the good grace to look properly chastised, and
when he took his hat off to rub a hand over his short cap of
hair, I noticed a nasty-looking gash that now decorated the
side of his head.

"What on earth happened to you?"

He looked confused until his fingers grazed the shaved
spot and the tiny metal sutures holding his scalp together.

He slammed his hat back on his head and the grin that
had been dancing around his mouth fell totally away.

"Wrong place at the wrong time, I have a knack for finding myself there."

I didn't understand how a guy who clearly had so much going for him—good looks, a loving family, hordes of people that cared about him, a successful career, and obviously a rigid sense of duty and honor—could be so unconcerned about his circumstances and his impact on those around him.

I cocked my head to the side and regarded him closely. I didn't know Rome from any other stranger on the street, but there was something about him, something strong and magnetic that I was having a hard time denying made me want to figure out what made him tick. Maybe it was the idea of having a distraction from how bummed out I was becoming the closer the date to Jimmy's wedding got. Maybe it was because he was so ingrained in the lives of everyone I cared about. Maybe it was because he was just so much larger than life and impossible to ignore, but the longer we stared at each other the more my curiosity was piqued.

I was going to tell him he should be more careful, when a heavy hand fell on the back of my neck and gave it a slight squeeze. I knew Rule well enough to take it as the warning it was: *Don't meddle.* Rome didn't need me trying to dismantle him and reassemble him in proper working order. He was a grown man and was going to have to find his way on his own.

Rule's client looked back and forth between the brothers with huge eyes and then at me, like I could explain why the room suddenly seemed full of tension and hostility, making it almost impossible to breathe. I forced a smile at her and climbed out of the chair.

"Let me just check you out and get you paid up. Why

don't you two take the brotherly love outside before you scare the rest of the customers into leaving?"

Rule gave the back of my neck another squeeze and let me go as he made his way around the counter toward Rome. The two brothers regarded each other stonily and Rule pushed out the glass front door without saying a word to his big brother. The antagonism passing between the two of them felt hot and heavy, which was a shame. They had already suffered the loss of one brother, they should be reveling in the fact they still had each other to lean on and give shit to. I had a hard time understanding how Remy's secrets had done more to drive the Archer brothers apart than his actual death had.

Rome gave me one last look that I couldn't decipher. "They're all lucky to have you."

I thought the same thing all the time, but it was weird hearing him say it in such an empty and hollow tone, like he was missing something crucial.

"Well, I'm lucky to have all of them, too, and so are you, Captain No-Fun."

Those blue eyes got big and then blinked at me and once again that little half grin that turned him from a good-looking dude into someone that made my heart bump against my chest in an erratic rhythm lit up his face.

"What did you call me?"

"Captain No-Fun."

He let out a chuckle that sounded rusty from lack of use and he shook his head at me.

"Staff Sergeant No-Fun is more accurate."

I gaped a little in surprise that a sense of humor actually lurked somewhere under all the muscle and broodiness.

"I call my dad 'Admiral Ass Hat,' he doesn't really think it's funny."

The scar on his forehead twitched again. "Your dad was in the navy?"

"Oh yeah. He was totally Popeye."

"Was he really an admiral?" There was a shade of respect in his tone.

"Yep, so you can imagine how thrilled he was trying to rein me in when I was younger."

He chuckled again and this time it didn't sound so much like it hurt him. His eyes glinted at me as he pulled the door open to follow Rule out into the Colorado sunshine.

"I don't know, Half-Pint, something tells me reining you in is probably a pretty good time."

I felt my next words die in my throat, and it occurred to me that I was openly flirting with a guy I had poured beer all over only a couple of days ago. Not to mention he totally wasn't my type and so far from what my idea of what the perfect match for me was that it was laughable.

I jerked my attention back to Rule's client, who was still waiting to pay for the peacock design he had inked along her rib cage. She was watching me with what I could only describe as envy, so I coughed a little and tried to get back down to business. It bugged me that while I ran her credit card and went over the after-care instructions with her, my gaze kept wandering to the big panes of glass that faced Colfax and the Capitol Hill area of downtown Denver. Rome had his back to the glass and I could see Rule gesturing with his hands, and he had a look on his face that was intense and serious. It looked like this was a confrontation the boys needed to have a long time ago.

"Here ya go." I handed her the slip to sign and wasn't surprised when she not only tipped 35 percent but also jotted her phone number down on the back of the slip. I would have given her a reproachful look or made some kind of snarky comment about it but she beat me to the punch.

With a shrug she tossed her hair over her shoulder and gave me rueful grin.

"You have the best view in all of Denver in this shop, and every time I come back it gets better. I saw his girl's name tattooed across his knuckles on his hand. If he won't take my number, give it to the big guy, I'm not picky and he looks like he could use a good time."

She swept out of the shop leaving me feeling a mixture of irritation and something else I wasn't sure of. It felt slimy and slippery and I didn't like whatever it was at all. I was possessive over my guys, that much was true, but Rome wasn't one of them, so I couldn't justify why the girl wanting him to have her number made me want to pull out her hair strand by strand.

Rome and Rule were still going at it when his next client showed up, so I set the guy up and had him fill out all his paperwork and stuff so that all Rule had to do was put the transfer on and do the tattoo. When I got back to the desk, Nash was sending his client on his way and had taken over my seat. He was watching me steadily out of those eyes that were way more lilac than blue. I crossed my arms over my chest, propped a hip on the desk, and met him look for look.

"What?"

He rubbed his thumb along the corner of his mouth and blew out a breath. "I need a smoke."

"I thought you were trying to quit."

" 'Trying' is the operative word in that sentence."

"Try chewing gum or something."

He grunted and arched back in the chair, lacing his fingers together behind his tattooed head. Nash was a really handsome guy, it just took a minute to notice it under that shockingly tattooed scalp and the tiny ring hooked through the center of his nose.

"Don't even try and go there with Rome, Cora."

I tried to keep my eye from twitching and my mouth from frowning. I had known Nash for a long time and there was no way I could pretend not to know what he was talking about.

"You all say he's a wonderful guy. Why wouldn't you want me to try and help get him back for you?"

"Because not everyone in the world needs your kind of help. Rome will find his way, we all believe that, and I was talking about the goo-goo eyes you two were just making at each other. That isn't something I think either of you needs to try and mess with."

I didn't like anyone trying to tell me what to do, even if I knew Nash was just looking out for my ultimate best interests.

"It's not like I'm Captain America's type anyway. Don't

worry." I pushed the edge of the chair with my foot, making him twist away from me. "Besides, you know I'm holding out for Mr. Perfect and that guy is so far from it there isn't a bridge on this planet that could get him from here to there."

He planted his Vans-clad feet on the ground and pushed up so that he was standing in front of me. He bent down so that we were nose to nose and I couldn't look away from those intense, pretty-colored eyes.

"There *is* no Mr. Perfect, Tink. You made him laugh, whatever that means. I haven't heard him laugh one single time since he got back into town. Just watch yourself because no one county can have two rulers and neither one of you likes to give up control."

I wanted to laugh it off, to brush off his warning as unwarranted and silly, but I couldn't ignore the fact that Rome Archer was enigmatic and that I found him more interesting than anyone I had encountered in a long time. Not to mention I really did want to see what he looked like without his shirt on, which was something because my libido had been missing in action for longer than I cared to admit . . . Ack, it all had the makings of something that was indeed bound to get complicated and messy if I didn't put a lid on it quick.

I sat back down just as Rule came back in the door. He didn't look overly upset, but he didn't exactly look very happy either. I was going to ask him if he was okay, but he waved me off and muttered that he didn't want to keep his client waiting any longer than he already had. Since that was a valid brush-off, I let it slide and went back about the business of keeping the shop running.

I know it was often hard to believe, given my big mouth and unusual appearance, but I had a killer mind for business and was really only a few college courses away from finishing out a full-fledged MBA. My dad and I had a difficult and convoluted relationship, but I always wanted him to be proud of me, and he had given me every tool and every opportunity to be the best me I could be. It had just been him and me for as long as I could remember. My mom had decided having a baby and being married to a guy who was deployed all the time was no fun, so I bounced from naval base to naval base and spent ungodly amounts of time with a series of nannies, distant relatives, and eventually Dad's girlfriends or live-in lady friends until I met Jimmy when I was seventeen and promptly decided he was my whole world.

Dad had eventually, after too many knock-down, drag-out fights, agreed to let me go live with Jimmy as long as I graduated high school and enrolled in college. I had no problem doing either of those things, and by the time I was a freshman in college, Jimmy had the shop open in Brooklyn and I was doing the same thing I did now for far less money. I had always had an interest in body modification, but I couldn't even draw a stick figure, so it was just a natural progression that I learned how to pierce and do dermal implants from the guy at Jimmy's shop. He was an awesome mentor and I liked having an actual skill that I could use in the world I lived in. Plus, it was fun to stick needles in people. What can I say, I'm a weird chick.

When things had gone south with Jimmy, my drive and ambition had taken a nose dive right along with my relationship. I barely finished my senior year and the damage done had a lasting effect on my GPA. I could go back and finish fairly easily but at this point in my career I made a good living at the Marked, I had a full life and generally was happy, aside from missing that magical connection with someone to make me a we instead of simply a me. I had been alone for too long.

Unbidden my thoughts went back to Rome and to that eerie and tight feeling I had in my chest when that girl had asked me to hand her number off to him. We were strangers, I was pretty sure I didn't even like him very much, but there was no doubt about it: today, while we were in each other's orbit, he got me to react. I wasn't sure what to make of that yet. The last guy who had gotten me to react had also destroyed my world when he decided I wasn't what he wanted. I didn't do well as a leaf no longer attached to tree. I needed roots, a foundation to grab on to, and when my perfect guy came along he was going to be so solidly planted it would take a hurricane to move him.

The rest of the day was busy and I had two more appointments of my own to get through. I lost track of time and was busy cleaning up my piercing studio and hollering at the guys to make sure they turned off the lights on their way out when I heard the bell over the door ring. Since I had locked it after my last client, I knew it could only be Phil. I poked my head out of the door to tell him I would be out in a second and tried to remember if I had done the "cash out" in order to hand it off to him for the nightly cash drop.

Phil was as opposite to my very clean-cut, straitlaced

dad as a man could get. He looked more like a biker than a successful businessman, but the two men had served together in their much younger days, Phil only staying in for a short four years, while my dad made a lifelong career out of the navy. I never really understood how they managed to maintain such a close friendship, considering they disagreed on everything under the sun. Phil was like a second father to me, and I treated him just like I did my own, so when I came out of the room snapping off my latex gloves, I frowned when I saw him sitting in my chair with his head in his hands.

Phil looked an awful lot like an older version of Nash; they had the same swarthy complexion, the same periwinkle-colored eyes, and the same stocky build. Phil had a riot of black hair that he wore pretty long for a guy his age, but with his sleeves of tattoos and neatly trimmed goatee, he pulled it off and still managed to be a babe even if he was in his late forties.

"What's going on, boss?"

He was typically an energetic and vivacious guy. He lived life at a hundred miles an hour and was constantly taking in strays. I personally thought it was his mission in life to save every wayward soul from themselves.

He looked up at me and I was surprised to see how tired and worn he looked. He had bags under his eyes and his normally full cheeks looked slightly sunken in and hollow, like he hadn't had a good meal in a few weeks. He rubbed his fists in his eyes and blinked at me.

"Just tired. I've been busy. I was thinking about opening

a second shop in LoDo and that's taken more time and effort than I thought." He even sounded exhausted.

"I didn't know you were thinking about opening an-other shop."

"You guys are the best, but there is a lot of talent out there. I see way too many bad tattoos, too much messed-up work coming out of other shops in this town. I have the re-sources for it, and frankly I think Denver needs it."

I went to the safe and pulled the cash dropout. There was definitely a profit to be made in having a second loca-tion. I was just surprised I had never heard a word about it before now.

"Have you told the guys about it?"

Phil took the bank bag from me and I frowned when I noticed that his fingers were shaking. Something was off here and I didn't have a good feeling about it at all. He gave his head a little shake and pushed up from the chair. It looked like it took far more effort than such a simple act should have taken.

"No. Rule was busy getting a house and settling down with his girl. Nash would ask too many questions, want to be too involved, and I haven't made enough firm decisions about anything yet. Jet ran off and got married, so we know where his head is at, and Rowdy . . ." A little grin tugged at his goatee. "Rowdy will just go with the flow. The others won't be affected by it one way or the other, so I don't think anyone needs in on it until I know for sure what I'm dealing with."

I had the very distinct impression we were talking about something other than a second tattoo shop, but I had no clue what that might be, so I just stared at him hoping he would clue me in. When he didn't I sighed and ran my hands through my short hair. I decided to change the subject.

"How well do you know Rome?"

He gave me a strange look. "That's an odd question, Cora. Why do you ask?"

I tried to shrug nonchalantly but I wasn't sure I pulled it off.

"Now that he's back from Afghanistan, he's around a lot. We don't exactly click. I poured a beer over his head at the barbecue on the Fourth. I thought he would be pissed about it forever but then he showed up here today all contrite and conciliatory. I'm just trying to figure him out."

He started to answer me but broke into a cough so loud and hacking that I thought maybe I was going to have to catch his lung if it flew out of his mouth. I settled for patting him on the back until he waved me away.

"Stop it. I'm fine."

"You sound the opposite of fine."

"I think I'm just coming down with a cold or something." He cleared his throat and rubbed the center of his chest like it hurt. "I don't know Rome as well as the rest of the boys. He had it okay at home, his relationship with his folks was nowhere near as contentious as Rule's was. I know he loved those brothers of his and took care of them like it was his God-given mission from birth. They were a solid unit and I was glad when he took Nash into that fold. It didn't surprise me when he enlisted, or that things got rough when the folks let the truth out about Remy. Rome was always going out of his way to play hero for his little brothers, I'm sure it stung something fierce to find out one of them was protecting him all along."

"I don't get it. Why would anyone have cared if Remy was gay if they all loved him so damn much?"

"It wasn't that. Rome would have tried to stand between Remy and the rest of the world, he wouldn't have tolerated anyone trying to say anything bad about his baby brother, regardless if Remy needed the help or not. I think he was saving Rome from himself by not telling him the truth, but knowing someone you loved so fiercely kept such a huge secret from you is rough. You know that, Tink."

I did know that, but I was so used to fighting my battles alone that the idea of having someone love me as unconditionally as that was pretty foreign. I mean my dad loved me, but he didn't necessarily protect me. I knew my friends here would die for me, would stand between me and anything that wanted to hurt me, but I was always the one that charged headfirst into most situations, regardless of the blowback that tended to end up on me. There were times when I wondered if I was going to be too much for them to take.

"He comes across very intense."

"He's a guy that has been at war for too long. I'm sure that's left its mark."

I thought about that scar that cut across his forehead, marring an otherwise beautiful example of masculine perfection. The marks that had been left on him from that life weren't just the ones on the inside, I guessed.

Another round of coughing broke through my thoughts and I scowled at Phil as fiercely as I could to let him know that I meant business.

"You need to get that checked out. It sounds terrible."

"Yeah, yeah, as soon as I find the time. It's just a little tickle."

"No, it's not. It sounds like you have the Black Plague."

He shook his head at me and bent over to give me a little kiss on the cheek.

"You worry too much. You take care of those boys, I can take care of myself." He lifted a dark eyebrow at me. "While you're at it, why don't you find someone to take care of you? That would make your old man so damn happy."

I snorted and went to grab my purse and cell phone from the drawer I kept them in while I worked. I was trying, but everyone came up short. It was hard to trust someone enough to let them all the way in when I didn't think they deserved to be there.

"Nobody fits the bill. Everyone keeps telling me my expectations are too high."

"Are they?"

We walked out the front door and I hit the last of the lights. I folded against Phil as he tugged me into a tight one-armed hug. I tried to fight down a swell of panic when I realized I could feel his ribs through his shirt. He was typically a solid guy, this wasn't good.

"My expectations are what they are. I'm never going to end up in a situation like I did with Jimmy again."

"Ah, honey, you gotta get over that burn. It was a long time ago. It should all be scar tissue by now and there are plenty of good, if not great men out there, and not a single one of them is going to come wrapped up in a bow of perfection."

"I expect a lot because I deserve a lot."

"That you do, Tink, but you also gotta keep your eyes open or the right one is going to pass you by because you were too busy looking for the white whale."

Again, against my will, my thoughts flipped to Rome Archer. I had told Nash that the older Archer was as far from perfect as I could imagine and I wasn't lying. He was moody, unpredictable, and I had a feeling that he was dealing with some baggage that even I couldn't help tackle. However, by all accounts he was also loyal to a fault, steadfastly honorable, and I had firsthand knowledge that he appeared to be honest and up-front about what he was feeling. There would be no guessing where you stood with the big guy, and something about that was alarmingly appealing.

Jimmy had been tall, not nearly as tall as Rome, but a lot taller than me. He had also had ink from his neck to his toes and had been pierced in all the most fun places. He wasn't drop-dead gorgeous like Rowdy, unforgettable like Rule, even just handsome like Nash, or rock-and-roll sexy like Jet. He was just a guy, and I had loved him beyond measure. But now, looking back on things, I was beginning to wonder if maybe I had been selling myself short because Rome was most definitely the most attractive guy I had ever seen up close and personal and he thought I had pretty eyes. Jimmy had never told me I had pretty anything. Rome felt dangerous and exciting at the same time even if perfect was nowhere in the picture. It made me all kinds of tingly and that was more than anyone else had done since Jimmy broke my heart.

CHAPTER 4

Rome

RULE LOOKED PISSED WHEN I finally pulled myself away from Cora and made my way outside. I wasn't looking forward to this little chat and flirting with the blonde was a great distraction. While she had been occupied with something on the computer I slipped in the front door and watched her unnoticed for a few minutes. She wasn't my type. I didn't normally go for girls that were so tiny. I liked them built sturdy and able to handle everything I had to give them. I wasn't a huge fan of all the ink and metal. I was used to it because my brother was covered in it and I had to admit that I liked the snowflakes that Shaw had across her neck and shoulders, but it wasn't my thing. I had enough permanent marks forever etched in my skin that I had never asked for and I couldn't imagine voluntarily adding any more. In fact I wasn't thrilled about the new addition on my head, considering that since I wore my hair so short, the bald spot from the scar was bound to show.

Cora was different. She didn't come across as delicate even

though she probably only reached my chest when we stood toe-to-toe. Her eyes were outstanding. I had never seen anything like them; the dual colors were unique in themselves, but the fact that whatever she was feeling literally ran from one color to the next was fascinating. I had never met a woman that transparent or that open with her emotions before. It was like she had zero artifice in her. She was also damn cute. Not beautiful or stunningly pretty, but she was cuter than any girl with that much attitude had a right to be, and somehow the bouquet of flowers that colored her skin in every shape and variety seemed like it belonged there. Even the pink eyebrow ring and the little gauges in her ears didn't distract from the fact that she was pretty much a hot little number all around.

I had to drag my attention to my brother when I could feel the heat of his anger blazing off the distance separating us. His icy eyes were hard and I knew simply throwing out a generic apology wasn't going to cut it.

"Rule, I'm sorry." I took my hat off and rubbed the back of my neck. "I'm sort of spiraling out of control right now and I don't want you to get caught up in it."

"Well, I am, and more importantly Shaw is, and I'm not down with that at all."

I cringed. "I'm sorry."

"For what? For ruining my barbecue? For making Shaw cry for no reason? For calling my relationship a mistake? For getting wasted and acting stupid all the time? For ignoring Mom and Dad? For getting your ass kicked by a bunch of bikers and calling Nash and not me? Narrow it the fuck down, Rome. What exactly are you sorry for?"

Damn, this wasn't my carefree and *I don't give a shit about anyone* brother. This was a serious-as-all-get-out young man who was rightfully pissed, and it was all directed at me. I sighed and I hung my head. Ever since the twins could walk, I had felt like they were mine to protect, mine to guide in the right direction, and mine to help groom into the men they were supposed to become. I didn't know if it was because Rule was such a troublemaker and always flitting from one catastrophe to the next, or because Remy was so coddled, so babied and in real danger of becoming a pansy, that I was so invested in their care, but whatever the reason, their well-being had always been my top priority and I felt now like I had let both of them down.

"All of it. I'm sorry for all of it. It's been rough trying to settle back into civilian life and I'm sucking at it. I shouldn't be taking it out on you guys. I know it, but I can't seem to stop it."

"We love you, dude, but I swear to God, if you put me in a position where I have to pick between you and Shaw, she is going to win every single time, hands down. Know it."

That took me aback for a second. After Remy died, it had just been me and Rule against the world. He wasn't only my little brother, he was also my best friend, and I had never been able to picture a scenario where someone would mean more to him than me. I sort of loved and hated that Shaw was that person. It also galled me to admit that I was damn proud of Rule for standing that particular ground with me.

"It won't come to that. I can't lose another brother. I'll make it right with Shaw. Mom and Dad might take some more time, but I'll get it together, swear it." I wasn't even ready to admit to myself the underlying reasons—beyond their dishonesty—that made dealing with my parents impossible for me at this juncture.

He looked skeptical, so I shoved my hands in my pockets and tried to explain.

"I love Shaw like a sister. I always took care of both you and Remy. It sucked that Shaw didn't tell us about Remy, but it sucks more that he used her and she let him get away with it. I'm mad at him and I was mad at her and I just didn't know what to do with any of it, so she suffered the brunt of it because I was leaving again anyway. We're family, all of us, there shouldn't have ever been secrets like that. It makes me feel like I was fighting for the wrong things all along, for people I didn't even really know."

"Remy made his choices. It sucks he didn't want us to know, didn't trust us to let him live his life the way he wanted, but he's gone and Shaw is here and she's mine. I'll protect her from anyone that wants to hurt her in any way, and that includes you, dickhead. I'm pissed at Remy, too, but I would rather keep the good memories alive, so every single day that's what I try and do."

Rule had a valid point, but he didn't understand that what I was battling against was so much bigger and harder to process than coming to terms with the fact that Remy and our parents had lied. I had so much death, so much blood in my dreams, that Rule would never be able to relate to it. No one would.

I blew out a heavy breath and slammed my hat back

down on my head, wincing a little as the interior scraped across my newly acquired wound.

"I wish it was that easy for me." I reached out and punched him in the shoulder. "Seriously I'll talk to Shaw and try and lay off the doom and gloom. Being Captain No-Fun really is no fun."

Rule rolled his winter-colored eyes and went to reach for the handle on the glass door we had been standing in front of. "Ignore Cora. We do all the time. She's a handful."

She did indeed look like the perfect handful, but I don't think Rule would appreciate me saying that. I wasn't even sure why I was thinking it.

"I really am sorry about the emergency room. I was pretty drunk and had lost a ton of blood; plus it's embarrassing. There's no way some scrawny biker prospect should've been able to get that good of a lick in the first place. Speaking of which, I have to roll to the bar and make amends. The owner took care of my bike, and when I went to collect it he wouldn't take a dime for the repairs to his place. He told me to swing by today and we could work something else out. He's a really legit guy, so I need to make it right by him as well."

"Cool, but next time you get cut open, call me. Put the shop number in your phone so that you can get in touch with me during the day. I don't answer my cell when I'm with clients. Cora can get me if you need me."

I tapped the number in my phone and regarded my brother seriously.

"We good?"

His eyes were so much cooler than mine, so much more guarded, and I could tell he wasn't a hundred percent on board with forgiving me just yet.

"For now we are."

It didn't sound like he had much hope for me being able to act right in the foreseeable future. I didn't like that at all. He told me he needed to get to his client, so we said good-bye and I found myself looking back through the glass to get another glimpse of the intriguing blonde. Too bad she had her back to me and appeared to be deep in conversation with Nash about something. I turned and went back to where I left my bike on the street to head down to Brite's bar.

I asked him the name of the place when I went to pick up my bike on the day after the Fourth, and he said it was called whatever I wanted to call it. The place had no official name, no signage, nothing. He told me most of the regulars just called it the Bar. That worked for me and it fit the simple, no-frills ambience of the place. So did the primarily classic rock that rattled off the old sound system Brite kept behind the bar. Plus he said that when most of the regulars grumbled to their pissed-off spouses that they were headed to the Bar, the vagueness of the name offered them a little breathing room while the angry wives called around town looking for which bar exactly.

When I got there, I was surprised that there was already a line of older guys seated at the bar top. I was having to work really hard at not disappearing into a bottle every night, and seeing them was a stark reminder that I could very well be them if I didn't get it together sooner rather than later.

I didn't want to be the lonely guy at the bar before noon, no one wondering where I was, no one concerned about my well-being, no place better to be or nothing better to do, with the bottom of a glass offering my only absolution. It didn't escape my notice that a lot of Brite's regular clientele, the guys that had been in here steadily since I wandered in a few days ago, were ex-military. The last thing I wanted was to become just one more . . . of anything.

The big man caught my eye from behind the bar and waved me over. I tried not to cringe when I had to walk over the lovely rust-colored stain that spread across the old wooden floor, courtesy of yours truly. I whipped my hat off, because even though we were from two different branches, and I probably outranked him in the reality of things, there was just something about Brite that demanded you show respect. I don't know if it was the eyes, so dark and serious, or that epic beard, but I had enough years in the service to know when to show proper regard for a fellow serviceman.

I leaned up against the end of the bar. I figured that kept me from looking like the sorry sacks that were posted up at it, already three or four rounds in.

"Thanks again for watching the bike, and the run to the ER. I really do appreciate it. I wish you would let me pay you for the damages."

I had more money in savings than I knew what to do with. I wasn't married, there wasn't a girlfriend, I didn't have kids, or a house and a dog, so while I was deployed, all I had to cover was the Harley and my truck. I wasn't a millionaire by any stretch of the imagination, but until I figured out

what in the hell I was going to do with myself for the foreseeable future, I most definitely had enough stockpiled to live
on comfortably. I could clean up the mess I made in the Bar
and not even notice it was gone. Only Brite just shook his
shaggy head, and that rueful grin split his beard.

"I don't need your money, son."

I lifted the eyebrow that was under the scar, it was the
only one I could arch independently, so I did it a lot.

"No? Well, what did you mean when you said we could
work something out?"

I had to wait as he was called to the other end of the bar
by one of the patrons. It startled me to realize the new customer was probably only five years older than me. I also recognized the Army Ranger insignia tattooed on his bicep and
felt a shiver of apprehension slide down my spine. I didn't
want to see myself in these guys, in this place, but it was getting harder and harder not to.

By the time Brite made his way back to me, I had given
up the fight and propped myself up on an empty stool. My
thoughts had drifted down a rather dark path, and I was
having to struggle really hard to stay in the present. I wondered briefly if it showed on my face. I used to think I was
pretty good at hiding all the turmoil that was crawling, satu-
rating, filling me up from the inside out. After the blowup
with Rule, and the way Brite was looking at me as he lum-
bered in my direction, I wasn't so sure that was the case. I
cleared my throat and forced myself to meet that charcoal
gaze as he leaned on heavy forearms across from me.

"How handy are you?"

I tilted my head to the side and considered him in puzzlement. "What exactly do you mean by 'handy'?" I mean I could break down pretty much any weapon you put in my hand and have it back together and firing in seconds, I could field-dress any number of injuries, I could tinker with the motor on the Harley and probably troubleshoot the basics of anything thrown at me. I was a problem solver by nature, but I wasn't going to go out and build a house from the ground up or anything crazy like that.

He gave me that grin that I was starting to think meant the guy had something up his sleeve.

"You're a guy with plenty of time on his hands and I'm a guy with a bar in serious need of some TLC. I already spend too much time here and I have no desire to be stripping floors and refinishing this bar top at my age. You bled all over it, you can fix it."

We stared at each other in a tense silence for a long time. I was trying to figure out if he was serious and I think he was waiting to see if I was going to waffle or not. Finally I had to blink, so I leaned back in the stool with a sigh.

"Are you sure you don't just want me to come regulate, like watch the door for you for a few weeks or something. Then no one would have to worry about bleeding on the floor in the first place."

He barked out a laugh that made me cringe.

"No offense, son, but last time you were in a scuffle in here, you were the one that had to get dragged to the doc."

I made a face and tried not to let the truth of it sting my already wounded pride. "I was drunk, and outnumbered."

"It doesn't matter. I don't need a bouncer. I need a help-ing hand, someone I can trust, and someone that can be in here and not judge, because maybe, just maybe, he sees a little bit of himself in some of the regulars."

It took every single fiber of self-control I had not to react to his dead-on assessment of how I was feeling. I had to fight not to fidget but to just sit still and try and think of any good excuse not to do what he was asking me to do. When noth-ing came to mind, it made that dark place I was hovering on get just a little bit wider.

Not even six months ago I was in charge of over a hun-dred men. I planned clandestine missions, I was the go-to guy for all the answers and solutions, and none of that trans-lated to any kind of goddamn real-world job experience. I indeed had way too much free time on my hands and no end in sight for it. It made my head hurt and my heart speed up a little in my chest, so I cleared my throat and told Brite thanks when he set a glass of water down in front of me.

"Are you sure you wouldn't rather me write you a check?"

He shook his head and that grin I was really starting to mistrust broke through once again.

"Nope. I don't need your cash, I need you."

Seeing that there really was no way around it if I wanted to be a man of my word, I nodded solemnly. I wanted to show this burly man who I respected without question, be-cause I felt like we were kindred spirits, that I might not know where I was going or what I was doing but I still had more honor than one man needed in this lifetime.

"All right. I can do what you need me to do. How long do you think it'll all take?"

He laughed long and hard, so hard that some of the other regulars looked our way in curiosity. I didn't see why it was funny but I kept my mouth shut.

"As long as it takes, son."

That seemed vague and open-ended, but before I could make him hammer down a more definitive time frame, he slapped his meaty hands down on the bar in front of me and leaned across the wooden expanse so that we were eye to eye. It was unnerving to have those dark eyes peer so intently into my own, but I immediately understood that whatever he was going to follow up with was to be taken seriously. This was without a doubt Brite's *I'm serious as hell* face.

"No drinking while you're working. I mean it."

I frowned a little. "Okay."

"I'm serious, Rome. I know firsthand how easy it can be to lose track of what it's like trying to live outside the bottle. What you do in your free time is of no concern to me, you want to pickle your liver that's your choice to make, but while you're here, I won't watch another good man go down."

"Weren't you the one pouring me endless shots of Wild Turkey the other night?" I would rather have all my teeth removed from my head by rusty pliers than admit how often a bottle of Belvedere was putting me to bed these days.

"It was the Fourth; every soldier should be allowed to celebrate what they have given up to support freedom, no matter how long ago that victory was."

I considered him carefully, but couldn't fault him his reasoning, so I just shrugged.

"All right, I don't think that should be a problem."

"It won't be a problem."

Jeez, this guy sounded like the very first drill sergeant I had when I enlisted.

"Okay, Brite, it won't be a problem."

His teeth appeared through the tangle of facial hair again and he smacked his palms flat on the bar.

"Excellent. You'll meet the rest of the gang eventually as we go along. The Sons of Sorrow haven't been back in, but if they come, I'll have a talk with the chapter president and let him know he better rein his prospects in. I don't mind a fistfight here or there, it gives the place character and keeps things interesting, but I have a hard-and-fast rule and no one, and I mean no one, touches servicemen or women when they're in here. Everyone knows that."

I laughed a little and climbed to my feet.

"It's the American Legion."

Brite laughed with me and picked up a bar towel. "Civilian life can be a real bitch to settle back into, sometimes it helps to have a place that feels more familiar. That's what the Bar is all about, son."

Since I was feeling so adrift myself, I had to admit what he was talking about sounded not only nice but also particularly necessary. I slapped my ball cap back on my head and shook Brite's hand. I agreed that I would be back tomorrow when he opened the doors at ten in the morning. I wasn't exactly excited about it, but it was the first time since I got back to the States that I actually had someplace to be. And that felt more right than anything had in a long time.

I WOULD'VE GOTTEN UP early the next morning, but considering I was sleeping fitfully at best, I was wide-awake already when my alarm went off at eight. Since Nash normally didn't have to go into work until noon, we usually tried to hit up the gym before he went in—that is, if he made it home from wherever he spent the night before. I think he felt bad for me, because while he and Rule had a pretty lax gym ritual they usually adhered to, I went every morning, and since I'd moved in he had managed to trudge along or at least made the effort to try. I needed the gym to work out the things chasing me in my subconscious, and even if I didn't feel like a warrior anymore, at least I could still look like one. Besides, I was just too big; if I didn't go to the gym, I would turn into a blob of a man in no time flat, especially since I was no longer out running PT and ops with kids ten years younger than me on the regular.

I was rubbing my eyes and making coffee when Nash's bedroom door opened. I never knew if it was going to be him coming out or some dewy-eyed young thing that looked like she had been through the sex spin cycle. Nash and my brother both had a way about them that drew attention from the opposite sex in a way I just never really understood. Not that I lived like a choirboy in my youth, but I had never been the kind of guy who wanted quantity over quality. That made my momentary lapse with the trashy redhead even more stupid. Man, maybe I really did deserve having my ass kicked the other night.

Nash was flying solo this morning, which was unusual. He was pulling a T-shirt on over his head and muttering a few swearwords under his breath. I handed him a cup of coffee and asked him what was wrong.

He just shook his head and cracked his neck.

"I'm trying to get my uncle to go to the doctor and he's being stubborn. Cora called after work last night saying he sounds like he's hacking up a lung and looks pale. He's insisting that it's just a cold, but even over the phone I can tell he sounds terrible."

I knew they were really close. Uncle Phil had raised Nash and been more of a parent to Rule than my own folks. I didn't know much about the man, but by all accounts he was a real stand-up guy and I knew the guys held him in really high regard.

"Maybe it really is just a bad cold."

Nash nodded and pointed at the half-smoked pack of cigarettes he had abandoned on the counter.

"I picked up the habit from him when I was younger. It makes me nervous."

"Then quit."

"I'm trying."

I snatched the pack of the counter and tossed it in the sink. Nash hollered my name and swore at me as I turned on the garbage disposal.

"Try harder."

He glared at me. "You're a douche bag."

I shrugged. "I've been called worse." I rolled my heavy shoulders and popped my knuckles.

"You ready to do this?"

He was still scowling at me. "No. I'm gonna swing by his place and see if I can harass him into getting a checkup, at the very least. Plus I have an early appointment."

"All right."

We said good-bye and I headed to the gym. I worked out harder than I had in a while, I think I was trying to burn out the memories, sweat out the coil of dread and unease that always felt like it sat in my stomach. I was sore and worn out by the time I showered and changed into an old pair of jeans and a faded tee with the word ARMY stenciled on the front. I opted to take my pickup in today since I was already dragging and didn't feel up to muscling the Harley through downtown traffic.

When I got into the bar Brite was already waiting with a list and a huge-ass BLT. It was too early for lunch, but considering the beating I had just put my body through, it was welcome. We chitchatted for a few minutes, he introduced me to his cook, a lady who was about the same age as him named Darcy, who apparently was also wife number two, and he ran down the list of the regulars that my too tired brain tried to process sluggishly.

The list of tasks he handed over was impressive. He wanted the bar stripped, stained, and varnished. He wanted all the tables and chairs tightened and cleaned up. He wanted the battered wood floors stripped, sanded, and refinished. He wanted all the heavy kitchen equipment moved and the whole joint power-washed. He wanted all the lights changed out. He wanted the entire place primed and painted. He wanted me to build a stage. He wanted me to reorganize the liquor stock room, including adding new shelving and storage. It was all stuff that was fairly easy and mindless, nothing I didn't think I could handle. In fact I was arrogant enough to think I could knock it all out in a couple of weeks.

It took two days for me to realize I was going to be at the Bar forever. Every time I would get started on a particular project, one of the grizzled veterans would wander over and I would find myself stuck in a conversation about the best way to do, or how they would do, or what I was doing, who I was, where I was from, my rank and designation, which inevitably led to talk about the military and endless amounts of war stories. Before I knew it, the day had come and gone and I hadn't accomplished much of anything. I mentioned it to Brite and he just shrugged it off and told me once again that it would be done when it was done, like I had all the time in the world. Like I didn't need to figure out what in the world I was going to be now that I was a grown-up and no longer in the army. I tried not to let it rub me the wrong way.

It was late Friday night, or rather super early Saturday morning and I was lying in bed staring at the ceiling. I was making a conscious effort not to use vodka as a sleep aid, but tonight I was regretting it. Luckily Nash hadn't been home, because this nightmare, when it woke me up, was violent enough that my own screaming had jolted me awake. I was sweating and shaking and getting a drink sounded awesome. I didn't do it, though, I just lay there and let the images that had been too harsh to sleep through roll endlessly through my head. I knew logically that if they didn't go away, I was going to have to get help, that I probably had bits and pieces of PTSD courtesy of the desert and too many years at war. I wanted to think I was tough enough to handle it on my own, that it would just fade away with enough time, but I wasn't so sure anymore.

I swung my legs out of the bed, thinking a nice predawn run would get my shit back on straight, when my cell phone suddenly rang from the desk where I had it on the charger. Icy fingers of dread raked down my back. Early-morning calls like this never led to anything good. It rang four times and was going to get sent to voice mail before I talked myself out of being scared enough to answer it. I didn't recognize the number, but it was long and the connection was barely audible and broken, so I knew immediately that it was coming from overseas.

"Hello?"

"Master Sergeant?" I barked out a bitter laugh and propped myself on the edge of the bed. I noticed absently that my hands were shaking.

"Not anymore. What's up, Church?"

Dash Churchill was my sergeant first class, and I recognized his slow Mississippi drawl even across the bad connection and with my mind being sleep-deprived. We had moved up the ranks together and served in the same unit for the last six years. We were soldiers first and friends second, but I trusted him implicitly and knew that if he was calling with no consideration to the time change and the fact I was no longer his commanding officer, then shit had to be bad.

All I could make out was a garbled bunch of words, stuff like "bad intel," stuff like "FUBAR mission," things like "outgunned" and "hidden explosives." I heard "insurgents" and "loss of life" and my brain went haywire. I went immediately into commando mode, trying to get him to give me just the pertinent details, only to get shut down by things like it being classified and on a need-to-know basis.

I swore at him and had to refrain from throwing my phone at the wall. With gritted teeth I asked why he called if he wasn't going to tell me anything. My heart was pounding so hard in my chest I could feel each thump, each beat in every tip of my fingers.

"Three KIA, four in serious condition getting airlifted to Germany. They were ours, just thought you would want to know."

The line went dead and I let the phone fall from numb fingers. I put my head in my hands and tried to stop myself from freaking out. I wasn't in anymore, they weren't my men anymore, it wasn't my mission anymore, but none of it seemed to matter. If they were in my unit then I knew two things: they were too young to be dead, and if I hadn't been such a mess, both physically and mentally, maybe I could have stuck around and prevented it.

I couldn't stay in this house. I couldn't be alone with just my wayward thoughts for company, so I changed into track pants, put in my earbuds, and went running. It was either that or cash the bottle of vodka and be useless the rest of the day. I ran until I couldn't see the blood and bodies anymore. I ran until my muscles burned and my lungs felt like they were turned inside out. I ran until there was so much sweat on my face no one could notice the moisture building in my eyes was anything but exertion. I ran until my heart thudded and hurt for another, more tangible reason.

When I got back to the Victorian, I took my time in the shower and contemplated calling Brite to tell him I had zero motivation to be at the Bar today, but then the idea of just sitting alone in the apartment with silence and too much time freaked me out, so I forced myself to go. When I walked in I didn't say anything to anyone or touch the sandwich Darcy had left for me. I was pretty sure my nasty mood was transmitting to anyone that crossed my path, because for the first time since I started spending time at the Bar, everyone gave me a wide berth. There was no chatting, no stories, just everyone looking at me suspiciously out of the corner of their eyes. Even Brite didn't impart his sage wisdom on me today, he just left me to my own devices, which was nice, or possibly dangerous.

I was pulling the wood trim off one of the walls in the back. I was working on autopilot, my mind in a place so far away from this dank bar in Denver that I wasn't paying attention to what I was doing. I put my hand on the wall and it landed on a missed finishing nail that was sticking out. It jabbed into the flesh of my palm, which was startling and hurt, but in no way deserved the reaction it got. I swore and threw the hammer I was using across the room. Unfortunately my anger added force to it and my aim sucked, so it smacked into one of the neon beer signs that decorated the wall and shattered the thing into a million pieces. I swore again and let my head fall forward like I just couldn't hold it up anymore.

When a weighty hand fell on my shoulder, I didn't have to look up to know it was Brite.

"You need the day off, son." It wasn't a question.

"Fucked-up mission. Too many KIA in my old unit. They were just kids, Brite. I shoulda been there."

He signed and hauled me toward the bar.

"No, you shouldn't have been. That was your life then. Had you been there, you very well might have been one of the casualties. Now sit here, get drunk and feel shitty for a minute, but shake it off and live in the now. You got someone I can call for a ride?"

I shook my head but didn't push away the double vodka and soda he put in front of me.

"You said no drinking while I was here." I was still reeling and trying to get it together.

"Grief is a hard mistress to have, Rome. She eventually wants all you have to give her. Take a breather someplace you know is safe. All of us have been in your shoes, kid. I just want to make sure you have someone to take care of you later."

I stared at the drink and blinked stupidly. I shoved my cell phone in his direction. "My brother. Call him when it's time to go, he might be pissed but he'll come and get me."

Brite nodded and put the phone on the bar rail. I rubbed my tired eyes and looked at him to see if he maybe had some of the answers I so desperately needed.

"Does it ever get easier?" Life and death, before and after, then and now, I was just having such a hard time finding my footing. I felt like I was going to fall off a ledge and there would be no going back and the inevitable landing would be the end of me.

He sighed and reached across the bar to clap me on the shoulder.

"No, son, it doesn't. You just eventually learn how to process it so that it doesn't end up killing you."

Well, that sucked. The vodka was cold and oh so welcome going down.

CHAPTER 5

Cora

I WAS CASHING OUT the last client of the day and waving to Rowdy as he left when the shop phone rang. We always had late clients on Friday and Saturday night, so I wasn't surprised by it, only I was alone in the shop because everyone else had taken off already. Nash swore up one side and down the other that Phil was actively avoiding him, so when his last client bailed on the appointment, he left early in order to ambush him at his house. Rule had jetted out early after getting a panicked call from Shaw. Something about the water heater leaking and the basement flooding. I never would have guessed Mr. Live By His Own Rules (pun intended) to be so concerned about home repair. Rowdy had stayed until his last client was done and all the other artists had left on time.

I didn't recognize the number on the display, so I answered it a tad more professionally than I normally did.

"Thanks for calling the Marked, this is Cora. What can I do for you?"

A long pause followed and I hear noise and commotion in the background. I was going to say hello again and then hang up if there was no answer when a gruff voice came across the line.

"I'm looking for Rome Archer's brother."

A shiver of apprehension slid up my spine. "Why?"

Again I was met with silence that dragged on.

"Do I have the wrong number?" This guy sounded frustrated and like he meant business.

"Rule is Rome's brother but he isn't here right now. Can I take a message?"

There was a sigh. "I hate these new cell phones, I can't ever figure out how they work. Is there another number where I can reach him?"

I wasn't in the habit of handing the guys' numbers out to anyone. If I did that I would have a line of desperate girls stretching from here to Coors Field.

"Can you tell me what it's regarding? I'm friends with both of them." It was stretching the truth a little but I didn't feel too bad about it.

"The big guy is having a pretty bad day. He needs a ride home and I thought his brother would be the best candidate for that particular job today."

I frowned and tapped my fingernails on the counter. "It's only eight o'clock."

The guy laughed. "Darlin', I don't think you can really understand just how bad a day it was. I can put him in a cab, but I can't take him myself because it's tournament night and the Bar is packed. But I need to see that he gets home safe and sound."

I puffed out a breath that sent wispy strands of short hair floating over my forehead. Rule would go get him if I called him, so would Nash, but there was already enough tension between those guys that I figured I would just take care of it myself and save everyone a headache.

"I'll come get him and see that he gets home in one piece."

"Ahh . . . no offense, darlin', but that is whole lot of un-wieldy soldier in a piss-poor mood and three sheets to the wind. You might wanna let the brother handle this one."

I wasn't a girl who backed down from a challenge, and Rome Archer drunk and grumpy seemed to be his default anymore. I wasn't scared of him. Plus it always galled me being told I couldn't do something just because I was a girl.

"I have to do a bank drop and I'll come get him. Where is he at?"

The gruff voice gave me directions to a bar located off the beaten path down on Broadway. He once again mentioned I might need physical help trying to maneuver all the intoxicated bulk that was Rome out of the bar. I shook my head in disgust and told him I was just going to have to figure out how to fit the giant into my Mini Cooper. The guy laughed so hard that I thought he was going to hurt himself. When he finally stopped he told me that he had long since hijacked Rome's keys and he would just help me pour him into his own truck. After I got him home I could come back for the Cooper. It sounded like the best plan, even though I would have loved to have a picture of all that brawn crammed in my little car. It would have been hilarious.

In the time it took me to do the deposit for the shop, find

the bar, find a place to park, and find the front door since there wasn't any kind of sign, or door guy, or any indication of where I was going, Rome's condition had apparently gone from bad to worse. He was actually slumped on the bar, his head hung low like his neck couldn't hold it up anymore, and the dim light was casting dark shadows on his face. He looked terrible and tired, and most definitely wasted. His pretty eyes were open only half-mast, watery and bloodshot. His mouth was twisted in an ugly frown and even though the air-conditioning was on, I could see a thin film of sweat covering his skin. His big, battle-scarred hands were shaking where he was holding an empty tumbler between them, and it looked like he was having an argument with the huge bearded man behind the bar.

I carefully walked up behind him and caught the eye of the guy who looked like he had given birth to every Hells Angel ever to walk the earth.

"Hi, I'm Cora."

The guy gave me a quick once-over and lifted an unruly eyebrow. "Tiny little thing, aren't ya?"

I was actually two inches taller than Shaw, but since I didn't have half of her curves, I think I looked a lot smaller and more delicate than I actually was. I lifted a shoulder and let it fall.

Rome turned on the stool and I saw his eyes widen and then try and focus on me. I wasn't sure he recognized me at first, but then the blue lit up like the base of a flame and a drunken and sloppy grin spilled across his face. I tried to keep my eyes focused on the scar on his forehead, because he was lethal when he smiled like that and I knew he wasn't in his right mind at the moment. That slight imperfection made me remember exactly who I was dealing with, Captain No-Fun, not flirty-fun-drunk Rome.

"Rule had an emergency at the house, so I'm gonna take you home, okay?"

"Where's Rule?"

At least I think that's what he asked, but it sounded like his tongue was too big for his mouth. I put a hand on his arm as he leaned toward me and almost toppled off the stool.

"He had something to take care of. So you're stuck with me."

He lumbered to his feet and I thought I was going to get dragged down with him. Luckily he seemed to have pretty good balance even when he was hammered because he caught himself on the bar and blinked those killer baby blues at me.

"I'm so tired."

I nodded, even though I wasn't sure what he was talking about and peered around him at the burly bartender who was watching us with serious, dark eyes.

"I know. I'm gonna get you home and put you to bed." Man, that shouldn't sound nearly as appealing as it did. I needed to stay away from this guy. He made my head go wonky.

"You need a hand getting him to the truck?"

I shook my head and hooked a hand around his lean waist and tried not to wince as he leaned all that considerable weight onto my side.

"If I can't get him in on my own, there is no way I'm getting him out on my own." I took the keys he brought me and gave Rome a little nudge with my hip. "Let's go, Goliath."

"If he's functional tomorrow, let him know he has the day off."

"What happened to get him in this state?"

The guy shook his head and stroked a hand over what was seriously the most awesome beard I had ever seen.

"Life happened, darlin'. Sometimes it just gets the better of us is all. Take care of that boy, he needs someone, too, especially right now."

I was going to answer that I took care of all my boys, but I never got the chance because Rome chose that moment to lurch toward the door. He put a thick arm around my shoulders, pulled me so that I was pressed flat against his chest, and buried his nose in the short hair on the top of my head. He awkwardly marched me backward while he struggled to stay upright and headed for the parking lot.

"You smell good."

Typically when I got off work I smelled like antiseptic and all the cleaners used to keep the shop sterile and safe. I had to wiggle free enough to breathe, but since Rome was going in the right direction and seemed steady enough on his feet, I didn't make him let me go. I tried to subtly steer him toward the shiny red Dodge that the bartender had indicated was his, but he suddenly stopped and stared intently down at me.

"You really do have the prettiest eyes."

I cleared my throat and tried not to blush since I had never really been the blushing type.

"So you've mentioned."

His words were still hard to understand, but the way the blue in his eyes was glowing wasn't. I was hardheaded to a fault, but I wasn't going to deny I thought he was hot, I mean I was only human and there was something about all that plain, old-fashioned beefcake that was hard to ignore. But I was surprised that he seemed to return the sentiment. I didn't for one second think I was any more his type than he was mine.

We stumbled, half stepped, and shuffled to the truck. It took some maneuvering and some wiggling on my part to get him to let me go and get him to climb up into the monstrous vehicle. I closed the door on him as he was humming an awful rendition of Lynyrd Skynyrd's "Simple Man" and closed my eyes for a second. I had plenty of experience dealing with moody, drunken boys—Rule was a pro at being a handful after too many cocktails—but there was something about the abject sadness, the visible sorrow hanging around in those azure eyes that made Rome just a little trickier to handle. I had an inkling that he could go from malleable and sloppy to really difficult in a heartbeat.

The truck was big and I had to slide the seat up as close to the steering wheel as it would go. I was lucky it was a newer model, because there was no way I would have been able to reach the pedals if had been one of the old-style bench seats. It was also an automatic, which was nice since I hadn't had to drive a stick in forever.

I glanced over at my passenger and found him slumped over so that his head was resting on the window. His eyes were closed and his chest was rising and falling in a steady rhythm. I was going to take him to the Victorian and have Nash help me wrestle him inside, when his voice cracked out from someplace so deep and dark it gave me goose bumps when it whispered across my skin.

"Do you ever wonder 'why you?'"

I frowned at him and shot Nash a text to see if he was home.

"Why me what?" I didn't understand what he was rambling about and his eyes were still closed, so I wasn't entirely sure he wasn't talking in his sleep.

"Why am I the one still here? Why was I the only one to walk away? Why did I dodge one bullet only to end up useless and unnecessary anymore? Whose plan was that? Why was I someone Remy couldn't tell? Why didn't he trust me? Why? Shouldn't there be a point to it all?"

It was incoherent for the most part but the sentiment behind it was heartbreaking and shouldn't be coming from someone so vital and thrumming with life. I didn't really have a working understanding of how survivor's guilt affected a man that had seen so much, but in Rome's case it seemed to be eating him alive.

"That is probably a conversation you should have with a professional and maybe not when you tried to drink your liver into submission."

"People die every day that shouldn't die. It isn't fair and it isn't right. There should be some kind of rhyme or reason to it." But there wasn't, and when he was sober he had to know that, didn't he?

My phone dinged at me and I had to wait until I stopped at a stop sign to check the message. I swore softly because

Nash wasn't home and had no plans on returning. I didn't want to bug Rule, not to mention he wasn't the most sensitive of guys and there was no way Rome was in any state to be left to his own devices. I was just gonna have to take him to my house and put him on the couch until he sobered up. Jet was on the road and Ayden was working late, so that meant I was only going to have to deal with a million questions and speculative looks from Asa.

"A lot of bad things happen every day that shouldn't happen. Unfortunately it's part of life."

"It shouldn't be."

I looked back over at him and noticed those bright eyes were wide open and focused on my face. It was unnerving to be the target of such intense scrutiny.

"Maybe not. Hey, I'm just gonna take you to my place for a minute. I'll let you catch a quick nap and put some food in you and you can run me back to my car when you're back at full operating power. Okay?"

His eyes slid back shut and his broad shoulders rose and fell like he couldn't care less. I hated to admit that I was worried about him, but whatever blanket of despair he had wrapped himself up in, it was thick and it was fibrous and I could almost feel the weight of it suffocating him.

We made it to Washington Park, where the cute little house I shared with the gang was located. I thought Rome might have finally settled in to sleep for real, but as soon as the motor of the big ol' truck shut off, his eyes popped open and he was once again staring at me fixedly in the dim interior of the cab.

"Why did you come get me?"

I fiddled with the key and pushed open the door. "Because I love your brother and he loves you and I want to keep it that way. I'm much better at dealing with something like this than he is."

"Something like what?"

He managed to get his own door open, but I heard him mutter a string of swearwords and a loud thud as he lost his balance and fell against the fender of the truck. I sighed and walked around to collect him.

"Something like a guy who is clearly hurting and lashing out at those that are closest to him because he knows they'll take it. We can go as many rounds as you want, Captain No-Fun, you don't scare me."

The uneasy way he made me feel did scare me but no one needed to know that. On the outside I was always rock solid, no one knew that on the inside I struggled every day with the holes left from not getting my perfectly planned future and happy-ever-after after Jimmy left in me. Growing up primarily on my own had sucked. I thought with Jimmy I would never have to be untethered again. Once that security had gone away, I knew there was no way I could risk my heart and dreams on someone who wasn't ready to offer me forever, stability, and family ever again.

He blinked his eyes at me and we had a stare-down, for a second I wasn't sure if he was going to scoop me up or push me down. Instead he just shook his head and whispered so quietly that I thought it could have been my imagination had I not seen his lips move, "That's good, because most of the time I'm fucking scared shitless of myself."

I didn't know what to say to that, so I took his rock-hard arm and half tugged, half guided him into the house. Asa was propped up on the sofa doing something on the computer and I could have sworn a look of guilt flashed quickly over his face. He gave me and my unwanted guest a questioning look and went to lumber to his feet. I waved him back down and kept tugging Rome across the living room, past the kitchen, to where the master bedroom was located.

"Don't get up. I'll put him in my room in case all that booze tries to come back up and he needs the bathroom close by. He just needs a little nap."

Both blond eyebrows went up. "He couldn't have taken one at his house?"

"Not now, Asa."

Rome stumbled and knocked a picture of me and the guys at the shop off the wall. I was fast enough to catch it before it hit the floor, but not strong enough to keep him upright as he toppled into the open doorway of my room. Luckily it was an older house and the room wasn't giant, so he half hit the king-sized bed. It took a little bit of work, some tugging and pulling, some swearing and grumbling, to get that big body spread across hot-pink comforter. He was breathing hard, his eyes slid closed, and I didn't bother to try and make him any more comfortable or tell him where the facilities were. I just left him alone, figuring sleep was the best thing for him.

Asa was right where I left him, only now the computer was closed and he looked like he was waiting for me to come back into the room.

"What's that all about?"

I groaned and sank down on the couch next to him.

"He was at a bar and the bartender called the shop looking for Rule. I decided to intervene since they just started working toward a cease-fire, only I had no idea what kind of drunk he was gonna be."

"What kind of drunk is that?"

"Complicated. I'm just gonna let him get straight and then send him on his way. He looks like he hasn't had a good night's sleep in days; hopefully the booze will knock him out for a few and then he can go home."

"You're a really good girl, Cora."

"I have my moments. What were you doing on the computer when we came in?"

Those eyes the color of aged bourbon glinted at me. Asa was lucky he was such an easy guy to like, because I didn't trust him as far as I could throw him, or even as far as Rome could throw him.

"Nothing. Just checking up on some things."

"Things that ended you up in the hospital? Ayden will murder you."

He laughed. "No. I'm not the sharpest tool out in the shed, but I do eventually learn the hard lessons."

"Why do I think that might not really be the case?"

"Because you are surprisingly smart for someone that looks like a living, breathing cartoon character."

I got the feeling he wasn't going to give me anything else, so I got up and made us some grilled cheese sandwiches for dinner and brought us over a couple of beers. I liked hanging out with Asa, but he seemed a little sketchy tonight, and by the time midnight rolled around with no sound or motion from Rome, I was getting tired and bored of dealing with difficult men. Asa mentioned he was going go watch TV in his room, because if he was up when Ayden got home, she was going to harass him about whatever it was she was on his case about this week. She tended to be a bit of a terror when Jet was out of town for more than a few days at a time, and her older sibling bore the brunt of it. I knew she didn't want to live alone since Jet spent so much time on the road, but dealing with the intense dynamic between the siblings was often like watching a reality TV show without the relief of commercial interruption.

I figured it wouldn't hurt anything to let Rome keep my bed for the night while I crashed on the couch. I was small and the couch was huge, so it wasn't like it would be a major inconvenience. I did, however, need to sneak into my bathroom and grab a quick shower to wash the workday off.

Asa and I said good night and I tiptoed into the darkened room. At some point in his fitful stage of blacking out, Rome had managed to not only move to the center of the bed, but also kick off his boots and strip off his T-shirt. Even though I knew it was wrong, I had to just stand there and stare at all that skin on display, spread out over my pink bed set. It was so odd. He was all hard muscle and male perfection amid a totally girly and ultrafeminine backdrop. It would take a guy like Rome Archer to make all my girly stuff look tough.

He had one long arm flung out to the side and the other curled up behind his head. The lines delineating muscles and tendons used to hard and strenuous work made my mouth water. I felt like a voyeur. I shouldn't be blatantly checking him out while he was passed out and unaware, but I also couldn't muster the strength to look away. I had never seen a real-life, living breathing male that had that vee that cut between their hips and pointed downward, where a trail of dark hair disappeared into his jeans. The only men that really had that in life were underwear models, dudes on romance novel covers, and maybe professional athletes. But oh no, Rome Archer had it, as well as abs that put a six-pack to shame and endless amounts of lightly tanned skin that stretched over a canvas that looked like it was carved from stone. He was a massive example of all that was beautiful and male. He was built like a god, and I didn't want to acknowledge it but I had never, ever seen anything look better in my bed.

He also had way more pale white scar tissue dotting that landscape of total hotness than I wanted to know about. Even with the only light filtering in from the hallway, I could see the huge scar on his shoulder where his arm was bent up under his head. It was puckered and was wider than my hand; it looked like it still hurt. He had an ugly red welt all along the opposite side on his ribs that was about ten inches long and looked like it was healing. There was a nasty white line that zigged and zagged under his belly button and disappeared into the top of his jeans and that was only what I could see on his very impressive front side.

I was used to being around men and women who marked their body to define their individuality, to claim their skin as

their own. Seeing those scars, those marks that he most definitely had never asked for, I had to wonder how he felt about
being permanently marked up against his will. His skin also
reflected his life, the choice he made to go off and become
a warrior, a man who fought for the freedom of others, and
now he would carry those reminders for the rest of his life.
It was body modification on an entirely different level than
tattooing, with a different purpose.

I gave my head a quick shake and told myself to stop
being a creeper. He clearly needed the sleep since he didn't
so much as twitch an eyelash as I got out an oversized T-
shirt and a pair of shorts to sleep in. I wasn't exactly stealthy
as I banged around in the bathroom and got ready for bed. It
was early for a Saturday night but no one was out and Ayden
didn't like to party while Jet was gone, so it was just going to
be me and cable until I zonked out. I was back in my room,
trying to unplug my phone charger from the nightstand
next to Rome's head. I wasn't worried about bothering him
since he seemed like he was out like a light—that is, until I
suddenly had a massive hand curled around my bicep.

"Hey!" The startled word didn't get any force behind it
as I was yanked down and my back met the mattress with a
thud. I let out a startled shriek as the arm he had dangling
over the edge of the bed curled around me and pulled me
half under him as he rolled over. He weighed a freaking ton
and no amount of pushing at his broad shoulders seemed
to have an effect on him. His dark head buried itself in the
curve of my neck, his ridiculously long eyelashes were still
pressed closed and brushed against my skin. His breath was

coming in a steady stream as his chest rose and fell with no sign of alertness or wakefulness, even as I wiggled and squirmed to get free of his iron hold.

"Rome?" I tapped him on the side of the head lightly and felt him frown against my neck. "Hey, big guy, I need to get up."

I tried to shake him once more and he muttered something under his breath and settled more fully on top of me. One of his denim-clad legs slid between mine and the thick arm he had wrapped around me locked even more in place and that wide palm settled fully across the curve of my backside. He turned his head and rubbed his cheek against the side of my temple and sighed. It made me stop struggling for a second and I looked up so I could peer questioningly at him because the sound was just so defeated. It hurt me to hear it.

He felt like his motor was running at a thousand degrees and he had to weigh over double what I did, but he was holding on to me like I was a lifeline. Like I was a living breathing teddy bear, and whatever it was that was keeping him up at night, holding me would make it stay away. I huffed out a breath and tried to decide what the best course of action was. In hindsight I should have just given the bartender Rule's number and let him be caught up in this mess, but as usual I had to meddle. No good deed went unpunished.

There was no way I was getting free unless I kneed him in the junk or punched him in the face to wake him up, and that just seemed a little too extreme. I felt bad for the guy. He was obviously struggling, and clearly a bad day didn't begin to cover what he was trying to drink away. I figured it wouldn't kill me to just lie still until he rolled over or loosened his hold. Plus it had the added benefit of letting me enjoy all that hardness that battle-ready body pressed against mine. I doubted that I would ever have an opportunity like it again. The landscape of my sexual experience was pretty barren over the last few years. There had been a guy here or there, but not one that I had wanted to hang out with for more than a minute and none could ever compare to the sheer physical perfection of the guy I was trapped under right now.

I sighed in resignation and tried to wiggle a little in order to get some more breathing room. Rome just tightened his hold even more and settled more fully into me. I relented and wrapped one arm around his shoulders; they were so wide, so broad, I could barely reach the other side. I put the other hand on his ribs, right above that healing wound. I kept my eyes on the ceiling and not the clock, figuring he would get uncomfortable, realize he wasn't alone anymore, and roll over at any second. Only at some point I heard the front door open and Ayden's heels on the floor in the hallway, which meant it was well past two in the morning and my human blanket hadn't moved a muscle. I had been pinned to the bed for over two hours, and it didn't look like I was getting free before dawn.

Finally I was too tired to just stare at the side of his sleeping face or wonder at all the little nicks and tiny marks that dotted his skin. This close to him the scar above his eyebrow was really wicked-looking. It hooked from the arch up into his hairline and spidered off to web across his temple. It looked like he was a very lucky man to still have a functioning eyeball on that side of his handsome face. There was history there, a life lived hard and dangerously mapped out across his skin for the entire world to see and judge. It made Rome an even more difficult man for me to try and figure out, and frankly I was exhausted by all of it. My last thought before I gave up the fight of trying to wait him out was that not once in all the years Jimmy and I had shared a bed had he ever held me this close, like he never wanted me to go.

I WASN'T SURE WHAT had me stirring awake—if it was the sun coming in the blinds, if it was the feeling of being covered by an electric blanket in the middle of summer, or if it was the impossible-to-ignore fact that I wasn't in my frilly pink bed alone. I squinted against the morning light coming in the room, but all I could see for days and days was blue. A blue that no words could describe, a blue that was so hot and bright I felt like it could burn me alive from the inside out. I opened my mouth to ask Rome if he was feeling all right, to tell him to get the hell off of me, but nothing came out. We just stared at each other and the lack of clothing between us suddenly became a noticeable thing. I could feel his heart thundering against my own where our chests were pressed together, could feel his sides rise and fall as he sucked in a breath and let it out slowly, could feel the hardness of an erection that needed its own zip code press against the softness between my legs, not protected at all by my tiny sleep shorts. This was a compromising situation to be in any way you looked at it, and considering we were practically strangers, my normally nimble tongue was having a hard time finding its defenses.

His hand that was holding on to my butt gave the cheek a squeeze and I thought he was going to lever himself up and off of me, but he didn't. He used the other hand to hold his considerable bulk up off of me for the first time in hours and his free hand lifted and I went frozen still as he used it to oh so gently trace the curve of my bottom lip where my mouth was still hanging open like a dimwit. Hands that big, that rough, shouldn't be capable of being so reverent, so delicate. It made me gasp.

I should say something. He should say something. Neither of us did, though, and when those pretty, sad eyes moved closer to mine, when that mouth surrounded by a sexy shadow of scruff dropped to cover mine, all I could do was lie there and take it like it was inevitable. I had been kissed plenty in my lifetime—by good boys and bad boys, by boys I liked and boys I didn't, by boys I spent just a minute with and boys I had spent years with, but no one had ever kissed me like this. Something happened when that firm mouth settled over mine. My brain short-circuited, my common sense and basic rationality took a hike, and all I was left with was a bundle of raging hormones and a desire so sharp and pointed it almost hurt when it started to pulse under my skin.

I was surrounded by him, engulfed by him. He was just everywhere and it was overwhelming. I knew I should tell him to stop, that this wasn't right. I didn't do this kind of thing and I had a feeling he was still cut open and bleeding from whatever had sent him over the edge last night, but the words just wouldn't come and it wasn't like I could have used them if they did. His mouth was hard on mine, his tongue invading every corner, every hidden place I had in my mouth. Neither one of us had very much hair to hold on to, so I had to settle for grabbing on to his ears to keep him in place. I should be pushing him away, not pulling him closer, but there was no way that was going to happen, not with all that brawn pushing against me and those eyes making me drown in them.

I kissed him back, because really that was all I could do. I slid my tongue against his, let my teeth find the soft inner side of his lip, wrapped an arm around his neck, and we devoured each other. There was no other way to describe it. We writhed together, the rough denim of his jeans rubbing against my bare legs, his hands holding me in a grip that I couldn't break free from if I wanted to. We kissed, we sucked, we bit, and somewhere along the line it went from some kind of spontaneous combustion to a slow burn that had me wrapping a leg around his lean waist and not protesting when impatient hands started pulling at the T-shirt I went to bed in.

This was too fast, it was too wrong. He was not the kind of guy I had been holding out for. He was as far from my idea of perfect as could be, but there was no arguing that he fit the bill for building me up to something tingling and achy in no time flat. I gasped a little when the fabric cleared my head. I hadn't been naked with a guy in a really long time, and getting naked with this guy was all kinds of intimidating. Where he was all smooth skin and perfectly cut muscles, I was all swirly colors inked on skin that had a tendency to tan but was also dusted in freckles. Besides my left arm,

I had a riot of lilies inked along my rib cage on the left side. They were bright, full of every color under the sun, and the stamen on each of them was decorated with a transdermal piercing. I had four or five little rhinestones that twinkled and winked from the center of each flower. It was something I was sure this serious and intense soldier had never seen before, but it didn't slow him down. He tossed my shirt over his shoulder and touched the tip of his index finger to one, which made me shiver. We still hadn't exchanged a single word and things were quickly moving out of hand. I was running out of room to make a graceful escape.

I put a hand on the center of his chest, spread my fingers wide, and tried to marshal my wayward and heady thoughts. I needed a minute to catch my breath, a second to remember we were not two people who had things in common, who would not normally exist in each other's world. He didn't give it to me. He was rubbing his thumb between the little jewels dotting my side. He didn't seem weirded out by it or unnerved by it or all the ink that was now on display, in fact not once had he pulled that hypnotic blue gaze away from my own. He put his huge hand over mine so that it forced my palm flat against his skin. I didn't like to be bossed around by anyone, at any time, but something was happening to me, to us, and I just couldn't seem to stop it. He dragged my hand over his breastbone, across that corrugated and taunt plane of his stomach, over his belly button, and down that light happy trial, stopping when he reached the stiff material of his fly, the heat and hardness of his skin behind it burning instantly through the fabric into my fingers. He didn't press me any further. He removed his hand and lifted it to brush his thumb over my cheek. He was giving me an out if I wanted it; somehow without one syllable this guy said more to me than any other guy I could ever remember going to bed with.

It was right there hovering on the periphery—sanity, logic, rationality; all the things I needed to grab on to in order to stop this. They were hazy and foggy, but they were there and Rome was giving me a chance to grab on to them if that was what I wanted to do, and all at once I realized the refrain about him being a good guy at heart had to be true. He wasn't pushing, he wasn't trying to take advantage even though he was so much bigger than me and could obviously force his hand if so inclined. He was making it my call and I was about to surprise us both because I couldn't resist the allure of all that rock-hard skin throbbing under my finger-tips. I wanted to see it, wanted to touch it, wanted to see if it was as big and hard as the rest of him. I hooked just the tips of my fingers in the tops of his jeans and popped the button out of the hole.

He hissed a breath out between clenched teeth and dropped his head so that he could get his mouth around the tip of one of my breasts. It was so startling, the suction, and the moisture, the rough scrape of his morning beard across my skin, that I arched up and threw my head back. I wasn't overly endowed, my breasts were like the rest of me, on the small side and delicate but they were supersensitive. When he ran his tongue over the quivering peak, when he scraped the pebbled flesh with the sharp edge of his teeth, I was done.

There was no more thought to try and act right, no more worry that I didn't even know him that well, I just wanted and needed and he was going to give it to me. End of story.

I shoved both of my hands between us, got his zipper down without wounding him, and started pulling the denim off over his hips. No underwear, that was always hot, and he wasn't shy because he levered up and shoved the pants the rest of the way off. They fell on the floor next to my discarded shirt, and while he crawled back up over me I took a second to check out the goods and felt my eyes widen in alarm. I wasn't a prude, I knew dudes' business came in all shapes and sizes, I was intimately familiar with the good, bad, and the ugly. It was a hazard of my profession, but Rome was packing something that I wasn't sure anatomy and biology were going to let happen. Needless to say, he was huge, everywhere, and I was small, everywhere. I was thinking I needed to rethink this entire thing and start acting like the smart, responsible person I was, but he got his hands on my shorts and my panties and I was naked and splayed under him before the protest and panic could find footing. There was no way we were going to fit, even if I was so turned on I felt like everywhere our skin touched we were going to end up welded together. I could feel desire and liquid want pooling between my legs, saw that he felt it, too, when his eye flashed cobalt sparks in every direction. I didn't care how sexy he was, how unholy hot and bothered he had me, there was no way that weapon of mass destruction was going to work its way inside my body.

My apprehension must have been displayed on my face,

because the eyebrow under the scar danced up and he finally stopped touching me, stopped dropping sucking little kisses along my collarbone, and stopped running featherlight fingertips over the flowers decorating my side. He stared down at me and I was fascinated by a drop of sweat that started at his temple and crested over his cheek, wound its way down his neck, and tracked over a pec muscle that looked like it belonged on a marble statue. I wasn't familiar with this kind of restraint, this kind of will, so I just traced the track that little drop of moisture had trailed and stopped at his nipple.

"That's never going to fit."

The words were strangled, like I hadn't had anything to drink in a hundred years or more. We were so close, this was so raw and open I didn't know what to do with him, or with me. My words were meant to be funny, to slow things down, but I sounded scared, even to my own ears, and I knew it wasn't just because he was far more than any man I had ever been with, or maybe it was.

That single dark eyebrow danced even higher and that little half grin that undid me the other day flashed across his face. I guess he decided that my words were a challenge and not a warning because the next thing I knew, all his attention switched to that already damp and needy place between my legs. He pressed my legs open with one of his thighs, pulled my hips up, and delved his fingers into folds that were achy and electrified by his touch. He was about to find another surprise that guys only got to see, got to touch, when I took my clothes off, and I felt it the instant his questing fingers made contact with the small little hoop hidden down there.

Once he touched it, he stilled, just a fraction. I had had the hood piercing for as long as I could remember. Initially I got it because I thought it was edgy and cool; now that I was older I kept it because I had had enough sex with enough guys that needed a damn bull's-eye to get to the good stuff. Rome wasn't one of those, he also wasn't scared or put off by it. He gave the ring a little tug that had my eyes rolling back into my head and made me pant out his name. Seeing the results, he played with the slippery metal while playing with the rest of me, creating a tidal wave of sensation that was going to make me break at any second. He touched, me, stroked me, rubbed his thumb steadily and unrelenting over the hoop and the tight little bud underneath it. He worked me over like it had never been done before, and just as I was grinding into him, pressing my heels into the mattress of the bed, splitting in half and seeing stars, he removed those skilled fingers, shifted me under him, and pushed all that turgid, straining flesh inside of me. I wasn't ready for it, but he slid in up to the hilt and filled me up to the point I thought I was going to suffocate on all I was feeling, all I could see was blazing out of his bright eyes.

He stayed still for a second, waiting to see if I was going to push him away, tell him it was too much. At any other time I would have appreciated his restraint; right now I wanted to choke him. I felt impaled, pinned, stuck, and I hated that I loved it. This was an aspect to sex I had never experienced before, it added an element that took things to a different level.

"Okay?"

It was the only word he had spoken since this all began and really it was more just a breath of sound. I knew if I told him no, that it hurt, that it was too much, he would stop, let me out from under him, and walk away without question, so it was that instinctual understanding that had me giving him the barest of nods and sliding my hands up around his neck. I wanted to see him finish, wanted to know what happened to those spectacular eyes when he went over the edge. I was all in anyway, there was no point in reining it in now.

He moved slowly at first, I think there was a legitimate fear there that he could indeed do some serious damage with that weapon of his, but he had done an excellent job of priming me, of getting me ready for him, so soon I was writhing restlessly under him and urging him to move faster, go harder, to just let go. He was good at reading the cues, he watched my face, eyes locked on mine, and before I knew it both legs were up high on his waist and he was driving into me like he was trying to put me through the other side of the mattress. It was awesome.

The muscles on the side of his neck corded, a fine sheen of sweat pebbled up on those massive pecs, his biceps bulged just enough to offer a very nice show, and those eyes, man oh man, those eyes lit up like the fireworks display he had missed on the Fourth. Silver sparks exploded from the center, chasing midnight-blue lightning as he grunted his release and dropped his forehead to the crook of my neck. He was careful not to collapse his whole weight on me, careful to set my legs back down, careful to pull out nice and slow, which made both of us gasp.

He flopped back on his back and we both stared at the ceiling while breathing hard and still not talking. I wasn't sure what there was to say. In all my visions of what I was doing, of who I was waiting for, there had never once been a glimpse of anyone like Rome Archer. I sort of marveled that he seemed to be blocking out not only the sun, but whatever else was standing on that horizon waiting for me. He was a problem that literally was going to be too damn big to ignore, not that I wasn't going to try and do exactly that until I figured out what in the hell I had just done and what exactly it meant to all my carefully constructed plans.

CHAPTER 6

Rome

I THOUGHT I WAS dreaming. Somewhere between the haze of blood and death, and the swirly nauseating feeling of being almost blackout drunk, I had a dream that a pixie came in and saved me from everything. It was all a blur after the fifth or sixth drink. All I knew is that the mind-numbing effects of alcohol and Brite's gentle, kind reminders that the shitty things in life could not be directly tied to me, were the only things that kept me from going completely off the rails.

When I pried my eyes open because the sun was bitch-slapping me across the face, I had no idea where I was. Hell, I barely knew who I was: my head was throbbing, I felt a little like I was going to hurl, and all I knew was that I was surrounded by wall-to-wall pink. I also had all kinds of soft feminine curves trapped under me and she smelled like cotton candy and flowers. It had to be a dream because at no point in my reality did I ever get to wake up after a crap day to end all crap days and have those amazing two-toned eyes looking up at me with trepidation, but also with a healthy dose of admiration. Therefore it had to be a dream, and since I was dreaming, I was going to do what I had been dying to do since she called me Captain No-Fun and smirked at me like she already knew all my dark and dirty secrets. I was going to kiss that sassy mouth until neither one of us could breathe, until my head stopped hurting, until I forgot what had put me in such a vulnerable, sorry state in the first place.

Only I had no idea a simple kiss with this tiny, bossy, mouthy girl was going to turn my head around. I wanted to kiss her because she was cute, and soft, and I really did think she had the prettiest eyes I had ever seen, but mostly I wanted to kiss her because I knew she would tell me to stop, that she would no doubt push me away and get worked up into a tizzy of righteous indignation. I was already feeling about as low as I could, so there was no harm in taking it one step further.

Cora apparently didn't play by any normal set of rules, though. She did the opposite of what I expected, and before too long I was too scared to talk, too freaked out to even breathe, because I was worried that one slight movement in the wrong direction and she would call a halt to the only thing that had made me feel good in a really long time. It still felt like a dream, but she was so hot, so damn unexpected, it now felt like a dream come true.

When it was all over, as I lay there panting and trying to think of an appropriate response, because "thank you" just wouldn't cut it, she rolled off the other side of the big bed and looked down at me with eyes that were both bright and shiny and dark and swirling. That dual-color thing really was kind of a trip.

"I'm going to take a shower and then you need to take me to get my car from that hole in the wall you were at yesterday."

She turned around to rummage through a tiny closet on the other side of the very pink room and I took a moment to admire the view. She was lithe, all smooth lines and colorfully decorated skin. She had some kind of Asian-inspired water-and-fire image tattooed around the top of one thigh that danced almost to her knee, those flowers on her ribs with the shower of jewels implanted in her skin on her side, and that arm that had every flower known to man inked on it. She was petite but man, did she pack a punch. Who knew metal in places I never imagined a chick would want to put it would be so hot, be such an unbelievable turn-on. Everything about this girl was a surprise.

"Uhh . . . not that I'm not grateful for it, but how exactly did I end up here?" The *in bed with you* I left unspoken.

She put on a short robe that had tiny silver stars all over it and looked silky and shiny. She glanced at me over her shoulder and ran her hands over her short hair. I reached over the side of the bed and started to pull my jeans back on, but I had to take a second because my head started to throb in time to my heartbeat.

"The bartender called the shop looking for Rule but he was gone already. He was dealing with the crisis of being a new homeowner and Nash wasn't at the apartment. You weren't in any condition to be left alone, so I brought you here."

Not only was she smoking hot but underneath all that sass there was a really big heart. I was a lot to handle on a good day, and knowing where I had been at yesterday before the booze flooded my system, she was pretty brave to try and tackle all that on her own. Most people wouldn't do that for a virtual stranger. I rubbed hard hands over my super-short buzz cut; this hadn't been totally awkward thus far, but now it felt more personal.

She didn't say anything else, just disappeared into the bathroom, and I heard the shower go on. I found my shirt wadded up in a pile with my boots and finished getting dressed. I smelled like sex and day-old booze. I smelled just like Rule used to smell all the time. The wayward thought of my brother had me absently searching for my phone and my keys. I should have given Brite better instructions before getting tanked yesterday. Not that Cora seemed in any hurry to try and rake me over the coals, but this had all the hall-marks of a situation that could go slanted in a heartbeat and I couldn't shake the feeling that there was something I was forgetting.

Not sure what to do with myself in the outrageously girly room, I decided to brave the wild and go in search of a glass of water and maybe some painkillers for my head. The house was tiny and cute. Cora's eclectic style was on display throughout. The couch was purple, the rugs were polka dot, and I assumed the massive flat screen and game systems had to belong to Jet because they were the only things in the living room not splashed with color. I found the kitchen in the back of the house and cringed inwardly when I saw it wasn't empty.

Asa was at the little table drinking a cup of coffee and seemingly ignoring his sister, who was grilling him about something. Both sets of amber eyes got wide when I walked into the room. Asa lifted an eyebrow and Ayden blinked like she had no idea who I was. I felt an embarrassed flush start to crawl up my neck and cleared my throat. I wished to God I could remember what, if anything, I had done last night.

"Uh, hey."

I gratefully accepted the mug of coffee Asa handed to me and propped a hip up on the counter while they continued to stare at me.

"Is that your truck outside?" I liked Ayden's voice. It was tinted with just a hint of the South and all soft and smooth. I liked those long legs of hers in her running pants, too, but Jet was like a brother to me, so there was no way I would ever admit that aloud.

"Yeah. I needed a DD and Cora decided to be it."

"You spent the night?"

I didn't like the third degree, I was used to being on the other side of it.

"Yeah, well, I blacked out in her bed, so there really wasn't a choice."

I could see Asa doing the math in his head that Cora hadn't been on the couch or anywhere else this morning.

"Interesting." Asa just chuckled and didn't say anything, for which I was eternally grateful. There was just something about the way he looked at you, something about the way he sized you up, that was unnerving and unsettling.

"What's interesting?" Cora came in the room smelling

clean and fresh. I tried not to notice I had left whisker burn all along her jaw and throat.

Ayden made a face and handed her a banana. "That you had to take care of the supposedly responsible Archer last night."

Cora frowned and moved past me back toward the living room. She had on black shorts with a wide waist and a black-and-white-striped top that was missing most of the back. The only thing holding it up seemed to be a giant bow in the back; her rib tattoo with all its winking jewels was totally visible.

"We all have bad days. I need to get my car, are you ready?"

I nodded and handed Asa back the coffee mug. We exchanged a little nod, like he understood the potential for this to be the most awkward thing in the world, and I gave Ayden a small little grin. She lifted her eyebrows back at me and took my spot against the counter. I knew as soon as we left they would be picking apart what my stay-over meant.

I noticed Cora seemed to be moving a little more slowly than her usual hyperkinetic way. I wanted to ask her if I had hurt her, she was so much smaller than the girls I normally went to bed with, but we seemed to be on the same page about leaving the deed in no-man's-land and I didn't want to rock the boat. She fished my keys out of her bag and threw them at me.

"I left your wallet and phone in the glove box."

"Did I do, or say, anything out of hand last night?"

I needed to know if I owed her an apology for anything . . . well, for anything besides devouring her like she was my last meal.

"No. You were just sad, really sad."

I didn't know if that meant I was feeling sad, or that I was sad as in she felt sorry for me. There was no way I could look her in the eye ever again if that had been a pity fuck. It was too good, too intense, and if she just felt sorry for me, I would never be able to look myself in the mirror as a man again.

"I got a phone call from the desert yesterday. It was bad."

I pulled into the traffic and headed toward Broadway. I needed to find out if I had made an ass out of myself to Brite and the gang at the bar as well.

"So you said. You also mentioned that you being home makes you somehow responsible for what happened, which I hope you know is nuts. People whose job it is to fight a war have a high risk that they may end up injured or killed, you should know that. You being here or there makes no difference in the matter."

I sighed and tightened my hands on the steering wheel. "It doesn't matter. When I was deployed my brother died, when I'm here men in my unit die. I just can't get away from it and yet somehow every single time I manage to scrape by just past death's door."

She looked at me out of those odd eyes, compassion in the blue one, censure and warning in the coffee-colored one.

"That's too much for one person to try and carry around all the time, Rome. You can't be responsible for everyone or feel guilty all the time for being one of lucky ones."

"Like you?" I cut a sideways look at her. "You run around rescuing those guys, Shaw and Ayden, and now me. You want to save everyone just as much as I do." I wasn't going to touch the guilty part of that statement.

"Yeah, I do, only the difference is that when they suffer from their own choices, I don't take the responsibility for it. When Rule was acting like an idiot and walked away from Shaw, that wasn't my fault. When Ayden was pretending like she could live without Jet, that had nothing to do with me. I'm just there to love them through it and pick up the pieces after. You think that you directly impact the bad things and that's just stupid."

She kind of had a point, so I didn't answer her and as such we spent the rest of the ride in silence. I turned on the radio and let old Pink Floyd fill the cab. When we got to the bar I pulled around back and she pointed to a ridiculous Mini-Cooper that was painted a bright neon green. Of course that's what she drove. I wouldn't even fit in the thing. I pulled up next to it and killed the engine. I leaned across the seat and dug my stuff out of the glove box. I didn't miss the way her breath caught when my arm brushed across her chest.

We stared at each other in mute silence for a full minute before she reached for the door handle. I couldn't just let her leave without saying something about this morning, not that I had a clue what that should be.

"About this morning . . ." She held up a hand before I could start.

"Just don't." She shook her head. "It was what it was

and let's leave it at that. You're ridiculously hot, but I don't want to be alone forever and the kind of guy I'm looking for doesn't come with all the questions and inner turmoil that seems to be eating you alive. I want someone steady, someone ready to settle down for the long haul, and ready to be all in with me. You aren't even close to being in a place where you're all in for yourself, let alone someone else. I get that you've been through a really hard time, have seen more than your fair share of awful things, but I need a guy living his life like tomorrow matters, not like it's a curse. I'm sorry, Rome. My perfect guy has got to come already together and be good enough, no assembly required by me. I learned that lesson the hard way."

I barked out a laugh and leaned back in the seat. She looked at me in confusion and I nodded at her.

"You're right. I'm broken. Half the time I don't know if the stuff going on in my head is real or the memory of a memory. I just didn't think it was so obvious." I wasn't even going to touch on the "ridiculously hot" comment. She was right, I was in a million and one scattered pieces and there was probably more than one screw missing.

She shook her head and pushed open the door. "That's not what I mean. You're not happy and you're not even trying to get there. Jeez, Rome we have more military in this state than we do normal people. Go get help, go find someone to talk to. Let someone save you for once. I know your brother and the other people that love you would appreciate it."

And then she was gone just like that, like she hadn't turned my world on its axis. Like she hadn't been the best sex I could remember ever having in my life. Like she hadn't just dismantled all my parts and pieces and left them lying stripped and bare for the entire world to see. It made my head hurt even more.

The cell phone I had in my hand vibrated with a text, and I flinched when I noticed I had no less than ten missed calls. Everyone was checking up on me, making sure I hadn't drunk myself to death, and my parents had called to see if I was coming for brunch. The answer to that was hell no, the reasons more complicated, but the text was from Shaw and I didn't want to be an ass and ignore her.

Skipped family brunch. Want to get some food?
I could eat.
Rule is messing with the water heater. Bob Vila he is not.
Just me and you?

I hadn't been alone with Shaw since before she dropped the bombshell about not only her and Rule being a couple, but Remy being gay. I loved her like a sister, loved how good she was for my brother, but I still had some issues with her lying to us for so long. However, I had promised Rule I would get it on lock, so that's what I was going to do and a greasy-ass breakfast burrito sounded awesome right now

Sure. The Denver Diner?
Gross. No, if you want diner food let's go to Steuben's.
Okay.
It's uptown on 17th.
See you soon.

I had a cast-iron stomach and the Denver Diner would have been fine for me. Army food had come a long way over the years, but it still wasn't great, though as long as it was hot, I could eat it. Uptown wasn't terribly far from where the Victorian and the tattoo shop were anyway, so I had time to swing by and change before I met up with her. Nash was coming out as I was running in and he gave me a concerned look on his way to the Charger.

"You okay? You weren't here this morning."

"I had a rough night. It's all good."

He must have been in a hurry because he didn't stop to give me the third degree. I doubted Cora wanted the guys to be privy to all the sordid details, so it was nice I didn't have to chitchat with him in passing.

I rushed through a shower and decided not to bother running a razor over my face. I felt like hell, so I might as well look like it as well. I tossed on some jeans and a clean T-shirt. I slapped my sunglasses on over my seriously bloodshot eyes and drove up to the restaurant. Shaw's snazzy Porsche SUV was already in the parking lot and I was surprised that I actually felt a little nervous about seeing her one-on-one.

Shaw was a sweet girl. She didn't have a malicious or mean bone in her tiny body. She was all gigantic heart and unconditional love, which was how she managed to get my idiot brother to act right most of the time. There was just something about those innocent green eyes that made you want to be her hero, made you want to be the best "you" possible around her, which made all the resentment and irritation I felt toward her so hard to swallow. Her blond head was easy to pick out of the crowd and the fact that she was as uneasy with meeting as I was showed on her pretty face.

She gave me a wan smile as I slid into the booth across from her, and I saw the concern flash across her eyes when I took my sunglasses off and ordered coffee from the hovering waitress.

"You look awful."

"I feel awful."

She was fiddling with her silverware and I could tell she wanted to say something but was holding back.

"What, Shaw? Just say it."

She bit her bottom lip and wrinkled her nose up at me. "Rule is worried about you."

I snickered at her and nodded at the waitress when the coffee was set down in front of me. "Oh, how the tables have turned. I spent most of my life worrying about him."

It was true. I don't know where the all-consuming need to be my brother's keeper had come from, but it was as much a part of me as my sense of duty and honor were.

She frowned at me. "Excessive drinking, acting out, not talking to Margot and Dale, and pushing away everyone that cares about you: it's like you're purposely trying to make coming home as hard as it can possibly be. We all love you, Rome. Yes, we were all used to loving you when it was easy and took no effort, but we can all learn to love you in a different way now that it's harder if you give us a chance."

I cleared my throat and waited for the hovering waitress to take our order before answering her.

"Look, I'm trying to settle into my life the way it is now.

I've had a few hiccups here and there but I'll figure it out. I'm sorry I was such a dick to you. It's hard looking at you and not seeing Remy and his lies, it's hard seeing you and Rule as a unit. I'm not used to being on the outside looking in at my own family."

She hissed out a breath like I had smacked her. I saw the pain flash across that jade gaze and felt like a heel.

"It wasn't my secret to tell. Remy lived his life the way he wanted on his terms. I didn't agree with it, with the secrets and sneaking around, but it wasn't my place to force the issue. He was happy, he was in love, and he didn't need or want you and Rule to interfere, even if it would have been with good intentions. As for being with Rule . . ." She met my gaze head-on and unflinchingly. "I've loved him forever and you knew it. I earned him, Rome. I earned the right to be happy with him and to make him happy. I won't apologize for it, ever. I'm sorry the change is hard for you to adjust to."

The waitress chose that moment to put our plates down on the table. We stared at each other in a long silence for a moment before my pounding head and empty stomach couldn't take it anymore.

"I'm just trying to figure it out, little girl. Everyone let Rule muddle his way to something great, why can't I have a little leeway until I get there?"

She finally gave me a grin that lit her entire face up. I really did love this girl and missed having her in my life.

"Leeway I can do. The total freeze-out, angry giant you've been lately, I've had enough of."

"Captain No-Fun." She laughed and looked at me questioningly. "Cora calls me 'Captain No-Fun.'"

"She tends to call it like she sees it. I like that about her."

I scratched the stubble on my chin and tried to keep my face impassive. "She seems to be full of surprises."

She lifted her fork and pointed it at me. "How do you know? When have you ever hung out with her?"

Now, that wasn't a question I wanted to touch with a ten-foot pole, so I decided to change the subject.

"Were the folks pissed you canceled Sunday Funday?"

She blinked at me in surprise. "A little. It's not that uncommon. Rule and your mom still have a rough time of it and sometimes he's just not in the mood to go. They both try and I guess that's all you can ask for, but it's hard. They miss you. They ask about you all the time. Everyone is so happy you made it home in one piece."

This wasn't a conversation I wanted to have either, but it seemed less torturous than talking about my morning with Cora or how well I did or didn't know the blond dynamo.

"I came back in one piece physically, not so sure the same thing can be said for my head."

She frowned at me in concern as I pushed my now-empty plate away and picked up the coffee.

"What do you mean?"

I slumped back in the booth and twirled a finger around my temple like I was nuts. "My brain goes wonky. I see things that aren't there, I can't sleep so great, and I feel like people around me keep dying and there's nothing I can do about it. I can't figure out what I'm supposed to do with myself now that I'm not in the army, and it's making me crazy. I don't really recognize myself anymore."

She made a little noise in her throat and reached across the table to put her much smaller hand over my own where I had involuntarily curled it into a fist on the tabletop. I could say over and over again I was mad at my mom and dad for lying to me, for making Rule's life miserable, but the truth of the matter was I didn't know that I could handle them looking at me like they didn't know who I was anymore. I was so far gone from the son, the soldier they had seen last time I was home, I didn't know what it would do to me to have them look at me like I was a stranger.

"Rome." Shaw's voice was soft and I couldn't meet her gaze. If there was pity, sadness for me shining out of it, it would just kill me. I was so used to protecting her, to offering her advice and comfort, that the idea that she had to do it for me now slid under my skin like an icy splinter. "I'm looking right at you and see the guy that was always a wonderful brother, an amazing son, and the strongest, most self-aware guy I have ever known. You're amazing and maybe you're struggling right now, but seriously Rome, you've had to be strong for your entire life, haul around everyone else's crap, it's okay to put it down for a minute and let the rest of us carry the burden."

I looked back up at her and had to gulp down the clog of emotion that rose in my throat. I couldn't answer her, so I just gave her fingers a little squeeze to let her know the sentiment was welcome. My brother was one hell of a lucky guy to have this amazing girl be so gone for him. I thought I was

off the hook when I pulled out my wallet to pay for the bill
but it was easy to forget that Shaw was smart as a whip and
rarely forgot anything.

"So what did you mean before when you said Cora was
full of surprises? I didn't think you guys really knew each
other that well."

I wanted to groan. "Nothing. I didn't mean anything by
it. She's cute and says whatever she wants, she's just surprising is all."

She arched an eyebrow. "You know we're really close,
right? And anything she doesn't tell me, Ayden will."

Damn it, I forgot about the way girls were all so chatty
and in each other's business all the time.

"I got plowed last night."

"Obviously." Her dry tone surprised a laugh out of me.

"I gave the bartender my phone to call Rule to come get
me but he called the shop and Cora answered. Since he was
busy with the water heater and Nash was AWOL, she came
and got me. She made sure I didn't kill myself or anyone else.
I just was surprised she cared enough to do it because I don't
think I'm her favorite person."

Shaw regarded me solemnly for a minute. I had to fight
hard not to squirm like a guilty little kid.

"There's more to her than meets the eye."

Hell yeah, there was but I wasn't going to say anything
about it.

"She was engaged a while back. The guy broke her
heart and now she has all these delusions about meeting
some picture-perfect guy and living happily ever after. She

meddles in all our lives, doles out advice, and sticks her nose where it doesn't belong time and time again, but won't listen to any of us when we tell her she's reaching for something that doesn't exist. It just sucks because more often than not she's right and we should have listened to her all along, so it's no wonder she blows us off. Honestly I think she's terrified of letting anyone close enough to break her heart again."

I shrugged and started to slide out of the booth. "Nothing wrong with reaching for the stars."

"There is when what's available is only here in the ground level. I love Rule with everything I have, but he is far from perfect. Relationships are not tailor-made and people are flawed. You have to work around that and love the other person anyway. Our flaws are what make us unique, and while Rule might not be perfect, he is absolutely perfect for me."

I wrapped an arm around her neck and gave her a quick hug that had her squealing. Something warm and familiar settled in my chest when I felt her wrap her arms around me in a hug. I missed this and it was my own stupid fault.

"I missed you, little girl."

I felt her exhale against my chest and her hug tighten just a fraction. "I missed you, too, Rome. I'm so glad you're back."

I wasn't a hundred percent back, but for some reason my eyes felt more open, and I had a clearer view of what I had been missing lately. Shaw was right. I had always been a pretty steady guy, a reliable son, a steadfast older brother. I was still all those things but now I was other things that weren't so pretty, were harder parts to accept. However, the people in my life that loved me would always love me even if they had to do it in a different way now, and that made me a lucky guy. I needed to stop taking things like that for granted and, just like Cora said, stop feeling guilty for being one of the lucky ones.

CHAPTER 7

Cora

IT HAD BEEN A week since I let my inner slut out. A solid week that I hadn't thought of Jimmy and the upcoming wedding one single time, let alone done any Facebook stalking. It had also been a week that I walked on eggshells waiting for the Terrible Trio to lay into me, to grill me about the overnight visit with big brother, but it never came. Apparently the idea that Rome and I could be anything but mortal enemies was laughable, and aside from the third degree I had to suffer from Ayden and some curious looks from Shaw, it wasn't a big deal at all. Now, had they known that I let it go from babysitting a blacked-out drunk to something else entirely, that might have been a different story. It sucked because I couldn't get the something else entirely out of my mind no matter what I did.

Rome had stopped at the shop once to drop off Nash's cell when he forgot it at home and another time to ask Rule if he would come and help strip the floors at that dive bar he seemed to be spending all his time at. On both occasions he had been achingly polite and totally normal. There was no hint of anything inappropriate or even flirtatious. He acted like we had never been naked together, let alone screwed each other's brains out, and it irked me to no end. Especially since every time I saw him I was reminded just how out-of-this-world hot he was. It wasn't fair. Granted I had been the one to deny that the act meant anything other than scratching an itch, but it rubbed me the wrong way that he seemed so blasé and unaffected by it. I responded by being even more flippant and sarcastic than normal. It didn't seem to bother him at all.

I was at Cerberus after a particularly long day at the shop having drinks with everyone and waiting for Jet's band to play. It was a typical Saturday night except for the fact that instead of having fun with my friends, I was busy trying not to watch Rome and the chick in leather pants who was practically dry-humping him at the table. I knew it shouldn't bother me, we weren't even friends really, but it was taking every ounce of restraint I possessed, which wasn't a lot to begin with, not only to keep from screaming at him, but to keep from murdering the chick with her own tacky necklace. To Rome's credit, he didn't look like he was interested in what the girl was throwing at him, but he sure as hell wasn't pushing her away either. I wanted to dump the pitcher of beer in front of me over both of them.

"What's up, cranky pants?"

Rowdy's amused voice broke through my dark musings and I tore my gaze away from Rome to look at him. Jet had dragged Ayden off backstage with him saying something about how she needed to see the bathroom here as well; Shaw and Rule were deep in conversation with Nash about Phil, nobody had seen or heard from the shop owner in over a week and everyone was concerned. Rome was busy with Catwoman, so that left me and Rowdy alone at the table. There were way worse drinking partners to have, but at the moment I didn't need those perceptive ocean-blue eyes picking me apart.

"I'm not cranky, just tired. It was a long day."

He lifted a blond eyebrow and picked up his pint of Coors Light. "You've been off all week. Quiet. That's not normal."

I just shrugged and hoped silence would make him drop it, but then the girl with Rome threw back her head and let out a loud laugh that had me biting down on my tongue to avoid creating a scene.

"There is no way he said anything that funny. I don't even think he has a sense of humor." I was aware I sounded snarky and mean but I couldn't seem to help it.

Rowdy stretched one of his arms out along the back of my chair and wrapped his fingers around the back of my neck. I sighed a little when he started to rub some of the tension out of the muscles.

"You wanna tell me what's really going on or do you just want me to jump to my own conclusion, which is probably right anyway?"

I scowled at him and looked back at Rome and the leather-clad bitch. I couldn't hold back the tiny snarl that formed when I saw her tuck her fingers under the edge of the leather belt he had on.

"It's possible, I mean highly likely, that I think big brother Archer is a total babe."

Rowdy laughed. "No kidding."

I elbowed him in the side and rolled my eyes. "It's also entirely possible that said babeness is hard to resist, and I may or may not have let his sleepover get out of hand."

The gentle rubbing stopped and he let out a low whistle. I looked up at him and frowned when I saw that he was frowning right back at me.

"What?"

"That's just surprising and kind of messed up."

"Why? You guys do it all the time."

"Not with anyone the rest of us are related to. We like to get away clean."

I elbowed him in the ribs again. "Pig."

"If it was just a onetime thing then what's with the death glare you're giving the brunette that's all up on him?"

I heaved a deep sigh. "I don't know." And I really didn't. Rome was not on my agenda, he was not what I was looking for, but I couldn't stop thinking about him and all his imperfections. That wasn't good. I put my chin on my hand and looked at Rowdy.

"Don't you get lonely? Rule's with Shaw, Jet went and got married, for Christ's sake. Don't you look around and wonder when it's your turn? I know you well enough to know that the endless girls, the one-night stands, are what they are. You could do without, but if the right one came along you would be all over her."

He laughed without any humor and leaned back in his

chair. When the waitress came by he ordered us a round of Jäger shots.

"The right one came along forever ago, only I wasn't her right one, so now it is what it is and I'm just killing time."

I blinked at him in surprise. He never really talked about his past much. I knew he grew up in the system in Texas, that he used to play football, and that he had left the game and college unexpectedly and decided to tattoo instead, but that was really it.

"So you don't think there's anyone else after that? You're just going to spend the rest of your life going girl to girl and being alone?"

It made me think of Jimmy, of the life I thought I was supposed to have by now. I had invested everything in him, had thought he was my everything, and now I wasn't so sure. Nothing had flipped me upside down the way the pain and passion that burned in Rome's bright blue eyes had. I wasn't a person affected by a lot, but he affected me, no doubt about it. He was about as steady and secure as a tropical storm, though, and that made him more than a little dangerous to my sense of what was right for me.

"For now it's all about a good time and eventually someone will come along and I'll be her one, and if I'm lucky I'll like her well enough that that'll be enough to make it work. I don't think that idiot you left behind in New York was ever your one and only, Tink. I think you were young and tired of being bounced around by your dad, so you latched on to the first steady thing you could find. You thought Jimmy was going to be your family, your home, and when that didn't happen you ended up lost and scared. I think you'll know it when your one comes along, because perfect or not, he's going to knock you sideways and maybe for once shut you up and you won't have time to be scared anymore."

I didn't respond when his gaze flicked to where Rome was standing. Crap. I tossed back the shot and made a face at him.

"You suck."

"Only when asked nicely." We shared a laugh and I looked up in surprise when a shadow fell over the edge of the table. I hated that I had to crank my neck back to look up at Rome. The scar on his forehead stood out in stark relief in the dim light of the bar. A muscle was twitching in his cheek and his normally iridescent eyes seemed kind of cloudy and dark.

"Can you tell Rule and Shaw I've had enough? I'm gonna bounce." He sounded gruff and looked irritated at something. His leather limpet was nowhere to be seen.

"Enmity hasn't even played yet." Why I told him that I had no idea. Obviously the band hadn't gone on stage yet. I was just being snippy and argumentative.

He narrowed his eyes at me and opened his mouth then shut it again like he had to rethink what he was going to say. He gave his head a tiny little shake like he was marshaling his thoughts.

"I've known Jet since he was a kid. I've seen him play a thousand times. I'm trying really hard not to drink, and if I stick around here one more second, that isn't going to be possible."

We stared at each other in silence. I didn't know if I should take that as he shouldn't drink anymore to avoid making mistakes like the one he made with me, or that he needed to stop drinking because he was out of control and it wasn't helping matters.

Rowdy ordered us another round of shots and I saw Rome's jaw clench. I wasn't sure what was going on, so I defaulted to my usual glib manner.

"Captain No-Fun strikes again."

I saw his dark brows lower and felt Rowdy tense next to me. It was rude and it was uncalled for, but before I could apologize, he put his hands on the table in front of me and bent down so that we were face-to-face. There was a storm brewing in that blue gaze and I didn't think I wanted any part of it, or maybe I wanted to be the cause of it and that was why I was acting so awful.

"Pretty sure you know what my idea of a good time is. I'd be happy to remind you in case you forgot."

My breath got caught in my throat and I saw Rowdy shift uncomfortably next to me.

"No thanks. I think Catwoman wants a turn."

He sneered at me and started to walk away throwing over his shoulder, "You would know that there's more than enough to go around, Half-Pint."

It took me a second to catch my breath after he was gone. I couldn't bring myself to watch and see if the brunette ended up leaving with him or not. Rowdy let out another low whistle.

"Dude, I didn't think I would ever see the day anyone got the last word with you. Totally sideways."

I ignored him and picked my beer back up. I couldn't do this with Rome. Couldn't run him off, these were his friends and family, too. I couldn't be bitchy to him just because I was jealous and envious that his hotness was undeniable. I was going to have to put on my big-girl panties and have a showdown with him, have the talk that I really didn't want to have and clear the air. I wasn't sure what I was going to do with him exactly, but there was something in all the messed-up ways we were around each other I didn't think we could ignore. But first I was going to drink all the Jäger in Colorado and try to block out the image of that leather-clad skank with her paws all over him. I also was going to steadfastly avoid the knowing looks Rowdy kept shooting at me; either that or I was going to punch him in the nose.

THE NEXT MORNING I was feeling a little rough, but it was totally manageable, especially since all I had to do was throw on a cute sundress, slime some product in my hair, and slick some gloss on and be good to go. Short hair rocked. My sundress was bright turquoise, the same color as my odd blue eye, and it had a big sunflower in neon yellow on the hem. It was bright and cheerful, so I figured no matter how grouchy Rome was, he wouldn't be able to stay too mad in the presence of such an awesome summer dress. Plus it made my legs look great and made it appear that I actually had some cleavage.

When I pulled up to the Victorian, Nash was coming down the front steps. He had stayed to shut the bar down with me and Rowdy, so he looked about as haggard as I felt. He had a ball hat pulled down low on his forehead and dark sunglasses covering half of his face. He pulled up short when he saw me and walked over to lean on the fender of the Cooper.

"What are you doing here?"

I tried not to fidget and pushed my own sunglasses up on my nose.

"I need to talk to Rome."

I saw his eyebrows dip below the frames and the corner of his mouth turn down.

"Why?"

"Because I do. Leave it alone."

"I told you it was a bad idea."

"Yeah, well, it's my bad idea, so back off. I just need to talk to him. Where are you off to so early?"

"I'm going to talk to my mother."

I blinked in shock. It was no secret that Nash's relationship with his mom and his stepdad was anything but rosy.

"Why on earth would you want to do that?"

"Because something is going on with Phil and I need help pinning him down. He's dodging me left and right, so she's my last resort."

"Wasn't Phil your real dad's brother?"

He nodded and rubbed the back of his neck. I could see even mentioning those dynamics made him uncomfortable.

"Yeah, but ever since I was little, I mean long before I even understood that my dad took off, Phil has been unable to tell my mother no. She says 'jump,' he asks her what river she wants him to leap into. It's weird but I figure she's the only way to get some answers."

I patted his bicep and moved toward the front of the apartment they shared. "Good luck with that, it sounds like a whole lot of no fun."

"He's not here."

I pulled up a step and looked back at Nash over my shoulder. Unbidden visions of Catwoman and her hands in Rome's pants flew through my head. I didn't like the way that they made my stomach drop at all.

"He didn't come home last night?" I could hear the dissatisfaction in my tone and clearly it wasn't lost on Nash because he scowled at me.

"No, he was here when I got home. Alone. He just doesn't sleep so great, ya know? He was up really, really early. I think he went running or something. You want me to let you inside so you can wait for him?"

I nodded. I needed a cup of coffee and a second to formulate what I wanted to say to Rome.

"I hope you know what you're doing, Cora. Rome isn't the kind of guy you can just manipulate and twist around your cute little finger. What happened to holding out for Mr. Perfect?"

I made myself at home in the small kitchen and pulled my sunglasses off to set them on the breakfast bar that separated the very masculine living room from the even more manly kitchen.

"Stop being such a worrywart, I just want to talk to the guy."

He headed back toward the front door but his words stayed with me after he shut it behind him.

"Talking with you is what normally gets people into the most trouble."

I appreciated that the guys were worried about me. I didn't have the best track record with disappointment and boys, and I had been going on for a long time about my perfect man. They all knew I was after a guy that seemed rock solid, that wasn't carrying around a truckload of emotional baggage, that came across happy and set with his lot in life. They knew I was ready for a guy who wanted to promise me forever and a future that was as bright and shiny as I tended to be. I wanted the happy-ever-after that Rule had given Shaw and the peace of mind that Jet had given Ayden. I wanted a partner and someone who was ready to travel the long, twisting road of commitment with me.

It made sense that they could all see that Rome was almost the exact opposite of what I had been describing, so they were just trying to save me from more unnecessary heartache because by now it was obvious he was getting to me. I just didn't know if my idea of what I was holding out for was a viable option anymore. There was something happening between us—more than chemistry, more than wistful longing, and more than a little crush. I knew when a plan was falling apart. I had seen my first plan of a life with Jimmy go up in smoke and now I could see the idea of Mr. Perfect, this fictional ideal I had built up in my head, start to tatter under the force of everything that was Rome Archer. It didn't matter that he seemed to be as lost as a child in the dark, that his baggage was heavier and harder to handle than most, or that he couldn't even see his tomorrow, let alone a future with someone else.

I wasn't sure I was ready to fully let go of the dream just yet; only Rome was standing in the way of me getting my hands on it anymore. I couldn't ignore that something was happening between us and it was time to stop being scared and find the answers to exactly what that something was.

I heard the front door open and heavy footsteps make their way toward where I was in the kitchen. I was rinsing off the dishes in the sink, mostly because I needed something to do with my hands, but also because they looked like they had been there for a while. Gross.

"What are you doing here?"

The tone was not nice. There was no welcome, none of the flirty and teasing he normally tossed at me. It sounded like each word was having to fight its way out of somewhere deep in his chest and that they tasted bitter and sharp on his tongue. I wiped my hands on a dish towel and turned around to face him.

Holy hell. How was I supposed to have a coherent, grown-up conversation with the man when he was wearing only a pair of black track pants and an iPod holder wrapped around one bicep? His dark hair was even darker with sweat and all those muscles and planes that made up his amazing physique were standing out in stark relief since he wasn't wearing a shirt and had clearly just put himself through some serious paces. That just wasn't fair.

"The dishes. You're welcome."

He grunted and pulled the iPod off. He stepped past me to the fridge and pulled out a bottle of water. I tried not to drool in an obvious way when some of it missed his mouth and ended up running a damp trail over his chest. He just watched me with almost zero expression on his handsome, but obviously exhausted face.

"I was going to do them later this afternoon. I need to take a shower. I stink."

I cleared my throat and leaned back against the sink. "I was hoping we could talk real quick." And maybe he would go put a shirt on so I could form words and not sound like a moron.

He rubbed both his hands, hard, over his face and head and I noticed how really worn he actually looked. Those blue eyes were sort of faded and he had dark shadows resting underneath.

"Listen, Cora, I understand. I'm jacked up, you aren't into it, whatever. It just messes with my already overworked mind when you tell me one thing and then look at me like you want to lick me all over like an ice cream cone in the same breath. I'm trying to figure my own shit out. I don't have the mental fortitude or the patience to try and figure yours out as well. I just ran six miles on less than two hours of sleep. I need a shower and maybe if I'm lucky, a nap."

He didn't give me a chance to respond. He just turned on his sneaker and left me standing there gaping at him. For the second time in as many days, I was not only speechless but also left without being able to get a final word in. I hated it. The butt-head didn't even give me the opportunity to apologize for being needlessly bitchy last night. I shoved off the counter and went down the hallway to the room at the back of the apartment. It was Rule's old room when he had lived with Nash, so I knew that there was a bathroom attached.

I could hear the water running and he had the radio on somewhere in the room and it was playing Tom Petty. Oddly fitting, Rome totally struck me as a classic-rock kind of guy. His room was also neat as a pin. All those years in the military had obviously bred good habits into him. The big king-sized bed was even all made up. There wasn't so much as a stray sock on the floor, but there also wasn't much to define the space as his. The only personal effect that was visible was a black-and-white photo of a much younger Rome and the twins.

Rule looked like Rule, only without as much ink, and he was smiling, something he didn't do much of until he and Shaw had figured their situation out. Rome looked tall and proud, every bit the protective older brother. And the other twin, Remy—it was crazy to see an exact replica of what Rule would look like as a typical guy—still beautiful, but so boring, so common.

I was lost in thought, staring at the photo, so I didn't hear the water turn off. An arm shot out over my shoulder and picked the picture up. Startled I turned around and came face-to-face with Rome in a towel and that's it. Man, this was turning into a total test of my self-control. Track pants were nice, a towel was better. He smelled clean but still looked annoyed that I was all up in his space.

"This picture has been everywhere I've been. I took it to basic. It went to Korea. It's been to Pakistan and Iraq, and it just came back from Afghanistan with me. The people in it were always there to remind me what I was fighting for, who I was supposed to be keeping the country safe for."

I put a hand to my throat and was surprised to find that his words had tears building in the back of my eyes.

"You're lucky to have that kind of relationship with them."

He snorted, and I had to try really hard not to reach out and snatch that tiny knot holding the towel up. I don't know what it was about him that made my body take charge and my mind take a backseat, but it was potent and slightly un-nerving. I had never been so overwhelmingly attracted to any man before, not even Jimmy.

"I thought so, too, only then I found out Remy was hiding a secret life, and that Shaw could do a better job taking care of Rule than I ever did."

I cocked my head to the side and considered him thought-fully. "What about you?"

He cut me a look and moved back across the room to his dresser. The backside view was just as nice as the front.

"What about me?"

"You always talk about how you fought for them, how you made choices for them. What about you? Who took care of you? Who fought to make the world a better place for you?" I asked the questions in shock, because I couldn't really believe he didn't realize how important he was and had always been to his brothers. Those blue eyes never wa-vered from mine.

"I think you're trying to diminish all the things you were to Rule and Remy, and that's not cool. Remy might not have been honest, but by all accounts he was in love and happy. And yes, Rule was a hot mess, but he managed to get it together when it counted, so you did your brotherly duty. It's time to focus on your own life. "

He turned around to look at me, a T-shirt dangling from his hand. I took a deep breath and forced myself to focus on his face and not his naked chest, or the spot below his waist where that towel was hanging precariously below his belly button.

"Look, I need to apologize for being so bitchy last night. I think it's cool that you're trying not to drink anymore. Admirable even. Honestly, I was not a fan of the leather-clad bimbo and her hands all in your pants. It might have made me a little cranky, but I shouldn't have taken it out on you."

The eyebrow under the scar went up. "Who?"

"The girl from last night." He shrugged like he didn't remember and tossed his shirt on the bed.

"Well, you and Rowdy looked like matching rock-and-roll wedding cake toppers. Both so blond, pretty, and all kinds of pierced and tattooed. If I had to stand there and watch him rub your neck or whisper in your ear one more second, it wasn't going to be pretty."

I felt my eyes pop wide and my heart started to speed up.

"Rowdy is like my brother."

"And I don't remember any chick in leather."

We stood there in silence, staring at each other. I saw his pulse flutter in his neck and bit my bottom lip. It suddenly felt like we were the only two people in the world, like this room was standing still in time. I was starting to feel like what I thought perfect meant was absolutely boring and I was an idiot forever thinking that was what I wanted. Wild and unleashed seemed so much more exciting than stead-fast and firmly planted. Now I just needed him to get on the same page as me with it.

"So here's the deal. I don't need you to figure my shit out, I can do it all on my own. I look at you like I want to lick you all over because I do. I don't really know how to go about starting up something with a guy like you, but as long you promise not to lie to me, to not cheat on me, I want to."

And I did. I wanted to start it and finish it and enjoy everything in between. He was so different from Jimmy, and honestly, troubled or not, I could see he was so much better. Rome Archer was a force to be reckoned with, a storm brewing of broken thoughts and dangerous demons, of misplaced responsibility and unknown future. I wasn't sure, but I had a sinking suspicion I might be one of the few able to withstand the destruction left by that storm's aftermath, and even though my old fear was there, it wasn't as strong as the attraction I felt for this enigmatic man.

He didn't respond, but I saw his chest rise and fall as he sucked in a deep breath.

"Cora." I could hear the hesitation in his tone. "I don't juggle women and I don't think I could be any more honest with you than I already have been. But I'm still not the guy you're looking for, and that hasn't changed since the other morning. Perfect isn't even in my vocabulary, even if you are cute enough to make me want to try and be."

He tapped a finger to his temple, and I saw the shadow

move over his eyes. He might not be one hundred percent, but I was starting to think any portion of Rome was better than most men operating at full capacity. I was good with words, could tell him that something about him just got to me, that I thought he was hotter than any guy should be, that I liked that he didn't just back down from me. Instead I decided that since he was a man of action, I would just show him I knew what I was doing and knew exactly what I wanted. I wanted the last word in this and there really was only one surefire way to get it.

I grabbed the hem of my sundress and whipped it up and off over my head. The bright material landed in a heap on the floor and I was left in my yellow wedges and cute pink underwear. One thing about having small boobs was I didn't have to really worry about a bra if I didn't want to. Apparently Rome was a fan of small boobs, because his eyes lit up like a lighter flicking to life. Even in my chunky shoes, with him barefoot, when I made my way to where he was standing, stock-still, the top of my head barely reached his chin. I had to look up at him, and when I did, I put one hand on either side of his face so he couldn't look away from me.

Those blue, blue eyes got heavy-lidded and dropped just a fraction, which made my blood get all warm and slippery under my skin.

"Don't be scared, Captain No-Fun, we got this."

He put his big hands on my naked waist and started to walk me back toward the bed in the center of the room. It would be so easy to be intimidated by a guy like him, only he was looking at me like I was something so unique and so precious that all I could feel was anticipation. That grin that was probably going to make me fall in love with him broke across his face, and I knew that whatever it was I was doing with this man, who was so the opposite of what I thought I wanted, was the right thing. He wasn't steady, he was most definitely not a man content with his current circumstances, and I was pretty sure his idea of what being a partner to someone looked like was totally different from mine. I still didn't know that he wanted to be all in with me or even with himself but the pull, the undeniable current of want and need that seemed to loop around us, was just too much to dismiss for a dream that had yet to come along.

"I told you last night you know better than anyone what my idea of fun entails." His thumb brushed across the jewels dotting my side and trailed up over a nipple that was now straining and begging for attention. The back of my knees hit the bed, and before I knew it, I was on my back and he was looming over me all naked skin and glowing eyes. It was beautiful, he was beautiful, and no matter what happened after this point, I knew I was a lucky girl to be here with him.

"Are you actually going to talk to me this time?"

I put my hands in his short hair as he worked on getting my shoes off and the cute little underwear out of his way. I liked that he was kind of rough, a little impatient, but there was always reverence when his fingers brushed my skin. He kissed me once and dropped the towel.

"Probably not."

He put his hands under my hips and moved me toward the edge of the bed. I slid my hands down to his shoulders and propped his chin up with the edge of my knuckle so that he was looking at me.

"Why not?"

He ran his hands down the length of one leg and situated me so that my legs were off the bed and he was standing at the apex of them. I was exposed, open to him, and should have felt vulnerable or maybe even shy, but it was impossible to feel anything but appreciated and sexy with the way those eyes burned when he looked at me. My breath got caught in my lungs and couldn't escape when he touched that little tiny ring situated at the heart of me with just the tip of his index finger. Everything was slick and damp, and his touch just made it all burn hotter.

"Because I'm freaked out that whatever I say might be the wrong thing. And right now, being with you is the one thing that feels solid and real . . . You're so full of color, so vibrant you never get lost in all the gray in my head. I don't want to lose that."

My heart caught. Those were words a woman would never forget a man saying to her, especially when they came from a man like this. I got my arms around his neck and pulled him down for a kiss that I hoped conveyed how I felt. I arched up off the bed when his finger abandoned the jewelry and went in search of more intimate, deeper territory. I felt those thick digits slide through my folds, brush against quivering nerve endings, play with all the parts of me that were achy and greedy for his touch. He used his thumb to press down on my clit, which had the added benefit of rubbing the smooth edge of my piercing against all those tightly wound centers of pleasure. He knew just how to stroke me, to play me to get the best result.

I kissed him until neither of us could breathe, kissed him until he made me pant his name, kissed him until he got more fingers involved in what he was doing down there and I couldn't keep it together anymore. I broke apart, felt him drop his head and kiss the side of my neck. I was clutching those broad shoulders like a lifeline. I felt like if let him go, this thing we were building between us was going to disappear in a puff of smoke—it was just that magical and different. I think he might have even chuckled, but I was pretty sure he had just devastated what it meant to have sex for me.

He pulled me to him and I could feel that erection pulsing and throbbing at the apex of my core. My breasts flattened against the hard plane of his chest, and we were as close as two people could be without being joined. I could feel his stomach muscles tighten and contract against me. I ran a hand over the solid curve of his ass and blinked up at him lazily. I saw that he looked a little hesitant, which made me frown. I wanted all that rigid and ready flesh inside me, now.

"Did I hurt you last time?"

His voice was gruff, and I didn't appreciate that he was too strong for me to just pull him down into where I wanted him to be. I retaliated by wrapping both legs around his lean waist and lifting myself up to him. I heard him swear, but it only took a fraction of a second before he got with the program and sank all the way down into me. I sighed at the sensation, the stretch and pull my body had to do to accommodate all that length and girth. I dug my hands into the thick muscles running across his neck. I wanted to groan but I tried to answer him instead because those blue eyes were on mine resolutely and he wasn't moving.

"Noooo . . ." I couldn't really form words as he bent his head and put a nipple in his mouth. The scrape of his teeth nearly made me lose it again and the way he lapped at the turgid skin with the flat of his tongue made it almost impossible to breathe. "It was awesome. You were awesome, so what if I had to be careful how I sat down for a week? Totally worth it."

I choked out a laugh when he levered up on his arms to glare down at me. It was hard for him to look threatening when he shuddered as I squeezed him with my inner muscles.

"Not funny."

I moved my hands so that I could trace the tight line of his rib cage, pausing a little when I got to the part that was just recently healing. I liked the way he felt, liked the way he moved. I liked that he was so big and strong, yet able to admit he was struggling and human enough to have weakness. The fact of the matter was I just liked him, and even if it meant we had to get used to the size difference, it was a learning curve I had no trouble being a part of. My body wanted him, it was my head and all things I had told myself I was waiting for that had been my stumbling block up to this point. Looking up at him looking down at me like he had never seen anything he wanted more, I realized all the parts were on the same page right now. I kissed him on the center of his breastbone and worked on pulling him back down where all of that straining and aching flesh did the most good. I liked feeling surrounded by him, engulfed in all his maleness.

"It's fine. Now move or I'll have to hurt you."

He grunted his agreement and got back to business. He stroked along my legs until I bent them up along by his sides. One of his hands tangled up in the top of my short hair and all that lovely, sinewy muscle started heaving and pushing against me. With each thrust, each retreat, his eyes got hotter and burned brighter. I couldn't look away. It was even better, more intense than the first time. He didn't leave any part of me untouched. My mouth, my neck, my breasts, the part where I was open and sliding along him. His hands, his mouth . . . they did everything they could to pull me back apart.

He said my name, I'm pretty sure I screamed his when he reached down between the two of us, and right before he pushed me over the edge again started playing with that damn hoop. His thick fingers were so light, so gentle, but I was too gone, too ready to let go, so it just took a brush of skin and the slight tug of metal in aroused flesh to make me come unglued and throw my head back and arch up against him hard enough that he got an arm under my back. Holding me that way, he plunged into me with renewed vigor and less care for my well-being. It was awesome. I felt him shudder his own release, felt him flick his tongue along the cord of my neck that was throbbing in time to his heartbeat, and then he rolled over so that both of us had our backs on the bed and our legs dangling over the side. I swore that if he was that good at getting me off with just his hands, I was never going to survive if he ever worked his way to getting his mouth down there. He was dangerous in a whole different way now.

We were both breathing hard and silent. I was pretty sure that Rome was the best cure for a hangover I had ever come across. He picked up one of my much smaller hands in his own and trailed a thumb across my neon-painted nails.

"So you gonna let me take you on a date or something, Cora Lewis?"

I turned my head to look at him and had to bite back a laugh. He actually looked concerned about my answer.

"Do you want to take me on a date, Rome Archer?"

"Yeah, I think I do. Don't get me wrong. If you just want me to take you to bed anytime you feel up to it, I'm game for that as well, but I like you, so yeah, I would like to take you on a date."

I went to push up on my elbows so I could look him in the eye, when I realized we were both really naked and there was a whole lot of non-after-sex stuff happening. I felt my eyes get huge in my face and I must have looked panicked because he frowned.

"Seriously we don't have to if you don't want to."

"Uh . . . The date is fine, but we have a problem."

He scratched his chest and yawned. "The guys?"

I smacked him on the arm. "No, well yeah, maybe, but something more serious than that."

He copied my pose. "What?"

"I'm not on the pill."

We stared at each other for what felt like five minutes without talking. I was smarter than this, always had been. I couldn't believe I let something as basic as safe sex get away from me. Finally he flopped back down on the bed and threw his arm across his eyes.

"I knew I felt like I forgot something the last time."

Well, crap, I hadn't even considered the time before. I cleared my throat.

"And?"

He just shrugged a big shoulder. "It's not like we can go back and un-have sex."

I growled a little at him and narrowed my eyes. "What if the result is a baby?"

"Then we deal with it."

"Just like that?"

"Just like that. Don't freak out yet."

Oh, this wasn't even close to freaking out, but he didn't know me well enough to know that, which really was the entire problem with the possibility of getting knocked up by a virtual stranger. I was going to start hyperventilating, start spazzing out, but before I could, he wrapped his arms around me and pulled me down so that I was lying on top of him. I felt his lips brush the top of my head and felt that wide chest start to rise and fall in a steady rhythm. The jackass was going to fall asleep on me while I was having a major crisis.

"Cora." I put my head down over his heart and tried to calm down. "Don't worry, Half-Pint, we got this."

And then he was asleep and I was left wondering how such an obviously imperfect guy had invaded my world so thoroughly and how right Rowdy had been, *sideways*. Everything was most definitely sideways and right now I had no clue which way was up.

CHAPTER 8

Rome

I WAS SPRAWLED OUT under the pool table, trying it get the stupid thing level, when several pairs of worn motorcycle boots were suddenly the only things I could see through the legs I had jacked up off the floor. It was early afternoon, so the bar was dead and Brite had taken off to run some errands. I guess that left me sort of in charge, and if a bunch of bikers were going to show up and trash all the hard work I had put in to this place over the last few weeks, it was going to get unpleasant really fast. I took a quick count, noting that there appeared to be five of them, before I slid out from under the table and wiped my hands down on my jeans.

Bikers looked like bikers, but these guys were clearly the top branch of the club. I knew badass when I saw it, could feel the *don't fuck with me* coming off this crew. These guys were no prospects, no sidewalk bikers looking for a little action. These dudes were the real deal, and if they wanted a piece of me, I was going to have to work way harder at staying alive than I had the last time I tangled with a bunch of bikers.

The guy that was clearly the leader of the crew took a step toward me and I had to stiffen up to avoid taking an automatic step back. I lifted the eyebrow with the scar in it and crossed my arms over my chest. I could do badass as well as the next guy if I had to.

"You Archer?"

I nodded slightly and kept an eye on the other four guys who spread out to flank the man talking to me.

"Brite told me some of the newbies came in here and fucked shit up. Tried to start some business with you and then looked like little punks when you finished it. That true?"

I just nodded again. I wasn't sure what this was all about, and I didn't know if more detail would help or hurt my case at this point in time.

The guy shared a look with one of the other guys over my shoulder and moved to pull up the edge of his sleeve. I blinked in surprise when I noticed he had the exact same tattoo Brite wore on his forearm.

"Brothers-in-arms, kiddo. That shit don't fly with me and it don't fly with the Sons of Sorrow. The club knows the Bar is off-limits and that anyone who did service deserves respect. That little ass-wipe is getting his rocker cut off. We will not have prospects or anyone around us who can't abide by the rules and show proper respect."

I wasn't exactly sure what getting a rocker cut off meant, but it sounded like it was all in my favor, so I nodded once more and pushed off the table.

"Thanks. I'm just glad nobody got hurt any worse or the bar didn't end up even more trashed."

"Brite likes you. Thinks you're a good kid with a lot of potential. That means you're good people in my book. We look out for good people."

I wasn't sure if that was entirely true. I knew from Cora that Asa was still in a cast from a beat-down by a Southern chapter of the SoS, but I guess as long as they didn't want to start anything up with me, I couldn't look a gift horse in the mouth. I shook the guy's hand but didn't breathe a sigh of relief until every last one of them trekked back out the front door. I went up the bar to where Darcy had stuck her head out of the kitchen to keep an eye on things.

"That was intense."

She nodded and handed me a glass of water from the other side of the bar. "Brite ran around with them when he got back after his first deployment. He was into all kinds of bad stuff. That was why wife number one left."

"I could see that. Those are some scary-ass dudes."

"Brite was just as scary. Still can be when he puts his mind to it. You're lucky you remind him so much of himself when he was around your age."

I was starting to agree with her. I was thinking more and more that even though I was at some serious loose ends, I really was a lucky guy. I liked hanging out in the bar and all my diligent work had it looking less like a hole in the wall and more like an actual, respectable establishment. I was learning the regulars, learning their stories, and it made me feel less alone the longer I spent here. I had spent the last week with Cora, either at her place or mine, and the more time I spent in her company, the harder it was to want to be away from her.

She let me take her out to dinner and a movie and we ended the night back at my place. The following night she surprised me by showing up at the bar and demanding that I let *her* take me out. I had never in my life had that happen before, but I let her have her way because she was so damn cute and I could tell underneath her usually sassy attitude she was really freaking out about the unprotected-sex thing. I probably should be more concerned about it than I was, but I made sure I was prepared now and I just tried to do my best to stay calm about it since she seemed to be worried about it enough for the both of us.

My brother was not stoked at the newest development in my love life and I had been subjected to no less than five lectures from him, Nash, Shaw, Ayden, and Rowdy; even Asa had given me the what for about all the bad things that would befall me should I leave her high and dry or decide that her big mouth was too much to handle. I was sure Jet would have gotten in on the *rake Rome over the coals* action as well if he had been in town. I didn't even want to know what would happen if they found she was worried about a possible unplanned pregnancy.

I really liked spending time with her. She was spunky, said what was on her mind, and had no trouble letting me know if I was drifting off on her, getting too lost in my own head. We didn't see eye to eye on a lot of things, but she made me want to laugh, and looking at her made me smile. Not to mention I couldn't keep my hands and mouth off of her. She was just so sweet and so easy to get to respond. I had never been with anyone like her before. She was all glittery and shiny, so I had no difficulty finding her in the dark that sometimes clouded my vision, and so far I had been lucky. With her sprawled on top of me, I somehow managed to sleep through the night. Not a single nightmare, no incidents of waking up to bloodcurdling screams. It was a really nice change of pace and reason alone to keep her around.

I was going to ask Darcy if she would make me something to snack on for dinner before I headed over to the shop to grab Cora for the night, when the chair next to me suddenly pulled out and was occupied by the last person I would've expected to see in the bar. Eyes that matched my own looked back at me and it floored me how old my dad looked after nearly a year of no contact. We had similar dark hair and the same blue eyes; his were paler, more like Rule's, and he was tall and broad, but not nearly as tall as I was. He was always a sturdy, steady guy, but clearly since the last time I had been home, things had taken a toll on him. He looked almost as much like a stranger to me as I thought I would look to him after all this time. Today was apparently my day for unwanted visitors.

"What are you doing here?"

He sighed and asked Darcy for a cup of coffee. He looked at me out of the corner of his eye.

"That's all you have to say to me after ignoring me and your mother for a year?"

"How did you know where to find me?" I lifted an eyebrow and then answered my own question. "Shaw. That little girl can't stop trying to pull this family together."

"Rome." He sighed so heavily I felt it weigh across my own shoulders. I had always wanted to make my folks proud of me. They had never really been excited about my choice to enlist when I was younger, but as time went on they grew to understand my motivation, my drive to help others, be active in making the world a safer place for my brothers and for them. It bothered me to see the disappointment in his eyes and marked on his face.

"This has to stop as some point. I fought to bring Rule back into the fold, told your mother it was this family or I was done. I'm not going to let another one of my boys go, not without one hell of a fight. I let you stew, let you and Rule act like it was a personal affront we never talked about Remy as a family, but the time for that is done. We need to figure out how to move forward from this point on. End of story."

I felt like a little kid getting scolded for getting his clothes dirty while out playing. I rubbed a hard hand across the back of my neck and looked down at the bar I still needed to strip and refinish.

"It's more than just Remy and the secrets. It's the way Mom treated Rule, it's the way everyone just let Remy use Shaw. It's the fact I don't feel at all like the same guy I was when I left last time. I don't know how to fit into this family anymore. I don't know what role I'm supposed to be filling."

I didn't have the nerve or the right words to try to explain to him that I didn't know how I would make it through having him and Mom look at me like they didn't know who I was anymore. Disappointment I could handle, dismissal I could not, so instead I was hiding and avoiding it altogether.

He swore softly and reached out to clap me on the shoulder. "There is no fitting in. You're our son, no matter what;

that role is yours until the end of time. That's what I finally had to get across to your mother about Rule and what we should have let Remy know before it was too late. We take you any way you come, Rome, even if it isn't the same way you always were. The life you lived, son, that changes a man. I understand that and so does your mother."

He cleared his throat and pushed the bar stool back so that he was standing next to me.

"Come to brunch on Sunday. Shaw said you're seeing one of her girlfriends, bring her along. I work very hard every week to make sure your brother and that girl of his know how much I love them. We all owe Shaw more than we can ever repay as a family. She's done more for both those boys than we can probably imagine. Come spend time with your family, Rome."

He didn't give me a chance to say "we'll see" or "no thanks"; he just turned around and went back the way he came. Being an Archer was never exactly easy, but it was like a badge of honor to be one and survive it. I really wished I could just slide behind that bar and mix a drink, but I was doing a pretty solid job of staying sober and just beating back all the crazy stuff going on in my head with force of will alone. I didn't want to mess that up just because I was being a sissy and couldn't handle getting told off by my dad. It was hard to keep my head buried in the sand when he had single-handedly just annihilated all my misplaced fears about going home and facing them.

I asked Darcy for that sandwich finally and went to finish getting the pool table leveled. Brite was back by the time I was done and headed out. I told him about the guys from the Sons of Sorrow and he just snorted and told me the kid that attacked me was nothing but a young prick. He told me that I better watch my back, because getting a rocker stripped from a biker's cut was apparently a really big deal and the scrawny guy was likely to be pissed as all hell that it was happening. It meant there was no way in hell he was ever going to be a member of any motorcycle club, at least not here in Denver, and likely anywhere else. I blew the warning off, figuring it was all said and done, and besides, I was used to watching my six anyway.

What wasn't as easy to blow off was the conversation that he leveled at me after Darcy ratted me out about the awkward conversation she had witnessed between me and my dad. I was on my out the door to get my little punk-rock pixie, but he followed me out to where the Harley was parked. I threw a leg over the bike and looked up at him.

"What's up?"

He ran a hand down the length of his beard, a gesture I was getting used to. It typically meant he was going to say something to me that he really wanted me to hear.

"Your old man came by looking for you today?"

I nodded. "He found me."

He crossed his thick arms over his burly chest and tilted his chin down at me.

"You know that Darce and I have a girl?"

I shook my head in the negative. Neither had ever mentioned a daughter to me.

"She's younger than you. Just turned twenty and is a

handful and a half. She didn't take it well when her mom and I split. I can barely get her to spend five minutes alone in the same room with me before she's at my throat about this or that."

I picked the bike up off the stand and balanced the heavy weight between my legs.

"That sucks, but what does it have to do with me?"

"Nothing. I just know as a parent, we make mistakes. We aren't perfect but that doesn't mean we don't love our kids. You've got a lot of stuff going on in your life right now, Rome. Don't let the things and people that have always been there slip away."

I just stared at him because I didn't know what to say to that. I liked Brite a lot, looked up to him, was starting to really view him as a mentor, but I didn't need him trying to fix every aspect of my life. I was going to turn the engine on and take off but he put a hand on my shoulder to stop me.

"I've got some stuff going on over the next few weeks, and I would appreciate it if you kept an eye on the bar and the guys while I'm in and out. I can pay you for it."

"I don't know anything about bartending, Brite."

"I said keep an eye on it, not mix drinks. Darcy can tend bar, or you can find someone to help you out until the end of the month. Granted the tips aren't anything to write home about right now, but you're getting the place cleaned up real nice so that might change in the near future."

"So what exactly do you want me to keep an eye on?"

"The crowd in the evening. The regulars. Make sure the guys aren't going off the rails. Make sure everyone acts right and gets home safe. I appreciate all the work you've put into the place, and I figure you're not in any hurry to see it all messed up. I'll ask Darce to show you how I do the cash out at the end of the night and how to drop the deposit."

"I guess I can manage all of that. Just for a couple weeks?"

I thought I saw him grin at me but with all that facial hair it was kind of hard to tell.

"For now. Don't write your folks off forever, son. They need you just as much as you need them."

I wondered if that was true. They used to need me to keep Rule in line and act as a buffer, then they needed me to hold it all together when everyone vanished into a cloud of grief. Now I didn't really know how I fit into the fold other than as the troubled oldest son, and that was a big part of what made it so much easier for me to stay away.

I started the Harley and pulled out of the lot. It only took ten minutes to make it to Capitol Hill. I usually just left the bike or the truck at the apartment and walked to the shop since parking in the area sucked. Plus I refused to ride in that little neon clown car Cora drove, so we usually had to do some switching off on how we got from one house to another. I pushed open the door and walked up to the counter. She wasn't behind it, which was unusual, but my brother was leaning against the desk talking to Rowdy.

"Hey."

He tilted his chin up in greeting and motioned toward the closed door that was off to one side of the shop.

"She has a late client. She's probably gonna be a few. You wanna go get something to eat when she's done?"

"I ate at the bar. Speaking of which, do you know anyone that knows how to bartend that can help me out for a few days? Brite asked me to keep an eye on the place for the next few weeks and I don't know a thing about bartending."

"You know how to drink vodka like it's water."

I popped him in the shoulder. "I remember more than a few nights where Crown Royal made you its bitch, so let's not point fingers."

Rowdy chuckled and made his way over to join us. I really wanted to dislike the guy. I didn't like that he was so familiar with Cora, that the two of them had such an easy camaraderie, but he made it hard. He was just an easygoing and totally affable guy. Plus his quirky sense of humor made him entertaining as hell to hang around.

"Talk to Jet. He knows more people in this town than all of the rest of us combined. I bet he knows someone that can help you."

That was a good idea, but Jet was gone more than he was home anymore, and when he was around he was usually wrapped up in Ayden. I didn't envy them trying to juggle a new marriage and so much time apart, but they looked happy and it seemed to be working just fine for them.

"I'll do that." I turned to look at the door as a guy came out followed by Cora. Her hair was flipped up into a fancy curl at the front of her head today and she had on a short orange skirt. Her top was bright purple and she had on black combat boots that laced up to her knees. She smiled at me when she saw me leaning next to Rule and I caught the way the turquoise eye brightened just as the brown one darkened. She was like a kaleidoscope of color and emotion, and whenever I looked at her, I never knew what was going to be reflected back at me.

The guy leading the way out of the room looked at me then back at her as she took her seat back behind the desk.

"Remember, be careful with it. They take a long time to heal."

He nodded and forked over an amount of money that was surprising and gave her one last look. She just smiled sweetly and looked up at me.

"You ready to go?"

I shrugged as she started to do the cash out for the end of the day.

"What part of that guy's body did you just shove a needle through?"

She lifted her pale eyebrows at me, and I elbowed Rule in the side when he asked, "Do you really want to know the answer to that?"

I made a face. "Seriously?"

It was her turn to shrug. "Don't knock it until you try it, big guy."

The idea of having anything sharp and pointy down there made me break out in hives. No thank you, I would keep my junk metal-free. Not that I didn't like her sweet little hoop that was attached to all my favorite parts of her, it was hot as hell, but I didn't need a door knocker hanging from my dick.

"I'll pass, thanks."

She paused in her counting to smirk up at me, and I

wanted to kiss it off her face. "That's okay, little brother has enough down there for you and everybody else in the room."

Rule burst into laughter and Rowdy chuckled, probably because the idea of Cora with her hands on anything in Rule's pants made me scowl at both of them.

"I could have lived forever without knowing that."

She laughed and got up to make her way around the desk. She threw her arm across my shoulders and kissed my temple where the end of my scar hooked down by my eye.

"Don't worry, his was business, yours is all pleasure. Let's get out of here."

I followed her and the guys out so she could lock the door. The boys were gonna head to the Goal Line and grab a beer and some wings. I wanted to get Cora someplace alone and horizontal so I could make her forget she had ever been up close and personal with any part of my brother's anatomy. She wanted to spend the night at her place even though mine was closer because she had breakfast plans with Shaw and Ayden in the morning, so I told her I would just meet her there after I went and picked up the truck. It was kind of an even trade-off because my place was closer to the shop and hers was closer to the bar. My place generally had less people in it, but I liked Ayden and Jet, and Asa was a character. Plus her bed was awesome, even if it was covered in pink.

Cora was in the kitchen when I walked in the front door. She was puttering around making something for dinner and talking on her cell phone. I didn't want to interrupt, so I plopped down on the couch and looked up as Asa came into the room. The walking cast was off of his foot, but he was still moving pretty slowly.

"You get that off today?"

He sank gingerly into the recliner across the room.

"Yesterday. It feels like it's going to fall off."

"I had one when I got blown up last year, but mine wasn't as bad. My shoulder took the brunt of it."

"It blows."

I was going to tell him that maybe he should avoid situations where he pissed off a bunch of bikers but that seemed kind of hypocritical, so I just asked him if he knew when Jet was going to be back in town. He shook his head and bent down to rub his shinbone.

"No clue. I think he mentioned that he was coming back for a week and then he wanted Ayd to come with him to L.A. for a week after her summer classes were done."

"I need to find someone to help me keep an eye on the bar I've been fixing up, I thought he might know someone."

Those gold-colored eyes glinted at me from across the room.

"I can do it."

I tilted my head to look at him. "Really?"

"Yeah, why not? I'm sick of being cooped up in the house. Ayd is on my case about everything under the sun and I could seriously do with some . . . companionship, if you know what I mean."

I totally did but I wasn't sure the Bar was the kind of place he would find it.

"Have you ever bartended before?"

Asa laughed a little. "There isn't much I haven't done before. All you have to do is stand behind the bar and talk to people. Trust me, I can talk to anyone."

I thought it was probably a bit more complicated than all of that, but if he was willing to help me out, why not?

"Cool. It isn't like some high-end, swanky bar where you're going to be pulling tail and rolling in money."

"Rome, I just need to get out of this house before my sister and I kill each other. She's still working on forgiving me and frankly I'm sick of my own company. It'll give me something to do, until I figure out where I'm going and what I'm doing from here on out."

That all rang just a few shades too familiar, so even though I didn't really know Asa from Adam, I was willing to take the help. Cora wrapped her arms around my neck from behind the couch and put her cheek next to mine.

"What's on the agenda for the night, big guy?"

She and I and a whole lot less clothing were what was on my agenda, but I wasn't going to say that in front of Asa. Good thing great minds think alike because it didn't take much more than a look and the brush of some fingers across the top of her bare leg to get my plans for the night across to her. Seriously, having this girl in my life made everything else I was dealing with seem so much less important. My folks, my future, the bar . . . all of it took a backseat to the way those two-toned eyes flashed and sparkled at me.

IT ONLY TOOK UNTIL the next weekend for things to go to hell.

I wasn't able to spend as much time with Cora because I was at the bar until closing. It might not be a crazy-busy place but I had no clue how much went into keeping the natives from getting restless and tearing the walls down. I was surprised at how much I actually liked it, though. I liked the ebb and flow of the business, the interaction with the customers, the interaction with the liquor reps and the sales guys. I felt like I was actually working for the first time since I got back home. I missed my girl, but she was a champ about it, and I think maybe I needed some breathing room, because the more days that went by that she didn't have her monthly visitor, the more anxious and keyed up she seemed to be. She must have blabbed to the girls because there was no escaping the narrow-eyed looks I was getting from Ayden every time we bumped into each other, or from Shaw whenever I spent time with her and Rule.

I was also surprised at what a natural Asa was behind the bar. The guy was a born bullshitter, and by the end of the night, from even just a handful of regulars and jaded barflies, he made more in tips than I had ever seen Brite or anyone else take home. He was an all-right bartender, but his gift of gab and plethora of charm made up for it in spades. I even noticed an increase in the younger, female clientele in the few days he had taken up his spot back there. I figured maybe I could talk Brite into keeping him around when he got back.

On Saturday night I left as early as I could and put Asa in charge of shutting the place down. Jet had pulled me aside a few days after mentioning that we were going to be working at the bar together in order to give me a little of Asa's background. He warned me that essentially he was a good guy, but not to let all that Southern charm fool me. Jet said to watch my back and not to trust Asa as far as I could throw him. I always heeded warnings when they came from people I trusted, but so far Asa had been nothing but an awesome partner in crime and I missed spending time with Cora. Leaving him in charge for a night was a risk I was willing to take.

When I got to the house she was asleep on the couch. Jet and Ayden were gone for the night, so I scooped her up and took her in her room to put her to bed. She woke up when I was pulling her swirly hot-pink sundress off over her head. She blinked those wicked-colored eyes at me and tried to focus.

"Hey."

"Hey."

She yawned and stretched her arms up over her head. The one with all the brightly inked flowers on it curled around my neck on the way down.

"I'm exhausted."

I let her tug me down so I could kiss her on her waiting mouth.

"Long day at work?"

She shook her head and ran her fingers over the short hair on the back of my head.

"No. Just sleepy all day. I was going to stay awake and wait up for you but I couldn't keep my eyes open."

I kissed her again and she put her hands under the hem of my T-shirt.

"You don't have to wait up for me. I was just going to put you in bed and crawl in next to you."

"If we're going to be in bed together, neither one of us needs to be sleeping."

Man, this girl was just something else, and it only took about two seconds to get both of us naked and down to business. I fell asleep pretty quickly afterward and as usual she was draped across the top of me from shoulder to hip. In reality it had only been a very short time since we had invaded each other's life, but something about it just felt like this was the way it was supposed to be.

At least if felt that way until sometime in the early morning.

There was sand in my face and I couldn't breathe. I was hot, hotter than normal, in all my gear and for some reason I couldn't see past the red haze covering my eyes. My ears were ringing in my head and from somewhere really far away I could hear voices screaming. I wanted to lift my hand up to wipe my face, to pull my helmet off to see if that would make it easier to breathe.

I couldn't get my arm to work. I couldn't get most of my body to cooperate.

I managed to turn my head to the side, just enough so that the blood covering my face trailed down my nose and out of my eyes, barely letting me get a look around.

I wasn't in the Hummer anymore.

I was on my back staring up at the sky and a cloud of dust and dirt was sticking to all the blood and sweat coating any of my skin that wasn't covered by my gear.

I didn't have my gun in my hands anymore, and I couldn't see any of the other guys who had rolled out on the op with me. There had been six of us total in the Hummer.

I wanted to call out, wanted to scream because my shoulder was on fire and I wasn't sure what was going on under my helmet, but the river of blood covering my face showed no sign of slowing down anytime soon and I couldn't see that great. I just didn't know if our location was secure. Didn't know if it was an IED or enemy fire. If any of the other guys had made it out, I wasn't going to be the one who gave our location away to the insurgents, even if it meant I had to bleed to death on enemy soil.

I don't know how long I lay there. I went in and out of consciousness more times than I could count, and finally, what felt like days later I opened my eyes to a medic pulling my gear off and trying to move me without breaking more of my body. I think they told me it was an IED. I think they tried to tell me I was going to have to get airlifted home. I'm pretty sure they said brain injury and possible loss of motion in my shoulder, but all I really heard was "sole survivor of the blast."

It didn't matter that my ears were ringing. It didn't matter that I was probably minutes from bleeding out. It didn't matter that it was war and things like IEDs and dead soldiers were an everyday part of life. I started screaming and screaming and screaming until I felt like everything inside me was empty and hollow. I think they doped me up to get me to calm down and minimize the damage, because when I woke up I was in Germany and they were doing surgery on my arm and trying to sew my face back together.

Everyone thought I was so lucky. I got to go home and recover. I got to live.

Every night after that I woke up either screaming or choking on blood and tears that couldn't fall.

Bolting upright on the bed, I forgot all about the fact that

I was holding on to Cora. I had cold sweat pouring off my arms and chest, and I felt like I was suffocating on blood and sand even though the desert was a lifetime ago. My lungs billowed in and out, my chest heaved up and down, and I knew I had to get away.

I swung my legs over the side of the bed and scrambled to find my pants. I could feel Cora sitting up on the bed behind me. I flinched away from her hands when she went to lay them on my back. All I could see was crimson and dust. All I could feel was loss and desperation. I didn't want her anywhere near any of it.

"I have to go." My voice sounded like I was talking over razor blades and salt.

"What?"

She reached for me again and I lurched of the bed. I pulled my shirt on over my head and refused to look at her. I heard the sheets rustle as she sat up in the bed.

"Rome, what's going on?"

Her voice was quiet, like she was afraid she was going to spook me. She had no idea about the terrible stuff rolling around like a silent movie behind my eyes. It was so horrific.

I grabbed my phone and keys off her nightstand and made my way to the door. I couldn't even look at her. I needed to say something, to try to explain, but the crazy, the pain, the memories were too close to the surface and I just couldn't get to her through them. I was being an asshole, but it was either bail on her or break down in a sobbing pile of goo on her bedroom floor. I couldn't let her see me like that, didn't want her to be a part of the stuff inside me that was so ugly and hard to forget.

I didn't start to breathe normally again until I had the Harley under me and the wind in my face. The nice thing about the bike was that it didn't matter if some of the emotion working its way to the surface leaked out, the night air just whisked it away. I felt like I was never going to sleep again.

CHAPTER 9

Cora

THIS THURSDAY-NIGHT GIRLS' NIGHT was unlike any the three of us had ever spent together before. Ayden was propped up in the doorway of the bathroom off my bedroom alternating between texting on her phone and staring at me with concern. Shaw was sitting on the toilet practically bouncing up and down; her green eyes were huge in her pale face and I knew she was just dying to say something. I was sitting on the edge of the tub trying to decide if I wanted to scream, or throw up, or cry, or pull all my hair out, or just laugh. Maybe a combination of all of the above. What did I know about trying to raise another person? I had spent my entire childhood shuffling from one random adult to the next. I had no idea what being a full-time parent even looked like.

"Well?" Shaw just couldn't stay quiet any longer.

The little white stick on the edge of the tub next to me stared back at me with two glaringly bright pink lines. Not that I was really surprised. I had been tired and moody for the last two weeks, and not just because Rome had pulled a disappearing act and wouldn't return any of my calls. I was also queasy, and it was just my luck that forgoing Mr. Perfect was going to end up biting me in the ass for the next eighteen years. I had really started to think he was worth the risk of letting that dream of someone steadfast and secure go, that I was tough enough to weather the storm that came with him, only now I was high and dry and looking back on my long-held dream of perfect and shaking my head.

Ayden snorted and walked farther into the room to pick the pregnancy test up from where it was resting next to me.

"Seriously? Look at her face. It's totally positive."

Shaw let out a noise that was between a gasp and a squeal. I glared at her and she clasped her hands over her mouth. Her eyes were bright and shining at me from over the top of her fingers and I wanted to smack her. Ayden leaned against the sink and frowned at me.

"So what's the plan?"

I groaned and shoved my hands into my eye sockets. What was the plan?

"You mean besides never, ever having sex again? I don't have the first idea."

Having kids wasn't something I ever really thought about. When I was with Jimmy I just figured it would be something that came up after we were married for a couple years and in a financially secure place. Now . . . well, now, other than wanting to murder Rome and his stupid perfect face and body, I had no clue what the plan should be. I would never let a child of mine feel unloved or unwanted.

I would never let my kid feel lost in a sea of adults because I wasn't able to give them a home. I just wished with everything inside of me I could say Rome felt the same way about parenthood. The fact of the matter was, I had no idea what he thought about anything right now because he wasn't saying anything.

Shaw bit her bottom lip and said so softly I almost didn't hear her, "You have to tell Rome."

I sighed and pushed my eyes even harder. Of course I had to tell Rome. Eventually.

Telling Rome was going to be a lot easier said than done since the big idiot wasn't quite finished with his epic freak-out. I wasn't exactly sure what had happened the other night; all I knew is that he had run from my bed like the sheets were on fire, he was shaking and the color of paste. That was ten days ago, and I hadn't heard from him since. The first couple of days I called and called, sent text after text, and worried myself into a concerned lather. By the end of the week I was good and pissed and clearly had more important things to worry about than Rome Archer because I was pretty sure I was carrying his baby. I had heard from Asa he was spending all his time at the Bar and that his venture into sobriety had taken a nosedive. Apparently he was back to drinking like a fish and grumbling and growling at anyone that got within breathing distance.

I had enough pride, and enough bad history, and a healthy dose of fear working inside me, that tracking his stubborn ass down and making him talk to me wasn't a workable option. I refused to be in yet another relationship where I was the only person invested in the outcome. I figured he knew where I worked and where I lived, so if he wanted to make things right, he knew where to find me. Admittedly I thought he would have come around a lot sooner, but now it looked like the choice was going to be taken out of my hands.

"I know that, Shaw."

She cleared her throat and shot a look between me and Ayden.

"He isn't doing so hot right now. I don't know what happened, he was starting to get back to his old self, starting to fall into some kind of pattern, and then, boom, he's right back where he was when he came home from Afghanistan. I thought Dale was going to cry when he didn't show up for brunch last Sunday."

I brushed hard hands through my short hair and rolled my eyes up to the ceiling.

"I don't know either. Things were cool, I thought we had a pretty good thing going even though it was pretty brief. Then one night not so much. I can't believe I was so stupid."

Ayden clicked her tongue at me and waved her finger back and forth in my face. "Stop beating yourself up. Jet and I had a near miss right before we broke up. Sometimes those boys just burn too hot and common sense goes right out the window."

Shaw nodded. "Yeah, if I wasn't on the pill since like the dawn of time, Rule and I would've been in the same situation. You're just human, and Rome can be pretty overwhelming."

All of it was overwhelming.

"Fuck." That seemed to sum it up nicely.

Ayden laughed and reached down to pull me up to my feet.

"I think that's what got you into trouble in the first place. Let's go eat something."

I groaned but followed her out of the bathroom. "I don't think I can eat."

I pulled her to a stop and grabbed her and Shaw both by the arm. "You guys can't say anything. Rome doesn't need to hear about this from Rule or Jet. I'll talk to him when I'm good and ready."

Ayden just rolled her eyes but Shaw nodded gravely. "I can't believe Rule is going to be an uncle. Margot and Dale are going to flip."

Well, crap. That was a whole other headache I hadn't considered. "My dad is going to kill me."

They both laughed at me and I went to throw myself on the couch. Even though we had technically only be seeing each other for a few weeks, I really thought there was something bigger working between Rome and me. I felt it in the way the air changed when we were together. He was vital, so much larger than life. I could still see the fracture in those blue eyes, see the things he was trying to work through, but I thought we were doing fine. Now I didn't know what to think and there wasn't enough history, enough time to know which way to go with it. On top of it, there was this added complication and my life was one big pile of no-fun at the moment. I never would have let him get to me had I known he was going to have such an easy time walking away. I was too guarded, too careful with my heart, for that.

Shaw came back from the kitchen and put a plate of pasta down in front of me. Ayden brought in a bottle of wine and I glared at her. She just shrugged and plopped down next to me.

"Make a doctor appointment in the morning, Cora. This is a big deal, and you need to take care of yourself. I'll go with you if you want."

"Don't worry, Cora, we're here for you. Whatever you need." Shaw chimed in right on her heels, and I knew I couldn't ask for better friends to get me through this initial period of shock that had settled around me.

What I needed was for this kid's dad not to be such a complicated handful and not be so damn sexy. If he had just been an average guy, one of a million, I could have happily continued on my fruitless quest for Mr. Perfect and never taken the scenic route into forever, life-changing, and gloriously imperfect. Rome never made me feel like I was settling for less than I deserved, he made me feel like having a new dream, where he was the center of it, just made sense.

"I know *you* guys are. Rome might be a different story. That's a lot to level at a guy already dealing with a full plate from the emotional baggage buffet."

Shaw narrowed her eyes at me. "Stop it. He'll be fine. He needs some help, just like Margot did, but at his core, Rome is rock solid. He hates for anyone to see him weak, hates the idea that he isn't the one holding the entire world up by himself. If I have to beat it into him, I promise you he will be fine."

I shook my head and let it flop back on the colorful couch cushions. Rome wasn't solid, he was unhinged and wild. I think that was what drew me to him so irresistibly in the first place.

"I don't want to be with a guy who feels like he *has* to be with me, Shaw. I don't want to be with anyone that isn't one hundred thousand percent as into me as I am into them. Not even if I'm pregnant with his kid. I'm not ending up on the other end of what I did with Jimmy ever again."

She made a face at me. "Rome isn't Jimmy; he would never betray you like that."

"No, he's not. I thought he was better, but I don't have the option to let him walk out on me every time he's having a tough time. That doesn't work for me, especially not now." And I didn't want to talk about how bad his sudden desertion made my heart hurt. That kind of pain was unfathomable when it came from something so fragile and new, not to mention it freaked me out that the loss of him felt more potent, more gaping, than walking away from Jimmy ever had.

"He's worth the fight."

"Because he's an Archer?" I didn't mean to sound so snappy, but Rome and his issues weren't my top concern anymore. They couldn't be.

"No, because he's a great guy that hasn't had the easiest time of it lately. Don't you remember telling me how broken, how robotic, Rule was after Remy died? Rome went through all of the same things, Cora, only he had to do it while fighting a war and watching his fellow soldiers die. Maybe he just needs someone that makes him see he deserves a break finally."

I didn't want to fight with her about it, because I didn't entirely disagree with her, but I also was the one left alone and in the dark after he disappeared into the night without a word, and that hurt. Maybe because I didn't just hurt for me, but because I ached for him as well. The horror shining out of those blue eyes even in the dark and the despair stamped across those handsome features made my chest ache just thinking about it, but I couldn't force him to let me in. And we couldn't make anything work between us if he ran from me every time things got rough. I didn't need him protecting me from him. I was more than capable of doing that all on my own.

"Just give me a couple days to get used to the idea that I'm growing another human being, and then maybe we can talk about what I am or am not going to do with big brother Archer."

Ayden nodded in agreement and gave Shaw a pointed look.

"That's a good idea. Now, everybody calm down. Shaw, help me finish this wine. Just because Cora can't have any doesn't mean this shouldn't be a proper girls' night." She wiggled her eyebrows up and down and leered at me in an exaggerated expression. "Plus Jet hasn't been home on a Thursday in forever and I miss sloppy-drunk sex."

That was enough to startle a laugh out of me and I tried my best to relax a fraction and enjoy the rest of the night with my friends. The future was such a huge, looming unknown and I refused to get sucked into it. I would be okay, whether that meant I forged on ahead alone, or I strong-armed Rome into getting his head out of his ass. I was terrified, but kind of excited behind the wall of fear. It wasn't something I would have ever planned for myself, not without a firmer grasp on what I was doing, but if anyone could take an unplanned pregnancy and possibility of single parenthood in stride, I guess it would be me. I knew firsthand what it was like to grow up without a mom, without a sense of home and well-planted roots. There was no way any child of mine would ever have to go through that. I would move heaven and earth to make sure of it.

By the end of the night I ended up putting Ayden to bed, without Jet. He was still out running around with Rowdy and Nash, but I was sure he would have no trouble figuring out how to get her up and going when he finally got home. Shaw left earlier; I think it was driving her crazy not to fire a million questions at me and at the same time sing Rome's praises. She was a really good friend, but in this particular case she was caught between a rock and a hard place. If I hadn't been the hard place and Rome hadn't been the rock, I might have been inclined to work up a smidge of sympathy for her. As it was, I made her promise again not to say anything to Rule about the baby until I had it out with the older Archer. She readily agreed and left with a hug and a knowing look.

I knew all anybody wanted was for me to be happy, for Rome to find some kind of peace and balance. I just wasn't sure those things went hand in hand anymore. I felt like if he got close enough to break my heart, the damage done would as detrimental to him as it would be to me. I wasn't sure any of it was worth the risk. Not with so much at stake.

Getting up the next morning was a little rough. Wrapping my head around the fact that I was no longer operating as an autonomous person was weird. I didn't know the first thing about being pregnant or having a kid, so I figured I better start Googling stuff, like yesterday. I also called and made a doctor's appointment and tried to figure out what on earth I was going to tell my dad. What I didn't do was call Rome. I couldn't think of a conversation I wanted to have less than that one.

When I got to work the guys were already there and doing their prep for the day. We all usually went in an hour before noon to get the shop up and running. The guys typically finished last-minute drawings and I called and reminded appointments for the day. This morning everyone seemed pretty sedate and I was glad Rule and Nash both acted totally normal. Clearly Shaw had kept her word and not said anything to her boyfriend. I was staring at my phone like maybe it would magically have all the answers I needed when it suddenly dinged with a new message. It made me jump, and when I saw Rome's name at the top of the message box, my stomach lurched hard enough that I had to run to the bathroom before I hurled orange juice all over my fancy computer and desktop.

I stayed in the bathroom longer than necessary. I had to splash cold water on my face and take a minute to catch my

breath. I couldn't avoid him forever, and I really did want to
know what he had to say for himself after the last few weeks
of radio silence. I fluffed my hair up, put on some bright red
lipstick, and felt like I had some kind of armor in place to
deal with whatever that message might say.

Only, true to form, Rome liked to make things a million
times harder than they had to be. When I came out of the
bathroom I stumbled to a halt because Rome was standing
in the waiting room of the shop and both Rule and Nash
were all up in his face. Rule looked furious and Nash looked
nervous. Rome looked like crap, but he wasn't saying a word
as his brother screamed in his face and poked him in the
chest with a tattooed finger.

"We told you to leave her alone. Could you listen? No!
Like always you know better than everyone else, and now
look! She's been upset for the last two weeks, being meaner
than normal, and now she's so upset you made her sick."

Rule poked Rome so hard that this time the older Archer
took a step back. None of them noticed me just yet, and I
wasn't sure the best way to interrupt without making a
bigger mess of things.

Nash shook his head and pulled Rule back a step. "I told
you to leave it alone, dude."

Rome cast those azure-blue eyes toward the floor and
what little color was left in his face fled. He looked like he
hadn't slept in a month; his pallor was awful, the turn of his
mouth harsh and concerning. All I wanted to do was give
him a hug and tell him everything would be all right.

"You don't understand."

"No, I don't. You threatened to kick my ass all over the place if I was messing with Shaw. Well, you're doing exactly that to Cora and it's fucked up."

Rome sucked in a breath and released it. I thought for a second he was going to turn around and leave, but just then he looked up and his eyes locked on mine. He blinked, once and then once again, and I could have sworn I saw some kind of shadow lift and clear, letting the dazzling sapphire light shine through.

"Rule, I'm not messing with anyone. Like I said, you just don't get it, but I don't owe you an explanation. Cora, however, I owe way more than that."

Rule swore again and Nash had to literally hold him in check. "You owe everyone an explanation, Rome. This shit is tired and needs to stop. You can't just keep hurting everyone because you're unhappy."

Blue eyes clashed with blue eyes and I saw the fire light up in Rome. It was about to get real.

"You mean like you always did? Funny how you can be so sanctimonious now that you settled down with Shaw. Not too long ago she had to drag your hungover, booze-soaked, philandering carcass to Mom and Dad's because you had hurt feelings. Get out of my face, Rule. I don't owe you shit."

Okay, there was going to be a full-on Archer brawl if I didn't stop this now.

"Rome." They finally turned their full attention to me. "What are you doing here?"

He looked unsure of how to answer, so I made my way to where the guys were standing and inserted myself in between them. I could feel the hostility blazing off of Rule and the remorse bleeding off of Rome. I didn't want to drown or get sucked into any of it.

"Uh . . . I was hoping I could talk to you real fast before you started work."

I sighed. "Well, I wanted to talk to you all last week and you ignored me."

"I know. I'm sorry."

"I'm sorry, too, because now I don't know that I want to hear what you have to say. I'm not that hard to find, big guy."

He sighed. "I know."

We stared at each other for a long and silent moment until he finally dropped his eyes back to the floor. I felt Rule shift behind me and figured I better split the two of them up before I had to clean blood off the floor. I grabbed Rome by the arm and pulled him out the front door to the sidewalk in front of the shop. Rule shouted something ugly out the door after us, and I felt Rome tense.

"Stop it. One battle at a time."

He threw his hands up in the air in front of him. "That's the problem, Cora. I'm so tired of fighting."

His eyes were burning so hot I felt like they were going to leave holes right through me.

"I'm fighting with my folks. I'm fighting with Rule. I'm fighting my vices. I'm fighting my fear of the future. I'm fighting my own goddamn head, and I'm just tired. I'm retired. I was supposed to be leaving all the fighting in the desert."

I wanted to comfort him, to tell him I understood, but there were bigger stakes here than just me and him.

"So what are you going to do about it?"

That was the key. He could keep fighting, keep battling everything alone until he just wore himself into a husk of a man, into a shadow of the person he once was, or he could ask for help. I didn't realize I was holding my breath until he finally answered me.

"I got the name of a guy from Brite. He's a retired shrink and a vet. He only takes guys on referral. I went to talk to him yesterday. He was a really nice guy."

I let out the breath and felt my heart rate settle into something less chaotic.

"I spent the entire hour and a half we talked telling him about you. About how shitty I felt for bailing on you, how I thought something really awesome was starting between us, and how I blew it all to hell by being a pussy."

He looked at me and I felt my heart turn over in my chest. The pleading in his gaze, the clear, naked longing for me to understand just a little part of what he was dealing with, really touched me. All I really wanted from a partner was honesty, and it didn't get more honest than this.

"I don't ever want anyone to see me like that, Cora. It rips me apart to live that shit over and over again, and nothing, not even really great things, like you and me, makes it stop. It's embarrassing to be that exposed to someone else. I'm so sorry I didn't handle it the right way."

"Rome." I wasn't sure what I wanted to say, but I didn't get the chance to anyway because he grabbed me by my upper arms and pulled me up on my toes so that we were eye to eye.

"Please, Cora." His voice was husky and so sad. "You are so much better for me than a bottle of vodka every night. I can't be perfect for you, but I can be someone you rely on, someone you want to keep around even though it isn't always going to be easy."

I put my hands on his broad shoulders and barked out a laugh. I laughed so hard I had to rest my forehead against his throat to catch my breath. I could feel his confusion in the way he tensed up and set me back down. I pulled away from him and crossed my arms over my chest. He would never know how much those simple words meant to me.

"I'm pregnant."

His eyes widened to the size of dinner plates and his mouth sagged open in a way that would have been comical had the situation not been so serious.

"I took an over-the-counter test last night, and it was as positive as positive could get."

"You . . . I . . . we . . ." He trailed off and looked like he might pass out. "For real?"

"For real."

"Are you okay?" His gaze swept over me from head to toe like he was looking for some sign of change in me already.

"I'm fine. Look, I know this is a lot to take in. I don't expect anything from you, but if you're looking for a really good reason to pull it together, I think you have one now."

"What do you mean you don't expect anything from me?"

I sighed. "Look, Rome, we hung out for less than a month. We were never really friends, then we became lovers and now soon-to-be parents. That's a lot for anybody to try and handle. I care about you and I really do think you're an amazing guy, but I'm not going to risk this baby or my heart on someone that isn't all in with me. I've been there and done that and seriously I wish I could give the T-shirt back."

"Give me a chance, Half-Pint, I'm all in."

I could see it there, dazzling and bright in the blue that was as sharp as a razor blade. He believed it, wanted it, I just didn't know that I could trust him to follow through on it and not leave me hanging again.

"The drinking . . ."

He shook his head. "Done. I'm all over it. It doesn't do me any good and Brite won't let me hang at the bar if I'm loaded. He's been in and out over the last few weeks and finally told me that if I didn't get my act together, I was done. I was already feeling like I let you down. I couldn't stand the idea of disappointing him on top of that, which is why I finally called his friend for help." He made a face that resembled a grimace of pain. "There's a good chance I'm gonna be struggling with the aftereffects of PTSD for a long time. I'm not going to wake up tomorrow and be all shiny, polished, and perfect, but I can get better. The difference is I didn't really have the motivation to head in that direction until I lost it and couldn't face you. I don't want you to be part of my nightmares, Cora, but I'm selfish enough to ask you to want to be."

He was saying all the right things, he was putting more of himself on the line for me than Jimmy ever had, and I was selfish enough to want to believe that what he was saying was real. I didn't really want to let him go just yet, but I had to make sure he understood the rules moving forward.

"Nightmares are just bad dreams. If you want me to be part of your dreams, there isn't a better place I could think to be. Rome, I'm more than willing to stick this out with you, but this baby is bigger than both of us. You can't just walk away when you're freaked out or because something from the past is standing between us. You have to let me in, you have to stick around so we can work through it together. I'm not flawless either, Captain No-Fun, but I kinda think together we might get close to something spectacular, if we want it bad enough."

I squealed in surprise when he picked me up and crushed me to his chest. I didn't think I was ever going to get tired of the solid way he felt pressed against me. He pressed a hard kiss to my mouth, and I put my hands on either side of his face to hold him there. I missed him, missed this, but I didn't have any delusion that this was the last of the bumps in the road we were probably going to have to face if we managed to stay together. It took a special kind of man to stick around when the reality of fatherhood is looking him right in the eye. We didn't know each other well enough to know if this was going to be it for us, but he affected me enough, moved me in ways I was continually surprised by, that I liked to think with some work he very well could be my new dream, that he could indeed fit what my new idea of perfect might be.

When he set me back on my feet, I laughed a little and moved my hands from his face to his shoulders.

"We might need to slow things down between us a little bit. We're going to be moving full steam ahead, and while there is no question that we are sexually compatible, we should probably figure out if we can stand to be around each other for the long haul."

He dropped his head so that his forehead was resting against mine. "All right."

I tapped him on the chin with my index finger. "And you need to make nice with Rule. Family is important and he's going to be this kid's uncle. Plus Shaw is going to drive everyone nuts trying to fix things if you can't patch it all up on your own. Same goes for your folks." I would never squander family away, and he was just going to have to reconcile that fact if this was going to work.

He pulled back and bit the tip of my finger, which made me scowl up at him.

"Repentance is my new middle name. Rule and I are both afflicted with the Archer stubborn streak and I can't really be mad at him for wanting to protect you. He's right: I did do the same thing to him over Shaw. The only difference is I don't have the reputation of the Mile-High Lothario to warrant it. I'll work it all out, I swear this matters to me. More than anything I can remember since I started looking out for the twins."

I finally wrapped my arms around his lean waist and gave him the hug I had been dying to give him since I saw him standing in the shop.

.

OF COURSE, AS SOON as I walked back in the shop, the boys jumped all over me. Rule was still all fired up and pissed off, Nash was acting like a concerned big brother even though he was younger than me, and Rowdy was just watching it all with a maniacal grin that made me want to hurt his pretty face. There were only about ten minutes until we opened, so I dragged all three of them into the back room and faced off with them. Telling them to back off and mind their own wasn't going to cut it, so I laid it out for them in terms even stubborn, hardheaded, but well-meaning boys could understand.

I told them I was having Rome's baby and I didn't want to hear a single word about it because it was still so early and things were so tenuous. I thought Rule was going to go through the roof until I smacked him with the back of my hand in the gut and told him to calm down. Nash looked like he was in shock, and Rowdy was the only one to press a tiny kiss to the top of my head and tell me congratulations. I explained that what I was or was not doing with Rome had nothing to do with them and that everybody better play nice because the big picture was that I was having a kid and everybody I loved and cared about was going to be a part of his or her life, whether they liked it or not. Rule and I had a pretty lengthy stare-down, but really it was cute, and at his center he was a big ol' pile of mush, so eventually he caved and scooped me up in a rib-breaking hug.

He told me he was still going to whup Rome's ass if he didn't start acting right toward me and I informed him that he was going to have to get in line. Nash was harder to crack. He just kept looking at me, then down at my stomach, then back up to my face, and shaking his head slowly from side to side. I just waited him out. Nash was a softy; he was more rational than the other guys, but his own upbringing had left some nasty scars and I don't think he was really comfortable with any human smaller than a bread box.

"It'll be fine. I'll be fine. We'll be fine."

He wrapped his arm around my shoulder and gave me a one-armed hug that was so tight it almost hurt.

"Don't get me wrong, Rome is a cool dude. I've always looked up to him, but lately he hasn't been acting like any guy that's going to be a dad should act."

"I just found out yesterday."

"But you knew before that, didn't you?"

"Maybe."

"Just be careful. I love ya both and don't want to have to pick between either one of you."

"Stop. We wouldn't do that."

Nash smiled a sad smile that looked so out of place on that handsome face and under that ring in his nose. "That's what every parent says."

He walked away leaving me speechless. Rowdy slid up next to me and hooked my arm through his.

"You're gonna be a great mom. Everything else will fall into place and everybody else can get over their own shit."

I grunted and rested my head on his shoulder. "Thanks."

"What about the guy? He the right one to do this with?"

"I think so." And I really did. He might make me work a little bit for it, but I really did think he was worth the effort. I was so happy to hear that he had taken steps on his own to seek out some help for the nightmares chasing him from his time in the military. I could chase the shadows with him, as long as he was willing to let me bring the light in.

"He hasn't let me get upright since we started this thing." I wiggled my eyebrows up and down suggestively, which made him laugh. "Literally and figuratively."

"Sideways it is." Rowdy reached down and patted my still-flat tummy. "This is going to be so fun to watch."

I snorted at him and elbowed him in the side. The fact was, I could do sideways. I could do the unexpected. What I couldn't do was heartbroken and shattered, so big brother better be on board with that or there was no telling what I was going to do. Heck, I would even be able to blame it on hormones.

CHAPTER 10

Rome

TAKING IT SLOW SUCKED. Don't get me wrong, I was pretty sure I was falling love with Cora. I had spent the last two weeks trying to drink her out of my head and feeling like a royal asshole for ditching her without a word. It was another pussy move in a list that seemed to be growing by leaps and bounds. I was embarrassed by the fact I couldn't pull it together, ashamed she had seen me so broken and open. I had known going in that she was leery about all the dips and valleys in my personality, but having her bear witness to my own personal hell was just too much for my ego and already battered pride to take, so I ran. It was cowardly and it was weak, but I didn't think I could handle her looking at me like I was someone to pity, someone that needed to be fixed. So I buried my head in a bottle of vodka and tried to drink it all away. My reasons for avoiding her didn't hold any more water than my reasons for avoiding my folks, a fact that I couldn't ignore or drink away.

It became apparent the very next day that not talking

to her, not being able to touch her, to hold her, hurt way worse than my pride did. She was under my skin, buried far enough down that I realized if I had to get help in order to be someone she could be with, then that was my only option and it was time to stop running and just do it. I was so glad she was willing to give me another shot. I needed her, and now with the baby, messed up or not, I was pretty sure she needed me, too. I was willing to do whatever it took to make this thing between us work, even if that meant all the sexual attraction and potent heat that had drawn us together initially had to be banked. There was nothing quite like being put in the friend zone by your pregnant girlfriend.

I spent the entire month of September keeping my hands in my pockets and my dick in my pants. I went with Cora to the doctor, which was exciting and terrifying at the same time. We went to dinner, hung out like a normal couple that was just starting to date, and I even entertained the idea of making peace with my folks like I had tentatively done with Shaw, because I knew it would make her happy and I was sick of running scared. I was tired of trying to guess what others' expectations of me were and had to get my head around the idea that my expectations of myself were enough. The idea of bridging that gap did make her happy, which made me happy, even if the idea was like torture for me. I just didn't know what to say to them in order to get the conversation started.

It was fine, the slower pace. I liked spending time with her, we got along great, and when we didn't, the way those two-toned eyes flashed and sparked a million different colors made me have visions of makeup sex that were triple-X-rated. It wasn't like I was only with her to hook up, but I would be a big fat liar if I didn't admit that I missed it, missed her and all that colorful skin. Sex with Cora was unlike sex I had ever had before, and not just because she was pierced down there and had all those colorful jewels embedded in her skin. Despite her refrain that she was holding out for some unobtainable vision of perfect, she just got me, like really got me even though I was as far from perfect as a guy could get.

I didn't know how she could stand the lack of sex either. Her hormones were all over the place lately. She was more mouthy and a little snarkier than usual, but there was something in her eyes. I would catch her looking at me out of the corner of her eye, like she was feeling the same repressed desire as I was. Like we were sitting on the brink of something major, something bigger than everything we had experienced before, but it was like she was scared of the drop-off. She let me kiss her, let me cuddle her up on the couch while we watched movies, she was openly affectionate, holding my hand, wrapping her arms around me, and letting me know she was there. She was always the one who pulled away, who cut the contact short and stayed on the right side of sexually unfulfilled. I could see the regret, the frustration on her pretty face, but I wasn't willing to push my luck, so I didn't question it or try and push it with her. She was willing to take me as is. I was willing to take her and any obstacles she put in my way as par for the course. Sometimes I thought she looked at me like she was downright terrified, not of me, but of something I was making her think or feel.

I was making up for lost time at the bar as well as trying to get my relationship with Brite and the regulars back on track. Brite was back, mostly I think to make sure I didn't drink him out of bar and profit the way I had at the end of the previous month. I think he was worried I was going to spiral out of control again. To prove to him that I had no intention of ruining my life, of letting Cora raise that baby alone without me, I was working extra hard and had all the improvements he asked for nearly done. I had even found a few of my own to add to the upgrades. The place looked like a nearly new bar; it was spotless, polished, and not a surface wasn't touched up and brand-new. There was an influx of new blood coming in the door and business had picked up enough that Brite asked Asa to stay on as the permanent evening bartender. My personal thought on that was that he liked the view. There wasn't a night the bar wasn't surrounded by pretty young things all clamoring for the blond country boy's attention. Asa was just that good.

I still didn't know what I was going to do when I was done with the Bar, but I was making a conscious effort not to lose sleep over it. I was losing sleep over enough other things. My future had enough twists and turns in it that beating myself up over not having all the answers was just exhausting and I didn't have the energy to do it anymore.

It was also a day-to-day struggle to deal with the nightmares and the weird slips in my mind that drew me back to the desert and all that blood and death in a more healthy and positive way than drinking myself stupid. An occasional vodka tonic was one thing; trying to kill my liver was another. When I woke up now, I went running or took the Harley out for a long ride until I came back into myself. It took longer but it worked just as well, and talking to Brite's friend was making me realize that it was just like everything else in life: I had to work at it, had to practice getting better. He also made me see that if I let the people that loved me help, it would make the process go faster. Just like Shaw told me, everyone was just going to have to learn to love me in a new way and I had to be all right with that. It was okay to ask them for help, that didn't make me weak, and I should be appreciating still being around to listen to them, not feeling guilty about it.

One night Cora and I were sprawled out on the couch at my place. Nash was out with Rowdy and my girl was all cute and curled up in a ball resting against my side. She had picked some dumb girly movie to watch after dinner and it was all I could do to keep my eyes open, it was so boring. I liked the way she fit next to me, she was so small and so deceptively delicate, and she brought all the protective instincts I had to the surface, which was funny because she was more than capable of protecting herself. It was hard for me to recall what my boring black-and-white world looked like before she stormed into it and bled color into every nook and cranny. I just wanted to take care of her, be with her.

"You hate this, don't you?" She was rubbing her thumb along the back of my hand and across my knuckles. I could feel her stop and worry over the raised scars and marks that dotted my skin.

"Naw, it's fine."

She laughed next to me. "You're about to fall asleep."

I was, but I figured she didn't need to worry about it. My attention kept drifting in and out. She wanted to see the girl in the movie get her happily-ever-after, and I figured I could hold out for that long. Besides, crashing out on the couch next to her was the closest I'd gotten to sleeping with her in the last month. I shifted so I could curl my arm around her and pull her closer to my side. I dropped a kiss on the top of her soft hair and told my overly anxious lower half to chill out. She had one arm wrapped around my waist and her other hand resting on my thigh. It was all very innocent, but telling my denied libido that was another story. Taking a little catnap might be the only way I made it through the rest of this date night without getting myself in trouble.

Between one breath and the next, I was zoned out somewhere between being all the way asleep and awake. I couldn't concentrate on the stupid movie and my mind just took a detour down a path I wished it hadn't. Everything sort of just faded away and I was back to a day I relived over and over, it was a waking nightmare and I couldn't stop the avalanche of memories as they free-fell on top of each other. I would have given everything I possessed to make it stop, to keep that particular day locked in a box where it couldn't get to me anymore.

I had only been back from Pakistan for a few months, the twins were barely in their twenties, and I got word I was headed to Iraq. My folks were freaking out, everyone wanted me to leave the army after this deployment was over, but I was excited to go. Rule and Remy had moved out, Shaw was almost ready to graduate, and being at home alone with my folks was boring. There was only so much of "Rule is terrible, Remy is perfect, you're a fool and could be doing something more important with your life" I could take.

I liked being in the army. I moved up the ranks fast. I was good with the other soldiers and had a natural talent for taking the lead. When I was home I was just the oldest brother of the twins. It was all always about the twins. Not that I didn't love my brothers. Hell, I went to war to make sure they had a safe and secure world to live in, but it got old just being the guy whose job it was to keep Rule in check and to let Remy's light shine. In the army I was Sergeant Archer. I was the one calling the shots. I was the one running missions and I had an entire platoon of men and women to keep safe, not just two boys who were opposite sides of the same troublemaking coin.

Mom insisted on a family dinner on my last night. I didn't want to do it. Rule was always an ass to everyone, and something was going on between Remy and Shaw. They had an odd relationship anyway. They hardly ever touched, they acted more like girlfriends than a couple, and no matter how much they said they were just best friends, there was something more going on there, I just knew it. I also couldn't figure out why when she thought no one was looking, Shaw was making goo-goo eyes at the wrong twin. It all seemed complicated and trivial compared to what I had been dealing with day in and day out, so I was not looking forward to it.

Dinner was as expected. Rule showed up with blue hair spiked up in every direction and sporting a black eye. Remy was distracted and evasive, while Shaw seemed sullen and out of sorts. I did what I always did and tried to play the middleman. I asked about Rule's apprenticeship at the tattoo shop, I talked to Remy about his new job, and grilled Shaw about getting ready to start her freshman year at college. My folks let me be the intermediary, like they always did, while dropping not so subtle hints about how much I was missed around the homestead. It was irritating and annoying, but I powered through knowing I would be halfway around the world the same time tomorrow. We struggled through dinner and then Remy made excuses for him and Shaw to go. Something was happening there but neither of them seemed like they were in any hurry to share. The four of us walked outside after saying good night to my parents and stood in the driveway. Rule gave me a hug and then punched me in the gut.

"Be safe. I'll miss your grouchy ass. Check your e-mail more this time when you're gone."

I ruffled his stupid hair and punched him back. "Try and stay out of jail while I'm gone."

He snorted. "What's the fun in that?"

Shaw rolled her eyes and hugged me.

"I love you. Please come home in one piece. I'll send you a million care packages."

Rule drawled, "Send him porn." Which made her glare at him and started them off on a childish round of bickering.

Remy shook my hand and pounded me on the back. When he pulled back I swear I saw something move across those pale eyes. I wanted to sit on him and make him talk to me, but there wasn't any time.

"Be safe. Take care of yourself, Rome. This family couldn't function without you."

I laughed it off because he was the golden son. He was the one we all wanted to be like. I inclined my head toward where Rule and Shaw were standing and arguing still.

"I'll take care of me, you take care of them. Try and keep your idiot other half out of trouble."

He just smiled somewhat sadly. "Which one?"

"Both of them."

We all hugged again and I went back inside. The next morning I was back on my way to a different desert and all of it was just mindless chatter that I forgot all about. I hit the ground running, went into mission-critical mode and under total blackout as soon as I landed. I was doing reconnaissance with a spec ops team for nearly two weeks before I had any kind of contact with the base.

They had been trying to reach me out in the field for three days before they managed to find someone that could relay a critical message from home.

Remy was dead.

There was an accident. He crashed his car on the interstate and hadn't made it. I was being granted only a few days' leave to get home for the funeral and then was expected back in proper fighting condition.

I felt like someone had stuck a serrated knife right through the center of my chest.

Remy was the good one, the best of the three of us. He was kind, he was loving, he was careful, and there was no way he was the one of us that was going to die before his time. Rule was going to get shot by an angry boyfriend or piss off the wrong meat head at a bar. I was going to step on a land mine or get taken out by enemy fire. There was no way it was Remy's time.

I flew back in a daze. I couldn't think, couldn't feel. I was *numb. I think that was how I missed my mom going from being just distant and snappy to Rule into totally arctic freeze-out mode. We were all sinking into a well of grief and despair for our own reasons and there was no way any of us could offer the others a hand out.*

All I could think was that I hadn't even told him how much I loved him before I left. I had ordered him to take care of Rule, always told him to watch out for his more difficult brother, but never said anything about how amazing and impressed I was with the man he had become. I never let him know I might have been his hero, but he was mine. The regret that I squandered the last minutes I had with him was a bitter pill that I never managed to swallow. Add in the fact that I knew something was going on with him, something I needed to make him talk to me about, and a chunk of my heart, a part of my soul, went into the ground with him.

I went back to the desert without talking to my parents, without being able to look Rule in the eye because it hurt too bad to see Remy's eyes looking back at me. Every night for the next year, no matter what mission I was on, no matter what barracks I was in, no matter what part of the sandbox they sent me to, I went to bed at night thinking about everything I would do over again if I could. I had seen a lot of death in my line of work; it always sucked and it was always hard to forget, but nothing woke me up in the middle of the night with tears running down my face like the memory of those last wasted seconds with my brother.

There was a weight on me. Not the typical heavy, sucking weight of sorrow that I woke up with when that particular memory blindsided me, but a soft, warm weight that was whispering my name over and over again. I struggled up from the blackness and found Cora in my lap. She was literally straddling me, her hands on either side of my face. She was saying my name over and over again, whispering it against the scar on my forehead and against the twin tracks of moisture I could feel leaking out of each eye.

My baser instinct was to shove her off of me and get out of there. It was to bury the shame and sadness deep down inside and cover it with a layer of vodka so thick I couldn't ever feel it again, but I knew if I did that she wouldn't give me another shot, so I just stared at her and let her brush kisses all over my face until my heart rate slowed back down and I could breathe normally again. I put my hands on her waist and counted backward from twenty until I was absolutely sure I wasn't going to bolt on her again.

"Want to talk about it?"

No, I sure as hell did not, but I had promised to let her in, so I would make an effort, and if it meant keeping her on top of me, stroking her fingers along my scalp, I would struggle through it even if it felt like it was killing me.

"Remy. I was thinking, maybe sort of dreaming, about Remy."

If the thought of a man's dead younger brother wasn't allowed to move him to burning-hot, sorrowful tears in his sleep, then nothing was. I wanted to be embarrassed, didn't want Cora to see how fractured and torn on the inside I really was, but she just watched me and didn't say a word. The bluish green of her turquoise-colored eye was full of compassion and kindness; the melty chocolate of the brown one was much sharper, waiting to see what I was going to do now that I was naked and raw in front of her.

"The last time I saw him I was annoyed. My folks were on my nerves, Rule was acting obnoxious, Shaw was being weird, and something was going on with Remy that he wouldn't talk about. Now I know it was his secret and Shaw was all bent out of shape over Rule, but at the time all I wanted was to get back to work. I told him to take care of Rule, not that I loved him, or that I missed him, or that I was so proud to be his brother. I just told him to keep Rule out of trouble."

I had to swallow back the flood of memory in order to keep talking to her. She just kept her eyes steady on mine. She didn't interject, didn't tell me it would all be fine, she just watched me and let her fingertips run along my shorn hair.

"When I came back for the funeral everything had turned to shit. Rule decided that the best way to deal with the loss was to be even more of an asshole than he was already. Shaw turned into this conciliatory, peacemaking machine, and my parents immediately went into blame mode. It was Rule's fault for calling for a ride, it was my fault for not being home to keep an eye on him, and it was Shaw's fault for letting him go. They put him in the ground and every single one of us went with him."

I had to blink and strain to keep my eyes on her. My fingers flexed involuntarily as I tried to decide if I wanted to pull her closer or push her away.

"I went back to the desert and watched more kids die, gave more of myself to the sand and the enemy, and then when I came home last time, things went from bad to worse. Mom had turned into this grief-filled monster who wanted to eat Rule alive. Shaw was head over heels in love with him and he was oblivious and it was killing her. And then there was Remy. Gone but always there between all of us and his goddamn secret that everyone seemed to know but me and Rule. I was so mad at him. Mad at him for lying, mad at him for using Shaw, mad at him for being gone, but mostly I was so furious with myself for letting him go that last time without saying something that mattered. Maybe if I had been different, acted differently, he would have been comfortable enough to tell me about his life. It's all I can think about."

We sat there in silence for a long time, just looking at each other. She kept stroking my head and it was interesting to watch her thoughts play out in those odd-colored eyes. Remorse for me flashed in one, while disapproval and something else flashed in the other. She didn't like me beating myself up over something that couldn't be undone, but it was clear she wasn't going to condemn me for it either.

"You don't honestly believe that either of those boys ever doubted how much you love them, how much you sacrificed for them? Do you?"

I shook my head slowly in the negative. "No."

"Good. Because no matter what you said to him, the words didn't matter. He knew. Rule knows. You could have told Remy all those things, and he still would have gotten in that car that night. Losing him that way would still have you hurting and your family in disarray. You know he knew you loved him. That's all that matters, Rome. If he wanted you and Rule to know, he would have told you. That's all there is to it. That's not your fault, it's not your parents', and it sure as hell isn't Shaw's. At some point you have to just let it rest."

"I don't know how to do that." It was the truth.

"Is there anything that you think would put it in per-spective for you? Make it easier to move past this?" I liked that instead of just letting me be all defeatist and lost about it, she wanted to actively help me figure out a solution to the problem.

"Not really. Answers would help. Asking Remy what he was thinking would help, but since none of that is possible, I'll just have to figure it out on my own."

Her eyes flashed at me, and I saw a shadow of something cross from one colored eye to the other. I wanted to ask her about it, but she climbed up off of me and I got distracted fighting the urge to snatch her back. I wanted to kiss her from the top of her head to the tips of her toes. I wanted to put her in bed and never let her out. I wanted to breathe her in and let her spread all that color and brightness that poured out of her all over the cold and barren that was spread around inside of me, but I was still minding my manners, so I lum-bered to my feet prepared to walk her out to her silly little car and settle for a chaste peck on the lips.

I didn't necessarily feel any better after talking to her about it, but I also didn't feel any worse. I didn't feel the need to guzzle down a bottle of Belvedere and I was pretty sure I could make it through the rest of the night without having to outrun the nightmares. I almost ran her over when she stopped in front of me and turned around. I had to wrap my arms around her small frame to keep her from toppling over onto the floor. She laughed a little against the center of my chest and grabbed the fabric of my T-shirt in her hands and started to pull me back toward my room.

Not that I wanted to rock this particular boat, but I also didn't want to get into something she was going to be all worked up about later either.

"Uh . . . What are you doing, Half-Pint?"

Those blond eyebrows danced up on her forehead as she continued to walk backward, towing me with her. Her eyes were lively and shiny, a small smile was playing across that mouth I wished I had dreams about instead of the nightmares I was having, and she was looking at me in a way that didn't just make my dick hard, but made something in my chest wind up and release like a spring.

"You have bad dreams. I don't want you to. So I'm going to give you something better to take to bed."

Oh, thank you, Jesus. I kicked the door closed behind us and let her pull my shirt off over my head. She was too short to reach all the way, so I had to bend down for her to get it up and over my shoulders.

"I thought we were slowing things down?" Stupid sense of morality.

She cocked an eyebrow at me and bent her head down so that she could get her hands on my belt buckle.

"Do you like me any less since we stopped having sex?"

I snorted and just watched as she pulled the leather through the belt loops with a single yank.

"No. Why?"

She lifted a shoulder and let it fall. I was trying to follow her train of thought but my eyes crossed because she got those little hands under the edge of my fly and brushed against an erection that felt like it was trying to escape from my pants all on its own. I was missing something here. She was almost as vulnerable as I was, only I didn't have a firm grasp on her reasons.

"I dunno. I thought maybe it was all chemistry and sexual attraction, and once that went on hiatus, things with us would be clearer, make more sense."

"We don't make sense?"

She had my zipper down and was working my jeans over my hips and my ass. I wasn't going to be able to keep talking to her coherently for much longer, but I had a feeling I really needed to understand the things she wasn't saying to me.

"We do, but things with us just seem to move at warp speed."

She wasn't wrong.

"Is that bad?"

Those two-toned eyes flicked up at me and she slicked her tongue over her bottom lip. Holy hell, I was going to come just by looking at her.

"No. It can be scary and overwhelming, but I don't care anymore because I want you. I missed this part of being with you, plus I'm pregnant and horny and want to jump you all the time. Restraint has never been one of my strong suits."

I sucked in a breath as she got my pants down around my knees and then dropped to her own.

"Why didn't you say something sooner, then?"

"Because we're trying to do something right, trying to do something that lasts, and when you take your shirt off I can't think straight."

That made me laugh, but then the damp heat of her

mouth closed around the head of my cock and I couldn't breathe anymore. She was so pretty, so exotic, with all her colorful skin, and good God, did she know how to bring a man to his knees with just a flick of her tongue and the barest hint of the edge of her teeth. I wanted to grab the top of her head and shove my dick all the way in to the back of her throat, but not only wouldn't it fit, I doubted she would appreciate the gesture since she was trying to distract me from all the bad shit going on in my messed-up head. So instead I weaved the fingers of one hand through her short hair and let the other one clasp her on the back of the neck.

"Cora . . ." All I could get out was her name as one of her hands slid between my legs and the other wrapped around the base of my straining dick. It felt so good; she flooded all my senses. The way she looked on her knees in front of me, the way she hummed her pleasure when I bucked involuntarily against her mouth, the way her mouth was so hot, so wet, as it slid up and down over skin that felt like it was going to burst at the seams. It had been too long, she was too potent, I wasn't going to last for very long, especially not if she kept playing with my tight and achy balls the way she was. I knew her goal was to distract me, work me over so that I was spent and tired and could go to sleep and stay down for the rest of the night, but if she was going to open the door, I was going all the way through.

I let her suck, let her roll her tongue along the straining head just to the point where I was about to lose it all in that pretty mouth. Luckily I was a guy who had a gold star in discipline: I pulled her off right before she finished setting me over the edge. She made a disgruntled noise in the back of her throat that had my dick screaming at me in protest, but her eyes were shining and laughing at me. She gave the hand that was still wrapped around the base a tight squeeze and grinned at me.

"Oh, old friend, how I missed you."

I was trying unsuccessfully to get her shorts down her legs and her stretchy top over her head because she didn't seem to be in any hurry to let go of my throbbing erection.

"You talking to me or my dick?"

She giggled, the sound so carefree and full of joy that it knocked something loose inside of me. I could feel that ball of tension, that coil of despair that I held so tightly inside of me break free from whatever it was clinging to. I put my hands on either side of her face and tilted it toward me so I could attack her smiling mouth. I overwhelmed her enough that she finally had to let go of her hold on my cock and reach up to grab on to my wrists so I didn't knock her over backward. She tasted sweet. She tasted like redemption. She tasted like the future I didn't need to figure out anymore.

When she rubbed her tongue back against mine, when she rose up onto the tips of her toes to wind her arms around my neck, I simply fell backward on the bed and took her down with me. It made both of us laugh. I couldn't remember the last thing in the entire world I had found humor in, let alone while I was in the middle of trying to get laid. That she could do that to me, do it *for* me, made it clear to me that I wasn't going to be able to let her go. Ever. She wiggled on top of me so that I was supine under her and she was braced on top of me with her hands on the center of my chest. She still had too many clothes on but seemed far more interested in getting me all the way naked and taking her sweet time about it.

She hopped to her feet and got my boots off and my jeans the rest of the way off, then stood over me looking down at me with a fiery gleam in those different-colored eyes.

"You sure are pretty."

I didn't know about that. My dick was sticking straight up in the air, the veins in my neck were pulsating, and I'm sure I looked pretty frenzied. It had been too long to be without her, but if she liked what she saw, ravaged scars and all, I wasn't going to complain.

"I think I should tell you that." She gave a delicate little snort and pulled her shirt off over her head. I felt my eyes widen, because I had been naked enough with her to know those boobs were not normally that size. She took her sweet time wiggling out of her shorts and lacy, pink panties; by the time she was done, I was contemplating pouncing on her and just throwing her on the floor and going to town. I didn't get the chance because she climbed back on top of me, only this time she was all pretty tattooed skin and warm and willing flesh. I got my hand around the tattoo high on her thigh as she settled on top of me and reattached her palm to my erection.

I ran my other hand up over her ribs, stopping to rub each of those little jewels like they would bring me good luck. I pressed my thumb under the swell of one breast and lifted my eyebrow up.

"Nice." I continued my journey upward until I was circling a pebbled nipple.

She made a face and bit down on her lower lip. She was just unendingly cute; I wanted to eat her all up. If she didn't make a move soon, I was going to do it.

"One side benefit of unprotected sex."

The humor was dry and she wasn't interested in cracking jokes anymore when I suddenly rolled her tiny frame under me. I could look into those mismatched eyes until the end of time, especially when they were foggy with desire and heavy-lidded with the knowledge that I was about to return the favor. I kissed her hard, licked my way across her collarbone, took a second to pay homage to her breasts, twirled my tongue around the jewels embedded in her side, and made my way to all that colorful ink that circled the top of her thigh.

I pushed her bent legs apart as I traced the design where it decorated the inner curve of her thigh closest to my destination. I felt her shudder in anticipation, saw her stomach quiver and tip, and grinned against the soft skin I was pulling between my teeth when the very tips of her fingernails pricked impatiently into my scalp.

"Rome . . ." Her voice was low and breathy, reminding me that she had had to wait on this just as long as I had. It made me even harder, if that was possible, to know that she would never hesitate to ask me for what she wanted.

I licked a trail along the crease in her leg that led to her damp cleft. The little wink of silver buried inside all that pretty pink flesh was an allure I wasn't able to ignore. I sucked the entire ring and the sensitive flesh it was decorating into my mouth. The action made her entire body bow up off the bed, and her hands got even more desperate along my head and shoulders. She was a tangy mix of metal and aroused female, and nothing in life had ever tasted sweeter. I twirled that little hoop around and around and abandoned it just when I felt her get to the crest of what I was building in her. I heard her swear at me, laughed a little against the grasping folds as I buried my tongue inside her, which had her alternating between cursing me and telling me I was the best she ever had.

I left her wet, greedy channel and switched my attention back to her hard, begging clit. I kissed her all over, sucked on it, bit down on it hard enough to let her know I meant business, and by the time I got my hand involved and used my fingers in unison with my mouth to finally let her come, she making noises that were a cross between moans of surrender and sobs of relief. She came like she did everything else, full of color and light and blindingly honest in letting me know that what I did to her not only worked, but was incomparable. A man could get used to having a woman make him feel that way.

It took a few minutes for her to recover, so I pulled her over me and rolled us so that she was covering me like a warm, satisfied, human blanket. When she finally roused herself she wasted no time and sat herself down on me and sank all the way to the hilt. She was wet and slick and all the good things I had been missing by being a big jackass and a man scared of his own reality. Only a moron ran away from a girl like this, and while I was a lot of things, stupid wasn't one of them.

We both sucked in a surprised breath at the same time. Her eyes drifted closed and mine popped wide. She just felt so good, and when she started to move on me, my poor brain shut down. She moved one of her hands so that it was by my head and bent down to put her mouth over mine. That position opened her up just enough that I could get my fingers on the damn ring of hers while she moved herself up and down in a rhythm that had both of us swearing and straining against each other. The drag of her pointed nipples across my chest, the soft suction of her body, the featherlight press of those sassy lips against my own and it wasn't long before I had to roll her over and pound into her.

She squealed a little at the action and I tried to tell myself to take it easy on her, but she was just as wild, just as greedy as I was, and it only took a grasp of needy and convulsing muscles to pull me over the edge. I said her name, heard her whisper mine against my ear, and I very well may have blacked out for a second as pleasure and the finality of what this woman meant to me slammed through my body with a shudder. I didn't mean to collapse on her, but I did. I buried my face in her neck and gathered her close to my chest before mustering the energy to roll over.

She snuggled into my chest and tucked her head underneath my chin. I rubbed a hand up and down her spine and kissed her on top of her head. I could stay like this with her forever.

"Sweet dreams, Rome."

When I closed my eyes all I saw was her and the colors and shades of rightness she brought with her into my dull world. I fell asleep with her all around me, her soft breath on my skin, and all the best parts of her changing all that emotional shrapnel lodged inside of me. I slept like a goddamn baby.

CHAPTER 11

Cora

STOP LOOKING AT ME like that, Shaw. I think it's a great idea; no, I know it's a goddamn brilliant idea."

If she didn't stop gawking at me with those big green eyes, I was going to knock her upside her pretty blond head. We were at lunch. I met her downtown so that she could hop over to the Goal Line for her shift when we were done. It was Sunday afternoon and neither of the Archer boys was in the mood to go see their parents, so instead they had decided to spend the day together doing guy stuff, whatever that meant. Shaw insisted it meant they were going to go to the gym and try to beat the crap out of each other, either that or they were going to stay put in the living room playing video games. Rome wasn't much of a gamer, so I thought the gym thing sounded more likely, but it made me nervous because neither one those boys knew when to pull it in and one of them very well could end up hurt.

I had a brilliant idea to help my big, brooding soldier put at least one of his demons to rest, only Shaw seemed to think I had gone off the deep end when I explained it to her.

She just kept shaking her head at me and biting her lower lip anxiously. She could look worried and think I was crazy all she wanted, but Rome needed closure, needed some kind of answers so he could move forward, and there was only one way I could see for that to happen. I just knew bridging this gap would not only offer him the peace of mind he needed, but also do wonders for his current need to keep his parents at arm's length. He had already lost a brother; this self-imposed exile from those who loved him simply had to stop. Unfortunately I needed Shaw's help in pulling it off.

"I was there, Cora. I'm the one who saw the reaction, the one they ignored and abandoned when they found out about Remy. Trust me, the Archer boys do not like surprises."

I sighed and blew my bangs off my forehead. "Look, Rule sleeps at night. Yeah, he had a hard time of it there for a while but mostly he has handled his grief and the role Remy played in it. Rome hasn't. He is sinking in a mire of 'what-if' and 'what-now'; if I can throw him a lifeline I'm going to, with or without your help."

She tapped her fingernails on the table and we stared at each other steadily. "I've known those boys a lot longer than you, Cora. Trust me: it isn't an idea that either of them will welcome, not to mention the tailspin it might send Margot into. It will just open old wounds and hurt. I have no interest in doing that to Rule or to Rome."

I shook my head at her. "You knew the Rome that he was before he found out his little brother had a secret life and his other little brother didn't need him anymore because he found the love of his life. This Rome, Shaw . . . you don't even have a clue what's going on with him. I'm sorry but it's true. He's a different man now. He needs this."

I didn't mean for it to sound so harsh but it was true. Granted, Rome had a knack for keeping people at bay and hiding all the things he was constantly struggling with behind a glower and a snide attitude, but I knew if anyone bothered to look closely, they could see how he was fractured in his heartbreaking, blue gaze. I would move every mountain in the Front Range to give him this. Besides, this kid was going to have every kind of family I never did, even if it meant I had to rattle the Archer family foundation to do it.

"I love him, Cora. He's my family and I don't want to hurt him."

"He needs closure, he told me he doesn't know how to let it go, Shaw, and none of us can provide it or help him with it. I think Rule would benefit from having some answers that make sense as well, but he's yours to worry about; big brother is all mine."

He was mine. Every towering, unpredictable, floundering inch of him was mine, and I was going to do whatever it took in order to make things better for him. I took care of my friends because I wanted them to live the best life possible. I was going to take care of Rome because it did something to me to on a fundamental level to see him struggle, to see him hurting. I felt like if I could put him at the slightest of ease, it would be the most rewarding gift I had ever given anyone. Plus he deserved it. He was a good man. He had earned someone working to make his world a better place for once instead of the other way around.

She opened her mouth to continue her side of the argument but was interrupted by my phone going off. I had set Rome's ring tone to Creedence because he was such a classic kind of guy and it always made me smile to see his grim mug looking up at me from the screen. He would laugh if he knew CCR played "Fortunate Son" every time he called me, especially since I preferred girl rock bands as a rule.

"What's up?" He had seemed pretty committed to spending the day with Rule and hashing out some of their issues, so I was surprised to be hearing from him.

"Can you meet me at the Bar as soon as you can?"

He sounded stressed out and was talking really fast. I frowned and motioned for Shaw to get the bill so I could go.

"Yeah. What's going on?"

"The place got robbed."

I felt my eyes go big and I understood the underlying panic in his tone. He was really close to Brite, the owner of the bar, and if something had happened to the older guy, it wasn't going to be pretty for Rome. He needed me to keep him grounded; I knew it even if he didn't say it. He was asking for help and my heart turned over in my chest.

"I'll be there in ten."

I felt him release a breath and he sounded less anxious when he spoke again.

"Asa called me, the cops are already there. I don't know anything else."

I frowned and stood as Shaw signed for the bill.

"Who would rob a dive bar on a Sunday in broad daylight?"

"I don't know. But I sure as fuck don't like it."

I nodded even though he couldn't see me. "I'll see you soon."

"Thanks, Half-Pint."

"Anytime, Captain No-Fun."

Shaw followed me as I hurried out of the restaurant. I was practically running to the Cooper when she stopped me with a hand on my elbow. Her eyes were still big and unsure, but now there was a different kind of understanding shining out of them.

"Are you in love with him, Cora?"

I didn't know how to answer that, so I just stared at her for a minute. It was a question I was actively avoiding asking myself every day. The answer scared me because if I was in love with him and he bailed on me again, there was no way I would be able to forgive him for that and now our futures were inexorably linked through the child I was carrying, so that wasn't a viable option. If I kept my feelings in check, denied how important he was, if he broke apart on me again, I could still move past it and not fall apart like I had before. My kid deserved a parent who was always going to be present in every way possible.

"I'm having his kid, Shaw."

"But do you love him?" Damn, she could be persistent when she wanted to.

"I don't know. Last time I loved someone he nearly destroyed me and that didn't feel half as intense or as important as this thing with Rome does. I think loving him could be the end of me if it doesn't work out."

"What if it does work out, though? What if he's your imperfect Mr. Perfect?"

I pulled away because if I was in love with him or not, it was irrelevant to me right in this moment. He needed me, and I wasn't ever going to leave him hanging if I could avoid it.

"Then he'll be the first to know. Call Ayden and tell her Asa just got robbed. She might want to check in on him." I didn't bother to say good-bye; I was in too much of a hurry to get to my guy.

When I got to the bar, everyone was standing outside. Rome was with Brite talking to a couple of police officers, a few of the regulars were huddled together looking lost and nervous in the bright light of day, but what really had my attention was the fact that Ayden and Jet were also there. Only instead of worrying over her brother, she seemed furious. She was pointing a finger in his chest and Jet was doing his best to hold her back.

I walked up to Rome and put an arm around his waist. He had on black track pants and a black T-shirt. Clearly, he had been at the gym. He looked like he should be on the cover of a men's fitness magazine.

"What's that all about?"

"I don't know. She laid into him as soon as she got out of the car."

He gave me a squeeze as I pulled away.

"I'm going to see what's going on. You okay?"

He nodded and Brite just grunted.

"I'm getting too old for this shit. Bar brawls with bikers, armed robbery on a Sunday, this is getting to be too much."

I saw Rome wince a little but the older guy just clapped him on the shoulder and shook his head.

"I'll finish up with the cops; you go check on the Southern Casanova."

I took his hand in mine and led him across the parking lot. He nodded at a couple of the regulars and looked down at me.

"Thanks for dropping everything and racing over here. I couldn't get ahold of Brite. I was worried something happened to him. Asa only said he was robbed and then hung up. Every worst-case scenario I could think of started running through my head."

I bumped his shoulder with my own and grinned up at him. "But instead of going off the deep end, you called me and asked for help. That's all you can do, big guy."

He looked like he was going to say something back but ended up grunting in surprise when Ayden shoved Asa in the chest with both hands so hard that he actually stumbled back a few steps into us. Jet swore and wrapped his obviously angry bride up in a tight grip.

"Ayd, cool it. There are cops everywhere and I don't need to spend one of my few days home getting your fine ass out of jail."

She was breathing hard and her light eyes were glowing in a way only pure fury could provide.

I grabbed Asa's elbow and turned him around to look at me. His mouth was pulled down tight in a frown, and he was meeting his little sister glare for glare.

"Hey now. What's all this noise about?"

He pulled away from me and shoved his hands through his tousled blond hair.

"Ask her. It's not bad enough I just had a gun shoved in my face and had to hand over the entire till to some asshole in a ski mask, but Miss Perfect Timing has to show up and accuse me of being in on it."

Jet swore, Rome frowned, and Ayden stood stubborn, with her arms crossed over her chest.

"I know you better than anyone, Asa. I know it isn't beyond the realm of possibility."

"Ayd." Jet's tone was warning, but he was running soothing hands up and down her arms. "Maybe not the time or the place, yeah?"

She shook her dark head and continued to glare at her brother.

Rome looked at Asa out of the corner of his eye.

"What exactly happened?"

Asa sighed and started to pace back and forth in front of us. I knew he had a shady history, a spotty reputation at best, but this seemed pretty terrible. I didn't want to imagine he could have anything to do with it, but Ayden's stony expression made me have my doubts.

"I was setting up the Bloody Mary bar just like I do every Sunday. There were only a few regulars sitting at the bar and Brite told me he had to run a couple errands, so I was on my own. I went in the back to get a case of vodka, and when I came back to the front a guy in a black mask, wearing a flannel shirt and jeans, was behind the bar messing with the register. I was confused, so I asked him what he was doing there, and when he turned he had a freaking Glock pointed at my face."

As he told his sister the rundown he refused to look at anyone but her. It was like he was trying to force her to believe him, even though it was doubtful she would.

"He told me to get on the other side of the bar. He emptied out the register and took off out the front door. It happened in like a minute."

"He didn't say anything else?" Rome's voice was gruff and I could tell he was struggling with the robbery happening while he wasn't there. He cared a lot about this place, cared a lot about Brite. This was a surefire way to get all that guilt he struggled with on a daily basis churning up inside of him.

Asa shifted those glittering gold eyes in our direction. "He said, 'Payback's a bitch.'"

I looked up at Rome, who was now scowling.

"You know what that means?"

He grunted. "Did you tell Brite that?"

Asa nodded. "Yeah, and he told me not to mention it to the cops."

"What? Why?" Rome wrapped his hand around the back of my neck and dropped a kiss on the top of my head.

"I think he knows who was behind it." Rome switched his attention to Ayden. "Lay off on your brother, girly. People change, sometimes not always for the better, but they do change. You're never going to be able to move forward if you're always thinking the worst of each other."

He flicked his gaze down to me.

"Give me a couple minutes to talk to Brite and we can head out. Rule dropped me off."

I chuckled a little. "You're going to ride in the Cooper?"

He groaned and walked away without another word. I'm not going to lie: I watched his ass the entire way until Ayden's voice broke through my reverie.

"Asa." Her tone was half conciliatory and half resigned.

Asa held up a hand and shook his head. I thought he looked sad, or maybe reconciled to the fact that Ayden was only ever going to see him one way.

"Just don't. I appreciate all you have done for me, that you could have just left me in that hospital, that I will never, ever be able to repay you, Ayd. But I'm not always going to be the bad guy. I like it here. I like this bar, and believe it or not, I respect the hell out of Rome. He is a good guy. I wouldn't want to do anything to screw him over. I know you think I'm only capable of looking out for myself, but almost dying gave me a slightly new outlook on life. Having your little sister save your ass endlessly gets old."

Ayden seemed stunned into silence, so Jet tried. "Asa, man, come on. You guys can work this out later."

The blond head shook in the negative.

"No. Obviously there is nothing left to work out."

He turned those liquid-gold eyes on me and I could practically feel the sincerity shining out of them.

"I'll be out by the end of next week."

I sighed. "You don't have to do that."

"Yes, I do. Besides, you're going to need room for that baby at some point."

Well, crap. Why hadn't I thought of that? Rome and I hadn't talked about that part of our future. It still seemed so far off; besides bigger boobs, mood swings, and the barest little rounding in my belly, I didn't look or feel that different, so I guess it was easy to forget I had a baby I needed to be preparing for. We switched back and forth between his place and mine, but neither was really an ideal environment for a newborn. I mean my house was great and had the room, if it wasn't currently all occupied.

"I'm sorry." Ayden's voice was strained and sounded tiny. Jet just held her closer and muttered soft words into her dark hair.

Asa gave her a sad smile. "I'm sure you are and I am, too, but I can't be around you if you always think I'm going to be up to something."

She gave a broken little laugh. "You always are."

"I always *was*."

With that, he turned around and walked over to where some of the grizzled regulars were still gathered. I watched as they all shook his hand and clapped him on the back. Clearly, just like they had done for Rome, they had welcomed Asa's lost soul into their fold.

"You okay?" Jet's voice was light as he kissed Ayden lightly on the mouth. She put her arms around his waist and rested her forehead on the center of his chest. They just looked like the perfect matched set.

"I don't know."

"He'll get over it."

"But he's right. I do always think he's up to something. I

thought he robbed your studio, I could totally see him being behind the robbery of this place. There isn't much I don't think he's capable of doing if he thinks it benefits him. I love him but I just don't trust him."

"You'll work it out." I looked down at my phone as it beeped an incoming text message.

It was from Shaw and all it said was:

I'm in.

I breathed a sigh of relief and put the phone away.

"We are all family, Ayd. Good, bad, and ugly, we figure it out."

"With our history, I don't think it's that easy, Cora."

I was reminded of Rome and how everyone had such an easy time caring for him before he came back lost within himself. Everyone still loved him, they just had to find a new way to do it to get around the what-was. Asa was the same way.

"You can love him, Ayden. You just need to find a way to love the new him that's different from the love you had for the old him."

She didn't answer me, but Rome came up behind me and asked if I was ready to go. I nodded and Jet bundled Ayden into his Challenger and peeled out of the parking lot.

"What was that all about?"

"She's having a hard time aligning Denver Asa with Kentucky Asa, which is silly since she had to do the exact same thing with herself not too long ago."

He didn't say anything but made a face when we got to the Cooper. It made me grin.

"Hey." He looked at me over the top of the car and lifted that dark eyebrow that arched under the scar on his forehead. It made him look sexy and slightly sinister at the same time.

"We need to talk about what we're going to do when this kid is here."

He frowned and folded his massive frame into the tiny front seat. I had to admit he looked ridiculous. So I snapped a picture on my cell in case I needed it in the future. He swore at me and scooted around until he found a comfortable position in the limited space.

"What do you mean? We have it, we raise it, we send it to school, keep it from getting eaten by wolves or becoming a stripper, and we're good."

"Don't call it an *it*."

"What should I call it?"

"I don't know, but not *it*, and I meant where are we planning on rising him or her? My place? Your place? Together under the same roof or are we going to bounce back and forth? I feel like we didn't really think this through."

"Well, shit."

I cast him a look out of the corner of my eye. "Exactly."

We hadn't really been together long enough to take such a big step as moving in together, but considering having a baby together was the ultimate game changer, I wasn't sure we could play by the normal relationship rules. He was pretty quiet, so i glanced over at him. He looked like he was thinking pretty hard, but he didn't seem too freaked out or panicked by the questions. I let him muse over it in silence while I headed to the Victorian. When I pulled up out front, he turned to look at me with seriousness shining out of those cobalt eyes.

"What do you want to do, Cora?"

I wasn't expecting that.

"I don't know. I don't want you to do anything just because of the baby. I don't want you to feel forced into anything."

"I'm one hundred percent here by choice, Half-Pint." When he said stuff like that, it made my heart throb.

"I guess we don't have to figure it out right this very second, but it's probably something we need to have a plan for eventually."

"My plan is to do whatever you need me to do."

Every girl in her lifetime should be so lucky to have a guy like him say those words to her. I knew he meant it, so I figured now was as good a time as any to push my luck. I put a hand on his knee and turned pleading eyes on him.

"Good, then what I need you to do is agree to come see your parents with me next weekend."

I saw him go stiff and a moment of panic flare in his gaze.

"Why?"

"Because at some point they are going to need to know that they are going to be grandparents and I figure we should break the ice first. Come on, it won't be that hard and I'll be there to protect you." I wasn't going to mention it was long past time for him to put his fears at rest about how they would or wouldn't see him.

He swore under his breath and shoved the door of the

car open. I tried not to giggle when he struggled to get out, but it was just too funny. I followed suit and he stared hard at me over the roof.

"I haven't been in the same room with them for over a year."

"Well, then it's been long enough. I'm not asking you swallow all that resentment you have about the fact they didn't tell you about Remy or about how your mom treated Rule. I'm asking for you to deal with it and get a handle on it so it can be one less thing that keeps you up at night."

We stared at each other for a long moment of silence. Finally he pushed off the car and inclined his head toward the apartment.

"Can I think about it?"

I bit my lip and put my hands on each side of his waist so I could rest my cheek against the center of his back while he fiddled with the lock in the front door.

"You can, but I already had Shaw tell them we would be there."

He went stiff in front of me but didn't say anything back. Once he got the door open, he turned around and pinned me to the wood with my hands above my head. I looked up at him and refused to blink.

"You can be a major pain in the ass. You know that, right?"

I smiled up and him and lifted up so I could wrap a leg around his hip.

"I know. But I make up for it in other ways."

He chuckled and dropped his head so that he could kiss

me. It was so easy to just get lost in him. The more I did it, the less I wanted to be found.

"Prove it." Now, that was a challenge I was totally up to. Good thing I had the rest of the day to do it.

"WHY ARE YOU RIDING with us again?"

Rule and Rome were in the front of the cab of the big truck, and I was in the back texting back and forth with Shaw. I really thought this was a brilliant idea but now I had visions of it blowing up in my face and being flat-out catastrophic. It was already going to be a tense reunion and adding my little surprise to the mix might just push the entire family over the edge. I just wanted to help, but if Rome didn't appreciate the effort and I screwed things up beyond repair, I wasn't sure I could survive it. I had a feeling him abandoning me would literally kill me, unlike Jimmy's betrayal, which had merely wounded me deeply.

"Because Shaw told me that if I wanted to have sex again in the next century, I would get my happy ass to Brookside even though she had a migraine and wasn't going. She told me I needed to be there for you since you were going."

I laughed. "Atta girl."

That had both of them turning around to glare at me. Apparently it wasn't funny to mess around with a guy's supply of ready and willing sex.

Rule's hair wasn't green anymore, instead it was bleached out to a startling white, and it was as pale as his girlfriend's. The spiky mess was a contrast to his dark brows and the brightly colored tattoos swirling along his neck. It was actually pretty sedate for him, not that I thought his folks would appreciate the fact.

"She said if she felt better she would rally and meet us there a little later."

Oh, she was going to be there all right, but I didn't think either of them needed to be privy to that information just yet. It took a while to get to Brookside, because it was up in the mountains and summertime in Colorado meant that everyone headed to the mountains on the weekends for fun in the sun and the million outdoor activities this state offered. The house was really nice, and when we all clambered out of the truck, I felt breakfast start to roil in my stomach. It was probably a mixture of nerves and the baby, but I just forced a smile and let Rome guide me to the front door with a hand on the center of my back.

The boys both seemed equal parts apprehensive and resigned to spending the day stuck with awkward family interaction, and I really just hoped my surprise wasn't going to backfire epically. The door was opened after a knock by an older man who was the spitting image of Rome. He had the same bright blue eyes, the same strong build, but he was several inches shorter. His eyes snapped from son to son and then he enfolded both of them in a hug that had tears working their way into my eyes.

"Boys." He had to clear his throat before he could go on. "I'm so glad you're both here."

Rome was rigid but he didn't push his dad away; instead he dragged me forward.

"Dad, this is Cora."

I stuck out my hand thinking I was going to get a hand-shake; instead I was enfolded in a hug that was tight enough to make me squeak.

"I don't know how you got him here, but thank you for whatever you did." He said the words so low that only I could hear them.

He might want to hold off on that praise, but I wasn't going to say anything just yet.

"Let's go inside. Your mother is dying to see you."

We all trekked inside, the boys purposely dragging behind us as Dale chattered on happily. I found myself dis-tracted by all the pictures of the boys on the walls. Rome looked so different, so young and carefree. There wasn't a single picture of Rule that didn't have Remy in it as well, and it was really interesting to see Rule's transformation from typical teen heartthrob to sexy black sheep. I couldn't rip my eyes away from them. I felt like I was getting an entirely new insight into the Archer boys.

"Oh, Rome." A woman's voice drifted across the expanse of the living room and a lovely woman with dark hair moved toward my guy. I saw him stiffen as she enfolded him in a shaky embrace. "I missed you so much." Her tone was ach-ingly sad and it was all I could do not to kick him in the shin for making these people who obviously loved him suffer so needlessly.

"Hey, Mom." He sounded strained, but when she let go of him and moved to embrace Rule as well I saw the grim line of his mouth loosen just a little bit.

"Rule, thank you for coming."

I knew this family had a history of pain and struggle, but when people loved each other and were willing to try, it was evident any wound could heal. My kid was going to be part of the Archer fold and that was just how it was going to be.

"Sure thing, Mom."

Margot pulled away and looked up at him. I held my breath thinking she was going to say something nasty about his hair, but she just gave him a wan grin and stated, "Shaw bribed you, didn't she?"

He just shrugged and her attention turned to me.

"You must be Cora. Rule and Shaw have talked about you so much I feel like I know you already. Thank you for coming."

She shook my hand and I returned the gesture with my heart in my throat. Shaw had just texted that she was only about ten minutes out, so it was almost showtime.

"Thank you for having me."

"How long have the two of you been seeing each other?"

I opened my mouth to tell her it had only been a couple of months but Rome interrupted with a sharp "Long enough."

I narrowed my eyes at him in warning and he grunted back at me. We all lapsed into an awkward silence until Rule let out a dry laugh that broke the tension.

"So this it was it feels like to be on other side of all the family drama. I always wondered."

Rome swore, Dale said his name sharply, and Margot just sighed. I was going to interject something but just then the doorbell rang. Everyone turned to look at it in surprise, so I steeled up the reserves and gave Rome's arm a quick squeeze.

"That's Shaw. Give me a minute."

"What?" Rome and Rule barked the question in the same tone.

"I asked her to do me a favor; that's why she sent you on with us." I looked at Margot and Dale and offered a shrug. "I care about both your sons so much. Rule is one of my very best friends and Rome . . . well, Rome changed my entire life. This family loves each other, I think that's obvious, but the secrets, the loss of Remy, are poison that you all are still afflicted with. I'm about to bleed the venom out, so bear with me."

Rome growled at me, "What did you do, Cora?"

I just shook my head. "You all need closure, and this was the only way I could think to do it. You told me you had to figure it out on your own, and that's just not true, Rome."

I pulled away from him and went to the door to let Shaw and her guest in.

He was a blindingly attractive young man. He was tall and elegant-looking in a fitted gray suit. His shaggy auburn hair hung messily in kind brown eyes and he looked almost as nervous as I felt. Shaw was grinning from ear to ear, and when she hugged me I finally felt like maybe I could get through this without throwing up all over the place.

"Thank you."

"Don't thank me, thank him."

I blew out a breath and stuck out a hand. "Hi, I'm Cora. Thank you so much for doing this."

He smiled, and it was just as sad as when Rule or Rome did it. "Nice to meet you. I'm Orlando, but my friends call me Lando. When Shaw tracked me down I was surprised, but I'm happy to help. Remy loved his family; he would hate to know he was the reason they were divided or struggling."

"They don't know you're coming or who you are; it might not be pretty."

He nodded as they moved into the entryway, I saw both Rule and Rome hanging over the rail of the stairs watching our little party.

"I can handle it. I am well versed in how to manage an angry Archer."

"Who's the suit?" Rule's voice was sharp and had us all looking up. I felt Lando tense next to me as he released a long breath.

"They look so much alike." His voice was barely a hint of sound, and Shaw put a reassuring hand on his arm.

"Yeah, but it becomes apparent really fast that they are only similar on the outside."

"Cora?" Rome's tone brooked no argument, so I hurried up the stairs to where everyone was gathered. I clasped my hands together in front of me nervously and waited until Shaw and Lando were at the top of the stairs.

"I know all of you have questions about why Remy did what he did, why he hid behind Shaw and didn't tell you what he was doing in his life. I know Rome in particular has questions that keep him up at night. The only person that I thought might be able to answer them was the guy he was in love with. Orlando Fredrick, the Archers. Archers, meet

Remy's boyfriend, Lando. I asked Shaw to track him down for me. She didn't want to do it at first, but I convinced her it was what you all need in order to move forward. I would apologize for overstepping my bounds but I really feel this had to be done."

You could have heard a pin drop. It was so tense, so silent, I was waiting for the volcano to erupt. Shaw stood next to me while everyone else just gaped at each other. Lando couldn't take his eyes off of Rule, and the brothers couldn't look away from their late sibling's attractive lover. I thought I was going to have to do something, anything to move things forward, but my guy surprised me by clearing his throat and extending a hand. His voice was gruff, but he took the first step forward and clasped the hand Lando stuck out.

"It's nice to meet you. Thank you for coming." If I hadn't thought my idea of what was perfect for me was wrong before, I knew now, without a doubt, how wrong I had been. I knew it couldn't be easy for Rome, but he was making the effort, that is what a perfect guy did. And the idea of loving this remarkable man was as easy as it was terrifying; I was going to have to figure out what kind of risk I was going to take.

Rule followed suit and Lando had to visibly gather himself.

"Those eyes are pretty hard to forget."

Rule gave a wry grin and walked over to pull Shaw to his chest. "Tell me about it. I see him every time I look in a mirror."

Margot and Dale were a little slower to react, but when they did I was happy to see they were welcoming if reserved.

"Well, come in. Shaw, why don't you go set another place since we weren't expecting an extra guest and we can all sit down and get better acquainted." Margot's suggestion gave everyone a chance to process the shock for a little bit before trying to pull apart the past. Frankly I was surprised she was being so calm about it all.

We all sat at the table and I looked at Rome under my lashes when he put his big hand on the top of my thigh and squeezed it under the table.

"Always trying to make everything perfect, aren't ya, Half-Pint?"

I winked at him and put my much smaller hand over the top of his.

"No, I like things imperfect, I've found out, but if I have the ability to make things easier for you, I'm going to do whatever it takes to make that happen."

Brunch was actually pleasant. Lando was interesting, charming, and it was so easy to see in every word, every look on his face when Remy came up, how much he had honestly and truly loved Rule's twin. It was heartbreaking, but lovely to see nonetheless. It was also apparent that Rome's parents had missed Rome greatly and had suffered at the hands of his stubbornness. They weren't looking at him as anything other than a beloved member of the family, and I think as the brunch wore on he recognized it. I helped Shaw clear the table and we gave each other a sneaky high five in the kitchen, when I heard Rule finally ask:

"Why didn't he want us to know? Mom and Dad had it figured out, but he still didn't want Rome or me to know. Why?"

"Remy didn't want who he chose to love to define him. Rome was the hero, you were the troublemaker, and it was his greatest fear to be simply 'the gay brother.' It kept him up at night."

"He had to know we would never try and stereotype him, to pigeonhole him into any kind of role. We loved him."

Lando shook his head. "He was convinced that if you found out it would change your relationships. He was scared you would force him to live out in the open and that Rome would be so worried about him while he was supposed to be focused on staying alive in the desert that something awful would happen. He had his reasons, flawed as they may be. He believed he was doing the right thing and it was all done out of love."

"It made me feel like I didn't even know my brother." Rome's voice was raw and I just wanted to hug him, but the family had to get through this on their own.

"Why? He was still funny, kind, smart, and more loving than anyone I have ever met in my life. None of that changes when you know who he chose to take to bed. You were his hero, Rule was his other half, and Shaw was his best friend. He felt that way about all of you and he would have still felt that way be he straight or gay."

The boys lapsed into silence and Dale decided to inter-ject.

"What about you? The two of you apparently had a

pretty committed relationship for some time. How did you stand not being part of his day-to-day life? You weren't even at the funeral."

All the color fled from Lando's handsome face and pain etched into his expression. This was a young man who felt the loss of Remy Archer just as acutely as the rest of his family.

"I was tired of it. I never had any issues with who I was or how I lived my life. My family was supersupportive, and while I understood his reasons for wanting to keep our relationship secret, it never sat well with me. The night of the accident I gave him an ultimatum. It was me or the secret. He chose the secret. We had a huge fight and he hung up on me. The last thing I said to him was 'I hope your secret keeps you company for the rest of your life.' I never got to apologize, never got to make it right. To this day I regret it. I know he loved me, that we were meant to be together, and I can never take it back."

It sounded so familiar that I saw Rome flinch involuntarily.

"I did go to the funeral. I sat in the back. I wanted to approach the casket, but it was too hard. I left when Shaw was giving the eulogy."

It was all so sad. Grief and loss just permeated the air. I couldn't resist walking over to Rome and wrapping my arms around his neck from behind. I kissed him behind the ear, and he reached up to run his hand along my forearm.

Lando cleared his throat and pushed his chair back.

"You all need to know he loved you. He was proud to be an Archer, he was proud to be your son and your brother. He talked about all of you all the time and he honestly thought he was doing the right thing. As much as any of us might have regrets for the final ways we said our last words to him, I know deep down in my soul he would have regretted his secret tearing you apart the way it has. We all just have to forgive and forget and move forward. Remy's memory deserves that much. Now, if you'll excuse me, I need to get back to the city. I actually have dinner plans with my own family in a few hours."

Shaw got up and went over to give him a hug.

"Thank you for coming. Just let me get my keys."

Rule got up, too. "Can I ride back with you guys?"

Lando's Adam's apple bounced up and down in a slow slide. "I think I would like that a lot."

Dale cleared his throat and rose to shake the younger man's hand.

"Son, you are welcome here anytime you would like."

Margot nodded her head, though she had remained quiet throughout the entire exchange.

Hugs and good-byes were exchanged until it was just Rome and me and Rome's parents at the table.

His mom was staring at me and Dale was watching Rome. It could have been awkward, but instead it felt like a giant door had been slammed closed, leaving a ton of baggage stuck behind it.

"That was a bold move, young lady." Margot's tone wasn't exactly appreciative, but she didn't sound mad either.

"I'm a bold kind of person, Mrs. Archer."

Dale thumped his fist on the table and threw back his

head and laughed. "I used to think nothing would top Rule's antics at brunch, but that . . . that definitely did the trick."

Rome stood, then scooped me up and threw me over his shoulder. He thumped me on the ass with the flat of his hand and started to haul me toward the front door. I hollered at him to put me down, that this was undignified way to exit his parents' house after our first meeting, but he just laughed at me and tossed me over his other shoulder. "I can top it even more. Cora's pregnant. We're having a baby. Thanks for brunch. I'll see you next week."

I heard his mom scream and his dad swear and they both ordered him to bring me back, but he was already headed out the door. He put me on my feet next to the truck and then leaned into me until I had the warm metal pressed all along my back.

"You're trouble."

I put my arms around his neck and tugged him down until I could fit my mouth over his. His hair was longer than usual, so I tickled the dark strands that brushed across my fingers.

"But I'm totally worth it."

He kissed me again, and I tried not to groan out loud when his tongue brushed across my own.

"Yes you are, Half-Pint. Yes you are."

CHAPTER 12

Rome

I DUSTED MY HANDS off on the back of my Carhartts and looked around the liquor room. The new shelving I had built looked awesome, the place was spotless and organized, and not a bottle or keg was out of place. It was the last task I had on the list Brite had given me all those months ago. The rest of the bar was done. Polished, primed, and looking entirely new and ready to be part of this generation. The regulars were still posted up at their favorite spots all day long, but there was a whole new crowd and influx of younger blood wandering in. I didn't ask Brite about the change in revenue because he had been quiet and a lot harder to pin down lately. Ever since the robbery, he had been skipping out before it got busy at night, leaving me and Asa to run the show. I didn't mind, but I thought it was weird that he didn't seem more excited about all the improvements.

I was putting the tools away in the toolbox when the door opened. It wasn't a huge storage space, so between my massiveness and Brite's, there wasn't a lot of room to ma-

neuver. I frowned a little at him when he took a seat on the
top of an empty Fat Tire keg and motioned for me to do the
same thing.

"You all done?"

I pulled the bill of my ball cap lower over my forehead
and nodded solemnly. I was proud of the work I had done.
I felt like I brought the place back to life for him, but I was
going to be bummed to move on and not just because I didn't
really have anywhere else to go.

"I think so."

He nodded and clapped a heavy hand on my shoulder. I
tried not to grunt under the pressure.

"The place looks great, son. You did an amazing job. I
would have been honored to follow someone like you into
battle, Rome. I hope you know that."

I just stared at him. That was a pretty serious compliment from one soldier to another.

"Thank you. I'm not real sure what would have happened to me if I hadn't stumbled in here on the Fourth."

He snorted and pulled back to stroke his beard. "You
would've been fine., kiddo. A man like you . . . the universe
looks out for the good ones, Rome."

I didn't know if I agreed with that, but I was grateful
that he saw it in me. I was going to ask him what this little
heart-to-heart was about, but he surprised me by asking me:

"Hey, you got a hundred bucks on you?"

I blinked at him and dug my wallet out of my back
pocket.

"Yeah, why?"

He waited until I handed over the bill and then climbed to his feet. I followed suit since I was confused as to what was going on. There was a strange undercurrent flowing between us that I couldn't put my finger on. My anxiety ratcheted up a notch when Brite stuck his hand out like he was saying good-bye.

"Rome, there are not enough good men in this world. Men that fight for what they believe in. Men that are more than willing to sacrifice for the greater good. I watched you this summer, saw how you handled the vets' and your own demons that chased you back stateside. You faltered here and there, but you're a rock-solid young man and there is no one else in the world that I would trust with my bar and my customers. You put your heart and your soul into this place this summer. You earned it."

I just stared at him because I still wasn't sure what he was saying. I crossed my arms over my chest and watched him steadily. He held up the hundred-dollar bill and made a big production of folding it up and putting it in his own wallet. His steely gaze held me in place and his face was marked with unwavering determination.

"You just bought the Bar. Congratulations. I'll have the paperwork to you by the end of the week."

I swore and reached out to grab him as he went to walk out the door like that was the end of the conversation.

"What. The. Fuck."

He sighed and turned back around to face me.

"I'm too old. My family is fractured, I've served my purpose here. When I was a couple years younger than you, I wandered into this bar after a serious string of bad days. The guy behind the bar kicked my ass, cleaned me up, had me work my ass off to get the place cleaned up and back in the current century. He was a retired air-force colonel and he didn't take any shit from me. When I had put everything I had left in me into the bar, he asked me for twenty bucks. The next thing I knew, I owned a bar. I didn't have to figure out what I was going to do, where I was going to go. This place was my home. I trust you to take care of it and honor it, son."

I just stared at him because he had to be joking. I didn't know what to say to any of it.

"Keep Asa around. That boy has something good going on behind the bar. Keep Darce in the kitchen, she knows what she's doing. Don't worry about the robbery. I talked to Torch, the prez of the SoS and he's aware that he has a problem on his hands. Biker justice makes the long arm of the law look like preschool."

I shook my head and shoved my hands in the back of my pockets.

"The guy that smashed my head in with a bottle? He's the one you think robbed the place?"

"Yeah, and I don't think he's done. Losing your shot to get in an MC is a pretty big deal. You can handle whatever comes your way, Rome. The bar, the baby, that little spitfire you're all wrapped up in, these are the rewards for living a life of sacrifice. You gave all you had for other people, this is the universe's way of paying you back. You earned it all, son, so stop feeling guilty about it and goddamn enjoy it."

I was speechless. I lowered my head and let out a breath that felt like it held my entire life in it.

"Brite . . ."

"No, son. There doesn't need to be a thank-you. I don't want your gratitude just like I don't want your money. This is the right thing, the only thing that can happen for you and for this bar. You needed each other, son."

"I don't know what to say."

"Good, because half the time when you open your mouth, I wanna punch you. I'll be around, kiddo, not that I think you're going to need me."

I followed him out of the storage room still reeling. I was going to try to express my gratitude, my overwhelming appreciation, but Asa suddenly stuck his head around the corner and said my name.

"Rome, you need to go outside."

I jerked my attention to him and scowled. "What?"

He lifted a blond brow at me and frowned.

"You need to go to the parking lot and take a look at your truck."

Brite and I exchanged a look and headed out the back door. It was easy to see as soon as my boots hit asphalt what Asa had been talking about.

The big 4x4 was listing to its side, the windshield was shattered, all the headlights and taillights were busted out, and it looked like someone had taken a baseball bat to the entire body. It looked like an expensive but mangled red tuna can.

Brite swore while I just stood there in stunned silence.

"You want me to call the cops?"

Asa's drawl was more pronounced than normal. I hadn't even heard him come up behind me.

"Naw. Pretty sure it was the same guy that held you up the other day. He's pissed at me and trying to send a message."

"Pretty hard message to misinterpret, Rome."

I nodded in agreement. "You aren't kidding." I looked at him out of the corner of my eye. "By the way, you just got promoted to bar manager."

Asa reeled back a little and Brite burst out laughing.

"What?"

"Apparently I own the Bar now but I also have a kid on the way, so that means I can't be here all the time. I need someone to have my back, and I pick you."

Those amber eyes narrowed and I could tell he was trying to judge the validity of my statement.

"You trust me to do that?"

I shrugged a shoulder and fished my phone out of my pocket to call a tow truck. "I trust you until you give me a reason not to, Asa. If you are so inclined to fuck me over, you might want to remember all the ways in which I know how to kill a man."

I saw him gulp, and he turned around to head back into the bar. "Thanks, Rome. No one has ever really given me the benefit of the doubt before."

Brite motioned to the truck. "Want me to call the boys in the club?"

"Yeah, but you might want to pass along if I get my

hands on that little shit first, there isn't going to be much left for them to regulate on."

We shared a laugh and he stuck out his hand for me to shake.

"Thanks, Brite."

"You are more than welcome, son. Need a ride home?"

I took him up on the offer to avoid the indignity of shoving myself into the Cooper. I had him drop me off at Cora's and he refused to talk about handing over the bar. Apparently it was a done deal in his mind, even though it was still life-changing to me. Having something to do, something to invest my time and future in, had been my biggest fear since getting back home. In that single, selfless gesture, Brite had knocked it all down. It was amazing, and even though he said it more than once, I still wasn't sure I really deserved it.

I let myself into Cora's house. It was always so sunny, so cheerful, just like her. I didn't see Jet or Ayden, but my girl was in the kitchen singing along to something that might have been music if it hadn't had a chick screaming at the top of her lungs.

I propped myself up on the long bar of the counter that separated the kitchen from the living room and just watched her as she danced around between the stove and the sink. Her short hair was slicked down to her head today. She had on a short red skirt that was ruffly and fluffy that made her look like the princess in a punk-rock fairy tale. Her top was loose and flow-y over a belly that was just starting to round out in the barest hint of baby belly. The flowers on her arm, and the water and fire on her leg, looked vivid and exotic and

I couldn't imagine ever coming home to anyone that wasn't her. I was in love with her. Plain and simple.

"What are you doing?"

She gave a little shriek and spun around to face me. Her eyes were big in her face and she put a hand to her chest.

"You scared me. What does it look like I'm doing? Gymnastics? I'm cooking dinner."

I walked up behind her and put my arms around her waist. I flattened the palm of on hand on her stomach and spread my fingers wide. She put one of her much smaller ones over the top of it and ran her thumb over the scar that decorated my knuckles.

"I didn't know you could cook."

She snorted and turned in my arms to put her arms up around my neck. I liked that she was so short that she had to get on her tiptoes to get ahold of me. It made her skirt ride up higher and her curves press against me.

"It's not haute cuisine but it won't kill us either. I didn't hear the bike or the truck. How did you get here?"

"Brite dropped me off." I walked her backward until her back touched the counter. "I had a little car trouble."

She dropped her pale brows and squealed a little when I picked her up by her waist and set her on the flat top of the counter. Her legs parted immediately and I stepped between them. Her eyes were laughing up at me but got serious real quick when I ran my thumb along the curve of her delicate jaw.

"Cora."

She curled her hands around the back of my neck and

swung her legs so that her ankles were locked around my waist.

"Rome."

"Brite sold me the Bar today and I'm in love with you." That was my future in a nutshell; nothing else mattered.   .

Her eyes got huge in her pretty face and her mouth dropped open in a little O. Her legs tensed around me, but that could have had more to do with the fact I was working my hands under her poufy skirt with every intention of getting into her panties than it did with the L-bomb.

"WHAT?!"

I dropped a kiss on her mouth and nudged her with my hips so that I had enough room to hook a finger under the lace trim and work her panties down over her hips and decorated thighs. She was always so soft and smooth, which was such a contrast to her prickly and sharp-witted personality. I tucked the lace in my back pocket and kissed her on the shoulder where the neck of her shirt dipped down. She always tasted so sweet.

"I own a bar and I want you forever."

"Rome." She was breathless and I could hear the undercurrent of fear working in her voice. I knew she wasn't there yet. She still had reservations having to do with that douche from when she was younger, and because of my dumb-ass freak-out, she wasn't sold on the idea that I would never do that to her again, but she would get there. I had no doubt. Besides there was no other option. She was it for me.

I shook my head at her and flipped the edge of her skirt over my wrists and grinned down at her.

"You don't have to say anything, Half-Pint. I just want

you to know what this is for me, that I'm not going anywhere ever again. I promise you that, and I'll prove it to you
no matter how long it takes."

Her eyes were luminous as she stared up at me. I could
see a million and one questions chasing across the light to
the dark, but she didn't push me away when I bent down to
kiss her like I meant it. Her fingers tightened in the hair on
the back of my head and she pulled me closer with her legs. I
wanted to sink into her, to remember this moment, the look
on her face, forever. Whatever my future looked like, as long
as she was at the center of it, I knew I could handle it, even
the unknown.

I was really getting into the kiss. I had my tongue in
her mouth, one hand up her shirt and under her bra, and
the other working on my belt buckle while she wiggled and
squirmed on the counter in front of me when the timer on
the oven dinged loudly and had her jerking her head away
and panting to catch her breath. Her eyes were dazed and
swirling with a heat that I was sure matched my own.

"It'll burn. I have to take it out."

I leered at her. "I have something hotter you need to
take out."

I adjusted the bulge in the front of my pants for empha-
sis, which made her laugh like crazy. When she bent over
to pull the concoction out of the stove, it was all I could do
not to grab her and throw her on the kitchen floor and have
at that little peek of her bare ass under all that scarlet material. I would never, ever get tired of this girl; I knew it to the
bottom of my soul.

She plopped the glass dish on the stovetop and cranked

the dials off. She tossed the oven mitt off to the side and whirled around so that she was facing me. I grunted in surprise when she launched herself at me. I caught her with a hand under her naked butt and hefted her up so that we were eye to eye.

"As hot as the idea of you devouring me in the kitchen looking all handyman hot in your work pants and boots is, Ayden could walk in the door at any minute. And while I may have caught her and Jet in a compromising position on more than one occasion, it is not something I care to relive. Take me to bed, big guy."

I carried her to the back of the house toward her room. When I put her on the bed I hovered over her with my hands on either side of her head. We were almost nose to nose and she was smiling up at me. Right in that moment I knew that all was right in my world.

"We need to find our own place."

"Excuse me?"

I reached up over my head and pulled my shirt off with one hand.

"If I want to take it to you in the kitchen, on the couch, in the middle of the goddamn living room, I don't want to worry about being interrupted. This is it for me, Cora. We need our own place."

She might not be quite ready to tell me she loved me back, but the idea of being stuck with me for the long haul must not have been all that frightening because she lifted her hips when I tugged the skirt off and pulled her shirt off over her head. I kissed the slight swell of her belly and she tangled her fingers in my dark hair. I felt her sigh against my lips while I licked across the delicate skin covering our baby.

"Okay, Rome. We need our own place."

I wanted to cheer in victory, but now my attention was focused on all that pretty pink skin nestled between her legs. I licked across the fire inked on her thigh and felt her tremble against my mouth. Going down on a girl wasn't something that ever really took much effort. It was a surefire way to get them off so that I could take care of business and not feel like a jerk for not being more attentive to their needs. It wasn't ever like that with Cora. Maybe because she always took such good care of me, maybe because I cared more about her than I had any of the others, maybe it was the contrast of soft, giving flesh and hard metal that always made rolling her across my tongue a total treat.

I vaguely heard her gasp my name and felt her hands get more impatient in my hair. I flicked that hoop with the flat of my tongue and got the edge of her clit with my teeth. She swore and I had to hold her hips down as she bucked up against my face. She was all warm liquid and quivering flesh. She was shifting her legs restlessly against me and I had to move out of the way so she didn't get me in the junk. I laughed against her and swirled my tongue around inside of her while tugging ruthlessly on that piercing I decided I couldn't live without. It only took a minute to bring her to the edge, and when she went over I swore it was the most beautiful thing I had ever seen. She looked less like a pixie and more like a woman thoroughly worked over and very satisfied by her lover.

I pushed up so that I could get my Carhartts off and ditch my boots. I had every intention of just crawling over her and sinking down into her, but she urged me over onto my back and got on top of me. She looked at home up there. She put a hand on the base of my dick to hold it where she wanted it then sank all the way down. Her ready and willing slide had my breath catching in my throat. I crossed my arms under my head and settled in to watch her have her way with me. She traced the dividing lines between each of my abs and curved her hands over the dip on each side of my hipbones. She gave me a saucy grin and lifted herself up only to slide back down excruciatingly slow.

"You know you're going to have to work twice as hard when that hood piercing comes out."

I grunted my response because she was squeezing me with delicate flutters all along the inside. If it was possible, my cock got even harder and throbbed even more violently. I curved a hand over one of her breasts and tapped the puckered nipple none too gently with my thumb. I saw her suck in a breath and her pace picked up as she rocked back and forth on top of me.

"You can put it back in later, though, can't you?" I swore loudly because she worked a hand between us and raked her nails lightly across my balls. Like I needed any more stimulation. I threaded my fingers in her hair and pulled her down so I could suck her bottom lip into my mouth.

"Like it, do you?" She whispered the words against my mouth and I chuckled back at her. Every guy should be able to find a girl who made him this happy in bed and out.

"I like everything about you."

She arched her back and put her hands over mine where they were kneading the tender mounds of her breasts. She threw back her head and gasped my name, which turned into a moan as I moved my legs a little farther apart, stretching her out and giving her movements more friction. Sometimes the difference in our size totally worked to my advantage. Pulling her apart, filling her up, made it all the better for me and I could tell by the cloudy haze of desire in her eyes that it totally worked for her, too.

The drag and pull of soft and hard, the rubbing of her ring against turgid flesh, the flash of her flowers against my scarred skin was too much to hold out against and we both broke over the pinnacle together. I wanted to scream that I loved her, to tell her that she was the best thing to ever happen to me, but I didn't want to scare her any more than I already had today. She collapsed on top of me and kissed the place on my chest where my heart was starting to settle into a steady rhythm. I rubbed a hand up and down her spine and felt her quiver along me.

"You're trouble." The laughter in her tone was contagious and I chuckled, which made both of us suck in a breath since we were still joined intimately together.

"I'm worth it."

Her eyes flashed all those colors at me when she looked up at me. She dropped a bunch of little kisses along my jaw and hooked her pinkie finger in mine.

"It's about time you realized it. Now tell me exactly how you ended up owning the Bar."

We stayed naked and sprawled together while I tried to explain Brite's madness and my good fortune to have so many people determined to save me from myself. By the time we got around to dinner, it was ice cold but it was still the best thing I ever ate because she made it and because soon I was going to have her all to myself in a place all our own. Happiness wasn't something I remembered bright and clear, but this feeling, it was powerful enough that I understood why men went to war over it, fought to the death for it.

CHAPTER 13

Cora

I WAS RUNNING LATE. I had already called the guys at the shop to let them know they would have to open the doors without me. I was scrambling to pull on a pair of cute, glittery flats and tame hair that was all spiked up and out of control from Rome's hands. He had risen with the sun and gone running with Ayden. I don't know how he did it, because after his startling declaration, a drab dinner, and about five minutes of TV, he had decided that was enough and took me back to bed for the rest of the night. I was sore, totally worked over, and scared out of my ever-loving mind.

He had taken Ayden up on an offer of a ride so that he didn't have to wake me up. Well, that's what he said, but I was pretty sure he would rather ride a mule to and from places then ride in the Cooper. It was just one of the things about him I was pretty sure I loved right back. I just couldn't tell him that.

Love had broken me once. It gave me unrealistic expectations and had changed me on a raw and fundamental level.

What I felt for Jimmy didn't hold a candle to the emotions, the wealth of feeling, Rome Archer evoked in me. The big, gruff soldier had worked his way into places I didn't even know existed. I was filled right up to the top with him and I was really afraid if I told him how I felt, all those emotions would overflow and neither one of us would know how to clean up the mess. I didn't want to be without him, but I wasn't ready to hand my heart over to him carte blanche either.

Having a man like Rome use the L-word was a heady thing. All the great things that made him who he was, his strengths, his loyalty, his care, his unwavering conviction that I was who he wanted for the rest of forever . . . it would be so easy to just give myself over to him completely. I was so scared about what would happen if it didn't work out that I just couldn't do it. I could only hope the big guy would be patient with me while I tried to unravel it all in my head. There was a lot going on up there—the baby, moving in together, him taking over the bar, and being totally sex drunk on him and his ridiculous body. A girl needed a minute to catch her breath; only I didn't get one.

Just as I was running out the door my phone rang and I couldn't ignore it because it was my dad. I stopped and took a seat on the front step of the house. I kicked my legs out in front of me and steeled myself for the typical interrogation I got when I hadn't talked to him in over a month.

"Hey, Daddy."

"You staying out of trouble, sunshine?" My dad was a gruff, take-no-crap man, but I never doubted for a single second his undying devotion to me.

I looked at my boobs, which were way bigger than they

had been a month ago, and at the round swell of a belly that I had never, ever had before.

"Not exactly." I wasn't quite sure how to break the news to him. When I had fallen apart after Jimmy, my dad had done his best to put me back together, but there were just some things a girl's dad couldn't fix for her and a broken heart was one of them.

I heard him sigh. "So you saw that the wedding is off?"

I was clicking the toes of my sparkly shoes together and patting my tummy and only listening to him with half an ear.

"What wedding, Daddy?"

"Cora, are you even paying the slightest attention to me?"

"Yeah, I just have a lot on my mind. Things have been crazy here. You should come visit."

He laughed and it sounded like rusty pans banging together.

"There's no air there, baby girl."

He wasn't wrong. So I smiled and trapped the phone between my cheek and my shoulder.

"I met a guy, Dad."

"Oh, Cora."

I laughed at him. "No, Dad, you'll like him."

"I doubt it." He huffed and puffed like any good dad who never wanted to admit his daughter ever had sex did.

"He's different. Not like Jimmy at all. He was in the army."

"You're dating a soldier?" He sounded so incredulous I debated being seriously offended.

"I'm dating an ex-soldier, but more than that, I'm dating a really good man. He's special, Daddy."

"That's all I ever wanted for you. And with Jimmy calling the wedding off to that girl, I'm happy you have someone so you aren't tempted to contact that piece of shit. Let that dog lie exactly where you left him."

I almost dropped the phone. I had been so busy with Rome, so caught up with the baby and trying to figure out what I was going to do next, that I hadn't given Jimmy or the wedding a single thought, let alone spent a single second Internet-stalking him.

"What?"

I heard my dad sigh and swear under his breath.

"Apparently the little chickie he was stepping out on you with took a page out of his book. He caught her stepping out on him with one of the other artists at the shop. He tracked your aunt down looking for you. I told her to tell him it's been too long, too much water under the bridge. Next time I'll let him know you've moved on to someone else."

I had moved on. Jimmy was very much a part of my past, but that didn't stop my heart from thudding hard and heavy in my chest and my ears from ringing. I must have made a noise of distress because my dad demanded to know if I was okay.

I had to rapidly shake my head to get my thoughts ordered back together.

"I'm fine, Dad. That was just a blast from the past I wasn't expecting."

"But it doesn't matter because you've moved on, right?"

"Right." Only I didn't sound nearly as confident about it as I wished I did. I took a deep breath and let it out slowly. "Dad, I'm pregnant, so air or no air, you need to come to

Denver when this baby gets here." He was my only family and I needed him here for the birth.

Echoing silence met my declaration. I knew he wasn't going to give me a long-distance high five, but the absolute quiet wasn't expected either.

"Daddy?"

He cleared his throat and sounded even rougher than usual when he decided to speak. "You happy about it, sunshine?"

"I was surprised and I freaked out, but I'm happy about it. Like I said, he's a good man, Dad. He isn't going to let either of us down. He tells me that he's all in and I believe him."

"That's a lot of faith you're handing over to him after what you've been through, Cora." My dad, always the über-pragmatic sailor. I wish I could tell him I hadn't really handed anything over yet because I was too scared to let go. He would tell me to stop being such a sissy and just give it up.

"I know. But I do trust him."

"Well, I'm proud of you. I might not tell you enough, but the way you rebuilt your life, it was something else. I know I never knew how to handle all that girly shit with kid gloves, but you make me wish I had been a better dad, and I know you'll be a terrific mom."

I choked up a little and climbed to my feet. "No one is perfect, Admiral Ass Hat. I turned out okay and you did what you could. I should've been a boy."

He snorted at me. "Be glad you aren't, because then I would have to kick your ass every time you call me that. When is that baby due? I need to buy a plane ticket."

I told him around the end of March and he swore he would be there. He asked me a million questions about Rome and about how I was feeling, and I didn't realize that I was crying silent tears until I got off the phone with him. My dad and I had a complicated relationship, but I loved him and I forgot how much I missed him until times like this. Family was important, that's why I was going to make sure this baby had as much of is at I could. I rubbed my palms over my face and raced to the shop.

When I barreled in the door the guys were already busy with their clients, but Nash was the first one to look up and frown at me.

"You and Rome at it again?"

I made a face at him and threw my stuff on the desk and sat down.

"No. I'm pregnant and emotional. I'm going to cry and it isn't always going to be Rome's fault, so chill out."

He grunted at me and went back to his client while I fired up the computer. I told myself I wasn't going to look, that I shouldn't look, but sure enough, the first thing I did was log onto Facebook and pull up Jimmy's page. Of course all the pictures of him and the tattoo tramp were gone and his status had switched from engaged to single. I couldn't get my head around how that made me feel. Not happy, not sad, not vindicated . . . I just felt weird and I didn't like it. I was going to flip back over the appointment page and start weeding through the private messages on the page we used for the shop when one caught my eye. It had my name on it and it had been sent a couple days ago.

I felt my body still as I clicked it open and saw Jimmy's smiling face in the sender space. I needed to erase it, needed to get away from the computer. It had been too long for him to try and reach out to me, too much damage had been done, but despite all of that, I was compelled to read it.

Cora: I know it's been years and I don't deserve your forgiveness, but I want you to know that I understand now how badly I hurt you. It's hard to ignore when the exact same thing happened to me. Everyone in the shop knew Ashley and Drake were hooking up behind my back while she had my ring on her finger and no one said a word. I just wanted to try and make it right. You were a great girlfriend and I should have treated you so much better. Your aunt said you moved to Denver and I figured you would have hooked up with Phil. The shop looks nice. If you are open to it, give me a call. I would really like to make amends. I've missed you.

He left an e-mail address and a phone number, but I hit delete and just stared at the monitor. Well, wasn't that all kinds of a mind fuck?

"Now what? You look like you've seen a ghost?"

I spun the chair around and met Nash's curious gaze.

"Have you ever had your heart broken, Nashville?"

He growled at me, which made his client laugh.

"Don't ever call me that again." He never used his full name and got touchy whenever someone else did. "And yeah, my heart was broken by the girl every boy loves first. My mom. The second she picked that dipshit over me, she broke my heart."

"What did she have to say about Phil? Did she agree to talk to him?"

"She was all weird about it. She said Phil is a grown man, and if he doesn't want to talk about whatever is going on, I should be mature enough to respect it. I still can't run him down and it's all starting to piss me off."

Phil had been scarce around the shop lately, and when I did catch him on the phone, he still sounded terrible. I didn't like it at all, and the fact that he was still dodging Nash just didn't bode well.

"I just had a bit of my past bite me in the ass but it's fine. Nothing to get all twisted up over."

"You sure?"

That was the question I was struggling with myself, but luckily I had a girl coming in to get the same piercing I had done and I needed to get ready, so I moved to the piercing room to set up and made sure all the instruments were ready to go. I needed to keep busy or the past was going to drag me under, and that was the absolute last thing I wanted or needed.

ROME KNEW SOMETHING WAS off. I met him at the bar because he had to stay later than normal because of a band or something. He fed me and poked and prodded at me, which I tried to evade because I just wasn't sure what to tell him. He had nothing to worry about. I didn't want anything to do with Jimmy. He was history and his apology was beyond a lifetime too late, but a part of me couldn't deny that I was curious about what he thought he could say to me after all this time to make any kind of difference. I was avoiding handing my heart over to Rome, because I was still scarred from the damage Jimmy had done when he drop-kicked it back to me and I wondered if there were any words that existed that could make that fear obsolete.

Dinner was a little bit tense but he let it slide because he was awesome like that even though I could feel those eyes trying to vet me. I was mad he didn't tell me what happened to the truck and that Asa spilled the beans. I was worried that someone seemed to have it out for him or the bar and that he didn't seem to be taking the threat very seriously. He said something about Brite having an in with the Sons of Sorrow and that didn't make me feel any better about the situation, but since I was twitchy and off anyway, I just let it go.

I was mentally exhausted when I got home. I chatted with Ayden for a minute since she was in the living room with her homework spread out all around her. I told her that I was probably moving out and getting a place with Rome before the end of summer, so she and Jet would have the place to themselves. She was happy for me but bummed because Jet was on the road so much. I think really she missed Asa and just didn't know how to mend that bridge. That was something the gorgeous siblings were just going to have to figure out on their own because I was simply spread too thin at the moment.

I took a shower and crawled into bed. It was weird to be alone, but Rome said he would be home as soon as he could. I slept more on him than on the mattress, which led to my hands being in some very interesting and naughty places in the morning since he typically slept naked. He was just so warm and so solid, he made me feel like anything bad in the world would have to go through him if it wanted to get to me.

I put on a T-shirt and some panties and was out by the time my still-wet head hit the pillow. I vaguely heard my guy come in well after midnight and heard him rustling around in the bathroom, but I was too out of it to rouse. Even when he pulled me up and settled me back on top of him with a hard kiss on my sleepy mouth, all I could muster was a pat on his chest before getting sucked back into dreamland. I felt his arms curl around me, and for the first time since that call from my dad, I felt like I had settled back into my reality. This was now, my then was not something that was going to mess with this. I refused to let it.

I was jolted awake sometime near dawn. I had to blink to try to adjust my eyes to the hazy light coming in through the blinds, but before I could even adjust to it, Rome had rolled me over and was looming over me with a scary look on his face. His eyes were wild, his mouth was tense, and the vein that ran along his neck was throbbing in a rapid beat that I could see even in the low light.

"Rome?" I asked it as a question because this was the same way he looked the last time he disappeared into the night. I didn't want to spook him, but I wasn't sure he was even seeing me right now. His hands were harder than normal and shaking just a little when they pulled my shirt up over my head and he didn't even bother to slide my underwear off; they just disintegrated under the twist and pull of impatient fingers. He jerked his head up and the light blazing out of those blue eyes was tortured and foreign, but there was enough of my guy still caught in there that I told myself just to calm down and ride out the storm. I knew to the bottom of my soul he would never purposely hurt me. He just needed to get away from whatever was hounding him and this was the only way he could do it without taking off on me again. I had asked for honesty and this was as raw and honest as I could get from him.

He positioned me where he wanted me and then his head and shoulders disappeared between my legs. I was still half asleep and nowhere near ready for this kind of assault, so I just threaded my fingers through his hair, which was now long enough to curl and loop around my fingers, and held on. I arched up against his thrusting tongue and tightened my thighs around his head.

"Rome . . ." This time it was a gasp not a question. He wasn't much of a talker during sex at the best of times and I had had the silent, totally intense sex with him in the past. But this was something on an entirely different level. He was typically a very generous and thorough lover. He went out of his way to make sure I was satisfied and ready to take anything he wanted to throw at me. That wasn't the case this morning. He clearly had a goal in mind and it was to get me off as quickly and as violently as possibly. A goal he was quickly reaching with his oral attack. I couldn't really complain about it since it felt so good and I knew he needed it for some reason, but if he thought he was just going to fuck me senseless and then not talk to me about it, he had another thing coming.

I couldn't hold out long, not with his tongue and his teeth doing all kinds of really wonderful things down there, but before the first spasm of my climax started, he jerked up, rolled me over onto my front, and pulled me up so that I was in front of him on my hands and knees. His broad palm stroked over the curve of my ass and he whispered my name.

"Cora . . ."

I felt him ready himself behind me, and even though I was all mellow and malleable from the pleasure and intensity he had just forced on me, there was no denying I felt a little like I was splitting in half when he pushed all the way into me from behind. I swore a little under my breath, not because it hurt but because it was just a sudden, overwhelming flood of sensation. He was always so careful with me, aware of the difference in our size, but this morning it was like some different part of him had been unleashed. This wasn't one of my favorite positions in bed, but with him like this, I thought maybe I could learn to love it. He was just all over me.

I felt him along my back. His hands were between us and curved around my breasts. My nipples were already extra-sensitive due to the pregnancy, but with him tugging on them and rolling them between his thumb and index finger, I was pretty sure I could come just from that alone. I

groaned and peeked over my shoulder at him. He was a sight
I would never forget.

He was all straining muscles, sweat-slicked skin, con-
tracting abs, flaming blue eyes . . . he was a picture of pure
male intensity and there was no way I would complain about
being the focus of all of it. I liked how he was all hard lines
and planes where I was all soft and round, now more so than
ever before. I also liked the way his hands looked against the
parts of my skin that were stained with color. It was a beautiful contrast, one he seemed fascinated by as well. It would
also be hard to erase the image of him driving, thrusting,
pounding into me like he was chasing down his release or
else he was going to suffer some kind of unexplainable loss.
That was a whole lot of Rome Archer to take in; lucky for
me I was up to the task. Even if my head wasn't a hundred
percent sure I could take all he was forcing on me at one
time, my body was more than up to the challenge. My inner
muscles were squeezing him in time to his thrusts, my nipples were puckering and begging for his touch, and there
was no denying the flood of moisture where we were joined
that was easing his way. I tilted my head back to the side and
braced for the inevitable explosion and collapse; only that
wasn't what I got. Once he ruthlessly shoved me back into
mindless oblivion, he seemed to come back from whatever
brink he was on. I was practically in tears, worn out from
pleasure and the wealth of sensation he'd foisted on me, but
he flipped me back over on my back, kissed me hard on the
mouth, and sank back into me.

He was slow, the drag and pull of that erection a rough

torture on oversensitized skin. He kissed my eyelids, the corners of my mouth, the edge of my collarbone. He whispered my name over and over again, and when he finally shuddered and growled his release into my throat, I felt like there had never been a time in my life where I knew what it meant to be so fully and completely needed by another person. I just wrapped my arms around his thick neck and let him cuddle into me while he caught his breath and settled back down.

I thought I was going to have to poke and prod at him in order to get him to divulge what had set him off, but after five long minutes of silence where all we did was hold on to each other, he finally started to lay it all out for me. The accident. How he thought he was going to die. How he lived every day with the guilt of being the only one to survive. How he was mad that the accident was one of the main causes of not only his physical limitations but had been the precursor to a lot of the mental ones as well. It sounded like he put a lot of the blame on the accident for ending his military career. It was sad. My heart broke for him a hundred times, but when he was done telling me about it, he turned his face to mine and kissed me so sweetly on the cheek I thought I might cry.

He went to pull out of me, to roll over, but I wouldn't let him. I locked my arms and legs around him and held him in place. If he was going to bare his soul to me, not because he wanted to but because I asked him to let me in, I had to do the same. He deserved nothing less. If he was going to give me his all, I had to stop being scared and be willing to do the same. Baby steps.

I licked the shell of his ear and whispered, "I got an e-mail from my ex today. It totally threw me off my game. That's why I was acting so weird earlier tonight."

That big body went stiff all over mine, and he pushed himself up so that he was scowling down at me. We were still joined intimately together, so I thought it should be impossible for him to be annoyed with me, but I was wrong. His eyes narrowed and flared with something that wasn't very pretty, and the scar that decorated his forehead started to throb an angry tempo.

"The guy you were engaged to?"

I ran my hands up and down his ribs like I was trying to soothe a wild animal and gave a little nod. "Yeah. Apparently the girl he was engaged to turned the tables on him and did the exact same thing to him that he did to me. I guess he was just looking for someone to commiserate with."

"Why are you just telling me this now?" I didn't like the note of accusation in his tone, so I dug the edge of my finger-nails into his flesh.

"Because I deleted it. I don't care about him or anything he has to say to me. It was a long time ago, and at one point in time all I wanted was for him to apologize and realize how badly he hurt me. Now I don't need it. Now I have you."

I narrowed my eyes right back at him.

"Plus you didn't tell me about the truck or the fact that you have some pissed-off biker all over your ass looking for retribution because you didn't want me to worry about it. It's the same thing, big guy."

"No, Cora, it sure the hell is not." He rolled us over so that I was sitting upright on him. He crossed his arms behind his head and continued to glower up at me. This was the weirdest position I had ever been in while having an argument in my life. I was annoyed at him, but apparently all my lady parts were tired of being full of all that delightful flesh and not doing anything productive with it. I could feel my inner walls start to ripple along his cock. And of course Rome being the superhero that he was had no problem turning around and getting hard again.

"I wasn't in love with that little biker punk. I didn't agree to marry him. He didn't break my heart into a million pieces, making it hard for me to see what is right in front of me. This guy isn't just your ex, Cora. He changed your life."

I frowned at him because I didn't like that he could read between the lines that easily.

"I see you, Rome." I grabbed one of his hands and put it on my belly. "It's kind of impossible not to. And when it comes to life-changing, you win. Hands down."

He took his other hand from behind his head and put it on the other side of the gentle swell so that the little bump was framed in his palms.

"I know you see me, Cora. But do you just see me as this kid's dad? Do you just see me as a guy with a shit ton of problems slowly trying to figure it out? Do you see me as someone that is just okay for now because you know how much I care for you and that baby and something better might come along? Or do you see me as yours, as someone you are going to be with for the long haul? Because if you are just riding this out until your Mr. Perfect comes along, I got news for you . . . he's going to have a hell of a fight on his hands getting through me."

I just stared at him because I couldn't think of anything to say. All I wanted was for a guy to be one hundred percent in it with me, and here this amazing man was demanding the same thing from me. Like I said, Rome won in the game of life-changing every time.

"I see all of it, Rome, and whatever it ends up looking like is already perfect. This"—I put my hand over his heart and made sure he could feel me squeeze him from the inside—"is as perfect as it gets. You're my guy, no one else does to me or for me what you do, and that's all there is to it. I didn't know what perfect meant until you."

I couldn't tell him I loved him yet. I still wasn't ready to take that leap, but I sure could show him and hope he understood the message I was trying to say with my body. I saw Rome Archer as clearly I saw my own face in the mirror. He was just simply the best of all the imperfect things I could ever have asked for. I could only hope that he wouldn't get sick of waiting for me to put my fear to rest and tell him exactly how I felt.

CHAPTER 14

Rome

THE DIGITAL JUKEBOX I just paid a mint for was playing the Eagles and my brother was acting more twitchy and irritable than normal. He had an untouched beer in front of him, and every time I asked him if he was all right, he just glared at me. I don't know why he was down here when the bar he usually hit up with the guys was right outside the shop on the Hill, but I could see that he wanted to talk about something; he just needed to get there in his own time.

Asa was busy chatting up a really pretty coed at the other end of the bar, and Dixie, the very sexy redhead he had convinced me to hire not just to help him out, but to cocktail the floor because it was getting that busy, was taking care of the rest of the customers. I poured myself a soda, checked to make sure Darcy was doing okay in the kitchen with the dinnertime rush, and went to plop down next to my little brother. His pale eyes flashed up to me and his mouth pulled down in a frown.

"You and Tink have any luck finding a place you both like?"

"No." I wanted to stay on the Hill and she wanted to stay in Wash Park. We both agreed we needed to find a house to rent with a backyard and a garage, but that was about all we agreed on.

"Aren't you worried about taking such a big step with someone you haven't really known that long?"

I snorted and looked at him out of the corner of my eye.

"I think having a kid is a little bit more of a major step than just moving in together. It's what needs to happen. I love her, Rule."

He nodded his head and wrapped his hands around his beer.

"I've been thinking a lot about that lately."

I lifted my eyebrow. "The fact that I love Cora?"

He made a face and elbowed me in the side, which caused me to grunt.

"No. The fact that I love Shaw. I never thought I would feel about anyone the way I feel about her, ya know. She is just . . . my whole fucking world."

I clapped a hand on his shoulder. "I know. I can see it. I'm superproud of you for figuring it out. I know I was hard on you when I got back and that wasn't fair. You're amazing together."

He gulped and the frost in his eyes thawed just the barest fraction.

"I want her forever."

"Pretty sure you got her."

"I want to ask her to marry me."

I almost fell off my stool. Not because I didn't think he loved Shaw, or that he would make an awesome husband, but because he was my impulsive, wild, unhinged little brother. Rule was not a guy that I ever thought would settle into the role of responsible homeowner and faithful husband. I just stared at him until he got mad and snapped.

"What?"

"Nothing. I just never thought I would hear you say that. Has she been hinting that she wants you to ask her?"

He shook his head and took a healthy slug of beer. The beer signs were making his typically wild hair even more outrageous with the neon lights shining on the white strands.

"No. She's perfect. She doesn't fuss, doesn't nag, she trusts me absolutely no matter how dumb I act, and she never, ever holds the past against me. Which, come on, it would be really easy for her to do. On top of it, she's mind-blowing in bed and I can't keep my hands off of her. She's too good to be true, so why would she want to spend the rest of her life with me?"

I thought the answer was easy. Shaw had loved Rule forever. For longer than he probably really knew. He was it for her and always had been. I had never seen Rule self-conscious or in doubt like this. It was eye-opening. He really did love that little girl as much as she loved him.

"Just ask her. She's going to say yes. She loves you. She has always been in love with you and she will always be in love with you. For her, you were too good to be true as well. You're both lucky to have each other."

He dropped his head in his hands and sighed. The knuckles of his hand that had Shaw's name inked across them caught my eye. I pointed to them.

"You have her with you forever already, a ring isn't going to make that much of a difference, bro."

"I need to wait until she's done with school next semester. She needs to graduate and focus on starting med school. I don't want her worrying about me or a wedding while she does it. Honestly, talking to Lando made me start thinking about it. God forbid something happened to me or to her. I want everyone on the planet to know how much she means to me. How she changed my life and made me want to be a better man for her and her alone."

I shook my head in the negative when Asa lined up a round of shots on the bar rail and lifted an eyebrow to ask if I wanted one. I was doing pretty well with the no-drinking thing. I had a beer here and there, did a shot with Asa at the end of the night occasionally, but for the most part I was too busy with the actual running of the bar and keeping an eye on the customers to get tempted. Plus having easy access to my pixie and her particular brand of help with my stress management was so much more fun—and a much more healing balm for my soul—that vodka and the inevitable hangover held zero appeal.

"Rule, she's always been an Archer. Putting a rock on her finger is just a formality. No one doubts how much you care about her, or that you are committed to her and her alone. Screw her obnoxious family and whatever headache Mom and Dad might want to cause, you want her forever, ask her."

He looked up at me and lifted both of his eyebrows in question. The barbells that decorated them looked like they were winking at me.

"So you don't think you want to marry Cora? You're just gonna knock her up and live in sin?" Coming from anyone else, that would've pissed me off. Coming from him and hearing the humor underlying his tone, I was able to take it for what it was worth. I shoved him hard, which made him laugh at me.

"I don't know. Maybe. It's hard enough trying to make a new relationship work with an unexpected baby on the way."

"Yeah. How exactly did that happen? You used to shove condoms in my pockets before I snuck out of the house at night. You drilled safe sex into me before I ever even saw a girl topless. It seems pretty against character for you to have an accident of that kind of proportion."

I crossed my arms on the newly finished bar and leaned on the rail. I looked at my hands, the scars that dotted them.

"Sometimes things are just meant to be. I never thought about having kids, never thought about the kind of girl I would want to settle down with, never thought much beyond the next mission, and then when I got home it was beyond the next endless day. Everything was all shades of gray and I was just disappearing into the fog. I thought I needed direction, needed something to define me. I didn't. I don't. I can just be a guy, a guy that messes up, but as long as I'm accountable, that's okay."

Rule finished his beer and put his hands on my shoulders so that we were eye to eye.

"You will NEVER just be a guy, Rome. You're the best brother a guy could have. You're a fucking hero. No one, and I mean no one, has ever had my back the way you have.

You are an incredible person, be it in the army fighting a war or sitting on the goddamn couch watching the game. Don't forget it."

He was serious and that was important to me. We had always been close, but after learning about Remy and trying to navigate how I fit into his life now that he had Shaw, I had let distance and my own pride come between us.

I clicked the edge of my glass against the edge of his beer mug.

"I lucked out in the brother department as well. Not only do I think you will make a rocking husband, but I think you'll be that baby's favorite uncle."

He laughed and turned around so that he was looking out into the bar. "Won't I be the only uncle? Cora is an only child."

"Semantics." I copied his pose and was going to see if I could work any info out of him about Cora's ex when the door to the bar opened and we both went stiff and on high alert. Now that I wasn't under the pool table, I had no problem recognizing Torch and his lieutenants from the motorcycle club. Not that there was any missing those cuts or the badass biker vibe that rolled right in with them.

"Brite said he sold you the bar, kid. Congrats."

I shook his hand because really, what else was I supposed to do? I introduced Rule and cocked my head to the side.

"Why do I think this isn't just a friendly social visit?"

"Because it's not." The prez tilted his head toward the back of the bar where the pool tables were. I nodded and asked Dixie to go make sure the area was cleared out for just a few minutes. Rule put his hand on my arm and gave me a concerned look.

"Do you know what you're doing? Those guys put Asa in a coma and left him for dead."

"Not those guys in particular, and as I understand it, Asa messed up good in order to get to that point. Torch, the chapter president, has history with Brite. He kicked the guy that trashed the Dodge and robbed the place out of the club. I need to see what he has to say."

He didn't look happy but he didn't stop me when I followed the herd of bikers into the back room.

"The place looks brand-new, kid."

"I worked hard to make it that way."

"I had a feeling about what that old goat had in mind the minute he mentioned you. The Bar is a Sons' place; that means you got us at your back, kid. This shit with the rogue prospect isn't how we do business."

"You don't mess with a man's ride."

"No, you don't. You need to know he's gone to ground. I've had eyes out for him since Brite called about the robbery, but we haven't seen or heard anything. His old man was patched into a club for years, went to the pen for some heavy shit, so the kid knows some people. Not hard for him to lay low or get his hands on all kinds of stuff that can make trouble for you and yours. You read me, kid?"

Yeah, I totally read him. The scrawny punk was not only pissed but he was pissed and probably armed to the teeth. It sounded like Asa was lucky he just took the cash.

"I hear about the people in the Sons' circle. I know you're

a good one, kid. I also know you got some heavy baggage you're carrying around from the desert. You okay to deal with that and keep an eye on your six?"

I don't think I wanted to know how this guy, this m.c. club leader, knew anything about what was going on in my head, but I couldn't deny that he looked more understanding than most people who tried to talk to me about it. I cleared my throat and leaned a hip on the pool table. I met his gaze because that's what you did when you were trying to be on the level with a man that not only offered you his respect, but also his protection and approval. The gray wasn't going to suck me under, not when I had so much color in me because of Cora.

"Most of the time I'm straight. Had a few bad months, almost blew it with the best thing to ever happen to me, pre- or postwar. Brite made me feel like shit, gave me Neil's number, and told me to go talk to him. When I can't get out from under it on my own, I do. Otherwise that best thing takes all kinds of care of me and nothing in this world could matter more for me to keep an eye on my back."

Torch laughed and nodded in agreement.

"I had one of those once. Was too much of a stubborn idiot to hold on to it. You got a girl that stays by you when you wake up in the middle of the night shaking, covered in sweat, and not knowing where you are, that's a girl you don't ever let go of."

I could do him one better and say that I had a girl who not only stayed but generally put me back to bed by sucking me off or riding me until I couldn't see straight, but I doubted Cora would appreciate the baddest-of-the-bad biker club in the union having that much info on our sex life.

"I have no intention of letting her go, or of letting some little punk with a grudge get anywhere near her, or me, for that matter. It all needs to be put to bed, and the sooner the better."

"We are on the same page. Anything else comes up, you call me not the cops."

I wasn't sure how I felt about having his number in my phone, but I also didn't think telling him that was a good idea. I programmed it in and pushed off the table, when he stopped me with a hand on my shoulder.

"We were all you at one point in time, kid. Dismissed, lost, and trying to figure out what was next. For some of us, what was next came out of the blue. The open road, the brotherhood, the family, it was like being back in but on our own terms and fighting for things that mattered here." He thumped a hand over his chest where his biker heart was covered by a leather cut. "Some of us found it in the love of a good woman and making a family; others, like Brite, found what was next by helping the most lost of us onto a better path. Whatever your next is, kid, it'll find you or you'll find it. Don't beat yourself up about it."

With that profound bit of advice, he and all his seriously threatening and intimidating cohorts made their way back out of the bar. I took a minute to gather my thoughts, to ponder the dramatic ways my life had turned on its head in the last few months, and made my way back to where my brother was waiting nervously at the bar.

"Everything okay?"

Typically I would have just brushed it off, told him it was my problem and that I would handle it. I was the big brother, the protector, but I was starting to see that all the things I had used to define myself for so long needed to be tweaked, needed to be redefined, as life moved forward, as I wasn't the same guy I had been when we were kids.

"Nobody seems to know where the punk with the grudge is at. Torch and the club said he has connections, could be armed, and he is good and pissed that picking that fight with me got him eighty-sixed. They want me to watch my back, and Torch was concerned that with all the stuff going on up here, I might not be able to give the situation the attention it deserves." I tapped my temple with two fingers and he frowned at me.

"Are you? Okay to keep an eye on yourself, I mean?"

"I think so. Protecting myself and survival is second nature to me."

"If you need anything from me, from the guys you know, all you have to do is ask, right?"

"I know. Just keep an eye on my girl. I don't want her to worry, not with the baby and not with her acting all twisted up over that e-mail from her ex."

I saw Rule's pale eyes go diamond hard and his tattooed hands curled into fists on the top of the bar.

"That asshole had the nerve to e-mail her after all this time?"

I dipped my chin in agreement and cocked my elbows to lean back against the bar. I didn't want to appear too eager to hear what he had to say about Cora's ex, but information was power, and the more I had the more I could break through that shroud of fear I saw in her multihued gaze every time I brought up the L-word.

"I guess his old lady was stepping out on him with another one of the artists at the shop. He apparently had a revelation that all the crap he shoveled Cora's way might just have made him a douche bag, so now he's all fired up to make amends. She says it's all water under the bridge, but sometimes she shuts up and I can tell she's somewhere else, but she doesn't say anything to me about it."

He let loose a litany of swearwords and his hands clenched and unclenched.

"That guy did a number on her, Rome." He sighed and motioned for Asa to bring him another beer. "When Phil came back to the shop after going to New York and told us we were getting a new shop manager, none of us knew how to take it. But then Cora showed up and it was clear she needed someone to save her. She was wasting away. I mean she is tiny as it is, but she obviously wasn't eating, wasn't sleeping. She was quiet, withdrawn. We tried to joke with her, tried to shake her out of it, but nothing worked. She was heartbroken. I've never seen anything like it. She wasn't just some chick that was sad because she got dumped . . . she was dying from it." He blew out a breath and slowly shook his head from side to side.

"Rowdy always said she took it so hard because her dad was always gone and Jimmy was her only constant in life. I don't know if that's the case, but I do know that guy hurt her in a way I would like to skin him alive and let fire ants eat him from the inside out just to teach him a lesson. No man should do that to a woman that loves him, even if he isn't in love with her anymore."

I had a sinking feeling in the pit of my stomach. I didn't like the sound of any of that at all.

"What snapped her out of it? What kept her from just fading away?"

His mouth turned into a wry grin and he bit down on his lip ring. "Remy died."

I blinked in surprise.

"Remy died and I went off the deep end and she waded in to save me. She was so focused on me and my mess I think she forgot that she was suffering herself. Day by day she got better and held on to me with both hands. I was operating from a really bad place, but I stayed just on this side of redeemable because of Cora. She's more than a big-sister figure, she's my voice of reason."

I barked out a laugh. "Tinker Bell."

"Definitely Tinker Bell, but a Tinker Bell that can flay you with her sharp-ass tongue and put you in your place with a simple look. Don't let that guy get his hooks back into her, Rome. That's bad news all around."

I grunted. "You've met Cora, Rule. She's going to do whatever it is she's going to do. All I can do is hope what we have going for us is enough to make him getting anything into her an option that isn't on the table."

We shared a knowing look.

"Sucks."

"Definitely sucks."

We lapsed into an uncomfortable silence as the jukebox shifted from the Rolling Stones to the Clash. I walked back behind the bar to help Asa with the dishes and to have something to do with my hands.

"You like it here, Rome? You want to stay here and run this place or are you just doing it because you don't know what else to do?"

Rule's question made me take a second and think of an answer that worked.

"A little bit of both. I like it here; I like the clientele and the regulars, I like that I get to make my own hours and that I put this place back together board by board. But I don't have a clue what's next for me, what I should or shouldn't be doing with all the years of training I have. For now this feels right and I can't ask for more than that."

"Whatever you do, whoever you want to be in the long run, Rome, I am so fucking glad you came back home in one piece. I missed you, we missed you. Even when you were being a royal pain in the ass. Knowing you're here, that I can call you, that you have my back even when you're pissed at me, you don't understand how much I need that."

And there it was. My brother still needed me. Yes, he had Shaw to take care of him. Yes, he had become enough of a badass, and enough of an adult to protect himself from most things, but he still needed me to have his back. He needed me to be the guy who looked at him and always saw the guy who lived his life on his own terms, made his own rules, and didn't judge him for it. That was a redefinition of my relationship with my brother I had no trouble filling. I was working my way toward that with my parents as well. I was starting to figure out I could just be Rome, nothing more and nothing less.

"I missed your punk ass, too, and I am sincerely sorry it took me such a long time to get my head out of my ass."

He nodded, finished his beer, and went home to his girl. It was an interesting evening, to say the least, and after the cryptic warning from Torch and the club, I stayed until closing with Asa and watched him leave with not one but two of the pretty coeds. I wanted to make sure everyone got out of the parking lot safe and sound and that no one was lurking around. The guy had game like I had never seen before and I probably would have felt a twinge of jealousy had I not been going to my house, where a very sexy pixie was no doubt passed out in my bed, where she waited for me to get home.

Nash's muscle car was gone when I got to the Victorian, but the Cooper was parked in its spot. I was getting tired of playing ring-around-the-apartments with her. I wanted one place to call our own, but after Rule's revelations about her and her ex tonight, I was starting to wonder if her inability to meet me in the middle on a place had more behind it. I grabbed a beer out of the fridge and thought I would snag a shower and crawl into bed next to her, but when I pushed open the door to my room, I was surprised to find the light on the nightstand on and the bed empty. I frowned and set the beer down while kicking off my boots and pulling my shirt off over my head.

I was worried that maybe she wasn't feeling so great. So

far she had been lucky and morning sickness wasn't something she really had to deal with unless she got superemo-
tional. She was tired a lot and hadn't asked me to go get her
pickles and ice cream in the middle of the night or anything,
so I just assumed it would be smooth sailing for the duration
of her pregnancy. I tapped on the door with a knuckle and
called her name.

"You all right, Half-Pint?"

The knob turned easily under my hand and I walked in
the bathroom. She was naked, all tattooed and bejeweled
skin, staring in big mirror that hung over the vanity. Her
blond hair was sticking up all over her head like she had been
woken from sleep by something and she was biting down
on her lower lip. She was perfect. Everything about her was
just absolutely fucking perfect. I braced my arms over my
head on the doorframe and watched her watch me. Her eyes
did that slow roll over my chest, across my stomach, and
stopped on the front of my pants the way she liked to do.
I needed to remember to always come home and take my
shirt off . . . it really did make it hard for her to think.

"Look." She turned to face me, and I think she wanted
me to look at something besides her perky breasts and the
delicate junction between her legs, but I was a guy and she
was naked, so she was out of luck.

"Look at what?" I wanted to snatch her up and take her
to bed. I wanted to lick every single one of those jewels that
decorated her rib cage and trace the line of the lilies all the
way up her side with my teeth.

"Look at our baby." She flattened both her hands on the

very slight swell in her stomach. She was so tiny that the barest bulge did indeed have her looking more rounded out than she had a day or so ago. She was just too cute with those big eyes so full of wonder. "I passed out a few hours ago and rolled over on my stomach, which sucks when you aren't there to act as a pillow, by the way, when this woke me up. I've never had a belly in my life and now I do and there is a supersmall person it there. It's unbelievable." She just sounded in awe, and I wouldn't have traded this moment for all the assuredness or foresight in the entire world.

I pushed off the doorway and stalked toward her. I got so close that I was towering over her, staring down at her, and she just continued to watch me. I saw her suck in a breath and let it out slowly as I sank to my knees in front of her. I put my hands on her hips and pulled her to my face so I could put my mouth on the soft skin right above her belly button. I heard her gasp softly and twine her fingers loosely in my hair. I let my fingers dig into the sweet curve of her hips.

"I put that baby in there, Cora. Anytime you want to talk about it, you want to marvel at it, you let me know. Yeah?"

She let out a little laugh and dropped her cheek on the top of my head.

"Yeah, Rome."

I gave her a squeeze to let her know I was serious and decided while I was on my knees in front of her I might as well take advantage of the situation, so I stuck the tip of my tongue into the dip of her navel and felt her shudder against me.

"I love you, Half-Pint. Love that little baby. You understand where I'm at with all of that?" She nodded a little but I was working my way south with my tongue and I don't think she had the ability to form words anymore. I breathed out a little puff of air against her cleft that I could see was getting slick and ready for me. "I know you aren't on the same page as me just yet, Cora, and for right now I'm happy enough we're reading the same book. Eventually you have to turn the page, though, you got me?"

Her fingers got tighter in my hair and I knew there was no one else on this planet I would willingly get on my knees for, but this girl with all her mouthy ways and swirling eyes, I would do it for her whenever she asked and even when she didn't.

"I got you, Rome." And she did. She had me any damn way she wanted me, and I was more than happy to show her since she was already naked and wet for me.

CHAPTER 15

Cora

W HY DON'T YOU JUST admit you're changing the subject and that we aren't going to find a house until our kid is walking?"

He sounded disgruntled and I couldn't really blame him. We had looked at three houses this morning before I had to go to work, and none of them fit the bill. I was having a hard time explaining to him that I had an ideal idea of what a home should be, where I wanted to be with him and raise our kid. I spent so much time bouncing from relative to relative while Dad was deployed, I knew exactly what I wanted and I wasn't going to settle, even if it made my guy all kinds of grumpy. It wasn't just about finding a house, it was about finding a home and starting a family, and I had to fully let go of the fear that was still holding me back to do it.

"Just be patient, big guy. It'll come along. Besides, that last place only had a one-car garage and we both know you don't want to leave the Harley parked on the street."

He grunted at me and scowled. I was glad he finally had

the truck back because he didn't want me on the back of the bike in my current condition and it was like pulling teeth to get him in the Cooper. At least having him drop me off at the shop on his way to the bar didn't result in an argument.

"I leave it on the street now."

"But you bitch about it all the time and it hasn't even started snowing yet."

He knew I was right, so he just grunted again and tapped his long fingers on the steering wheel. He had been getting impatient with me lately. Not outwardly, but I could tell every time he told me he loved me that it did something to him when I didn't just say it back. I just couldn't. I wanted to. I was sure I did in fact love him more than I had loved anyone else ever, but giving him that . . . I simply couldn't do it. Seeing this man, this warrior, on his knees in front of me, ready to give me anything and everything I ever wanted, I knew I had to get over it. Kick the fear to the curb and just *know* Rome Archer would never undo me the way Jimmy did. I couldn't say it to him, but I knew I could show him how I felt, which was why I had asked him if I could borrow his dog tags for a couple days.

I was changing the subject because I was tired of fighting about the house even if I thought he was sexy as hell when he was disgruntled.

"So can I have them or not?"

"I don't understand what you want them for."

I was surprised he didn't still wear them since they had been a part of his uniform for so long. I figured since he kept the hair and the strenuous workout routine, he would have kept the tags as well. Plus I thought they would look hot around that thick neck. Maybe I would ask him to put them on for me sometime and nothing else.

"It's a secret. I promise not to lose them and to treat them with all the respect and reverence they deserve. Stop being Captain No-Fun because we didn't agree on a place and hand them over." I tried to keep my voice light and teasing, but I couldn't shake his black mood.

He cut me a look out of the corner of his eye and pulled the big truck to a stop in front of the shop. I could already see people milling around in the waiting room and Nash waved at us since he was out front smoking.

"They're in a box in my underwear drawer. Grab them the next time you're over at the apartment. Just put them back whenever you're done with them."

I giggled a little and leaned across the seats so that I could wrap my arm around his neck and pulled him down so I could kiss him. Even when he wasn't overly happy with me, he never stopped me from loving all up on him. He was pretty much a gentle giant, not that I would ever dare tell him that to his face.

"Why do you even have an underwear drawer? You don't ever wear underwear."

He shrugged a broad shoulder and kissed me back.

"Right, so I have to have a place to keep it all in because I never use it."

"You are so weird." I pushed open the door and hopped down onto the curb. I was going to blow him a kiss or maybe flip him off just to be ornery, but since I forgot my purse and he was nice enough to get out and bring it around to me, I decided I would just kiss his face off some more instead. I heard Nash chuckle at the spectacle I was making, heard Rome groan against my mouth while he curled a hand around my ass, and heard a voice I never thought I was ever going to hear again say my name.

"Cora?"

I slid back to my feet from the tip of my toes and peeked around the solid wall that was my guy to see the last person on earth I ever wanted or expected to see again. I felt Rome's arms tighten reflexively around me and Nash moved from his spot by the front window to come stand next to us. I turned in Rome's rapidly stiffening grip to face my ultimate worst mistake. I felt that big body go absolutely rigid behind me, but thankfully Rome didn't say anything. His irritation was like a lash in the air as Jimmy took a hesitant step toward us.

The years had been kind to Jimmy. He was less skinny and more filled out. He had way more ink curling over his arms and neck than I remembered and he wore it well. His sandy-brown hair was artfully tousled and topped by a cool, plaid skully-cap. He was the epitome of Brooklyn cool and I hated to see that he had genuine regret shining out of his dark brown eyes.

"Jimmy. What are you doing here?"

"Uh . . . you didn't answer any of the e-mails I sent you and your dad refused to give me a number to reach you. I just . . ." He trailed off and I realized he was staring at Rome and not really looking at me. He sighed deeply and shook his head. "I wanted to see you. To get some kind of closure and tell you how very sorry I am for what I put you through. I know it's too little too late, but I just had to do it now that I understand how wrong it was."

If Rome was stiff before, he turned into a statue behind me now. I pulled out of his grip and walked toward my ex. The blood that was rushing to my head was making me deaf and the shining light of my past staring me in the face was making me blind. I think Nash said something to me, think Rome called my name, but all I could see was Jimmy and all I could feel was everything I had wanted to do to him, all the things I had wanted to make him realize five years ago. Seeing him thrust me back in time even if I had strong hands trying to hold me in place in the present.

Operating on ancient rage and embarrassment, I pulled back a hand and socked him in the gut as hard as I could. I owed it to him, but it didn't do anything to make me feel any better. In fact all the old feelings of betrayal and hurt were starting to fade simply because they were irrelevant in the face of how ridiculous it was that he thought I would want to hear anything he had to say. I was still mad, but for other reasons. He let out an "oof" and doubled over. I contemplated smacking him across the face as well, but Nash got to me first and handed me off to my chuckling guy, who locked down my flailing arms and cut off the steam that I felt was pouring out of my ears. I should be overwhelmed with joy that I had escaped the life I would have had if I had stuck with a guy like Jimmy. But all that old duplicity and sting had greatly affected my ability to give everything over to the man I now considered my life, and I was all kinds of newly furious at Jimmy for that.

"Fuck you, Jimmy. I don't need an apology from you. I

don't need anything from you. As far as I'm concerned, you got exactly what you deserved. You're wasting your time here."

Rome growled behind me, which was all kinds of alpha sexy, and ran a soothing hand over my arm. I was shaking, and it made me mad that Jimmy could affect me in any way still. Apologizing for shattering my young heart into a million pieces was just laughable, like any words could go back in time and undo the damage he had done, could fix the current predicament I found myself in with Rome.

"You actually deserve a shit ton more, but considering her condition, I'm not going to let her at you." Rome sounded gruff and even less happy than he had been originally.

Jimmy's gaze widened and then flicked over my now slightly extended belly. I wasn't huge but I was obviously rounded out more than normal and clearly pregnant. I wanted to hit him again when he looked at Nash and asked:

"You're knocked up?"

Nash choked on a laugh and hooked a thumb at Rome.

"You might wanna look at the guy holding on to her, genius. Not mine."

Jimmy's eyes got huge when he took in the protective stance Rome had taken behind me. He looked at me, at my belly, and then back up to the thunderous expression of the man standing behind me. It irritated me to no end that he automatically assumed Nash would be the dad just because of his outward appearance. Why hadn't I ever realized how shallow and awful he was before I had fallen in love with him? Gross.

"Seriously, Cora? What the hell happened to you? This

isn't like you. You used to be nice and funny. The old you would have forgiven me in a heartbeat, and we could have gone and had a beer and a few laughs for old times' sake. You loved me."

Oh, the nerve of him. How did I ever think anyone that stupid was my Mr. Right? I could read between his lines. The old me would have been head over heels to have another shot at being with him and he could have used me for a quick hookup to soothe his battered ego. Uh, no thank you.

"*You* happened to me, Jimmy. You have the nerve to talk about how I loved you? How about because of you I can't love someone else? Where is the apology, the regret for that?"

I heard a sharp intake of breath behind me. I knew I needed to stop—that I was risking ruining the thing that mattered—but in my fury I was stuck in a cycle of past and future, anger and remorse, and there was no turning back.

"Cora." Jimmy rubbed the back of his neck and looked at his feet. "We were young. I was immature. I never meant to hurt you that way. You were the first girl I ever loved. Can't we just grab a coffee or something and mend some fences. I really am sorry."

"No. Just because you're sorry doesn't mean I'm obligated to accept your apology. It sucks you came all this way in search of absolution, but it's not my job to offer it to you. I don't owe you anything. I never did. You were just too stupid to see that I was offering you the world and then you decided to toss it away. Never again, Jimmy. I'll never do that again." My voice dropped an octave and my chest heaved up and down. "The embarrassment, the loss of the only family

I thought I had, it made me lost, made me search and search for some kind of perfect I'm never going to find. You ruined my idea of happy-ever-after."

When my words hit Jimmy they made him shudder, and they made me feel free. But any satisfaction was brief, disintegrating as what I had just said hit me square in the chest. It was too late, I couldn't force the words back in. I turned to look at Rome, and those blue eyes had gone dull, distant, his face like stone.

For five years I had needed this moment to let go. But now that the anger was starting to bleed out, I knew the harsh words I had thrown out in a blind rage had hit the wrong target.

Rome had offered me everything over and over again, and still I'd held back. I'd never been absolutely clear to him why I was so hesitant to just hand my heart over, and here I was laying it all out there to the last guy who deserved any consideration. Jimmy might have damaged my ability to freely offer my love, but I had to be accountable for my part in being scared to give everything over to Rome. I knew we were meant to be and holding back fell entirely on my cowardly shoulders.

"Cora . . ." Jimmy didn't get the chance to add anything else because Rome's tolerance ran out. He moved around me faster than a guy that big should be able to move and grabbed Jimmy by the collar of his trendy pearl-snap shirt. The toes of his hip boots dragged across the sidewalk and his eyes popped wide. I saw Jimmy gulp and heard Nash chuckle.

"Not helping, Nashville."

"No plans to, Tink. Let him wrestle with the bear. He deserves it."

"She said she doesn't have anything else to say to you. That ends the conversation. You want to continue it, you continue it with me. A lot of time has passed for you, but I'm brand-new. I know what I got with her, and I'm not going to let you dirty it up or twist her up anymore." He shook Jimmy like he was a rag doll and I had to bite back a grin. "She's having my baby. I love her. There is no room in any of that for you to show up and try to make her responsible for your bruised ego and hurt feelings. Maybe if you weren't a dick to begin with, you wouldn't have ended up getting fucked over in the long run. Are we clear?"

I had never seen this side of Rome. He was always kind of dangerous, always kind of coiled tight like he could take care of business at any minute. I had to admit it was fascinating to watch, and I wasn't surprised that Jimmy couldn't hold up under the threat of the kind of guy Rome was. I doubted many could. He nodded and Rome shoved him away. Jimmy stumbled off the curb and looked at me one more time.

"For what it's worth, I do really understand now how bad what I did to you hurt. You always deserved better."

I snorted. "I deserve the best and that's what I found. Good-bye, Jimmy."

The three of us watched him walk away, me with a new clarity, Nash with unbridled amusement, and when I looked up at Rome, everything I had been afraid my thoughtless words were doing to him was shining out of his hard gaze. He was angry, but more than that he was hurt, and I couldn't fault him for it. I wanted to reach out and touch him, to try and soothe the unintentional burn I had caused, but those sapphire eyes flashed at me and I could feel the blaze of his anger burning in his tightly locked muscles and granite-hard expression. I took a step back and started when he did the same thing. There wasn't supposed to be space like this between us anymore.

"What just happened, Cora?"

The words were gritted out between clenched teeth, and I blinked at him in surprise.

"I thought this entire time that you couldn't tell me you loved me, that you were struggling to find a house with me because you were still working through all that stuff that idiot left you with when he cheated on you. I thought I was letting you find your own way to where I was waiting for you, and I just watched you annihilate the only excuse I thought you had for holding back on me. You just told that idiot you could never love someone else because of what he did to you, I heard it loud and clear. "

I reached out for him, my hand was shaking, and I could feel Nash recoil next to me when he backed away another step. This couldn't be happening.

"Rome." I tried to get him to calm down. To get a word in edgewise, to tell him he didn't understand, but he wouldn't let me. The thing I was best at, talking, seemed to be my worst enemy at the moment. If I had just been able to tell him I loved him back, he wouldn't be reacting this way now. Of course I loved him. I was just terrified.

"Dude, chill. She just got ambushed by her ex. She's pregnant. Take a breath and calm down."

"I know she's pregnant, Nash. I had something to do with that, but I can't give you everything, let you see all the broken, ugly parts of me, if all I get in return is only what you deem as safe. I'm not Jimmy. I won't let you down like that, and I thought I had proven that to you over and over again. If you can't be in love with me because of what that loser did to you five years ago, which one of us isn't all the way in, Cora?"

Beyond the rage in his voice I could hear the sounds of his heart tearing loose in his chest. My fear and hesitation had caused this. There was no one to blame but myself. But no matter how hard I tried, I couldn't pry the words he so obviously needed off of my tongue. I did love him, but this wasn't a way I was ever going to tell him that. He would never believe me if I blurted it out to prevent this ugly scene.

The driver's door slammed shut, and he took off in squeal of tires and roaring engine. I was glad he wasn't on the bike. That would have been dangerous and scary.

Nash pulled me into a one-armed hug and I rested my head on his chest.

"He'll calm down. I think seeing Jimmy was as much of a shock to him as it was to you."

"He's right. I should have told him how I felt forever ago. I just couldn't. I was scared telling him I loved him would mean it would all fall apart and it would destroy me if it didn't work out. He always tells me I color his entire world, but he did the same thing for me. If what I felt for Jimmy is beige, then what I feel for Rome is a damn box of Crayola crayons. I shouldn't have been such a baby and just let him know. He is perfect for me, Nash."

Nash swore a little bit and turned so that we could go into the shop.

"When two people feel that way about each other, they figure it out. Just like Rule and Shaw did and just like Jet and Ayden. It'll be fine, Tink. I promise. By the way that was a nice gut shot. You shoulda aimed for the nose, though."

Normally that would have made me laugh, but I felt like everything I had was swirling around in that cloud of wrath Rome had ridden away on. It had to work out, there was no other option. He was it for me, I just needed to pull my head out of my ass and tell him. He was right: I asked him for everything and he gave it without question. He wanted one thing from me, to hear that I loved him like he loved me, and I had been unable to do it for him. I sucked. Plus I was sick and tired of the big jerk always somehow managing to get the last word in every time we had a fight. That was really annoying.

"I wish that was a promise I could be sure you could keep, Nash. Don't say anything to the guys. You can tell them about Jimmy because you all gossip like teenage girls, but leave Rome out of it. I need to fix this mess on my own."

And fix it I would, because there was no other option for me or for our baby.

When we walked in the door, the guys all wanted to know what was going on. I let Nash fill them in while I asked Rule if I could talk to him in the back room.

He followed me, his face screwed up in a total look of confusion, but he was kind enough not to grill me.

"That was Jimmy."

"I figured. Looks like Rome made it pretty clear he better leave you alone."

"Yeah, he also made it pretty clear I better figure my shit out or I'm going forward alone."

I thought Rule would get riotously indignant on my behalf, but he didn't. He narrowed those pale eyes at me, which made me twist my plugs around nervously. I felt like a bug under a microscope.

"What? Stop looking at me like that."

"Like what, Cora?"

"All judgy. I was your biggest cheerleader when you were acting like a dipshit over Shaw, so knock it off."

"He loves you, Cora. That isn't a joke. He's never laid himself on the line for anyone like that before that wasn't family."

"I know, I know. I'm working my way there, all right. I don't want to be without him."

"Do you love my brother, Tink? Because if you don't, even if it kills him, you need to walk away now. You can't do that to him."

"Rule." I sighed and started to pace back and forth in front of him. "I wanted someone perfect, thought it would keep me safe, save me from another broken heart, and all it did was insulate me and make me too scared to tell a wonderful man that I love him back. I thought I could show him, that he would just know, just feel it pouring out of me the way I felt it from him. I screwed this up royally and I don't know if he's going to let me fix it."

I started crying and he swore and pulled me into a hug that crushed my ribs.

"Everything is fixable. He had the same reaction when Shaw let us know about Remy, only then he had all my idiotic outrage on top of his own to keep it going. He works his way out of it and I know how much he needs you, Cora. It'll be fine. Love is a goddamn scary thing. Facing it takes brass balls, and we all know you have a pair."

I didn't want to laugh, but I had to. I pulled away and wiped a hand over my face. "I used to think I was pretty tough, but your brother has turned me into a big pile of goo."

"He makes all of us look like marshmallows."

I straightened my top and tried to make sure I looked presentable before going back on the floor.

"I want you to design a new tattoo for me. That is the real reason I asked you to come back here, not to sob all over you like a big girl."

He lifted the eyebrow that had the rings in it and looked me over. "More flowers?"

I told him no and explained what I wanted. I was gratified to see his eyes grow big and to see some of the frost that was always in there melt a little in appreciation.

"I'd be honored to do it. Just let me know when you're ready."

I tilted my head to the side and winked at him. "Gotta get big brother to forgive me first."

"He will."

"You guys keep saying that. I just hope you're right."

CHAPTER 16

Rome

EVERYONE AT THE BAR was giving me a pretty wide berth. I came in breathing fire and lit up. I knew my anger was disproportionate to the situation, kind of like it had been when Shaw broke the news to us about Remy, but I couldn't seem to stop it. I felt like I was losing my grip on things, like whatever I had been building with Cora was crumbling to dust right in front of my eyes. I was so wound up in my own bruised ego, and my own sense of loss, that I knew I was on the brink of spiraling out of control with no way to stop it.

I told myself over and over that we couldn't agree on a house because we were just two very different people. When it crept up on me that she couldn't tell me that she loved me, I convinced myself it was because she was still working around the fear Jimmy had left with her. I tried to reason that she was scared to see forever with me because I was still rocky at the whole family and stability thing, but I tried to show her in everything I did, with every dark memory or tortured dream I let her touch, that I was getting there.

Watching her face her ex, dismiss him out of hand as insignificant, unimportant, and irrelevant, didn't give her a wall of excuses to hide behind anymore. I couldn't get my head around a real reason she might have for not feeling about me the way I did about her until she told him that he'd made her unable to love anyone. I knew she was holding parts of herself back and I understood fear, but I felt hopeless and furious at the idea that she had forced me to open all my hidden places, to bleed all the worst parts of me out in the open for her to see, while she still got to play it safe. It wasn't fair, and it wasn't a way for us to move forward together.

As tempting as it was to just grab a bottle of vodka and disappear into the back room and drown my sorrows, I knew it wouldn't get me anywhere, so I just made sure I kept busy and tried to avoid snapping anyone's head off needlessly. Asa was watching me closely and running pretty good interference for me. I didn't know why everyone else thought he was such a shady character; so far he had done nothing but have my back. I would even consider him a friend at this point, so when I got a text from Cora at ten telling me she was in the parking lot and wanted to talk, I just nodded to him even though the bar was packed. The crowd on a Friday night was something to be proud of now, but I was so twisted up about a certain wild-card blonde I didn't even stop to acknowledge it.

I knew she didn't want to come in the bar in case I was going to make a scene or because she was worried that I would be unbending and unreasonable. I had given her good cause to believe that, which made me feel like a major jerk. There was no need for her to be cowering in the parking lot like she did something wrong. If she didn't feel about me the way I felt about her, I was just going to have to accept it and move on. The one thing she had been so instrumental in teaching me was that there was nothing wrong with holding out for what you ultimately decided you deserved. I wanted her, wanted a life with her and the baby, but she needed to want me on the same level or it wasn't enough.

I saw the bright green car parked next to my truck. When she caught sight of me making my way toward her, she climbed out of the driver's side and started to make her way toward me. I was going to tell her to just follow me inside, that I would have Darcy make her something to snack on while we talked. I never got the chance because I heard the roar of Harley pipes at the same time all my *oh, shit* instincts fired up. I saw her head whip around, felt time slow down the way it did when danger and doom were breaking on the horizon, so I did what I had been trained to do. I knew what gunshots sounded like. Knew not to panic, but never had I been so scared. I had been shot at plenty of times. I had never had to worry about someone I loved getting shot, though. It made me move faster than I ever had in my life.

I sprinted across the asphalt like it was made of lava. I got to her right before the first bullet made contact. My head jerked back and blood started immediately rushing down the column of my neck and soaking into the collar of my T-shirt. I saw her wild eyes go huge in her face but didn't have time to say anything to her. I was lucky she made such a tiny target because the next gunshot didn't miss either, nor did the next as I took her to the ground under me. I'd been hit with bullets before, but had always had body armor to dull the impact. Bullets tearing through unprotected flesh felt like Satan flicking his tail across bare skin. My flesh burned and the calm night air instantly filled with the coppery scent of my blood. Man, there was a lot of it. I could see it flowing out of me and onto her and the pavement below her. How could have I forgotten there was a pissed-off biker all set to get vengeance on me? Cora shouldn't have been in that parking lot alone.

I had her whole body under me. Could feel her shaking and whispering my name against my throat. I hoped I hadn't hit the ground with her too hard, but I couldn't move to check on her. In fact I knew I needed to get off of her so I wasn't crushing her into the hard ground, but none of my limbs were obeying my commands. In fact her lovely and beloved face was blurring in and out as breath wheezed in and out of lungs that felt like they were suddenly full of cement. I was suffocating. I was bleeding. I was hurting all over, but she was looking up at me in shock and fear but alive. So full of life and color, and that was all that mattered.

"Cora . . ." I wanted to tell her I was sorry. That I would never be done with her, not ever, but there wasn't a way to do that. I was going under. I could feel blood pooling under us. Could feel fire blazing in more than one place from my prone body. I think Cora screamed my name over and over again. I think I heard Asa tell her he was calling for help. I was pretty sure my little pixie had a death grip on me where I covered her, but I couldn't feel anything. I was also fairly certain my girl was about to watch me die, and the last thing

I heard before it all just went absolutely black was her tell me that she loved me over and over again.

"ALWAYS HAVE TO BE the hero, don't you?"

His tone was kidding, but it had been so long since I had seen him that all I could do was gape at him in shock.

"Rem?"

"Who else? Got yourself in a bit of a pickle, didn't ya?"

I tried to shake my head, tried to reach out and put my hands on him, but all I could do was just stare at him while he paced back and forth in front of me, hands shoved into the pockets of impeccably pressed, pin-striped pants. He looked good, way better than a guy who had been dead going on five years should.

"You look good, bro."

He smiled at me. A smile so different from Rule's, and I felt my heart flip over. I missed him so much.

"I always looked good, Rome. We need to have a serious heart-to-heart, big brother."

"About what?"

"You."

"What about me, Remy?"

"You seriously have any doubts over whether I knew, absolutely, without any kind of shadow of a doubt that you loved me, Rome? That you were proud of me?"

I felt something happen in my chest, like lightning burning where my heart should be.

"I should have told you. I shouldn't have asked you to keep an eye on them. That was selfish."

"Oh, Rome," It sounded like a sigh, but I wasn't sure what

was going on or where I was at, so maybe it was just the last of my breath escaping my no longer working lungs. "I was always so proud when you asked me to keep an eye on Rule or on Shaw. It meant you trusted me, you believed that I could do as good a job as you always did keeping everyone safe. Those words meant more to me than you can know."

I took a minute to let that process and heard him laugh. It sounded happy and there was no regret in it.

"The girl, the one you just took three bullets for, she's the one for you." It wasn't a question, so I didn't feel obligated to answer him. "You don't think she loves you? You don't think her heart is breaking right now? Because I can assure you that it is and it has nothing to do with being afraid of having to raise that baby alone. She's scared for you. Her heart is shattering for you."

I tried to scowl but I didn't have any control of my facial muscles.

"She's never said anything to me."

"But don't you just know, Rome? Just like I knew you loved me without question. Love doesn't always have to be spoken out loud. Shaw loved Rule from the beginning of time and never said one word one about it, but if he had ever bothered to look at her, he would have seen it shining out of her like a beacon. The same thing can be said about your little spitfire. It's stamped all over her, Rome, you just have to look past the fear, hers and your own, to see it."

That point was burning and hot in the center of where I thought my chest was. I knew all about fear. The fear of the unknown, the fear of not being good enough, the fear of not having anything to offer. I hoped I hid it well, but I hadn't taken one second to think *that maybe Cora was hiding behind a cloud of terror as well. Our experience made us; what we did with that knowledge is what defined who we were going to be, and somewhere along the line I got caught up in all the noise of "what if" and forgot that.*

"I should have just known."

"You have time to make it right."

"I do?"

He laughed again and I felt warmth embrace me, something like rightness settle around my shoulders.

"Someone had to set you right. I knew I could do it. Love is never perfect, big brother. It's what you make of the imperfections in it that makes the ride worthwhile."

"I met Lando."

That sound that could have been a sigh or something else whirled around me.

"He is how I know all about unconditional love, Rome. He deserved better than my secrets. Frankly everyone did. Who we are is always shifting, turning, and changing. Soon you'll be a father, a husband, then an uncle, and then later on down the line, you'll be a grandfather. Who you are never stays the same. It's called living life."

I felt like if I could control any part of my body, I would wrap my arms around my brother and never let him go, but as it was, things inside me were starting to burn and those pale, winter-tinted eyes were getting hazier and farther and farther away and I was flared up on the inside like an inferno.

"Oh, and Rome." I tried to focus on him but it was getting harder and harder to hold on to where I was at. Pain was starting to pull me apart at the seams and I wanted to scream. "Remy

is an awesome name for either a little boy or a little girl. Just saying."

    I felt rather than saw him disappear, the warmth, the joy that was my brother, poofed away and I went crashing back to a body that was on fire with pain and flooding with blood in places there shouldn't be blood.

CHAPTER 17

Cora

I DIDN'T REMEMBER MUCH of anything after I hit the ground, all of Rome's weight and bulk pressing me into the hard asphalt. One second I had been sitting in the car trying to figure out how to talk my way out of this mess and try to fix everything, and the next I was wide-awake in the middle of one of Rome's nightmares.

I had sent the text letting him know I was outside the bar, and then I waited while I held my breath for him to answer me back. My big mouth had hurt the one person I never wanted to cause pain, and I needed to fix it. It didn't matter if he ignored me. I would march right in that bar and make him talk to me. As it turned out, I was getting all worked up for no reason because it only took a minute until his unmistakable silhouette came out the door and he was making his way toward where I had parked. I was nervous, but more than that, I was filled with regret. I never should have held on to what Jimmy had done to me and used it as an excuse to keep my heart insulated from all the wonderful things Rome was trying to fill it up with.

I only made it past the hood of the Cooper when there was a sudden roar that sounded like it was right behind me. I went to turn my head to see what it was because it was so loud, but before I got my neck cranked all the way around, I was bulldozed to the ground and deafened by the repeated *pop-pop* that sounded like extra-loud fireworks. I hit the ground with a grunt and clung to Rome, because those blue eyes were huge in his face and a typhoon of panic and fear was working its way across the shimmering surface.

"Rome?" I said his name because he wasn't moving and something warm and wet was seeping into his T-shirt where I was gripping it in my hands.

His mouth moved. He said my name on a gasp but no sound came out. Something coppery-smelling and hot landed on my cheek as it leaked out of his neck and splatted on my face. His eyes flickered like a flame going out, and the next thing I knew I was trapped completely under him as all his strength fled. His blood was covering both of us and starting to pool on the ground beneath us. I couldn't get to my phone, couldn't move, because even when he was unconscious, even when he was furious at me and hurt by my selfish and thoughtless words, he was still trying to keep me and our baby safe.

"Rome!" This time I screamed it and clutched at him. "You have to open your eyes. Come on, big guy."

I was screaming his name over and over but he wouldn't move, wouldn't react. I'm sure we were only there for a minute, but it felt like an eternity until Asa's blond head appeared over Rome's prone form and he told me he had called the police and an ambulance was on the way. It took three of the regulars to move him off of me, in part because I refused to let him go. I was crying and had so much of his blood on my hands it made it hard for me to hold on to him as the regulars from the bar worked to separate us and put pressure on the gaping wounds that were spilling his life out onto the ground.

I think Asa put an arm around my quaking shoulders and tried to tell me everything would be all right, but I knew that was a lie. Through the tears and Rome's blood smeared all across my face, I could see that his eyes were still closed and that his massive chest wasn't moving up and down. He was going to die right in front of my eyes, and I was never going to get the chance to tell him that I loved him. I absolutely couldn't let that happen.

I broke free of Asa's grasp and ran to where people were trying desperately to stop him from bleeding. The entire side of his neck looked like raw hamburger, flayed open and gushing vital red onto the ground. I fell on my knees, not caring that the asphalt ripped my skin open, and put my hands on his cheeks.

"Rome, please open your eyes, please. I love you so much. I need you. Please, big guy." I was sobbing and I doubted the words made any sense. Somewhere in the distance I finally heard the sounds of sirens screaming toward us. The ambulance was too far away to do him any good.

"I love you, I love you, I love you." I just told him over and over again, trying to will him to breathe. Because it was true. Being scared of handing over my heart to him because

I wasn't sure what he would do with it had nothing on the choking fear that I would never get to tell him how I felt because he wasn't going to make it. He had always been a hero, and right now I almost hated him as much as I loved him. If he hadn't been so perfect, so honorable, so devoted to me and his child, he wouldn't be lying in a puddle of blood. It was just wrong on so many different levels.

"Please don't break my heart, Rome. I can't do this without you." Somewhere along the line, police and the ambulance crew arrived, and again I had hands trying to pull me away from him. I bent down and put my mouth to his. I cried even harder when I felt how cold his lips were.

I kissed him, tasting the salt of my tears and the iron burn of his blood, and whispered that I loved him again and again. I had to succumb to the impatient hands of the female paramedic that pulled me away from him. I couldn't take my eyes off his deathly-still face and his unmoving chest.

"We got him, honey."

I shot my gaze to hers. "He has to be okay."

"We'll do everything in our power to make that possible. The blond hottie said you're pregnant and that you might be hurt. We need you to get checked out."

I shook my head vehemently. "No. Just worry about him."

The medic opened her mouth to argue, when there was suddenly a gasp and Rome's bright blue eyes shot open only to flutter immediately closed again.

"Cora . . ." My name was just a whisper of sound, but it was enough to have me screaming his name again and to have everyone moving twice as fast as they had before. The paramedics had him on a stretcher and in the back of the ambulance in no time flat.

They didn't say a word when I scrambled in after them. I wasn't going to let him out of my sight until I knew for sure he was going to be okay. There was just so much blood and it wouldn't stop flowing out of the holes that decorated his entire right side.

The female paramedic was all business as she went about hooking an IV into him and started to cut his clothes off so that she could work on getting all that blood to stop pouring out of him. She kept talking to him, telling him over and over that he had to fight, that he couldn't leave me and the baby. She was rattling off info about the shooter and the bikers, but all of it was a dull buzz. I just wanted him to open his eyes and look at me. She told me to hold his hand, to let him know I was there. Once again the thing I was best at, talking, using words, had fled. All I could do was stare at him and cry. He was my entire world, he was everything I ever wanted, and it was going to turn my heart to stone if I didn't get the opportunity to tell him that.

Suddenly the paramedic swore and started moving around frantically. Her sharp tone cut through my haze of despair. She told me I had better convince Rome to stay with us because my stubborn soldier wasn't listening to her. I squeezed his hand, leaned over him and kissed that scar on his forehead. I told him everything, begged him to open his eyes. I told him that he had done his job and fought for me and the baby; now it was time to fight for himself. I would pull him back from the brink of death over and over again if that was what it took to keep him with me. I didn't think it was doing any good, but when the ambulance rolled to a stop outside the hospital, I saw his eyes flutter open again. He didn't look good and it didn't take a medical professional to see that he had lost way too much blood, but those eyes were bright and looking right at me, so I made sure that if it was the last time he saw me, the last thing I ever got to say to him, I would make it matter. There was no way Rome Archer was going to fade away again without me telling him I loved him and needed him.

CHAPTER 18

Rome

"THERE'S THOSE PRETTY BABY blues. Keep fighting, big man, we're almost to the hospital."

I didn't recognize the voice or the girl who spoke them. She was hovering over my head and I was having a hard time tracking her. I hurt all over and I couldn't breathe. I was trying to suck air in and out but it didn't seem to be working. I vaguely heard the sirens overhead blaring and the radio in the ambulance squawking. I couldn't feel anything other than the hot blaze of pain from the top of my head to wherever my toes were.

"You have some pretty powerful friends. The guy that pulled the trigger already got picked up. I guess he was so scared of what the Sons of Sorrow would do when they found out he shot you, he took his happy ass to the station and turned himself in. Idiot. I guess he doesn't know how many Sons are doing time."

She prattled on and on while moving all around me. I didn't care about the guy that shot me, I cared about Cora.

I didn't know if one of the bullets had gone through me and hit her, didn't know how hard I had taken her to the ground, didn't know if the baby was okay . . . The thoughts ran around and around and I couldn't hold on to any of it anymore. The pain was too much. I couldn't get any air and I was tired. So tired, and I felt some of the fire licking across my skin start to dull.

"Hey now, soldier, none of that." The girl's voice rose and slapped across me. I thought I heard another sound, a whimper or something that sounded like a wounded animal, but I couldn't turn my head or even move my eyes to track the noise. They wouldn't even open when I commanded them to. Something clamped on my hands and squeezed. I was surprised I could feel it amid the living fire that was scorching me up from the inside out.

"You didn't make it all the way home to have some punk take you out. You need to fight. You got too much riding on coming out of this battle a winner. Fight."

This chick was good at her job. Had I not been on the brink of death, I would have admired her a lot more. I didn't know how she knew what I had to lose—my girl, my baby, a future and a family that I was finally, at the worst possible time, starting to understand that I deserved. It was all beyond worth fighting for, but I was so tired and I needed air. It was so much easier to just close my eyes and let the pain and fire take me.

"Shit, he's crashing." The stranger's voice rose and everything around me started to fade away once again. I could hear Remy screaming at me to stop being an idiot, could hear my heart starting to slow down, and felt the pain start to drag me under and the fire shift from hot to freezing cold. "Honey, you better convince your man to stay with us, because he isn't listening to me."

Something jabbed into my side and into my arm and the stranger's voice vanished to be replaced with the one I think I had been searching for all along.

"Rome." She sounded like she was crying but I couldn't pry my eyes open to look at her. "Come on, Captain No-Fun, I need you to look at me." She sounded so sad, so scared, and it pissed me off there was nothing I could do to make her feel any better. I wanted to look at her, but it was hard. My eyes were so heavy. I felt soft hands stroke along my jaw, across my forehead and trace the scar that was there. "I can't tell you thank you for saving my life while you aren't looking at me, big guy. You saved us, me and the baby. Now I need you to save yourself. Come on, Rome, you can't leave us now. You need to wake up so I can tell you how much I love you."

I never wanted to leave her, not even when I was mad at her and acting like an idiot. I wanted to apologize for flying off the handle like a hothead, wanted to make sure that if I didn't make it, my last words to her were words of love, words that expressed how important she had been in bringing me back to myself. I wanted her to know that I thought she was as close to perfect as I was ever going to get. I just couldn't do it. My eyes wouldn't open. My limbs wouldn't work and I still needed air and felt like I was in a vacuum where there was none.

Something wet and warm slid across my face. I thought

it was just more blood, but then it dripped more, slow and steady, and I heard Cora's soft sob. I didn't want her to be sad about anything. I wanted her to be happy and safe, to know that I loved her. It took every ounce of strength I had left, every morsel of fight I possessed, to pry my eyes open to look at her, and when I did the pain slammed back into me full force, enough to make me gasp and to have moisture flooding my eyes. I had never felt anything like this. I was turned inside out and losing my grasp on reality fast. I was sinking in pain and suffocating on lack of air.

Her eyes were liquid blue and brown. She was crying and her blond hair was stained pink with what had to be my blood. She was pale as a ghost and her hands were shaking where she was touching my face. Our gazes locked and her mouth broke into a trembling grin.

"Please be okay. You have to be okay. I love you so much, Rome." She was pleading with me but there was nothing I could do to reassure her.

The movement of the ambulance stopped and the strange voice was back.

"We're here. We gotta get him into surgery."

I wanted to scream when Cora's unusual eyes were replaced with the stranger's. I was moving but I wanted my girl. The sky flashed overhead for a brief second and then all I could see was white ceiling tiles and industrial lights, what I didn't see anymore was Cora and she was all I wanted.

"I thought I told you to stop messing around with angry bikers." The pretty nurse with the gray eyes was now hovering over my bedside. She was more familiar but she still wasn't who I wanted. "They're ready for him in the OR; just take him back. We need to prep and get him under like yesterday."

I wanted to scream that I needed my girl, that she had to know I was going to be okay, but I was poked and prodded some more and then there was no more fire, no more ice, there was just darkness, and I was gone.

"ROME ARCHER, IF YOU don't wake up right this second so I can tell you that I love you, I swear I'm going to name this baby something ridiculous like Daffodil or Rover and I'm going to let your brother be in charge of haircuts until he or she is old enough to complain."

I could breathe again. It hurt, I mean really, really hurt, but my lungs seemed to be inflating and deflating on their own. I cracked an eye open and immediately wished I hadn't because the light behind Cora's head made me nauseous. I tried to say something back to her but there was something shoved in my mouth, so all I could do was look up at her and blink. She was really just a colorful blur against a bunch of stuff shifting in and out of focus.

She was still crying, or maybe crying again, but I was pretty sure she had told me that she loved me, so it didn't matter. I felt her hand on mine and then the redheaded nurse was next to her checking out the machine that was beeping somewhere over my head.

"There he is. You have more lives than a cat, Mr. Archer. You sure are one lucky guy. Not a lot of people could lose that much blood and still be with us. I told your girlfriend to go buy as many lottery tickets as she could."

I sure was lucky, but it didn't have anything to do with getting shot and surviving. It had everything to do with the woman holding on to my hand and looking at me like I was some kind of miracle. The nurse turned to Cora and put a hand on her shoulder.

"Honey, he's awake. You need to go take care of yourself and that baby. This is a huge hurdle crossed. We can't take him off the ventilator until we know that lung is stable, so he won't be able to talk to you for a while still. Go home. Take a nap. He's in good hands. Plus there is a waiting room full of people out there waiting to see him. He won't be alone. I promise you."

I saw Cora blink. She looked awful . . . well, she looked wonderful and she had said she loved me. Even if it was just the painkillers I was sure they were pumping into me that made me think she said it, it was good enough. She smiled at the pretty nurse and bent over to kiss my temple.

"But he's mine." Her voice broke and I managed just barely to move my fingers under her death grip.

The nurse offered up a very kind smile. She really was a stunningly pretty girl and her genuine kindness just seemed to pour out of those soft gray eyes. When Cora mumbled her name in aggravation, I thought that Saint really was a fitting name for her. She seemed blessed with infinite patience.

"I know, sweetheart, but you aren't doing him or your baby any favors by not taking care of yourself. It's been a couple days, hon. This is all good news, trust me. He didn't save your life just to have you pass out on us and end up in a bed next his. Trust me. It's not every woman who can actually say her man took a bullet for her." There was a strain of envy in the nurse's tone. "You're just as lucky as he is. Now go take a breather. I got your fella."

I couldn't agree or disagree, but then Cora was hanging over my face and all I could see was her different-colored eyes. The turquoise one was glowing so bright I could see her heart in it, the brown one was all velvety and warm and I could see my future plain as day. She leaned over and kissed me on the plastic machine helping me breathe in and out. I think that made me jealous of some kind of medical machinery. She brushed a thumb over my eyebrow and smiled at me. Remy was right: actions were important. I needed to pay closer attention.

"I was so mad that you kept getting the last word in every argument we seem to have, but this—good Lord, Rome, this is an extreme way to win a fight." I would have laughed if I was capable of it. "I love you. I need you to know that. Please know that. What I said to Jimmy . . . it was stupid and thoughtless. I was acting as dumb as he was. I've loved you from the beginning; I was just too cowardly to admit it. You're my family, my everything, Rome, you have to know that."

Her voice dropped an octave and tears flooded her eyes again. All I could do was blink up at her. I knew it before she said it. I was just being a typical stubborn and blind guy. She kissed me on the forehead again and disappeared after telling me she would be back as soon as she could. She must have been exhausted because my girl didn't acquiesce that easily.

The nurse was back. She was taking my vitals and writing things down in my chart. She looked down at me and smiled.

"That is one fireball of a girlfriend you got there. The OR team was drawing straws to see who would go out and update her and your family. I think she actually had them scared."

Sounded like my girl.

"One bullet in the neck that magically misses your carotid artery, another one that shattered a rib and deflated your lung, and lastly one that lodged in your thigh just millimeters from your femoral artery . . . you look like Swiss cheese, but you are so incredibly fortunate to be alive."

She put the chart down on the end of the bed and crossed her arms over her chest. She lifted a russet-colored brow at me.

"When you make it through something like this, you can't squander the second chance away. I hope you know that. If you're up to it, I'll send the rest of your fan club in one at a time."

I wasn't up to it and didn't make it past my mom and dad coming in and alternately crying and swearing at me for five minutes. My eyes were too heavy and there was too much blood loss and pain meds in my system for me to power through, and I was once again dragged into oblivion. The next time I managed to pry my eyelids open, it had to be late into the next night. The lights were off and the only sound

I heard was the steady *beep, beep* of the machines checking my heart rate. The ventilator was gone, but I still had tubes sticking all over the place and moving any part of my body besides my eyes wasn't something I was excited about.

"'Bout time you woke up, asshole. I've been waiting for a week to tell you how fucking pissed I am at you."

Rule did indeed sound seriously pissed, but he also sounded hoarse and all kinds of torn up. I wasn't sure why he was in the room when it was so late, but my brother had never been one to let other people's rules dictate his actions.

"I understand why you did it, Rome. I get that you couldn't let anything bad happen to Cora or to the baby, but for the love of God, did you stop and think what would happen to me if I had to bury another brother." His voice cracked and I wanted more than anything to tell him I was sorry, to offer him some kind of comfort, but all I could do was blink rapidly at him. "I swear, when you are back on your feet I'm kicking your ass and you're going to let me."

I would have laughed if I didn't think it would turn me inside out.

"It took both Shaw and Ayden to get Cora to go to the house and clean up. You should have seen her. She had more of your blood on her than you had in you. She had everyone worried she was going to run herself into the ground. None of the nurses would come anywhere near her, and if you had died—" He had to clear his throat. "If you hadn't made it, Rome, I don't know that she would've either; she was a mess. She was forcing her will for you to pull through so hard I think we all knew there was no way you wouldn't make it. It's a good thing you're a fighter, brother. I wouldn't want a pissed-off, pregnant girlfriend haunting me for all of eternity."

That was all nice to hear but none of it touched the fact that she loved me. Rule got up and hovered over the edge of the bed. Those pale eyes were rimmed in red and he had more than a couple days' growth of stubble covering his jaw. He looked awful. I wanted to tell him I saw Remy, that I understood it all now, but I still couldn't make my mouth and tongue work. He nodded a little and rapped the knuckles that had his name inked on them against mine.

"Thank you for not dying, big brother."

It was entirely my pleasure but he was going to have to wait until I had a little bit more get-up-and-go to tell him that.

He talked to me for another hour even though I couldn't respond to him. He told me that Brite had showed up as soon as they rushed me into surgery. Apparently Cora had lit into him the second she saw him. My girl was mad that the shooter was in the safe arms of the law. The bloodthirsty little minx was all for brutal biker payback, but Brite had talked her down. He had also pulled Rule aside and assured him that, prison or no prison, the little punk would get his due. Torch and the boys would make sure of it. Rule was pissed enough and just unhinged enough to approve of this eye-for-an-eye method of payback, I was just glad the threat was gone. I didn't mind taking a bullet for my girl, but if I had nine lives, I was down to the last one after this stunt.

He told me that Shaw had been working night and day

to keep my mom from going off the deep end. Me getting shot had almost undone all the good that had happened with her since she started therapy. All the guys were taking turns keeping an eye on me, or rather keeping an eye on Cora so she didn't overdo it. She didn't want to go home, but they were making her now that I was out of the woods for sure. He told me that she had yanked Nash's nose ring, pulled Rowdy's hair and socked him in the gut, when they tried to make her leave before she was ready. It was funny, but it also made me happy to hear.

He talked to me until I fell back asleep, and when I woke back up, a doctor was buzzing around me asking me a million questions that I could only slightly shake my head or tilt my chin down to agree or disagree with. The consensus was that I was the luckiest bastard in the world and it was a miracle of fate that I was still here. The pretty nurse popped back in a couple of times and I was poked and prodded more than I ever wanted to be again in my life when Cora appeared like a punk-rock angel. I wanted to talk to her, but every time I tried, I broke off into a fit of coughing that made my injured lung feel like it was full of razor blades and barbed wire. I couldn't even tell her that I would take a million bullets for her if it made her look at me the way she was looking at me now. She fed me slivers of ice and kept touching any part of me she could reach over the rails of the bed. It made me feel better than whatever the redhead was putting in my IV bag. I had a lot I wanted to say, but in the interim I just kept writing down that I was okay, that we were okay, on the tablet of paper we had resorted to for short conversations.

After lunchtime, Shaw and Ayden both showed up and tried to harass her to go and get something to eat, which she flatly refused to do. They were forced to call in reinforcements, and before I knew it, my hospital room was full of people. Rule and Nash walked in together, followed shortly after by Rowdy and Jet. It took about fifteen minutes more for my folks to show up and ten more for Brite and Asa to make an appearance. It was crowded, but everyone was just so overwhelmingly grateful that even though I couldn't talk or interact, I was awake and aware . . . it was palpable in the antiseptic-scented air. It was almost like a celebration; only I was one big party pooper.

Cora curled her hand around mine and dropped her head down so that our foreheads were touching. Her eyes were right above mine and any question I had about what or what might not be in my future was answered right there. I would look into those eyes every day and know that any decision I made to make her happy, to keep her safe, would be worth any kind of sacrifice or suffering I might endure on the back end.

The chatter in the room was loud and I thought it was strange that the nurse made herself scarce once again when she caught sight of Nash. Maybe she didn't like the flames on his head; they did make him look intimidating, but it didn't justify the way she flat-out bolted when he told her a simple hello. If I could get my face to work, I would've asked her about it after everyone cleared out for the night.

"Everyone that matters in one place." I looked up at my brother as he leaned over the other side of the hospital bed and looked down at me. I gave a slight nod and something flashed in his eyes. Oh, shit, I totally knew what he meant by that. He walked the few steps across the room to where Shaw was standing between Ayden and my mom and got to his knees in front of her. The entire room that had been full of talking and laughing went silent.

Shaw put a shaking hand to her mouth and I heard my mom gasp.

"I don't have a ring. I don't have a pretty speech prepared. All I know is that I love you more than life itself and I want every single person in this room to know that I want you forever, Shaw Landon. I love you. Marry me." Typical Rule: he didn't ask, he just told her. "Be an Archer. Be mine."

Crystal tears worked out of Shaw's glimmering green eyes and she almost looked like she was going to fall over from shock. Everyone held their breath because Shaw still hadn't given Rule an answer. She was just staring at him and then she screamed so loud that a couple of the nurses poked their heads in the room. She was crying and laughing so hard she looked a little crazy. She would have to be stuck with my brother for the rest of eternity.

She launched herself at him so hard that they tipped over and Rule ended up on his back with her holding him in a choke hold. A collective "awww" went up as she started to kiss him all over his startled face. There was no doubt she wanted to be his wife as much as he wanted her to be.

"I'm always yours, Rule. I will so totally marry you and it would make me happier than anything in the entire world to be an Archer. I don't need a ring or a speech. All I ever need is you."

I squeezed Cora's hand as everyone cheered again as Rule kissed Shaw like they were alone and not on the hospital floor surrounded by family and friends. Like everything I was learning, it was just perfectly imperfect. Cora looked back down at me and dropped a kiss on my forehead as everyone else rushed to congratulate my brother and his new fiancée. I was happy for him, proud of him. He had made the right choice and had picked the right girl.

"I don't care where we live, Rome. I just want to be where you are. I was trying so hard to make choices that kept me from getting hurt again . . . it was weak and caused unnecessary grief between us. I've been chasing my idea of perfect for so long I didn't know what to do when it was right in front of me. You were right, you are perfect for me because I'm just as imperfect as you are, but with you, it's all just flawless. I thought I was terrified of what would happen if I gave you my love and you decided you didn't want it anymore. That's got nothing on watching all the life flood out of those beautiful blue eyes. I thought I lost you for real, big guy, and my heart stopped. It wasn't broken, it wasn't hurt, and it flat-out stopped working because I thought I was going to have to go on without you. I love you, Rome. I'm not scared of letting you have all of it anymore. I'll give you everything and then some more. I'll give you everything I have, big guy."

That was all I wanted to hear. Too bad I still was all messed up and couldn't tell her any of that awesome mushy stuff back. She had already given more than I could ask for. She gave me myself back, she was giving me a baby, she gave me herself, and that was all I really needed. Just like Remy said, just like she had told me all those months ago, she was just going to have to *know* it. Just like I would *know* it from here on out.

CHAPTER 19

Cora

SHAW WAS GLOWING, AND not in the typical *just got laid and it was sooooo good* way. Her green eyes were radiant and I think the smile on her face was contagious because Ayden couldn't stop grinning back at her, and I kept laughing. There was no missing the elegant and absolutely perfect solitaire diamond sitting on a simple platinum band on her ring finger. She was happy, and Rule had done a killer job picking out a ring that was just the right amount of rock and class.

"It's beautiful. I'm so happy for you guys."

We were back on the deck at Shaw and Rule's house for a cool, fall barbecue before the full chill of October set in, and this one was going a lot smoother than the last one. Rome was still in a badass mood, but that had a lot to do with the fact he was on crutches and sick and tired of physical therapy, not because he was mad at the world in general anymore. He was sprawled out in a lawn chair next to the grill, and he and Rule were alternately arguing about the best way to grill steaks and drinking beer. He didn't normally let loose like that, so it was nice to see him with a grin on his face, even if it was hidden behind a scruffy beard he refused to let me help him shave off.

"What about you guys? The house hunt going any better?"

I shook my head and took a sip of water. "No. I thought I was being difficult but now he can't decide on anything. Nothing is safe enough. No neighborhood is right. I'm ready to strangle him, and not just because he's the worst patient in the history of injured men."

Rome was a warrior. He bounced back at a rate that left the doctors and nurses baffled. He told me that he didn't want to be in the hospital anymore, he wanted to be home with me, and that was his motivation to get better so fast. The bullet in his leg had done a number on him. It tore through muscle and tendon, making it impossible for him to immediately get back on his feet and be mobile. The shattered rib made moving and lying down a chore and hindered his movement with his right arm, so he was just generally grumpy, and I think he was sexually frustrated because the doctor had told him no action for at least six weeks and we weren't even to the halfway point yet. He was a big, grumbly teddy bear.

He was also annoyed that he couldn't be as present at the bar as he would like to be. Brite was back to watching over things until Rome was back to a hundred percent. I secretly thought the old marine felt guilty that Rome got hurt on his watch. They had a pretty intense bond and I was so glad Rome could rely on him. Brite made him talk to his friend after the shooting. He didn't give my guy any chance to slip back into the black place he had been in before, and as a result there had only been one episode since the shooting where Rome woke up in a cold sweat and shaking. We both considered that a win, and I couldn't wait until he was better so that I could just take care of him in my own special way and we could both go back to sleep exhausted and smiling. Brite had also shown up at the hospital while Rome was still unconscious, stroking his beard and looking like the cat that ate the canary. It seemed like the shooter had made bail, but he had missed his court date and no one had seen hide nor hair of him since. I wasn't vindictive, but after I'd been bathed in the blood of the man I loved, there was something to be said for brutal and swift biker justice.

Ayden cleared her throat and took a swing of the Coors Light she had in front of her. Her amber eyes considered me thoughtfully.

"What about just keeping your place? Jet's been talking about taking part of the studio and converting it into a loft so he's closer to work when he's in town. It's right downtown and close to work and school, plus if Jet follows through, then I could actually see him more when he's in town and not working."

I looked at her in shock. "Seriously?"

"Yeah. I want to be with him whenever I can. I'm actually thinking about putting grad school on hold for a year so I can travel with him. He's going to the UK at the beginning of next year and I want to go. Grad school will always be there; traveling the world with Jet is an opportunity I might not get once I have a steady job."

I loved my house, loved my neighborhood, and if all the other rooms were empty, it would have plenty of room for me, Rome, and the baby. I bit my lip and tilted my head to consider her thoughtfully.

"What about you and Asa?" Her brother wasn't at the barbecue. Since it was a weekend and the bar was going to be busy, he had offered to go in so Rome could come hang out with me and the rest of the hooligans. My guy and the Southern charmer had some kind of bromance going on. I didn't question it, but where I knew Asa could be slippery and scandalous, Rome only saw a coworker and a buddy. It was actually kind of cute and I felt bad for the girls who came into the bar trying to get in between them. I think Asa was one of the few who didn't give my guy a hard time when he got lost in his own head. He just waited it out until Rome was back to being Rome.

"He's still ticked off at me. He acts like everything is fine, but I can tell he hasn't forgiven me, and I don't really blame him. He comes by sometimes, but mostly he just shoots the shit with Jet and pretends like I'm not even there. He's nice enough when we talk on the phone and whatever, but I really hurt his feelings when the bar got robbed. I'm not really sure where he's been staying, but he seems happy with whatever he has going on, so I don't pry."

I could see that she was upset about it but I didn't know what to tell her in order to make it any better.

"I'm sorry, Ayd. That blows. I'll ask Rome about staying

in the house. It would suck for you to go to all the trouble of moving out if he won't go for it."

She nodded and Shaw tapped her finger on my left hand. "What about you guys? You think you'll join the ranks of the hitched and the engaged anytime soon?"

I put a hand over my rapidly growing belly and felt a little tremble under my hand. I wasn't far enough for Rome to feel when it happened but I knew my baby was in there safe and sound thanks to Daddy, and it always made my heart swell and overflow with love. I didn't need a ring or a wedding to make that any better.

"We've had a lot of excitement in a short amount of time. I think we're both just looking forward to things settling down and being normal for a little while."

Shaw threw back her head and laughed while Ayden rolled her eyes.

"Cora, nothing with you is every normal."

She wasn't wrong, so I tossed the cap of my water bottle at her.

"Shut up. Besides, you know Rome has to get better so he can be Rule's best man. We already have one wedding to focus on. We don't need another."

Rule wanted to wait until after Shaw graduated to get married; Shaw didn't. The compromise was they would have the ceremony in December—a Christmas wedding before she and Ayden went back for their final semester in the spring. That was almost no time to plan a wedding, but with all of us chipping in and Shaw's determination to be an Archer, I had no doubts it would happen and be wonderful.

I wasn't excited about being the size of a whale in my brides-
maid dress, but I would do it for her.

"How did your parents take the news?"

Her green eyes darted away and she chomped down on
her lip.

"I maybe, possibly haven't told them about it yet."

Ayden shook her head and I rolled my eyes. I looked
pointedly at the rock on her finger.

"That's gonna be kind of hard to hide, girly."

She fidgeted nervously. "I know. It's just a fight I don't
want to have. I've never been so happy. I never, ever would
have thought Rule would want to do something as tradi-
tional as get married. No one, and I mean NO ONE, is going
to rain on that parade."

I understood where she was coming from and I didn't
envy her going forward. That was a battle that wouldn't be
fun and I think we all knew it.

I looked up in surprise when Rowdy was suddenly looming over me with his hands on my shoulders.

"Tink, you might need to rally your man. I think beer
and pain meds might've done him in."

I spun around on my chair, and sure enough Rome was
zonked out on the lawn chair. Rule and Nash were hovering
over him, trying to decide if they should find the situation
cause for concern or hilarious. I patted those tattooed hands
and got to my feet.

"My turn to save him."

That's what we did. We saved each other. He forced me
to see that living in fear got me nowhere and that holding

out for some unobtainable ideal of perfection was just silly. I made him realize that whoever he wanted to be and whatever he chose to do was enough. He didn't have to be anything more. He wasn't perfect, I wasn't perfect, but the love we had for each other . . . nothing was more perfect than that.

I elbowed my way between Rule and Nash and bent down so I could put a hand on one of Rome's prickly cheeks. He didn't look bad with a beard; in fact it made him look almost too rugged. The last thing he needed was anything that accentuated his raw and undeniable man-ness. But I liked his pretty face and missed it hidden behind those bushy whiskers.

"Come on, Captain No-Fun, time to go home."

His dark lashes fluttered along the high ridge of his cheeks and those breath-stealing blue eyes blinked open. It was strange to see him so vulnerable, so open, but he had never hidden from me and apparently he was done hiding from himself because it was all there in his gaze when he looked at me. Everything he was—hero, lover, stubborn pain in the neck, and a man with or without a plan—I could see it all and it just made me love him all the more.

He had to have both the other guys help him to his feet and it was slow going on the way to the truck. Even though it took some maneuvering and the use of every swearword in his vocabulary, he insisted on taking the Dodge instead of riding in the Cooper, which I thought would have been easier. He was going to have to get over his hatred of my car because sooner rather than later it was going to be too hard for me to hop up into the massive 4x4. He didn't argue when I held out my hand for the keys and tossed his crutches in the back. I noticed that he had white lines of pain fanning out around the corners of his eyes despite the meds and the booze. It looked like he might have overdone it a little.

I reached out and patted his knee.

"So I have a question for you."

He shifted his gaze to mine and just grunted. Okay, Captain No-Fun was in serious effect.

"Ayden told me that she and Jet are more than likely moving out. He wants to convert the studio. How would you feel about just moving in with me and staying at my place?"

He was quiet, which made me nervous. I looked over at him and was surprised to find he had his eyes closed and his head resting against the window. I thought maybe he was asleep and I wondered how I was going to get him inside and had a sense of déjà vu.

"Can we tone the pink in your bedroom down just a little bit so my balls don't shrivel up and fall off?"

His snippy tone made me laugh as I pulled into the driveway.

"Sure thing, big guy."

He sighed and shifted his big body so that he could maneuver himself out of the door.

"I love your place, Cora. It's colorful and cute just like you. Plus it's a rental, so we can stay there until we decide we want to buy something and stay there permanently. That totally works for me."

Man, I wasn't sure I was ever going to be able to contain how happy this big, gruff man made me.

"It works for me, too, and it would make me really happy."

I went ahead of him to let him in the house. When I got to the door he followed me in and I guided him to the room so that he could sprawl on the bed.

"If it makes you happy, Half-Pint, you don't have to ask. That's all I want." He threw the arm on his good side across his eyes and sighed. "I love you, Cora."

Every time he said it, I kept it in a place deep down inside of me to cherish and hold on to forever. It was a special place full of special things, and even if our time together had been relatively short, that place had enough love in it to last a lifetime. I sat on the bed next to him and ran my fingers over his scruff.

"I love you, too, Rome." It was so easy to tell him that now. To hand over everything I had been so foolishly afraid of giving to him. I realized now love didn't do any good if you held on to it in a death grip. It only had purpose, had power, when you had the courage to hand it over to someone else for safekeeping.

"I know."

It's what he always said to me. "I know." Like without the words he just knew how I felt. I asked him about it and he just smiled at me and told me he needed someone to point it out to him. When I asked what he was talking about, he just asked me what I thought about naming the baby Remy. I loved it.

"I also love your face and I'm sick of trying to find it in all of these whiskers. I know you can't use your arm very well right now, so why don't you let me help you shave?"

I ran a finger over the delicate curve of his ear and the eyebrow with the scar danced upward. I was hoping the pain meds and the beer were enough to make him more agreeable.

"You don't like it?"

"I miss your face. It's too pretty to be covered with all of this."

"Is that why you won't kiss me?"

I frowned at him and leaned down to drop a kiss on his sullen mouth. "No. I'm not kissing you because with you, kissing always leads to more and the doctor told you that was a no-no. I don't want to hurt you."

"Not kissing hurts me and you don't even want to know what no sex does to me."

I had a pretty good idea—after all, I was on the other end of the ban—but his health and well-being were more important than an orgasm no matter how good he might be at giving them. I kissed him again and levered myself up off the bed. I stood over him and put my hands on my hips. I didn't miss the way his eyes narrowed on my chest.

"I'll run you a bath. You can relax and I'll help you look less like a mini Brite. How does that sound?"

He grumbled that real men didn't take baths, but he didn't argue or try and stop me when I went into the bathroom and turned on the water. In fact by the time I made it back into the room, he had wrestled his shirt off and had his pants unbuttoned. I could just stare at him like that for-ever. Even with the angry scar that now decorated the side of his neck right above his collarbone and the ugly wound on his side, he was the most beautiful thing I had ever seen. I just gaped at him like a dimwit until he laughed at me and ordered me over to help him up. It took some maneuver-ing and some shuffling, and by the time he got his pants the rest of the way off, there was no doubting that nearly dying hadn't had any effect on his libido.

I looked at the erection that was now pointing straight upward at his rippling stomach and then up at him. He gave a small shrug.

"My dick doesn't give two fucks about doctor's orders."

I laughed and helped him into the steamy water. He was so big the liquid spilled over the sides onto the floor. He gave me an *I told you so* look but settled his broad shoulders back and closed his eyes as I brushed a thumb over his cheekbone and along the strong line of his jaw where it was covered in a soft layer of facial hair. I used my other hand to grab a washcloth and roll it over his shoulders and neck, careful of his new battle mark.

"Rome." Those unbelievable eyes flicked open and I thought I was going to drown in the blue of them. "We might not be perfect, but you and I are so perfect for each other. I just want you to know that."

He grabbed the hand that I was using to stroke his face and sucked the edge of my thumb into his mouth. Between the heat from the interior of his mouth and the tickle of his beard, I was beginning to doubt I could keep this all business.

"Kind of funny how that worked out, isn't it?"

He ran his hand up my arm and tangled his fingers in my hair, and before I knew it, he had my entire upper half bent over the edge of the tub and I was not only soaking wet but sprawled across his chest as his mouth sealed itself over mine. Kissing him while he was furry was interesting, and maybe I had been too hasty in wanting to get rid of the beard. His tongue rubbed against mine, his teeth nipped at the delicate skin on the inside of my lower lip, and I realized he had completely maneuvered me into the position with the use of only one good hand. Tricky soldier.

I pushed up off of him and shook my wet bangs out of my face.

"The doctor said no."

"I say yes."

I should have fought harder when he moved my hand under the water and wrapped it around his prominent erection. I told myself I didn't want to hurt him, but the truth was I missed the feel of him, the weight of him in my hands and in my body. I gave that impressive flesh a light squeeze and bit my lip as I waged an internal war with what was right and what was right now.

"Come on, Half-Pint. I only have one working side, I got more holes in me than a golf course, and I haven't seen you naked in way too long. Climb on and give me something to smile about."

God, how I wanted to, but I just didn't want to hurt him and I wasn't sure about what he was going to say when he caught sight of my little surprise. I thought I was going to have more time to show him, maybe break him into the idea slowly in case he hated it, but his good hand was working into the neck of my tank top and his strong fingers were tweaking my nipple, making it hard to think.

"Rome . . ."

"Cora . . ."

I don't even know why I thought I could fight it. I didn't have it in me to deny this man anything. I scooched up so that I was propped up on the edge of the tub next to his bad arm. I made him lean his head back so that his neck was resting on the rim, and I kissed him long and hard. He tasted like beer and forever.

"When I take my shirt off, don't freak out."

That single eyebrow shot up and he chuckled a little. "I've seen your miraculously growing tits, Cora. I think it'll be fine."

I made a face at him and pulled my tank top over my head. There was no missing what I had been talking about and I heard him suck in a hard breath then swear when the action hurt his still-tender side.

"Oh my God."

The tattoo was pretty big. It started on the back of my shoulder blade, the chain meticulously detailed and so real it looked like you could pick it up off my skin. Rule had tattooed the little metal beads that made up the standard chain so that they were in the shape of a heart. The design twisted and twined under my arm and high across my rib cage. The twin tags with all of Rome's vital statistics hung next to each other under the soft swell of my breast. He was there, forever on my skin. I didn't know a better way to show him how much he mattered to me, and apparently it had the desired effect because his eyes shot up to mine and for once the man that always had the last word was silent.

"That's what you wanted my tags for." His voice was husky and there was no mistaking the emotion in his tone. "It's beautiful."

So was the way he kept touching it.

"Rule did it for me. I thought I was going to have more time to surprise you. I wanted to show you when I couldn't tell you that you were it for me, too." I reached out and brushed a knuckle along the spot that cut across his neck that was still raised, angry, and red. "You permanently marked your skin for me, Rome. I wanted to do the same for you."

He got his good arm around me and pulled me fully into the tub with him so that we were hugging but so much more.

"This, Cora . . . this is as perfect as two people can be."

He was right; he was also aroused and sexually frustrated because the hug quickly turned from a sweet moment to something much hotter. The fingers of his hand snaked into the back of my damp shorts and his mouth latched on to the side of my neck and started to play with the sensitive skin there.

"You're gonna have to do all the work, Half-Pint."

That wouldn't be a problem, not with his straining cock practically calling my name and his questing fingers already working their way to the place where I needed them most.

"We're going to flood the bathroom." He pushed up and

helped me get my shorts and panties off. A wave of water cascaded over the edge of the tub and soaked the floor.

"Who cares?" He was all impatient male and grabby hands. Rome was big, the bathtub was not. By the time he finagled me to where he wanted me, more water was on the floor than there was covering him and swirling around our hips. I made sure to keep most of my weight on my knees and braced myself, using my arms on the porcelain instead of on him like I typically did. His eyes flared up at me when all the best parts of me lined up with all the demanding parts of him. I was starting to rethink my stance on the beard when his mouth closed over the tip of one breast, making me gasp. It tickled, but not in a funny way, in an *oh my God don't stop ever* kind of way.

It was a rough ride. Even with me trying to be as gentle and as careful as possible, there was no missing that mixed in with his grunts of pleasure there were gasps of pain. Trying to have sex with jacked-up ribs just wasn't a good idea, but my guy wasn't one to give up, and his determination and perseverance were two of the things I loved most about him, especially when it meant he had to get really creative and inventive with his one good hand in order to keep me distracted so that I didn't call the entire episode off in order to save him unnecessary pain.

I dropped my forehead so that it was touching his and lifted my arms so that they were resting loosely across his shoulders. The water swirling around where we were so intimately joined was warm. Rome was warmer. On every glide up and every slide down, I made sure that he could see how I felt shining through our locked gaze. I didn't just see him and all that he was: to me he was the only thing worth looking at. I knew by what was staring back at me in the endless depth of those blue eyes that he felt the exact same way, and that was undeniably precious.

We'd never had sex that was slow and agonizingly drawn out. There was something to be said for the anticipation, the heady throb between my legs, and the pulse at the base of my neck. There was reverence in the way we touched each other, like we both knew just how lucky we were to be able to touch each other like this still. Every brush of his mouth across my skin, every nip of teeth against a tender place, reminded me that I had almost lost him and this was life-changing and life-affirming. With each up-and-down drag and pull of aroused skin against pulsing flesh, I could see the vein in his neck and the muscle at the side of his mouth twitch. It was the best kind of torture and probably did more to make him feel better than any of the medication he was currently on. Even if he was normally a more hands-on-type lover, there was no mistaking the fact that he needed this right now.

In typical Rome fashion, all the sexy wait-for-it was only enough for a few minutes. Narrowing his eyes, he flashed me a wicked grin and drove those talented fingers between us so that they were hooked around my ring and pressing against my clit. There was no holding out against that kind of sensual assault and it had the desired effect. I forgot we were supposed to be taking it easy and went to work getting us both off in a matter of minutes. It was more of a sweet cresting than a brain-boggling explosion like it normally was, but it still made my limbs heavy and the rest of me flush with satisfied pleasure. Anything this man wanted to give me was going to end with both of us smiling, there was no doubt about it.

I giggled a little bit and rested my cheek on his shoulder. His thumb left the metal between my legs and skated up my ribs to stroke lovingly back and forth across my new tattoo. I could feel the edge of his blunt fingernail trance the outline of his name even though he couldn't see it because I was lying entirely on top of him.

"You okay?"

He grunted and wiggled the fingers on his bad side so that he could stroke my thigh.

"Better than okay. Doctors don't know what they're talking about. Sex makes everything better."

I sighed because it might have felt great, but his eyes were darker than normal with shadows of discomfort and those white lines of pain were back next to his eyes. I tried to disengage from him as carefully as possible, which only led to getting the rest of the bathwater on the floor. I just shook my head and wrapped myself up in a fluffy towel. He was cradling his injured side and his thick thigh muscle was clenching and unclenching involuntarily. He looked sated but not in any kind of hurry to move.

He stroked a hand over his still-furry face and looked up at me in question.

"Thought you wanted this gone?"

I considered him thoughtfully for a second, then reached

down both hands to help him lever himself up. We almost ended up back in a tangled heap in the tub due to the wet floor and his unwieldy bulk, but somehow I got him to his feet and a towel wrapped around his trim waist.

"I think I might want you to keep it until you're all the way healed up."

I got him to the bed and scooted around the room, throwing on some stretchy yoga pants and an oversized T-shirt so I could clean up the tsunami we left in the bathroom. I could feel his eyes follow me as I bopped around.

"Why?"

I froze for a second and looked at him over my shoulder. Was he really going to make me spell it out for him? I could tell by the half grin dancing around his mouth that he already knew.

"Why what?"

"Why keep it if you don't like it?"

He always had to have the last word, so I slid up next to his hip on the bed, yanked on the long hairs at the tip of his chin, looked him dead in the eye, and told him, "It tickles. I want to know what it feels like when you can get yourself back down between my legs. Can't wait, big guy."

The blue in his eyes blazed so bright and hot I was surprised steam didn't start to come up off of the water droplets still clinging to his damp skin. I laughed and pushed up off the bed, only to be stopped with his hand on my wrist. His look was serious but his voice was soft when he told me:

"You are everything to me, Cora."

Seriously . . . and I worried about him not being the perfect guy? If that was what imperfect got me, I was the luckiest girl in the world. I was going to tell him I felt the same way but he tugged me over him, grinned up at me, and told me to climb up and straddle his face so that he could tickle me the rest of the night. I wanted to laugh but I was equal parts turned on and angry that once again he got the last word.

Thanksgiving

W E NEED TO GO to the hospital."

I dropped the Allen wrench I was using to put the crib together on the floor and jumped to my feet. Cora was in the doorway to the nursery twisting her hands together.

"The baby?" I didn't want to ask; the worst thing I could think of started chasing through my mind even though she had just had a checkup and come away from it the epitome of good health. We also knew we were having a little girl, which blew my mind and already had me in a state of perpetual panic.

"No, it's Phil. Nash just called. It's bad. Dad's already in the truck waiting on us."

Cora's dad, Joe, had finally flown out for the holidays and to my relief I got on with the older sailor just fine. Instead of going to Brookside with Rule and Shaw for Thanksgiving with my folks, we had stayed in town and done the holiday thing with just the three of us. Cora had tried to get Nash to bring his uncle, but Phil was still acting strange. He was still avoiding Nash and not showing up at the shop, which had prompted Nash to plan a surprise Thanksgiving invasion of his uncle's fishing cabin on the outskirts of Boulder.

"What's wrong?"

She shook her head and I could see the worry etched on her pretty face. I pulled her into a tight hug and her arms immediately went around my waist.

"Nash didn't know. He said when he got to the cabin he thought it was empty, but Phil's bike was there. He broke in the door and Phil was unconscious on the floor. He had to call Park Service to get help to get him out. They apparently airlifted him here. I called Rule and he and Shaw are on the way down the mountain. Rowdy, Jet, and Ayden are at the bar with Asa, doing Thanksgiving for the vets, but it's almost over. Ayden said they would meet us there, but if it's as bad as Nash made it sound, I don't know that he's going to want a crowd around. Dad and Phil go way back, so there's no way I can keep him from going."

"If I need to run interference I will, Half-Pint. You know it."

She gave me a hard squeeze and I saw her put her protective mask in place. She was a warrior in her own right, always ready to march into battle and protect the ones she loved from anything she thought could do them harm or hurt them. I gave one last look at the delicate, white crib and followed her out the bedroom door. Disarming a roadside bomb was easier than putting together baby furniture. All the little parts and pieces were not designed for a guy with paws like mine. At least Cora found it hilarious every time she walked in to find me swearing and threatening death upon inanimate objects.

We put the nursery in Asa's old room because Jet and Ayden still had a few months until the remodel of his studio was done. Jet was gone so much and Ayden was so busy with work and school I hardly saw either of them. In fact, aside from my girl and brunch on Sunday with the family, the only person I really saw a lot of was Asa. I was busy with the bar because the bar was busy and he was simply my right-hand man. I didn't know if we clicked because we both filled the role of big brother, or if it was because we were both men trying to redefine how we saw ourselves and how others saw us, but we just did. I knew enough to know that he was wily, and crafty; the last two bar fights I had been forced to break up had been because of girls he left high and dry or who hadn't bothered to remember they had a boyfriend before going home with the Southern charmer. There was no doubt he was trouble, but so was Rule. I knew all about how to handle it and I liked to consider the guy a buddy.

I hoisted Cora up into the cab of the truck and roared on to the hospital. She was quiet and her dad was tense. I didn't bother with platitudes because one military man didn't try and fool another. The situation was unknown, but with Phil's strange behavior and the way he had been avoiding everyone who loved him, it didn't bode well. I grabbed Cora's hand and felt the way it trembled in my own. She was scared, but she would power through it like she always did.

We filed into the hospital, following behind her dad. He had a take-no-prisoners kind of demeanor that was very similar to Cora's, and he got us to the emergency wing way faster than we would have had we been on our own. We came around the corner of the waiting room and there was no missing Nash. That shaved head with the flames tattooed on either side of it was bent down and he was staring intently into the gray eyes of the very pretty redheaded nurse. I kind of considered her a good-luck charm, so I was glad she was there. Cora called his name and his head jerked up to look at us. Something twisted in my chest when I saw that there were very obvious tracks of moisture on his face. Those periwinkle eyes were liquid with sorrow and heartache.

The nurse put a hand on his cheek and he reached up to wrap his fingers around her slim wrist. She said something to him and he nodded solemnly. She pulled her hand away and walked the opposite direction down the hallway. I inclined my head in the direction she went and tapped Joe on the elbow.

"You might want to talk to her. Let your little girl handle Nash. She's good at dealing with her boys."

He gave a sharp nod and took off after the nurse. Cora pulled free of my hold and went and wrapped herself around Nash. His big body gave a shudder and he buried his face in the curve of her neck. I didn't know what to do with myself, but when he looked up, those lapis eyes locked on to mine.

"Cancer. Fucking lung cancer. They're calling in an oncologist right now, but it's bad."

I sucked in a breath and saw that Cora was shaking, too. That wasn't good news.

"I'm so sorry, man."

He blinked like he was in a daze and pulled away from my girl. He scrubbed his hands roughly over his bald scalp and started to pace back and forth like some kind of wild animal in a cage. I pulled Cora back into my arms and ran my hands up and down her back when I felt her tears slide against my neck where she shoved her face.

"I knew something was wrong. For months and months he's been acting weird, not returning calls. He was all gung ho to get a new shop opened, and then that just fell off the map. I let it go and let it go. Hell, I thought he had a new girlfriend he didn't want anyone to know about, but no, it's motherfucking cancer. Jesus Christ, smoking. All from god-damn smoking."

"Nash, take a breath. You don't know how bad it is or if it's treatable yet. Don't jump the gun."

He swore some more and kept moving rapidly back and forth in front of us. His nervous energy was like an electrical charge making the hairs on my arms stand up. I wanted to tell him everything would be fine, that it would all work out, but before I got the chance to say anything, a petite woman with jet-black hair, dressed like she had just left high tea, followed by a man who clearly wore a suit every day and bossed peons around for a living, burst into the small wait-ing room. I didn't know who they were, but Cora went stiff in my arms and Nash stopped pacing. The look on his face would have been enough to frighten a herd of stampeding elephants, but not this lady. She shrieked, "Nashville. Oh, honey, the hospital just called us. Are you okay?"

She hugged him hard, and I didn't miss that he didn't

return the gesture. He looked at me and then back at the woman, then purposely took a step away from her. I peeked at Cora, who mouthed "his mom," and turned my attention back to the family drama that made the Archers look like the Brady Bunch.

"What are you doing here, Mom? Why would the hospital call you?"

The woman fiddled with the strap on her purse. I was having a hard time seeing any of Nash in her. She was small and pale of complexion; he might have inherited his dark hair from her, but that was all I could tell.

"I'm Phil's next of kin on all his paperwork. The hospital had to call me. I'm also his power of attorney."

Nash glared. "Why you? Why would he have you on all that stuff, Mom?"

The woman took a nervous step away from her obviously emotional and enraged son. "He was going to turn it all over to you once the final tests came back."

You could've heard a pin drop. I felt Cora gasp and let go of her because I was actually worried I was going to have to physically restrain my brother's best friend.

"You knew? You knew how sick he was?" Nash's voice blasted across the hospital walls like a gunshot. The man that had followed his mom in—her husband, I assumed— went to take a step toward Nash, but I reached out a hand and shook my head.

"Wouldn't do that, friend."

He sneered at me and looked at my hand like it was covered in shit.

"And who are you?"

I lifted my eyebrow.

"I'm nobody, but if you think you're going to get in the middle of that, I'm the guy that'll be happy to stop you."

His eyes slid over the top of my head, across my shoulders, and looked at where my pixie was shooting him the death glare from my side, where she was safely tucked away. Apparently he saw that I meant business because he huffed and crossed his arms over his chest like a sulking child.

"Nash." The woman was pleading but he wasn't having any of it.

"How long, Mom? How long has he been sick? How bad is it?"

She looked away and bit her lower lip. Nash put his hands on her slight shoulders and gave her a little shake. I thought for a second the hospital security might show up or the rest of the crew, but so far it was just us and Nash's life unfolding in front of him.

"He got sick at the end of last year. They had to remove part of his lung. He didn't want anyone to know. The doctors thought it was contained but it metastasized and spread. He's in stage three. It's possibly moved to his lymph nodes. He was waiting on the test results. He didn't want you to worry, Nash."

Nash swore long and loud, and Cora pulled away from me to go and soothe him.

"Worry! You don't think a heads-up would've been nice before I stumbled across what I thought was his corpse. Jesus Christ, Mom!"

"You need to calm down."

"The last thing I need to do is calm down. Why would he tell you all this and not me? I'm his family. Hell, I'm more his son than his nephew."

I saw the woman flinch and the suit made a strangled noise in his throat. Cora narrowed her eyes at the woman, and at the exact same time as Rule and Shaw came racing into our little party from hell, the pretty nurse came back around the corner followed by Cora's dad.

"Mom?" Nash's voice was downright scary, and for being a typically mellow guy, he looked like he could take the hospital apart brick by brick if he wanted to right now. Rule took a step toward his buddy but I shook my head. The nurse walked up to Nash's other side and put a hand on his shoulder. His gaze snapped to her and something in the lilac depths shifted fractionally.

"He's awake and asking for you."

"For me?"

She tilted her fiery head to one side and blinked up at him.

"He asked for his son. That has to be you, right? I mean you guys look identical."

Nash's mom gasped and looked like she was going to faint.

"Holy shit." Rule's outburst got him an elbow in the gut from Shaw and a dirty look from the suit.

"Nash." Cora's tone was stern and no-nonsense. "Now isn't the time. We can work out all the details later. They don't matter. You have to appreciate that he's still here and focus on the now." Her bright eyes danced over to me and then slid back to him. "Plus you can't hit her and get away with it. I can."

Saint—I still thought the nurse's name suited her perfectly—hooked her arm through his and started to guide him away from the mess that particular bomb had left in the waiting room.

"I got you, Nash." Her tone was kind, and instead of being brisk and businesslike, there was something else lurking in those dove-gray eyes.

"Do you?"

"I do."

They went around the nurses' station, and we all collectively turned and stared at Nash's mom. I saw Cora cross her arms over her chest and stamp her foot. If this prissy lady thought this was over, she had another thing coming.

"Phil is Nash's father, the father that supposedly took off when he was a baby?"

The woman looked at her husband and then around at all of us. Rule growled something under his breath and stalked toward her until he was right in her face. I saw her cower but I wasn't going to intervene.

"How could you let him believe that lie? It tore him up, it made him feel lost. He loved Phil like a father all this time; hell, we all did, and neither of you could bother to share! Fuck you and fuck that piece of shit you picked over your son. You better hope to God Phil has a fighting chance to beat this, Ruby, or I will make sure your dirty laundry is spread all across the Front Range."

The small woman bristled in that way only someone who thought they were inherently better than you could do.

"I don't owe you an explanation, Rule. I don't owe any of you anything." Her husband shoved past me and went to stand by her side. They both glared at us like we had something to do with this life-changing secret coming to light.

Cora came back over to me and curled back into my side.

"You're wrong. Nash is ours, not yours. We love him, we take care of him, and we're going to be the ones that help him through this. You didn't want him, we do. I think you need to go. You are not wanted, or needed, here."

The couple bristled and I could see they were going to put up a fight, when Cora's father stepped around our motley crew and got between us and them.

"I know you don't know me, but my name is Joe Lewis and Phil and I go way back." They might not have known the sailor but they both had clearly heard of him. The fight visibly drained out of them. "I know all about you, Ruby, and you, too, Grant. I know your story, I know about the boy, and trust me, if you want any chance at making this right with your child, you will turn around and leave his family to take care of him. Am I making myself clear?"

Apparently he was, because with one last haughty look they turned and walked out of the waiting room without a backward glance.

Shaw let out a little whistle and fake-whispered, "Your dad is a serious badass."

I snickered a little and dropped a kiss on top of Cora's wild hair. "You come by it naturally."

"So what now?" Shaw propped herself in one of the uncomfortable plastic chairs and took out her phone.

"If Phil pulls through, they can work it out. If he doesn't, I don't know." Rule's voice sounded strained.

Cora kissed me on the cheek and wandered over to sit next to her friend. My brother arched one of his dark eyebrows and nudged me with his shoulder.

"So what was up with the hottie nurse? They know each other or something?"

"You guys went to school with her."

"Ah . . . no, I didn't. If I went to school with a chick that looked like that, I would've remembered . . . don't tell Shaw I just said that."

I snorted because that was typical Rule. "She's Saint."

He frowned in confusion. "She's a saint?"

"No, her name is Saint, but she might *be* a saint as well."

I sure hoped she was because it looked like Nash was going to need all the help he could get dealing with this particular mess. Sure, he had all of us in his corner and at his back, but there was no denying that a saint might come in handy.

Nash and Saint's story to be continued . . .

Rome's Playlist

Deer Tick: "Twenty Miles"
(Do yourself a favor and listen to this song before you start reading the story . . . This is totally Rome's song for Cora . . . it's perfect!)
The Gaslight Anthem: "Boxer"
(This song doesn't fit with Rome's classic-rock theme, but when I was writing, for some reason every time I got stuck, or was wondering about what direction the big guy would go, this song made it make sense.)
Creedence Clearwater Revival: "Fortunate Son"
The Rolling Stones: "You Can't Always Get What You Want"
AC/DC: "You Shook Me All Night Long"
The Weeks: "Sailor Song"
The Clash: "Should I Stay or Should I Go?"
Eagles: "Take It Easy"
Neil Young: "Rockin' in the Free World"
The Kinks: "You Really Got Me"
Pink Floyd: "Comfortably Numb"
Tom Petty: "Free Fallin'"

Cora's Playlist

Nikki Lane: "Walk of Shame"
The Detroit Cobras: "Can't Do Without You"
Devil Doll: "You Are the Best Thing and the Worst Thing"
Sleater-Kinney: "You're No Rock n' Roll Fun"
Le Tigre: "Nanny Nanny Boo Boo"
Bikini Kill: "Rebel Girl"
Spinnerette: "Ghetto Love"
Pretenders: "I'll Stand by You"
Naked Aggression: "Pros and Cons of Dying"

ACKNOWLEDGMENTS

I HAVE A BUNCH of people who help me do what I do on a professional level. My agent, Stacey; my editor, Amanda; an entire team at HarperCollins that is dedicated to making sure whatever I create gets polished and put out to the reader in the best way possible. It's been an interesting and often challenging process to learn how the publishing world works. I have a publicity team whom I work with to try to get my boys all the love and exposure they deserve. They are wonderful ladies, kind, easy to work with, fun, and a great source of information and support, and I can't tell you how grateful I am to be able to pass the ball occasionally . . . remember I am a complete spaz. Check them out if you are in the market for some promo, marketing, have questions, and even if you want to venture a toe in the big bad writing water: http://literatiauthorservices.com/.

At times I frankly want to run away from it all because it's new and can be intimidating. But it's also humbling and at times overwhelming to have so many different people be-lieving that I have the talent to create something memorable and meaningful. I can never express how grateful I am for all the exciting experiences this journey has brought me and the fabulous people it has given me the opportunity to work with. I am very fortunate and I have to remind myself every day to take a minute and enjoy it because I am such a spaz, and I let all the good things that go with being thrust into a new experience pass me right by.

My usual cast of characters who I couldn't live without. My family, my bestie, my dear friend Melanie, who goes by many names and wears many hats but really is the kindest, most thoughtful person I have had the pleasure to meet. We don't always agree, but I trust her to be honest, and she is an awesome sounding board for all the crazy characters and stories rolling around in my head. She is and probably always will be my book bestie . . . she just gets it. And she lets me borrow her husband and his awesome design skills.

I have to thank my mom specifically for being such a trouper. She's let me drag her all across the country this year as I get used to being in public and meeting readers. I hate to fly . . . HATE it. So she's the best because she comes with me and that makes traveling less of a nightmare. She also toler-ates me when my nerves get the best of me and I turn into a snappy, sarcastic monster. She's just the best mom out there and it's always nice to know after a long day working, meet-ing people, moving and shaking, that I always have someone to keep my head in the game and grab a drink at the hotel bar with. That's right: I'm totally a grown-up, a professional with a busy and crazy life of my own, but I still want my mommy at the end of a long day! ☺

I couldn't do what I do without my wonderful readers. I just think you're all spectacular, and there isn't a way to express my gratitude to you without sounding like a complete sissy. Really the only part of this new career I've taken on that I understand inside and out is the role of an avid reader. I love a good book, great characters, and moments in a story that you just can't stop thinking about as much as the next book lover. Every time I start a book, or think about a story line, I run it through my reader brain and ask myself if it is a book I would read, is it a story that needs to be told? If the answer is yes, I tell it in the best way I possibly can. Those of you who have contacted me or left stunning reviews, it touches me every time and makes me feel like we are kindred spirits. I never thought I would be on the other side of the pages of a book. Have no doubt that all readers are invaluable to authors; we wouldn't exist without you, so thank you. You rule!!!

Last year at this time, I had no idea what a blog was. True story. Now I know that blogs and the bloggers behind them are a serious driving force behind the word-of-mouth success of a book. It seems pretty selfless to operate a blog just to share your love of reading and books with the world, because you love reading and interacting with other readers. It's where like minds can meet and collude, which I wish I had known about back when I wanted to talk about this book or that book and my friends looked at me like I was a nut. I cannot imagine investing my time and energy in something like that when I didn't get paid for it! Anyway, I thank all the bloggers who had a hand in taking my boys from the small time to the big time, for pimping the series out, and for wanting to have anything to do with me, frankly. It's been a delight working with and learning from you; those of you who had my back and supported me from the beginning know who you are and I hope my gratitude is evident. If it's not, I heart your faces off and appreciate everything all of you have done for me.

Lastly I'm shouting out to my pack. It doesn't matter how long I'm on the road for, how long I'm sitting at the computer, if a walk gets missed or a ball doesn't get thrown, they just love me endlessly. They make my day and my heart smile, and really they are my fuzzy, furry little family.

IF YOU WANNA TALK at me you can. I always welcome hearing from my readers:

E-mail: Jaycrownover@gmail.com

Web: www.Jaycrownover.com

Twitter: @jaycrownover

Facebook: http://www.facebook.com/AuthorJayCrownover

COMING UP NEXT . . .

Nash

BY JAY CROWNOVER

Saint Ford's life is exactly how she likes it—calm, serene, and all about work. Since she was a little girl all she wanted was to be a nurse, a caregiver. Not on her agenda: doing a back-and-forth dance with the guy who nearly destroyed her in high school. Dark, brooding Nash Donovan might not remember it—or her, for that matter—but he changed her life forever . . . and now he's trying to change it again.

Nothing in Nash's life is what he thought it was. And after a deeply buried secret about his family hits him like a one-two sucker punch, he has a lot to sort out. He absolutely doesn't have time to try to figure out the sizzle between him and the hottie he keeps bumping into, or why she seems so desperate to avoid him. But Saint is far too pretty to ignore and much too kind for him to give up on without a fight. And just when she becomes the one person who can help him out of his tangled mess, Nash learns he may have given up his right to her heart years ago . . .

April 2014
From William Morrow Paperbacks

If you loved *Rome*,
Meet the rest of the Marked Men in Jay
Crownover's wildly addicting series!

Rule

A MARKED MEN NOVEL, BOOK 1

Shaw Landon loved Rule Archer from the moment she laid eyes on him. Rule is everything a straight-A premed student like Shaw shouldn't want—and the only person she's never tried to please. She isn't afraid of his scary piercings and tattoos or his wild attitude. Though she knows that Rule is wrong for her, her heart just won't listen.

To a rebel like Rule Archer, Shaw Landon is a stuck-up, perfect princess—and his dead twin brother's girl. She lives by other people's rules; he makes his own. He doesn't have time for a good girl like Shaw—even if she's the only one who can see the person he truly is.

But a short skirt, too many birthday cocktails, and spilled secrets lead to a night neither can forget. Now Shaw and Rule have to figure out how a girl like her and a guy like him are supposed to be together without destroying their love . . . or each other.

Jet

A MARKED MEN NOVEL, BOOK 2

With his tight leather pants and a sharp edge that makes him dangerous, Jet Keller is every girl's rock-and-roll fantasy. But Ayden Cross is done walking on the wild side with bad boys. She doesn't want to give in to the heat she sees in Jet's dark, haunted eyes. She's afraid of getting burned from the sparks of their spontaneous combustion, even as his touch sets her on fire.

Jet can't resist the Southern belle with mile-long legs in cowboy boots who defies his every expectation. Yet the closer he feels to Ayden, the less he seems to know her. While he's tempted to get under her skin and undo her in every way, he knows firsthand what happens to two people with very different ideas about relationships.

Will the blaze burn into an enduring love . . . or will it consume their dreams and turn them to ashes?

Rome

Fun and fearless, Cora Lewis knows how to keep her tattooed "bad boy" friends at the Marked in line. But beneath all that flash and sass is a broken heart. Cora won't let herself get burned again. She's waiting to fall in love with the perfect man—a baggage-free, drama-free guy ready for commitment. Then she meets Rome Archer.

Rome Archer is as far from perfect as a man can be. He's stubborn, rigid, and bossy. And he's returned from his final tour of duty more than a little broken. Rome's used to filling many roles: big brother, doting son, supersoldier—but none of these fit anymore. Now he's just a man trying to figure out what to do with the rest of his life while keeping the dark demons of war and loss at bay. He would have been glad to suffer it alone, until Cora comes sweeping into his life and becomes a blinding flash of color in a sea of gray.

Perfect may not be in the cards, but perfectly imperfect could just last forever . . .

Don't Miss NEW BOOKS from your FAVORITE NEW ADULT AUTHORS

Cora Carmack

LOSING IT A Novel
Available in Paperback and eBook

FAKING IT A Novel
Available in Paperback and eBook

KEEPING HER An Original eNovella
eBook on Sale August 2013

FINDING IT A Novel
Available in Paperback and eBook Fall 2013

Jay Crownover

RULE A Novel
Available in eBook
Available in Paperback Fall 2013

JET A Novel
Available in eBook
Available in Paperback Fall 2013

ROME A Novel
Available in Paperback and eBook Winter 2014

Lisa Desrochers

A LITTLE TOO FAR A Novel
Available in eBook Fall 2013

A LITTLE TOO MUCH A Novel
Available in eBook Fall 2013

A LITTLE TOO HOT A Novel
Available in eBook Winter 2014

Abigail Gibbs

THE DARK HEROINE A Novel
Available in Paperback and eBook

AUTUMN ROSE A Novel
Available in Paperback and eBook Winter 2014

Sophie Jordan

FOREPLAY A Novel
Available in Paperback and eBook Fall 2013

J. Lynn

WAIT FOR YOU A Novel
Available in eBook
Available in Paperback Fall 2013

BE WITH ME A Novel
Available in Paperback Winter 2014

TRUST IN ME A Novella
Available in eBook Fall 2013

Molly McAdams

FROM ASHES A Novel
Available in Paperback and eBook

TAKING CHANCES A Novel
Available in Paperback and eBook

STEALING HARPER An Original eNovella
Available in eBook

FORGIVING LIES A Novel
Available in Paperback and eBook Fall 2013

DECEIVING LIES A Novel
Available in Paperback and eBook Winter 2014

Shannon Stoker

THE REGISTRY A Novel
Available in Paperback and eBook

THE COLLECTION A Novel
Available in Paperback and eBook Winter 2014